BELEAGUERED TRUTH

BOOK II: THE SHATTERED TRIANGLE TRILOGY

WILLIAM P. MESSENGER

ISBN: 978-1-61296-570-3

PUBLISHED BY BLACK ROSE WRITING

www.blackrosewriting.com

Printed in the United States of America

Suggested retail price $17.95

Beleaguered Truth is printed in Traditional Arabic

I lovingly dedicate this book to my mother,

Marilyne J. Messenger

Having seen each of us through to adulthood, she earned the right to
echo the words of Rome's greatest general,
"I came, I saw, I conquered."

ACKNOWLEDGMENTS

Caesar did not boast idly. An unparalleled military genius coupled with his success in war, earned him the right to herald his own laurels. Still, perhaps such conquering bravado should be proclaimed less by those who emerge victorious from military campaigns, and more by those who overcome the more mundane conflicts of life, such as poverty, prejudice, disease and inequality. And, of course, the most fundamental of all, parenthood.

My siblings and I were raised in a poor household, one that was filled with music and literature. Embraced by loving parents we were taught to appreciate the arts. We were taught to sing, dance and read. My mother instilled in each of us a love of books, by teaching us to read well before entering kindergarten.

I am extremely grateful to others who assisted me in the preparation of this book.

Adolfo Batres schooled me in the inner workings of the Los Angeles Police Department and in the policies governing international and inter-agency cooperation.

Perry Leiker, Taylor Lilly and Marilyne Sherwood gave hours of their time to read through multiple drafts, correcting errors and ensuring that the storyline was integrated and complete so that the book would have wide appeal.

Barbara Fandrich once again lent her extraordinary editing skills so that this story would be consistent and grammatically correct.

Frank Hicks allowed me use of the Writers Loft as a place for quiet composition.

Thank you all!

BELEAGUERED TRUTH

PROLOGUE

December 28, 2000

My wife and children were murdered in September. It was now December and the investigation had been going on for three months without progress. Tom Moran was the lieutenant in charge of the case. He was a skilled detective, but the murders had been flawless. It was only his knowledge of me, his closeness to my brother and my family that enabled him to suspect the sinister truth. But he had no evidence.

As Moran left my office, I knew I was safe. I had won. When the door closed, I stopped smiling. There had been nothing funny about our meeting, but I had been laughing from disdain. We had grown up together and I knew all his strengths and weaknesses. I would have respected him if he had shot me. But he didn't. Instead, I was left with victory, contempt, and a cloak of silence.

That last little item was essential. I was embarking on a completely new life and I knew that the public tends to cut more slack for entertainers and Hollywood stars than it does for politicians. The right person can even elicit empathy and warmth. No senator, for example, could mock his own life the way Frank Sinatra did in the song "My Way" and still maintain a strong constituent base. No, I would never be able to adequately explain myself. So why try? Silence would be my new spouse.

My name is Giuseppe Lozano and I am a United States Senator from the state of California. Although representing the largest state in the Union, I am still only one of one hundred votes—a situation I intend to rectify.

CHAPTER 1

January 2001

I was elected on November 7, 2000, only six weeks after my wife and three children were murdered in our Los Angeles home. Historians will debate what effect those deaths had on the outcome of the election. They certainly had an impact on the campaign. My opponent, Anthony Gottesman, could not have been more temperate or judicious following the murders, and his restraint may have cost him the election. Regardless, I remain grateful. He gave me time and space in which to grieve. Anyone who read Lt. Moran's account of the events may suspect me of cynicism. The truth is, I do miss my family.

During the six weeks following the election, the presidency remained undetermined. Although Al Gore won the popular vote by a substantial majority, George W. Bush was eventually declared the winner with a one-point Electoral College edge. In California there was no question about the senatorial race. My margin of victory was comfortable. And so, in the ensuing months I prepared for my move to Washington, D.C. But first, I had unfinished personal business.

·   ·   ·

I have never liked cemeteries. I find them artificial. The more magnificent the grounds and elegant the buildings, the greater their illusion. Holy Cross cemetery is modest by comparison with other Southern California graveyards. Still, it sprawls over the hills of Culver

City, its gently sloping and sculptured lawns providing plots with spectacular seascapes of the Pacific Ocean. But to what benefit? It certainly is not appreciated by the dead. In the end, these places only exist to comfort the living. And for some, it works. A manicured grave creates calm: an opportunity to seek relief from pain; to find hope in loss; to soothe a disturbed conscience; to escape unresolved conflicts; to put the past, if not the dead, to rest.

Given that so many funerary grounds resemble city parks, it is not surprising that people plan picnics and family outings to visit the gravesides of their relatives and friends. But the dead are dead, and cannot be visited in any real sense of the word.

My wife and children were buried in the Visitation section at Holy Cross. By every standard, it was beautiful. And, of course, there was the ocean. But it was beyond their sight. Nor did the view particularly appeal to me.

Other than the burial itself, I had been to the cemetery three times after my family's murder. Partly, it was an attempt to keep up appearances. In the waning days of the campaign, in the wake of the election and throughout the investigation, I had to be perceived as the grieving husband and father. At some point, I became aware that I was running. Not from the murders. Not from death. I was running from myself. Suddenly I realized that I could not relocate to Washington without visiting the graves unaccompanied. As the man I really am.

Very few people can possibly understand my feelings as I drove through the gate, parked my car, ascended the hill and approached their tombs. I had been responsible for their deaths, and from my vantage point, their murders served a greater purpose. But I also mourned their loss. I perused the surrounding grounds. Unlike my previous visits, I was not accompanied by security guards, and the media no longer chronicled my daily activities. I was alone. Or so it seemed.

I am not a man given to hallucinations. And yet, I could almost see the bodies rise from the ground. I felt an uncertain quiet envelope me. Haunted by their memories, perhaps tinged with guilt, I looked around again. No one. I was securely sequestered and alone with my thoughts. I began to speak aloud.

"Yolanda, kids, I'm sorry."

Despite the fact that people often use those words when responding to tragedy, that was not an empty sentiment on my part. I felt a great deal of pain and loss. Besides, what other way could I begin? I wanted to reach out and hold them, but I could not. They were dead and I was ringed by isolation. I was not prepared for these feelings. I felt my knees begin to quiver and become unsteady. I had maintained control of these personal emotions, carefully locking them away for months. I could not afford to falter now. I had to remain resolute and focused.

This was not just about my ambitions. The world I grew up in, where I fell in love, the world I brought my children into, had ceased to exist. From my perspective, America was facing an unclear future and most politicians were unprepared or incompetent. I believed, I knew, I still know that I can do something special for this country.

Suddenly I had an eerie feeling that someone was watching. I glanced around again. No one in sight or earshot. It was just my imagination. That, or Yolanda was reaching from beyond the grave. But I don't believe in restless spirits. Nor was it my conscience, for I wasn't really looking for forgiveness. Still, she was with me. She had always stood by me, even when she did not approve of my decisions. Giovanni and Tom would never understand or accept what I had done. Without her, I had no place to turn.

I sat for a while, lingering longer than I had planned, unsure if I deserved to be that close to them. Finally, I stood and turned away. The evening was approaching as the sun slipped ever closer to the sea. I knew this was my last visit to the cemetery for there was no need to return. I had learned something that day in the city of the dead. The fallen cannot impart pardon or grant solace. The only peace I would find would come from speaking my piece, leading and influencing others. From that point on, I would always be alone. This, too, I knew was inevitable. I was prepared.

. . .

Congress is an interesting amalgam of people. The purest of politicians run for office to serve the common good. Others run to achieve recognition, to be or to become somebody, to escape a common, undistinguished, and potentially forgotten existence. Still others run to become kingmakers. Or at least prince-makers. To decide who climbs which ladder, how fast and how far. I ran for office for one reason only—power. And that power is not held by a kingmaker. I am not seeking to be anointed by anyone and I intend to be beholden to no one. For me the U.S. Senate is merely a stop. A stepping stone. My ambitions lie elsewhere.

While my name is not unfamiliar, my story remains unknown, save for two people—Lt. Tom Moran and my brother, Fr. Giovanni Lozano. Yet even they do not know me, for the events of any life are, at most, the building blocks for knowledge. In and of themselves, they do not convey understanding.

To truly know another person, it is necessary to link the facts of that person's life with values and motivation. Even then, more than observation is required. Communication is essential. Giovanni, Tom, and I grew up together, and they have known me all my life. They possess many facts about me and so seem to think they comprehend me. They do not. Our values parted ways when we were young, and over the years I kept my own counsel as regards motivation. Tom and Giovanni will never understand me. They will forever inhabit a darkness they cannot fathom.

. . .

My parents, my sister, and her family all attended my oath of office in Washington, D.C. The solemnity of the U.S. Senate prohibits photography in the chamber itself. Notwithstanding that tradition, cameras are essential in the world of politics. So, although the actual oath is administered during Senate proceedings sans pictures, a reenactment takes place in the Old Senate Chamber, photographers eagerly welcomed.

During the official ritual, a newly elected senator is escorted down the aisle by another senator, frequently from the same state. I know the importance both of tradition and appearance. A woman leading me down the aisle would play well in my home state. Barbara Boxer and I both represent California, but since she is very liberal and I wanted to demonstrate my fealty to the Republican Party, I asked Kay Bailey Hutchison of Texas to escort me. Still, I could not ignore that I had been elected from a left-leaning state. For purely symbolic purposes, I asked Boxer to accompany me during the reenactment. The photos of this second rite would cement my commitment to all the people of California.

The monuments and structures of Washington are a majestic tribute to democracy. But the handsome intimacy of the Old Senate Chamber sets it apart, evoking memories of a storied past with senators enlisting elegant rhetoric in their efforts to lead and preserve a nation. That was not just the Golden Age of the Senate; it was truly a more mature and elegant time of governance.

Above the vice-president's desk a gilded eagle keeps perpetual watch over a fledgling nation with the depth of a mother's pride and anticipation as one eaglet after another takes wing. Documents lying upon various desks resurrect the discussions and disputes of ages past. Standing within those walls one can almost see the great orators rising up to engage each other in the debate over slavery: Daniel Webster, Henry Clay, John C. Calhoun, Robert Hayne, and Stephen Douglas. Within that room, I had one of my rare moments of uncertainty. Would I be able to live up to the standard set by these predecessors and lions of history?

Neither Giovanni nor Tom was in Washington for the swearing in. Nor had they attended the family Christmas dinner the previous month. Though both of these absences were highly unusual, the circumstances surrounding the death of my wife and children forestalled normal suspicions. Both men had professions capable of masking reality with passable explanations: Giovanni claimed that parish duties required his attention, while Tom was still officially pursuing the murder investigation. I saw no reason to steal illusion from the family. And I was not in any position to reveal the truth. They were not in Washington, and no explanation was needed. Unfortunately, my sister, Bianca, fancied herself the family problem solver. She knew that we were all affected in different ways by my family's deaths. Still, she sensed there was something more at work. As we exited the chamber, she pulled me aside and began her own mild inquiry.

"Sep, what's going on with the three of you?"

Bianca was not given to an overabundance of subtlety. Neither did she need to explain the reference. We three men had been so inseparable as children that people could barely conceive of one without the other two. Like many a myth, that impression persisted long after our lives diverged in adulthood.

"Nothing." I hoped that my response was neither too quick nor too curt. Then I softened my reply with, "Why?"

For a moment I was transported back to my childhood, for it was a child's response, not unlike a mischievous boy trying to veil the truth about the frog in his pocket or the grasshopper in the jar. My sister continued, "I have not seen the three of you together since Thanksgiving."

That was more than just an impression. It was, in fact, the last time we had been together. Tom's mother had invited our entire family over for the holiday dinner. At that time, my brother and Tom had no way of knowing the truth behind the murders. For now, I was in no mood to pursue this conversation with Bianca. But how would I exit gracefully? I thought, *Hell, I'm a politician. This should be easy.*

"Look, sis. You know them almost as well as I do. I think they have been riding emotional waves since September. We all have. And we each have to deal with it in our own way. There are times when being around family is comforting and supportive. There are also times when it is just too stressful. Even recalling good memories can be burdensome.

I imagine that deep down they both would have liked to be here, but I decided not to pressure them about it."

I hoped that would put her concerns to rest, at least for a while. She was not naïve. On the other hand, she tended to believe me when I spoke. And, for the moment, it seemed to work.

"Maybe you're right, Sep. Things just aren't the same. I guess they never will be. But I would hate to see the three of you drift apart. You need each other now more than you ever have. Just remember that."

I had no desire to pursue this line of conversation and certainly could not tell her the real reason for their absence. I managed a disconsolate expression and said, "Thanks, sis. But I assure you they have not forgotten me. We had dinner together every Thursday until after the election. Following that, I was too preoccupied with setting up my office and residence here in D.C. Listen to me. I know you love us. And I appreciate your concern. But you don't have to worry. Everything will be fine."

Of course, that was not true. Nothing would ever again be fine among the three us. Still, she seemed to believe me and I found myself easily slipping into the role of professional politician.

CHAPTER 2

My relationship with Giovanni and Tom had deteriorated precipitously during the month of December. I was not aware of it at the time, but as my life and career were on the ascendant, both of theirs had begun downward spirals. I had been too driven by my own ambitions to notice. Nor, at the time, would I have cared.

For Giovanni the routine nature of parish ministry initially provided cover. Even though he was frequently in front of a congregation, maybe even because of that, he was able to hide behind his liturgical posture, managing to keep his emotions private. Yet he was under tremendous strain. Nothing less would be expected from someone who lost a family under such horrific conditions. For Giovanni, however, there was the added issue of my confession. I had suspected that he would eventually figure out who was responsible for the murders. Either that, or Tom would inform him of his discoveries. My only choice was to bind him to silence.

It is difficult for many non-Catholics, and even some Catholics, to understand the quandary he was in. I, on the other hand, understood fully what I had done. The closest example is attorney–client privilege, in which information obtained from discussions and meetings can never be divulged. This confidentiality remains intact after a lawyer is no longer the attorney of record. It also survives the death of the client. In the Catholic Church, confession is held to an even higher standard—the only thing that is truly inviolable. Although it may sound hyperbolic to some, St. Thomas Aquinas suggested that what the priest learns in confession he knows "as God knows it." As such, the sacrament requires absolute secrecy.

Giovanni was not insensitive to the effect of this seal, and frequently thought back to the night I asked to go to confession. Had he known what I would say, he might have refused. In retrospect, he blamed himself for the situation he was in. From his perspective, my request to confess my sins was an offensive and insidious manipulation, and he had been too blind and trusting to play caution. The agony that was becoming his constant companion was also beginning to eviscerate his emotional heath.

•   •   •

In the immediate aftermath of the murders and funeral, Giovanni was more fortunate than Tom. He had a powerful support system in place and he was not under pressure to investigate the crime or to seek out the murderers. On the other hand, he encountered extreme emotional stress but still needed to provide steady leadership for his parish community. As more information about the murders came to light, Giovanni's brokenness gradually stepped from the shadows to be bathed in light. In the meantime, he was not alone.

St. Catherine parish had been in disarray for many years before his assignment as pastor in 1992. Multi-ethnic and divided, it included Anglos, Filipinos, blacks, and Latinos. It was also near the University of Southern California where the priests at the Catholic Center, if not conservative, were certainly lacking theological depth. As a result, many of the university's students chose to worship at St. Catherine Church.

Upon his arrival, Giovanni immediately began developing programs and events to unite the parishioners. In this, he proved himself to be a community builder par excellence. He genuinely liked people and found that care, creativity and commitment were the only requirements to bring them together. There was, of course, the expected resistance from those individuals who did not like change, especially of a demographic nature. But there was no holding back the tide, and for most parishioners the sense of togetherness was welcomed. Within a year, St. Catherine was unrecognizable. It truly had become a community and was developing a reputation as the place to be—for both priest and parishioner.

That same year, 1993, Giovanni's friend, Fr. Bill Messenger, was appointed director of the Catholic Center at USC. As a result, the university students had another progressive place to worship. Giovanni and Bill had been friends for many years, and at first a friendly competition arose between the two priests. But Bill's presence at the Catholic Center was also freeing for Giovanni. He no longer needed to be concerned about students seeking refuge from a regressive religious environment. Instead, he was able to focus on the diversity of his own parishioners and spend more time on the activities that consume a typical parish. The proximity of the two churches also meant that Giovanni had a friend and ally close by.

When my wife and children were murdered, the news spread quickly. This was due in part because I was a candidate for the U.S. Senate. Giovanni was overwhelmed by the warmth and support both from his parish and the university. The parishioners at St. Catherine sent cards and gifts of food and arranged a major reception following a parish memorial Mass. Bill concelebrated the Mass and coordinated a group of students to represent the university's Catholic community. Genuine though it was, Giovanni knew this outpouring of support was also unsustainable. He would need to turn elsewhere if he was to endure this crisis.

While in the seminary, Giovanni had been exposed to the Jesus Caritas movement—a fraternity of priests inspired by the life and faith of Brother Charles de Foucauld, a French cleric killed in 1916. Since diocesan priests do not live in community, the fraternity was conceived as a means for them to encourage one another and to develop a spirituality appropriate for the demands of their more individualistic and secular lifestyle. And it worked for many of his colleagues. At the same time, the movement allowed some priests to remain substantively aloof from their parishioners—comfortably perched on pedestals, perceived as men of wisdom without weakness. Giovanni looked for something more realistic.

In his first year of priesthood, Giovanni became part of a less formal support group. It began with a married couple, Brian and Judy Henderson. Brian was a doctor and researcher at the University of Southern California. Judy was a teacher. Also part of the group were Sr. Barbara Nixon, principal at All Souls Parish, and two other priests, Bill Messenger, also from All Souls, and Perry Leiker, from Saints Felicity and Perpetua Parish. The group was rounded off by two deacons, Gilbert Cruz and Tim McGowan, both in the final year of seminary training. Although not as conventional as Jesus Caritas, it was effective. The eight of them came from differing levels and experiences of parish life, but they possessed common concerns and questions about Jesus, theology, their personal faith, and the work of the church. This small band of Christians formed a modern example of the house churches of early Christianity, meeting regularly at the Hendersons' home in San Marino, a suburb of Los Angeles that also neighbors Pasadena.

Although this was early in the papacy of John Paul II, he had already initiated a conservative and authoritarian drift for the universal church, the full impact of which would not be discerned for years. It is true that the pope was to achieve a rock star popularity, but an uncanny prescience pervaded the meetings in San Marino, recalling the words of Jesus in Luke's Gospel, "Woe to you when all speak well of you, for that is what their ancestors did to false prophets." This is not intended to be an unfair judgment on John Paul II. The truth is that religion and politics are not too dissimilar. An overly enthusiastic acceptance of politician or cleric often leads to uncritical evaluation of ideas and the institution of policies that have long-term damaging effects. I believe that history will not be too kind to John Paul II.

On the one hand, I did not care. I had already begun distancing myself from organized religion, but I also loved my brother and regretted seeing him struggle with the institutional church. I admired his persistence and believed that his endeavors would have been fruitless without his support community. As they shared their struggles and doubts, the little "house church" in San Marino encouraged its members to be faithful and fierce in their commitment to Jesus. It was not surprising then, that he should turn to them following the murders. Nor did they disappoint. Their daily presence in his life strengthened him to survive the first couple of months of grief. Then came the fateful night in December and that damned confession.

A week after the confession, the group met again at the Hendersons', but there was a noticeable difference. On the surface, everything seemed normal. But Giovanni could not contain the tension. It oozed from him as easily as breath. There was truly something in the air, and everyone was aware that it originated with Giovanni. But none knew the cause.

Gilbert was the quietest and sometimes seemed the most perceptive of the group. His initial thought was to remain silent. It fit his personality. But he was concerned, and he voiced that concern. "Gio, what's wrong?"

Giovanni had developed the ability to keep things to himself, sharing only what he wanted, and even with this group of friends he knew how to keep things hidden.

"Nothing, Gilbert. I'm just exhausted. I haven't been sleeping well, lately." That was very true, but it was quintessential Giovanni. He spent years mastering various ways of deflecting the queries of his inquisitors with just enough truth to avoid lying. "You know what it's been like since September."

Gilbert, however, was not completely convinced. "I do. But you're not the same. You seem even more tense tonight than you have for the last couple of months."

Giovanni could always count on Barbara to come to his rescue. She interjected, "Maybe it's finally catching up with you. You haven't rested since this whole thing started. You can't keep going like this, Gio."

"Maybe not," he replied. "But I couldn't have made it this far without all of you. And for that I'm grateful."

This was not a prayer group. And as supportive and serious as their gatherings were, they also included fun and relaxation. Nobody knew this better than Brian. He and Giovanni were intellectuals who sometimes seemed to communicate better over scotch. He stepped to the bar and suggested, "Let's start with a drink, tonight." Perry, Bill and Tim were also scotch drinkers, and they readily seconded the idea.

That had the welcome effect of momentarily shifting the conversation. It was the middle of the holiday season and Giovanni seized the opportunity to speak about Christmas and plans for New Year's Eve. The rest of the evening, he expended a great deal of energy masking his inner feelings so that no other suspicions were raised. But it took its toll. He knew he could not do that forever.

Ultimately the greatest effect my confession had on Giovanni was the loss of his support group. Collectively, they were too observant even for his powers. When it came to Tom, both of them knew what had transpired in the sacrament, even though it remained unspoken. With his other friends, Giovanni could not even tell them that a confession took place, let alone what he knew about the murders. He began skipping some of the meetings and holding people at bay on the telephone. Eventually he stopped returning calls. Hiding behind his clerical duties, he became more distant. The days stretched into weeks, but he was losing himself by the hour. Aging from the inside out.

· · ·

The fallout for Tom was different, but still severe. He had botched, or so it seemed, a high-profile murder investigation; he had to face his critics on a daily basis. He found no ally in the truth. Although he had solved the case, he was unable to surface the requisite evidence. To the novice and expert alike he was viewed as a failure. Then again, Tom had no major aspirations saddling his career. In that he was fortunate, for after the Lozano murder inquiry stalled, his career was at a dead end. Although others were involved in the investigation, he seemed to be the only one singed by the inability to find justice.

In all fairness, one could not lay the blame for failure at Tom's feet. There is no other individual or any agency that could have succeeded at the task. This was a murder in which nothing was left to chance. If anything, more information was discovered because of Tom's involvement than would otherwise have been the case. Still, he would not be able to voice what he had learned nor would it lead to arrest and prosecution. He would forever bear the dark secret of truth alone. Or at least in silence, for there was one other who knew.

The telephone rang at nine o'clock in the evening. Giovanni had already settled back into his chair, a glass of scotch on the table beside him, Giuliani's Guitar Concerto No. 1 playing on the stereo. The prior evening he had begun to re-read Mary Doria Russell's *The Sparrow*. He had discovered long ago that good science fiction provided an intriguing and successful escape from reality. His first reading of the book was engrossing, a rather realistic encounter with extra-terrestrial life. In this second read, he wanted to focus more on the interaction of the characters, both human and alien, and their responses to events of the story. There was a subtle interplay between elements of the plot and circumstances in his own life. His reading was interrupted by the ring. He reached for the phone.

"Gio, this is Tom. Are you busy?"

"Not really. I just sat down and started to read."

"Do you mind if I stop by for a visit?" Tom asked.

Giovanni did not really feel like having company, but this was his best friend. And although things had been uncomfortable between them over the last couple of months, he could not turn him down.

"Not at all. Come on over."

In preparation for Tom's arrival, Giovanni lit a fire in the fireplace. A thoughtful gesture. It was now the middle of February, and although a fortnight of bitter cold cycles itself through Los Angeles each winter, those weeks had already passed. Nonetheless, a gently glowing hearth is unequalled at creating an atmosphere of relaxing intimacy. There was no guarantee that the blaze would ease the strain between these friends, but it was a good counter to Giovanni's unhelpful greeting.

Tom walked into the room looking unkempt, if not completely disheveled, the vestige of a stressful bachelor's existence.

"Geez, Tom. You look like shit."

At another time that would have been a friendly, if throwaway, welcome. Tom replied, with just a touch of sarcasm, "Yeah. Well, the last several months have taken their toll."

"I'm sorry, Tom. What I really meant to say is that you look like Columbo. Minus the overcoat. Here." He handed him a glass and with a conciliatory tone said, "I poured you a scotch."

"Thanks, Gio."

Not many things went unseen by Tom. He was, after all, an excellent detective. Then again, it did not take any special effort to notice the fire. As he sat down, he gestured toward it and said, "Nice touch."

"Thanks," Giovanni replied.

"Gio," Tom continued, "you haven't asked me anything about the investigation for a long time. That would seem to prove I was right."

"About?" Giovanni asked.

"I'm too tired to play games, Gio. You know what I'm talking about. Your sister told me that you did not go home for Christmas, and you did not go to Washington last month for Giuseppe's oath of office. Face it. You have not been the same person since he confessed to you."

Giovanni looked away for a moment, not sure how to respond. When he turned back, he was firm and almost expressionless. "I'll repeat what I said to you back in December: *'You have no idea what he told me. And I can't say anything.'*"

"Look, Gio. I've been a cop for over twenty years and I've seen more violence and death than I care to acknowledge. This case was different and I put everything on the line. Don't you think you owe me a little help? Surely this sacramental seal of silence isn't more important than your own family. Deep down you have to agree with me."

"I'll give you this much, Tom. You are tenacious. But there's a reason I've avoided you for so many weeks. I don't want to have this conversation. I'm not at liberty to say anything more than I already have. And I wish you'd let it go."

"Let it go? Can you imagine what it's been like for me at the division? Officially, the case is still active, but the investigation is obviously at a standstill. And my reputation is crap. The only thing that diverted the attention of the media and the public was the Bush/Gore election fiasco."

Giovanni did not even attempt to deftly change the subject. "What do you do for relaxation these days, Tom?" Then reaching for the book beside him he continued, "You really should read this. It's an excellent novel about first contact with aliens from another solar system."

"I'm not a *Star Trek* fan. You know that," Tom replied.

Unlike Tom, Giovanni had always been energized by astronomy and the possibility of life elsewhere in the universe. His first homily in the seminary expounded on the Ascension of Jesus; a metaphysical reflection on its significance for life on other planets.

"This isn't *Star Trek*. It's far more realistic."

Tom just rolled his eyes, replying, "Science fiction bores me almost as much as detective stories. Give me a good historical novel, or even pure history."

Giovanni had succeeded. Almost without knowing it, Tom instantly seemed to relax, even though the subject did not particularly interest him. But now it was his turn to alter course.

"How do you do it?" he asked.

"Do what?"

"Live without sex."

"Well, that's rather abrupt," Giovanni replied.

"No, I'm serious," Tom said. "I've often wondered. When we were teenagers, you were just as interested in girls as I was." Then somewhat impishly he continued, "Of course, you also liked those dead saints!"

Giovanni simply smiled.

"I'm serious, Gio. Don't you ever even think about it?"

Slightly tilting his head and cocking his eyebrows, Giovanni inquired, "Why are you asking?"

"Because I do. And I'm not satisfied. It's been seventeen years since Emily and I split up. During that time I've been with"—he paused briefly—"a few women."

Giovanni did not react. Nor was it his habit to judge. Still, Tom felt it necessary to assure him.

"Not all of them were one-night-stands, either. I just haven't found any of them fulfilling. I suppose deep down that's the real reason I came by tonight. To get some advice. No one knows me as well as you do."

"I don't know what to say to you, Tom. I look back over the years, especially after what happened to Yolanda and the kids, and I wish you and Emily were still together. She was good for you. Since the divorce there's been something missing in your life. You need someone, but when it comes to relationships you lack permanence and commitment," Giovanni suggested.

"Maybe so. But I'm not looking for that. I want to know your secret." His look became more quizzical as he said, "I'm presuming you haven't broken your vows."

"I didn't take any vows," Giovanni said matter-of-factly.

"What are you talking about? I was at your ordination. I heard you."

"No," corrected Giovanni. "You heard me make promises. There's a difference between a vow and a promise."

"Now you're playing semantics," Tom replied.

"No, I'm not. First of all, the canonical consequences for violating vows are far more serious than for profaning promises. Secondly, priests in religious communities take a vow of chastity. Diocesan priests make a promise of celibacy. Technically, celibacy simply means one cannot get married. Still, since everyone is supposed to live a chaste life, I guess the vow and promise are the same in practice."

Tom expelled a breath of air and shook his head, his mouth courting a half smile. "I've watched you do this before, Gio."

"Do what?"

"Deflect a question so that you don't ever actually answer it. Sometimes people don't even remember asking. I've known you too long, and when I see you do that it makes me suspicious. So forget the distinctions and tell me. I'm not going to condemn you."

"Why does this matter to you?" Giovanni asked.

"Because on the surface you seem to have things together, and I'm pretty sure you're fundamentally faithful. If you've figured this out, maybe I can, too."

For a moment Giovanni did not know how to answer. They had been friends forever, but had never pursued this conversation. Why not? And why now? But instead of questioning further, he decided this was a moment for truth. Honesty between friends.

"Well, Tom, it hasn't always been easy. And, yes. There were times I crossed the line. Not many, but a few. I had one relationship that lasted quite a while." He looked away with a betrayal of longing. "That was years ago, but those failures have always bothered me. And I've kept them to myself. Until now. These days, like other priests, I find different ways of compensating."

"Like what?" Tom queried.

"Everybody has a peculiar solution, a way of finding other things to consume one's time and attention. Some are a bit esoteric. I know a priest who spends his free time roaming through antique stores looking for uncommon orange glass. Another has been collecting postage stamps most of his life, and his portfolio numbers in the many thousands, some of them exceedingly rare. Yet another priest rides Harley-Davidson motorcycles. Flying down the highway at ninety miles an hour with eight hundred pounds of iron between your legs has to account for something!"

They both laughed at the amusing image he conjured.

"And you?" Tom asked.

"I try to lose myself in music. I attend concerts and occasionally dust off my violin and squeak through a sonata. Mostly I listen to CDs. There are few things that can lift my spirits like the unending melodies of Schubert or the virtuosic demands of the Giuliani concerto playing now. But the truth is every priest is merely trying to cope. Forced celibacy is abnormal. And until the Church figures that out, there will continue to be failures. Not just sexual ones, either. It seems to me that an inordinate number of Catholic priests are self-centered and authoritarian. Then there are the alcoholics. Speaking of which, let's have another drink."

The next couple of hours passed quickly. Finally, it was time to call it a night. I'm not sure Tom got the answer he was looking for, but it was a good visit. Some healing began to take place between them, and he knew not to raise the subject of the confession again. Giovanni would never tell. He drove home, opened the front door and looked around. There was no one there. And yet, he was not alone. He and the house were a perfect match. They were both empty.

CHAPTER 3

The real work of the Senate is not accomplished through flashy, constituent-oriented speeches from the floor, and certainly not by making the rounds of talk shows. It is carried out in committees. Like every other senator, new or returning, I had a wish list of committee appointments. But I was a freshman, and the 2000 election almost left the Senate in total disarray, with a split of fifty Democrats and fifty Republicans for the first time in history. This made for a very challenging 107th Congress.

The vice-president of the United States serves as President of the Senate, mostly a ceremonial role. However, he exercises his presiding role by administering the oath of office to newly elected senators, and most importantly casting the deciding vote in case of a tie—the only time he is allowed to vote in the Senate. This meant that for the first seventeen days of the new Congress, the Senate was controlled by the Democrats, since Al Gore was still vice-president. On January 20 the Republicans took over with the inauguration of George W. Bush as president, and Dick Cheney as vice-president.

Throughout, Tom Daschle was leader of the Democratic Caucus and Trent Lott leader of the Republican Conference. It was Lott's influence that enabled me to secure a seat on the Senate's Committee on Commerce, Science, and Transportation. I was also appointed to serve on the subcommittee for Science, Technology, and Space. My colleagues considered this my area of expertise, since my company, The Pegasus Group, though not a household name, was well known throughout the industry and in government.

The learning curve for a new senator is not as steep as I expected, but it includes a certain amount of grunt work. Even for someone representing the largest state in the union, the first step is the bottom rung. The Senate has its own version of hazing without the obvious life-hazards that define initiation rites in college fraternities and marching bands. This is particularly true for members of the majority party because they assign new members the task of presiding over the Senate during necessary, yet unimportant or routine, debates. It is also the best opportunity to study and learn the rules of the Senate. And there is a parliamentarian on hand at all times in case any presider makes a mistake. After one hundred hours in the presider's chair, a senator is awarded a golden gavel. Since my long-term goal was the executive branch, I was not overly interested in legislative work. Still, I thought one golden gavel would indicate a successful rite of passage. I had to earn it within five-and-a-half months, because on June 6 Jim Jeffords left the Republican Party and declared himself an independent who would caucus with the Democrats, thereby returning Tom Daschle to the position of Majority leader. It was a bit dizzying, but the golden gavel still looks good in my Senate office.

.   .   .

In polite company, at cocktail or dinner parties, and even in casual conversation, religion and politics rank among the great forbidden subjects. Either one of them can kill a social gathering. Yet they sinew through every discussion, for whenever two or three are gathered we make up a body politic. The popular prohibition is not intended to be generic or philosophical but is a precautionary warning about partisan politics and sectarian religion, and their ability to divide families and terminate friendships. In the United States there is no exception to the rule although one elected office comes close. The presidency.

No president is truly unifying. Some are downright divisive and all have their detractors. Yet each one belongs to the world's most exclusive club. Thanks to Presidents Truman and Hoover, former

White House occupants do not work against their successors, instead sometimes serving as powerful allies. This places the presidency in a unique position among all other elected offices. When the president comes calling, all doors open.

In mid-February the intercom in my office rang and my secretary informed me that Andrew Card, President Bush's chief of staff was on the phone.

"Hello, Mr. Card. This is Giuseppe Lozano."

"Hello, Senator. I'm calling for the president. He would like to invite you to lunch next week at the White House."

I hardly knew how to respond to this unexpected invitation. I simply said, "It would be an honor, sir."

"Good. How's Thursday?"

"I think I can clear my calendar," was my wry reply.

"Then it's settled. I'll meet you here at 11:45."

"Thank you, Mr. Card. Goodbye."

I was a bit puzzled, but must have been smiling when I hung up the phone. My secretary walked in and asked why I looked so pleased. "The president has invited me to lunch next week. Clear my Thursday. I'll come into the office first, but I don't want to bother with appointments."

When Thursday morning arrived, I was filled with anticipation. I also had mixed feelings, for I had not originally supported Bush's campaign. In the California primary, I voted for John McCain. Bush was too right wing for me, as he was for the whole state of California. McCain was more my kind of Republican—fiscally conservative but socially moderate. More in the mold of Ronald Reagan. During the primaries many in the Republican Party had their doubts about McCain's conservative credentials. Though not quite a flip-flopper, he was too willing to work with the opposition.

By the 2000 election cycle, the divide between right and left was growing into a chasm—a remnant of Newt Gingrich's term as Speaker of the House. However, an astute observer of politics realizes that neither the Democratic nor the Republican parties are monolithic and are frequently held together not by common purpose, but by common enemies. When Bush won the nomination, my allegiance was set. He was a better choice than Al Gore. In fact, there was no choice. Had there been a third candidate between the two, I probably would have supported him. In practical reality, however, the United States is a two-party system, so in the general election I voted for Bush. Still, I did not know why he invited me to lunch.

Meeting the President of the United States is unlike any other encounter. As a businessman I had met powerful people from around the world. This was different. There is no reservoir of nonchalance to draw from when approaching the White House. Inside I was churning with excitement. A schoolboy at his first dance. On the outside, I was calm and professional. Regardless of the thrill of the afternoon I would maintain my composure.

The morning was crisp as I walked from the Dirksen Senate Office Building to the White House. I started out early enough that I could meander along Pennsylvania Avenue. As usual, Washington was filled with many visitors, most of them seemingly paying no mind to the brisk weather. I arrived with sufficient time to stand outside the gates at 1600 Pennsylvania Avenue, appreciate the view, and anticipate the future. I knew where I was headed. In the meantime, I was a visitor at the world's most prestigious address. I passed through security and was admitted into the residence.

Surprisingly, Mr. Card met me in the foyer of the West Wing. This was more attention, and much more personal, than I expected or deserved. He did, after all, have other duties as chief of staff.

"Hello, Senator. Welcome to the White House."

"Thank you, Mr. Card. I've never been here before. This is great," I said exuberantly.

"The president is busy right now, Mr. Lozano. Follow me and I'll show you to the dining room. He'll join us there in a few minutes."

As we walked through the West Wing, I experienced the same sense of wonder and history that I felt in the Old Senate Chamber. Despite the Constitution's establishment of three branches of government, this was the real center of power in the United States. Other heads of state may occasionally address Congress, but they come to Washington to see the president. It is a stately city and this is the most intimidating building. Is it any wonder that I set my political ambitions so high?

The presidential dining room is far from pretentious. It is intimate and possessed of an elegant simplicity. As Mr. Card and I walked into the room I noticed there were only two place settings on the table. That was my first real moment of nervousness. Perhaps he noticed. I'm not sure. But as we awaited the president, he began to explain the history of the room and its furnishings. Presently Bush entered.

"Mr. President," Card said. "I would like to introduce Giuseppe Lozano, the Republican senator from California."

"Thank you, Andrew," the president replied. As Card quietly slipped from the room, the president continued, "Senator, it's a pleasure to meet you."

For the briefest of moments, I did not know how to respond. It was not that I lacked the words. There was something in Bush's manner. Something unexpected. Down home. Like the kid next door. Admittedly, he was new to the job, but he was not imposing nor did he seem consumed by his title or authority. That could have been because his father had also been president, so he was not entirely unfamiliar with his surroundings. As I stood there, I realized that he really was the guy you could have a beer with. My moment of hesitation went unnoticed and my recovery was quick.

"Mr. President. I'm honored."

"Of course you are." Then he chuckled with that up and down motion of his shoulders and continued, "I'm just joshing with you."

This guy was incredibly disarming. He knew just how to put someone at ease and it did not appear that he intended to stand on ceremony. He wanted me to be relaxed as much as possible under the circumstances. He had to know that I was a little off guard being alone with him.

"Senator," he asked, "may I call you Giuseppe?"

"Of course, sir."

"Did Mr. Card show you around the room?" he continued. By this time, we were completely alone. His chief of staff had closed the door on his way out.

"He did, indeed, sir. I must say this is nothing like I expected."

"Giuseppe, when you and I are alone in a room, you can call me George."

"I don't think so, sir," I laughingly replied.

"Whatever," Mr. Bush said. "I enjoy opportunities to be informal. Besides, I'm not quite used to the title yet. You know, for a while there, I thought Al Gore was going to steal it from me!" His humor was contagious and relaxing. He continued, "I understand your hesitation, though. Would you like a drink? Anything you want. I'm going to have a Diet Coke, but don't let that stop you."

I would really have liked a martini at that point. However, discretion prevailed.

"Actually, I'd just like some coffee, please."

Bush called his attendant and ordered our drinks.

As we waited, he asked, "How do you like Washington, Giuseppe? Have you settled in yet?" I doubted very much that he did not already have the answer, but it was a point of conversation.

"Yes, sir. I found a place over in Georgetown. As for the overall city, I'm still getting my bearings, but this has to be the most exciting capital in the world." I threw up my hands as I continued. "I know. That sounds very American of me."

"Well, nothin' wrong with that," he chuckled. Again, very homespun.

On a more serious note we talked for a while about our backgrounds, what brought us to Washington, and our recent elections. He chose not to mention the Florida disaster or the Bush v. Gore court battle. That was certainly a cue for me not to bring them up.

He turned somber and sympathetic as he said, "I was sorry to hear about your family."

I knew this had to come up at some point, and I appreciated the fact that he waited until I was somewhat at ease in his presence. I responded, "Thank you, sir."

"I also admire your tenacity," Bush said. "I'm not sure I could have continued my campaign if that had happened to me."

His was a genuine sensitivity, and my reply was equally honest. "It wasn't easy, but there wasn't much I could do at that point. The election was only six weeks away. Even if I had pulled out of the race, I probably would have been elected. Not unlike Mel Carnahan over in Missouri. That was a bad break for John Ashcroft."

Carnahan was attempting to unseat Ashcroft, the senator for the state of Missouri. He died in a plane crash three weeks before the election. In spite of being dead, Carnahan won.

Bush replied matter-of-factly, "Yeah, but now John's attorney general and we still control the Senate."

The attendant arrived with the coffee and cola. As we drank we talked a little more about families, notably our children. His twin girls were only four years older than my daughter Carmen. Nothing political came up in this part of the conversation. This was a getting-to-know-you encounter.

We sat down to a simple meal and it was obvious that someone on his staff had done some homework. We were served lobster bisque followed by spicy shrimp pasta. And for dessert there was freshly made ricotta cheesecake. That menu might strike some as stereotypical since I'm Italian. However, I was flattered and realized that there was more to this meal than the food.

As we were eating, the president turned the conversation to state politics.

"Giuseppe, I have no intentions of being a one-term president like my father. This last election was far too close and I'm a little embarrassed to be sitting here after losing the popular vote and only winning the Electoral College by one. This is a divided country and many people don't consider me a legitimate president. I want that to change in four years."

I tilted my head and assured him, "You have my support, Mr. President. I'll do anything I can to help."

"Listen," he continued. "Republican senators are not unheard of in California, but it's an increasingly liberal state. My dad barely won in 1988. In fact, if Dukakis had not made a fool of himself, dad might have lost. How did you get elected?" My facial expression must have changed because he quickly added, "I don't mean that the way it sounds. But I want to begin now to build a base of support in California. I got clobbered there a couple of months ago. You won in a walk. Your experience could help me."

I have to admit I was a little disappointed. Apparently, this conversation was why I had been invited to lunch, and probably the reason the president tailored the meal to my palate. Then again, I don't know what I expected, but I was hoping there was more to the invite. Perhaps tapping into my expertise in the world of electronics? Deep down I guess we are both just political animals and I should not have been so surprised. Besides, I was having lunch in the White House. If the conversation was unanticipated, my reply revealed no surprise. I was accustomed to spontaneity and I gave a thoughtful response.

"I don't know if the people of California are so liberal. In fact, except for a few places like San Francisco, I don't think they like the far left any more than the far right. I think Californians are more about inclusivity than ideology. That was my biggest difficulty running against Gottesman. Neither one of us was extreme, and except for fiscal matters we were not completely different. The fact that I won by several percentage points may actually reflect that California is not too divided a state. Truth be told, I think the people would have been just as happy if Gottesman had won." I took a noticeable breath and said, "But I'm glad he didn't."

Bush smiled. "That makes two of us. Giuseppe, I have several appointments this afternoon, so we need to conclude. But I'd like you to think about how I might make inroads into California. You're set for the next six years, but I have to run again in 2004. Over the next several months I want my team to stay in touch with you."

We stood up and began to leave the room. As if on cue, Andrew Card opened the door. Bush shook my hand and said, "Thank you for coming over today, Senator."

"Mr. President, it was a great honor. And I assure you I am always at your disposal."

Once again, I was surprised as Card walked me to the foyer. He was in the president's inner circle and fully aware of the purpose for the invite. As we made our way he said, "Senator, thank you. You're important to the president's future."

I thought to myself, *And he's important to mine.* But I was smart to leave those words unspoken. I simply replied, "You can count on me."

As I headed back to the Senate I began to process the lunch. I knew I could never deliver California on my own. Bush would have to prove himself to the people and I had my doubts. Nonetheless, he held the office I aspired to. I recognized that courting his favor could only build political capital for me.

CHAPTER 4

It has long been observed that Americans are obsessed with—well—America. This has some repercussions, for most U.S. citizens possess an appalling lack of geographical knowledge coupled with minimal interest in international affairs. Except when it comes to major natural disasters, at which point Americans make up for their shortcomings with an abundance of generosity. Underlying this myopic view of the world is another fully human foible—the attention span. News items cycle swiftly through the American media and just as swiftly through the American consciousness. This, however, proved beneficial to Lt. Tom Moran. As horrific as the murder of my family was, it was pushed from the forefront of the news by the 2000 presidential election.

The drama unfolding in Florida was far more gripping, even more significant. And it lingered. Florida's secretary of state, Katherine Harris, certified George W. Bush the winner of the state's electoral votes. Conflict of interest issues aside (Harris was co-chair of Bush's Florida election campaign), the excitement began on election night when Bush first conceded the election to Gore, then withdrew the concession, setting in motion a number of court battles that would ultimately end up before the U.S. Supreme Court. For thirty-five days, no one knew who would be the next president of the United States. Not only was this unprecedented, but in the modern world it was nothing short of chaotic. Nor was there a shortage of commentary (legal, political, and social), thus riveting the public's attention. In that environment it is easy to understand how people might forget even about the murder of a senator's family. And yet, not everyone forgot.

The Los Angeles Police Department, like many such institutions, has a long memory. Sure, most departments have a file of unsolved cases, but this was not a typical murder. Given that at the time, I was the Republican nominee for the U.S. Senate and the election was only weeks away, my family's murder was very high profile and almost a daily news item. The inability of the LAPD to apprehend a suspect fell squarely on Tom.

He was not the only one involved in the investigation, but since he maneuvered himself into the position of lead detective, the responsibility was his. His failure to resolve the case reflected poorly on the department, and the LAPD does not look kindly on an officer who tarnishes its image. In fact, following the civil service reforms that resulted from the Rodney King riots and the retirement of Darryl Gates, not even the chief is given a pass these days. Of even greater concern to the department than fulfilling its motto *"to protect and to serve"* is how the public views its competency. It is not inclined to forgive the ineptitude of one who holds the rank of lieutenant. Therefore it seemed unlikely Tom's career would advance any further. I told him as much in a conversation the previous December. Still, the LAPD suffers from a malady that characterizes many a large organization: The paradox of power. The higher one rises in rank, the easier it is to evade responsibility for failure. At the time of the murders, Tom's captain was Erick Haskell. He was a very decent man and only after much cajoling did he authorize Tom to head the investigative team. But when it stalled and produced no results, it was Tom, not Haskell, who was held to account. When in February of 2001 an opening occurred for the position of commander, Haskell's friends guaranteed that he was promoted, no questions being raised about the murders. In the upper echelons of power, the influential take care of each other.

Tom was resigned to his fate. He had never been driven by ambition for higher office. Even moving from patrol officer to detective was more a matter of accident than planning. Once there, he demonstrated such skill as an investigator that it was inevitable he would be made a lieutenant. He was content with that rank and did not begrudge

Haskell's promotion. To those on the outside, like Giovanni, that did not seem fair. Then again they both had enough worldly experience not to expect fairness out of life. What burdened Tom was not internal police politics but the knowledge of who was responsible for the murders that September night. Knowledge that came from his investigation, but that he could not discuss with anyone, even his best friend. The strain of the investigation and what he had learned fractured the facade he had so carefully crafted.

•　　•　　•

Tom and Emily had been divorced for nearly seventeen years. There had been no real animosity during their marriage. They had, like many couples, simply grown apart as their value systems and goals veered in different directions. In the intervening years neither had remarried. Tom pursued a few short-term affairs and enjoyed a number of one-night stands. Emily dated a little, but nothing ever developed from those encounters. Both were committed to their jobs—he becoming a respected detective, she a sought-after journalist.

Following the collapse of the *Herald Examiner*, Emily secured a position with the *Los Angeles Times*, eventually becoming chief foreign affairs' correspondent. This necessitated her traveling the world, occasionally placing her in dangerous situations. The weekend of March 2, 2001 Emily was in London en route to Afghanistan. She was sent to cover the story of the destruction of the two ancient Buddhas in the Bamiyan Valley. These magnificent statues, standing approximately 180 and 120 feet respectively, were carved in the valley's sandstone cliffs in the sixth century. They had survived an assault by Genghis Khan some eight hundred years earlier, but the Taliban would not be deterred—by history or international objection. The destruction was part of the Taliban's fanatical attempt to eliminate anything in Afghanistan that was not Islamic. Another example of the dangers of a religiously controlled government.

Emily's parents still lived in the Putney Bridge suburb of London and this gave her an opportunity to spend time with them. While there, she checked in at the BBC to meet with a colleague who would be traveling with her to Afghanistan. At 12:30 a.m. on Sunday morning, March 4, a car bomb exploded at BBC Television Centre, part of a terror campaign by the Real IRA. Like all major news centers, the BBC is staffed twenty-four hours around the clock. Fortunately, Emily was not present and although a number of people were injured, no one was killed. Tom had followed her career from a distance since their divorce. He knew she was passing through London on her way to the Middle East. He called a friend at New Scotland Yard and ascertained that Emily was safe. Still, he remained unsettled at the prospect that she could have been injured or killed. He decided to contact her upon her return.

Without hesitation on Friday morning, March 23, Tom dialed Emily's telephone number.

She answered. "Hello?"

"Hello, Emily," he replied. He did not need to identify himself. Although they had not spoken for years she recognized his voice. How could she forget the sound of the man she had so deeply loved?

"Tom. This is a surprise. I hardly know what to say." She had no reason to expect this call. "How are you? Is something wrong?" Several ideas raced through her mind as she tried to focus.

"I'm fine, Emily. I was actually calling to ask how you are. I know you were in London a couple of weeks ago when the car bomb exploded at the BBC. I was worried you might have been there."

"No, Tom. I was with my parents at that time. But how—"

"Emily, can we get together for lunch or dinner sometime?"

There was a brief pause. She was not seeing anyone, but she also had no idea where this came from. He didn't offer anything except the question. It might have been her imagination, but she sensed desperation in his voice. Or maybe it was dejection. Either way, he needed to see her.

She replied, "I just returned from Afghanistan yesterday and don't return to work until Monday. I'm free tomorrow and Sunday. What's your schedule?"

"Tomorrow would be great," he said. "Is dinner OK?"

Again she paused for a brief moment. "Yes. Let's make it seven. Do you have a place in mind?"

"How about Ruth's Chris in Beverly Hills?"

"Have you recently come into money?" she half-jokingly inquired.

"No. But we can get a quiet table. Besides, I don't have much else to spend my money on these days."

"OK. I'll meet you there at seven."

"Thanks, Emily. See you tomorrow."

Tom had to find ways to keep busy on Saturday. Every clock resembled a watched pot. As the evening approached, he found himself almost as nervous as he was on their first date. Just the sound of Emily's voice the day before unearthed feelings he had spent years trying to bury. After all, she was the one who wanted the divorce. He just did not stand in the way. Over the years he never found anyone to take her place. But then, he did not try very hard. Rather, he kept most women at a comfortable distance, even the ones he managed to bed.

As concerned as Tom was about seeing Emily again, he could appear neither uptight nor formal. For clothing, he chose smart casual: black shoes, cream-colored pants, a coral shirt, and charcoal sports coat. At six o'clock he headed to the restaurant, guaranteeing that he would arrive first. She'd had to wait too many dinners when they were married.

Emily was known for punctuality and at exactly seven she entered Ruth's Chris Steakhouse. She gave the reservation name and was escorted to the table. Tom looked up and was briefly caught off guard as her physical beauty created a flash of déjà vu. He quickly recovered, recognizing that they both had aged. But as he wore the years in rugged lines and graying hair, she defied those same years with gentle grace. And while most people look good in black, Emily was simply stunning. Her elegant one-shoulder dress accented every curve of her body. Tom rose and greeted her with a soft kiss on the cheek. He had always been aware of what he lost sixteen years earlier, but he would never acknowledge his continued longing, nor would he admit how deep the desire ran. Standing before him that night she unmasked all his defenses.

"Hello, Emily. You are as beautiful as ever."

"Thanks, Tom."

They took their seats and the waiter presented the menu and wine list inquiring, "Would you like something to drink? A cocktail or wine?"

"Emily, what would you like?" Tom asked.

"A Smith and Kearns," she replied.

Tom turned to the waiter and said, "One Smith and Kearns, and a Glenfarclas 17. Neat, please."

As the waiter left, Tom said to Emily, "I'm serious. You really look great. The years do not show on you at all."

"I see that you're still suave, Tom," she smiled. "The years are there. I just have ways of hiding them. Tell me, how are you?"

"I'm fine," he replied with a deft dishonesty. "But we'll get to that. I want to know how you are. I was worried when that car bomb exploded in London."

"How did you know I was there?" she queried.

"I've followed your career over the years, Emily. I always thought you were the more talented of the two of us, and I was pleased to see that management at the *Times* recognized your skills. I've read most of your articles. They've been excellent. You have a unique ability to make your readers feel as if they are with you on assignment."

"Tom, you almost sound as if you've been stalking me," she jested.

"If reading your articles makes me a stalker, I'm guilty. But you are a well-known figure at our city's newspaper. I just like to keep up with current events. Besides, I also read what other journalists write." He hoped that did not sound too defensive. He winked at her as he continued, "Of course, I do have my favorites."

The waiter returned and served their drinks. On the tray was a single yellow jasmine: white waxy petals with a yellow center, which he placed in front of Emily saying, "I believe this is for you."

Tom felt a momentary awkwardness with the waiter acting as his surrogate. When the server left, Emily took the flower and looked up. "It's beautiful, Tom. I can't believe you remembered."

Not only was it Emily's favorite flower, she was wearing one the first time they met. They were both attendants in a wedding at the police academy. All the bridesmaids wore green dresses with yellow jasmine. Tom and Emily were not paired in the wedding party but he found it difficult to take his eyes off her. During their marriage, Emily often decorated the house with arrangements of jasmine. Mostly they were white, but she was always partial to the yellow because it seemed more delicate. She asked, "Is this a date?"

He evasively replied, "Not really. I just wanted to do something special for you. It's been a very long time. And when I think about it, I did not do enough when we were married."

"You weren't a bad husband, Tom. In the beginning it was a wonderful marriage. We just ended up wanting different things."

"You mean like children." It was a matter–of–fact statement with a hint of resolve or defeat. Had it been a question he ran the risk of sounding snarky and he did not want to poison the evening.

"It's not that, Tom. I think children were more a symptom. In hindsight, I'm not sure we were ready for marriage. At least not for the sacrifices it requires." Then wistfully she concluded, "In any case, that was long ago."

She picked up the flower. Enveloped by its aroma she closed her eyes, briefly retreating into a world of memories. She looked across the table and queried, "Tom, why did you invite me to dinner?"

He let out a sigh and replied, "I just needed someone to talk to."

"About the murder of Giuseppe's family?" she inquired. The sound of my name made him cringe inside but his countenance betrayed nothing. Years of interrogation had taught him to withhold expression. "Your eulogy at the funeral was deeply moving."

"I didn't know you were there," he said with some surprise.

"I was there, Tom. I just stayed in the background and out of sight. Like much of the congregation I was in tears when Celine Dion sang the song Yolanda had written."

"Giuseppe shared that with Giovanni and me a week before the service. He had asked me to speak, and I was scared to death. You know me. I'm not really a public speaker. But after he played the song, I asked him if I could use it. I figured it would help me get through the eulogy."

"It was amazing and very effective. More than that, you shared a wonderful reflection on who Yolanda was." She sipped her drink and continued, "We don't have to talk about this if you don't want to."

"It's all right, Emily. I do want to. I just don't know what I can say or even how to say it. Let's order dinner first."

He called the waiter and placed the order. They began with barbecued shrimp as a shared appetizer. Emily requested lobster bisque soup and lamb chops for her entree. Tom ordered a Caesar salad and a rib eye steak. They chose creamed spinach and sautéed mushrooms to share as side dishes. When the waiter left they continued their conversation.

"Tom, I've followed the investigation from the newsroom but there doesn't seem to be much development. For a while the LAPD was taking a lot of heat from the media. It must have been very difficult for you."

"More than you can imagine, Emily. I put pressure on my captain and pushed myself into the role of lead detective. I made promises I couldn't keep. Ultimately I failed the department and the family."

"Tom, you're being too harsh. I know you. You're a skilled investigator. If you don't have any leads, that's not your fault."

"It's more than that, Emily. This investigation has taken me down an unexpectedly dark path. For the first time in my life I have seen the face of evil. And it's not some vague disembodied spirit. It's real flesh and blood."

"What do you mean?" she asked.

He replied, "I know who the murderer is. Or at least who orchestrated it. But I can't prove it."

Emily was silent. This was a turn of events she did not expect. And Tom did not intend such a blunt statement of fact. She knew he was not a careless detective nor was he given to extremes of speech, so she asked, "Tom, how can you be so sure if you don't have proof?"

"I'm sorry, Emily. I should not have said that. There are elements about this case that I'm not free to discuss. And there is information that has not been revealed to the media or the public. I really wanted to see you tonight to share my *feelings* about the case, not the facts. The last several months have been beyond stressful."

"That's understandable, Tom. This was no ordinary murder. Over the years you've remained close to Giuseppe, Yolanda, and the kids. They were family to you. I can only try to imagine what you've been going through. And now with Giuseppe in Washington, you and Giovanni are alone."

"Except," he replied, "I can't even talk to Giovanni."

"But he's a priest. And your best friend," she exclaimed. "And he's going through the same thing. Surely he understands."

"It's more complicated than that. I can't explain it right now. Maybe what I needed most tonight was diversion. Something to take my mind off the case. It's consumed me for the last five months." He looked intently at her and continued, "Can we change the subject?"

She could see he was uncomfortable and said, "Of course."

Tom leaned back in his seat and asked, "Do you mind if I ask you a personal question?" Then quickly added, "You don't have to answer."

Anticipating his query she said, "You want to know why I never remarried."

"It seems like a fair question," he replied. "Any guy would be lucky to have you."

"Thank you, Tom. I guess there are a number of reasons. For now, let's just say I didn't have time. After we split up, I was too focused on my career. I set my goals very high. And I've achieved most of them. There's more to it, but that's enough for now."

Tom suddenly realized how quickly the evening had passed. He did not want it to end, but it was getting late and he had no further designs for the night. He was fairly certain that his eyes betrayed no longing as he smiled and said, "I'm glad you came tonight, Emily. It was really good seeing you."

"Thanks, Tom. I enjoyed the dinner." She looked directly at him adding, "And the evening."

"Do you mind if we have dinner again sometime?" he asked.

"I'd like that," she replied.

He walked her to the valet and waited while her car was delivered. Then he said good night and gave her another gentle kiss on the cheek. As she drove off, he wondered what feelings she might still have for him. He decided he would find out soon.

CHAPTER 5

Giovanni and I are identical twins, but the similarity is merely superficial. In late adolescence, I began withdrawing from religion—at least internally. That has continued to the present day. For the sake of my wife, Yolanda, and our children, I celebrated baptisms and First Communions, and I attended Mass regularly. When I entered politics, that expression of faith proved a valuable asset in a society where a one-dimensional approach to religion is the norm. Fortunately, no one can determine the depth or strength of my faith based merely on outward signs. As for what I truly think or believe about God, that remains unrevealed.

Giovanni inhabited a different reality. As he grew into adulthood, he was drawn ever deeper into the world of religion—an understandable trajectory, given his vocation to the priesthood. Following ordination he embraced his public persona to perfection. He was at ease before a crowd and comfortable leading a congregation in prayer. In his personal life, however, he was reticent, deliberating in silence and stingily expressing his feelings. Not that he did not have them. But when it came to personal emotions he was quite content to be the still waters. He was not cold, but he could be aloof and judgmental. With a formidable intellect, he was comfortable in the world of theology and religion. And yet, that very world would emerge as his nemesis. For although his feelings were private, his opinions were not. Choosing to approach conflicts head on, he never shied away from challenges, believing all rules and regulations could be modified. He preferred not to limit his options.

In the early days after his ordination, he occasionally found himself at odds with church authorities. When needed, he had a place to retreat to and calculate his response. The Henderson home had a housekeeper's quarters but no housekeeper. Brian and Judy offered it as a respite for Giovanni whenever he felt the pressure of the institutional church, or just needed to get away. They and their children affectionately called it "Father Gio's room." More important, though, was that his eight-member support group met at the Hendersons'.

Here each person could express opinions freely and securely. No subjects were off limits, and no one was judged. Challenged, yes. Judged, no. The five young clergy, just starting out and trying to find their way in the church, found encouragement here that was not always present among other priests. Of the other three members, Brian was the most highly educated. Not just a medical doctor, he was a scientist and served for many years as the only Western advisor to the Chinese government in cancer research. On some levels, Giovanni had the most in common with him. They were both iconoclasts and believed in true equality among people. Judy was the most deferential of the group. She had been raised in a devout household and possessed a slightly exaggerated concept of priesthood. Combined with her innate gentleness she had a tendency to see only the good in people, even those who kept that good deeply disguised. This led to her holding idealistic expectations of the clergy. Sr. Barbara Nixon knew better. She entered the convent as a teenager and had already been a nun for several years. During that time, she had firsthand experience with a number of priests. She counted many as personal friends and respected the clergy collectively. But she was also aware of their weaknesses. To her priests and nuns should be collaborators in ministry. In her role as principal of All Souls School she was so responsive to the needs of the parishioners that many considered her their real pastor—or at least equal to the associate pastors.

Giovanni thrived in this group. But I worried about his relationship with the institutional church. I had been able to determine my own identity. In pursuit of wealth, I was able to choose both my field and my business ethics. I was accountable to no one. But when Giovanni entered the priesthood, identity was forced upon him. It was not just a question of duty and responsibility. He was expected to reflect someone else's idea of what a priest is or should be. Charting his own course and forming his own image would prove a constant struggle and was often confrontational, making it difficult for him to secure a comfortable niche in Catholic ministry. He took his beliefs too seriously and sometimes to the extreme. Occasionally this led to harsh judgments of his fellow clergy, and he was more than willing to be vociferous about them. I was pleased that he had his support group, but I remained doubtful that it would provide sufficient refuge.

In the early days of Giovanni's ministry, the house church in San Marino provided just that. It succeeded in strengthening and supporting all its members. At this time the Catholic Church in Los Angeles was still in the midst of renewals begun in 1962 when Pope John XXIII convened the Second Vatican Council. Pope John's vision for the council was to modernize the church's relationship with other faiths and with the secular world. This necessitated the church reexamining itself, beginning with how it worshipped. And it caused consternation and resistance among some conservative Catholics. Giovanni's support group was driven by a common attempt to faithfully live out the teachings of Vatican II. But even they had to redefine roles and parameters that had previously been presumed.

An example occurred in 1981 when Giovanni, Perry, and Bill were still new priests. Each was experiencing similar difficulties understanding their priestly role, and none was treated as an equal by their pastors. At one meeting all the members of the group were present except for Deacon Tim McGowan who was assisting at a funeral.

Giovanni shared a letter he received from Cardinal Manning reprimanding him for not using the title "Father" with the parishioners. "What difference does it make to him?" Giovanni asked. "I'm comfortable with people calling me by my name."

Brian was the first to respond. "That's just asinine. What's the purpose of the title, anyway? It's just like being a doctor. It doesn't mean anything in and of itself."

Bill easily latched on to this topic. He contributed by adding, "All titles do is separate people, pretending some are more important than others. I mean, seriously, is a priest more important just because he's ordained? Hell, I even let the kids in the school call me by my first name."

Judy chimed in, "Don't you think it's a matter of respect?"

Everyone was about to jump on that, but Giovanni spoke first. "How can that be, Judy? Words don't determine respect, attitude does. Someone can call any one of us "Father" with a venomous tone of voice. That's certainly not respect."

"I agree," Bill continued. "Our parents taught us to address all adults as Mr. or Mrs. But the truth is kids in the school can call me by my name and still be very respectful. It's all a question of demeanor."

"But," Judy interjected. "The title just seems more deferential. And a priest deserves that."

"Why?" Perry asked. "Just because he's a priest? People don't deserve respect simply because of their job. They deserve it because they are human beings. It doesn't matter what positions people hold or even what age they are. Dignity is a human right. It seems to me that all three of our pastors, even though they call each of us 'Father' actually disrespect us and discount us as partners in ministry."

Brian offered an example from his own life. "I agree with Perry. I worked hard to get where I am and I'm proud of being a doctor. But that does not make me better than my patients or the people who assist me in my research. The position may be important and may even convey expertise. But not the title. I don't insist that people call me 'Doctor.'"

"What about you, Barbara?" Judy asked. She was known to be persistent, to pursue topics and not easily give in. "Would you like the children in the school calling you by your name, without saying, 'Sister'?"

"Not really. I think teachers need a certain amount of distance, a boundary line from their students. For one thing, they need to avoid over-familiarity or the appearance of favoritism. From that perspective I guess I would prefer that the kids use the title."

Apparently, Judy had one ally. She also wanted to include everyone, making sure no one felt left out—another Judy trait. She turned to Gilbert and asked, "What about you, Gilbert?"

"I'm not in a parish yet," he answered. "But I think I agree with Giovanni. We don't use any titles in this group, even though our positions are all different. Yet we all respect each other. And whenever I call my nieces or nephews, I always say, 'Hello, this is Gilbert.' I guess I'm not completely comfortable with titles."

Perry started to laugh and said, "I was just thinking. Bill's mother makes all of her grandkids call him 'Uncle Father Bill.' In fact, they have to call each of us that. 'Uncle Father Perry.' 'Uncle Father Gio.' Gilbert, she'll do the same thing to you after ordination. Maybe that's why Bill hates the title so much!"

As the laughter subsided, Bill replied, "That's not the reason. But that 'uncle father' thing my mom created is ridiculous."

The house church was not supposed to solve any problems. And no conclusion was reached that night. In the course of the evening they were all able to vent a bit, and that was always helpful. In the end, even these gatherings would fail Giovanni, for the support group had a downside. It was insular. Whatever encouragement the members received from one another, it did not help the priests in dealing with other clergy, particularly their pastors. If anything, it further entrenched Giovanni's lack of patience. Although he saw the world in shades of gray, he judged other priests in black and white. In his mind, an unwillingness to bend the rules to help people equated with simple rigidity. It never occurred to him that some priests, like many parishioners, were struggling with the extensive changes sweeping over the church.

•   •   •

Giovanni benefitted from a post–Vatican II training, naïvely believing that all seminarians were internalizing the same education. Indeed, many were. Some proceeded to become model priests. But there were others who "submarined" their way through the seminary. This was a term used to identify those who mastered outward conformity, fulfilling all the requirements for ordination while raising no suspicions about their true spirituality or theological leanings. Like their military namesake, these seminary submariners skillfully avoided detection as they navigated the waters of formation—unseen and unidentified. Many of these became the epitome of clericalism: arrogant and authoritarian, parading about with a preeminent air. It was bad enough that some people put priests on pedestals. It was obscene that some priests put themselves there.

Giovanni's attitude may have been rooted in our family upbringing. We were not rich. We had no cooks or housekeepers. Those were chores we all shared and that he was content to continue after ordination. He did not understand other priests who expected someone else to perform even the simplest of tasks: making beds, washing clothes, cooking and cleaning. In theory, housekeepers and cooks free up a priest's time, making him available to serve the people. The truth is that most priests are quite comfortable living an upper–middle–class lifestyle. And many relish being served. Some even develop demanding personalities more befitting the church of the Middle Ages than the one of the twenty–first century. The institution is at least partly to blame. After all, to this day cardinals are still called "Princes of the Church," a title that is as anachronistic as the monarchical world from which it came.

Giovanni understood that the priest has a unique role within the church, but in his opinion, the priest is neither better than, nor superior to, the laity. Nor is he holier, at least not by virtue of ordination. Holiness is quite personal, and over the years he met many parishioners who had a closer and richer relationship to God than their pastors.

Giovanni's vocal displeasure with clerical indulgence was not limited to support group discussions. Occasionally, he would find opportunity at daily Mass to chastise other priests in his preaching. Though he was careful to criticize without naming, these homilies did little to establish esteem among his brother priests. An example occurred one weekday morning. The first reading had been taken from Paul's letter to the Philippians. The excerpt included the following verse:

Let the same mind be in you that was in Christ Jesus,
who, though he was in the form of God,
did not regard equality with God
as something to be exploited,
but emptied himself,
taking the form of a slave,
being born in human likeness.

Giovanni walked to the middle of the aisle, looked out at the congregation, and began to speak.

"Today's first reading is wonderful poetry. But it is much more. This passage is one of the great Christological hymns of the early church. Like many of our own hymns, it sings of the wonders of Jesus. Like hymns throughout the ages, it uses an economy of language that provides for hours of reflection and interpretation. Don't worry, however, I won't speak that long!

"As I began my reflection on this passage I asked myself this question: 'Who is Paul speaking to?' To me the answer seems clear. He is speaking to all the followers of Jesus, but not just in his own time. He is speaking to all who will ever come to believe in Jesus. He is speaking to us. However, Paul uses imagery that is all but alien to the church of today. And I'm afraid that in a special way, it is alien to many of today's priests.

"This hymn lyrically speaks about the Incarnation: the mystery of Jesus becoming a man; of God becoming human. We know this mystery. We celebrate it with great fervor every December 25. How can it be, then, that a church deeply rooted in the Incarnation can so easily be disconnected from the profound humility of Jesus? In another letter, Paul speaks of the centrality of the Resurrection. 'If Jesus has not been raised from the dead, our faith is in vain.' But even the Resurrection must first begin with Jesus's birth. And in today's reading, that birth is all about meekness, lowliness. Here is God declaring that being God does not mean as much—is not as important—as being human.

"The bishops and priests who are charged with ministering to God's people are not exempt. If anything, they should be models of Jesus's humility. But tell me. How many clergy act like servants? When was the last time you saw one humbling himself before parishioners?

"Instead what we often see is arrogance rooted in a false spirituality. One that claims the priest is sacred. That he is above the people and closer to God—not, I suggest, to the God who chose to become human, and certainly not closer to the Jesus who humbled himself to be a slave. This hubris mocks God. It demeans even the Eucharist—the very presence of Jesus on this altar. There should be no place in our church for a clerical attitude of disdain or superiority. I fear that Jesus's challenge of recognizing him among the least significant often goes unheard by a clergy clothed with and cushioned by lavish living. The question needs to be asked, 'Who are the servants?' Clearly, the answer should be 'all of us.' Priest and parishioner alike.

"We are a people on a journey, meandering toward perfection, drifting toward God. We need cathedrals that reach to the skies in a transcendent link with the divine. But we also need a church that discovers the divine here on earth, among people, among the least important, among the world's outcasts. Simply put, we need a church that serves."

These reflections rarely went unnoticed in the archdiocese. But Giovanni could always handle the fallout. He could always retreat to San Marino, to a gathering of likeminded individuals, each seeking a place in and attempting to survive a dysfunctional and frequently oppressive church. In that regard, the meetings were successful. But they were not really designed for his new situation. Following the murders, Giovanni was finally confronted with a rule he could not break—the inviolability of the confessional.

•   •   •

In the first few months following the confession, Giovanni found that few waking moments distracted him. Relying too much on his own abilities, he began to use each element of his ministry, each activity with friends, to weave a barrier within his mind. He had never had trouble compartmentalizing and was sure he could contain this area and keep it from breaking free. Relying on his friends for relaxation and diversion, he began to anticipate the freedom of Tuesdays—his day off. They were relaxing and the only times he had occasion to laugh.

The day frequently began on the racquetball court with Perry and Bill. This physically demanding game enabled him to release some tension and pent-up emotion. All three friends were about equally skilled, making for healthy competition. Afterward, Gilbert would join them for the remainder of the day: lunch, a movie, and dinner. It was all quite routine. Almost a rut, even. Yet that is exactly what appealed to him. Each day off provided a psychologically needed, if temporary, escape. The ritual of these Tuesdays freed him from discussing his feelings about the murders, allowing him to keep the more disturbing ones private.

Most of the time the others respected this decision. Perry, in particular, was sensitive to others' feelings, a characteristic of his own personality and ministry. Gilbert was practically defined by non-confrontation and never raised uncomfortable issues. On the other hand, Bill was a problem solver and willing to address unspoken subjects. Like Giovanni he also kept a lot of things to himself but tended to probe others when he saw them in distress. However, nothing in the seminary prepared any of them for Giovanni's situation. Even if he had wanted to talk, he was bound by secrecy. He could not even tell the others the reason for his silence. Over time, Giovanni's struggle became more and more evident and his friends became increasingly concerned.

53

One Tuesday in March, Bill decided to take a direct approach. Early morning provided some levity following a couple of hours of racquetball. Giovanni, Bill, and Perry were playing games of cutthroat on the court. After they had finished they went to the showers. The stalls were full and Bill had to wait. Finally, he entered the shower that Perry had just exited. Immediately he called out, loud enough for everyone to hear, "Perry, do you have to fart everywhere?"

At first Perry tried to deny it. With an inflection of feigned innocence he asked, "What are you talking about?"

"You know exactly. You farted in here and I can't breathe."

Perry started to laugh, undaunted and seemingly unembarrassed by the truth and replied, "It's not that bad."

Bill asked, "Are you kidding?" Then with a requisite mixed metaphor he observed, "The smell is sticking to the walls." Even Giovanni had to laugh at this, something he rarely did. As childish as it was, he appreciated the banter. Besides, there was some truth to it. Perry was notorious for his flatulence. And he never had the decency to do it in private. He preferred to wait until they were together in a room, sometimes even in the car. He claimed it was a family trait. A gift he inherited from a long line of ancestors. The humor of this retreat into adolescence was brief. When they left the club Giovanni was as withdrawn as ever.

Gilbert joined them for lunch at one of their favorite Mexican restaurants, La Adelita in Echo Park. The food was traditional fare and a cut above its competition. But the restaurant was really noted for its freshly made chips and salsa, and the owners never rushed their customers. Many problems had been discussed there on other Tuesday afternoons. Why not this one?

"Gio," Bill started. "None of us really knows what it was like for you last fall. The murders of Yolanda and the kids were horrific. I certainly don't know how I would have responded. But you haven't said anything about this for the last few months."

"And I don't want to now, either," Giovanni responded definitively.

Bill pretended not to hear and continued. "You act like you're in your own world. All our conversations these days are superficial. We're your friends, Gio. You know we're here for you."

"Leave him alone, Bill," Perry interjected. "He'll talk when he's ready."

For weeks they had all been uncomfortable watching as Giovanni withdrew, receding further and further into himself. It was not healthy. But each of them had his own approach to helping people. Bill sensed he was not going to get any assistance from Perry. He turned to the ever-quiet Gilbert who was enjoying his cocido, hoping not to be drawn into the conversation.

"Don't you have anything to say, Gilbert?" Bill asked.

"God, no!" he replied. Gilbert's signature, default phrase when seeking to avoid uncomfortable topics.

Bill turned back to Giovanni and continued. "We all have secrets, Gio. They're not all skeletons, but they are all burdens. And if I have learned anything from our priesthood and our friendship, it's that burdens are lighter when they are shared. Remember what Cicero said: 'Friendship doubles our joy and divides our grief.' We're your friends."

"Look, guys," Giovanni said. "I appreciate your concern and I've never questioned your friendship. But there's more going on here than you know. And I can't talk about it. It's not just the three of you or the group, either. I don't even talk to Tom or my family about what I'm going through. There are some things I have to process by myself. For now I'm content to hang out with you each week, to enjoy your company and a little superficial nonsense. It means a lot to me to get away from everything."

That did not really answer any questions, but it was good enough—for the moment. Even Bill was willing to let it go. On the other hand, it certainly did not solve Giovanni's problems. He knew he would have to find a way to live with his secret or be destroyed in the process. He understood and trusted his friends' concern for him. But these encounters only made him aware of how alone he truly was. On the other hand, there was one person who might understand.

.   .   .

Sunday, April 1, was the beginning of daylight savings time and Giovanni invited Tom to the rectory for a barbecue. The weather was mild and pleasant. In fact, one might say it was a perfect spring day for an outdoor meal. Usually, these evenings involved a select group of people. But the two friends had not seen each other in several weeks. This distance was part of Giovanni's attempt to avoid discussing the subject that had so alienated them. Besides, merely adjusting the clock to provide a later sunset changed nothing. For him this night was like all the others over the past few months—not made for entertaining. One friend was enough and he hoped there would be an opportunity to share with Tom something of what he was feeling, this in spite of being bound by secrecy.

He planned a simple but substantial meal: buffalo tri-tip, shrimp pasta salad, and corn on the cob. He was just getting set to fire up the grill when Tom arrived. One week earlier Tom and Emily had met for dinner, but this would not be the night to break that news to Giovanni, not yet. It might be that things would continue to go well with Emily. If so, Tom would have an ally in his own struggles adjusting to the murder. For the closer he and Emily became, the more he would be able to communicate with her. Tom thought it best to see how things developed before telling Giovanni. He knew that Giovanni would never find a similar outlet, for he was restrained by a different set of values. He did not craft them. They were thrust on him by the church. Nonetheless, he accepted this obligation. More than that, he believed. He had a profound love of the church and its rules and regulations had become an integral part of his life. Given the current circumstances, it would be cruel to tell him about Emily.

Tom walked onto the patio and found that Giovanni had already poured the scotch. "Hello, Gio." Then, as he was handed his drink he said, "Thanks. But what if I had been late? The ice would have melted and watered down my drink. You probably would have finished yours and you'd be one ahead of me."

"Really, Tom," Giovanni replied. "Do you think I'm stupid or that I would be so careless? The parking lot is on the other side of the fence. I heard your car when you drove up."

"Well, thanks again." As he raised his glass he toasted, "Here's to daylight savings time and the promise of long summer nights."

Toasting was a friendly formality, but as they raised their glasses and took a sip, Tom saw a different Giovanni. Parishioners who encountered him on a daily basis may not have noticed the change. Knowledge can be a terrific burden and exact an immense toll. Since December Giovanni seemed to be in a constant state of decline. His features were haggard, far beyond his modest forty-four years. He had lost weight and his hair was graying. He hardly looked like my twin brother anymore.

Preparing the food was a masterful demonstration of subterfuge. Giovanni was able to continue a lengthy conversation without eye contact. The only way he could compose his thoughts was by looking away from his friend. Tom helped matters along by opening with a bit of banter.

"Geez, Gio. You look like shit."

"I'm sure," Giovanni replied. "I feel like it, too. When I was in school I always worked well under pressure. But the last few months have been a different kind of stress."

"That's understandable, Gio. The murder of your family was a horrible event."

They had not seen much of each other for a while and there existed an unspoken agreement not to talk about the investigation. It would inevitably lead to the confession that Giovanni did not even admit had taken place.

"It's not just that, Tom. It's affecting my ministry."

"You're a fine priest," Tom assured him.

"That's not the point," Giovanni replied. "I have moments of reflection and clarity. And I don't like what's been happening."

"Like what?" Tom asked.

"I've been taking almost every opportunity, both in conversation and preaching, to criticize the clericalism of other priests. As if I would feel better bringing them down. I don't. At first I tried to convince myself that I was empowering the laity so that they would not fall prey to the lordship of the clergy. But it's not really about the people. It's not even about other priests."

"Gio, aren't you being a little hard on yourself? Everyone who knows you is aware of your commitment to collaboration and equality. You've always tried to right wrongs. How is this any different? Someone has to speak the truth and assail falsehood. Maybe it's just your lot in life."

"Don't get me wrong, Tom. I happen to believe everything I say. I never mention names, but I haven't been pulling any punches, either. And I don't care if word gets out and other priests are offended. Lately, however, I've been thinking that I'm attacking the wrong target."

"Meaning what?" Tom asked.

"Meaning there will always be weakness and imperfection in people. And they should be addressed. But my real problem is with the church, itself."

"Have you talked to your priest friends about this? To Perry or Bill, Gilbert or Tim?"

"No. Because it goes beyond the murder to embrace something I can't discuss."

"The confession," Tom said knowingly.

Giovanni didn't look at him. A blank stare overtook him. Neither nodding nor shaking his head, he gazed into the distance, momentarily transfixed in deep thought, clearly fighting a struggle within. Finally, he looked back at his friend and said, "I'm sorry, Tom. I can't handle this. I don't want to talk about my family or the church. Let's change the subject, OK?"

Tom began to wonder. Maybe tonight was the right time after all.

He said, "I had dinner with Emily last weekend." Right time or not, it peaked Giovanni's attention.

"Wow! That's out of the blue."

"Not as much as you think," Tom said. "I've followed her career all these years."

"Everyone in L.A. has," Giovanni responded. "She's become quite the journalist. And now she has an important position with the *Los Angeles Times*."

"Yeah. But for me it was more personal. I never wanted the divorce. I just didn't want to fight her. Even you said we should have stayed together."

By this time, they had finished their meal. Tom continued, "Emily was sent to cover a story in Afghanistan and was in London during the attack on the BBC. For some time I had wanted to call her. That incident gave me an opportunity. I phoned her when she returned to L.A."

"Just like that?" Giovanni asked.

"Yeah, but I was pretty charming on the telephone," Tom joked, "and even more so in person! It was a very comfortable evening. Damn, Gio. She's as gorgeous as ever. And she is still so smart and competent. Did you know she was at the funeral?"

"No. There were too many people," Giovanni replied. "I couldn't see everyone and I don't even think I can remember most of those who spoke to me. I know she didn't. I would have remembered that."

"She was very moved—by both of us." The same wistfulness that had invaded Emily's mood last weekend now found expression in Tom's voice. He exclaimed, "God, it was good to see her again!"

"It's been years since I've seen you like this," Giovanni said. "You sound like you did when you first met her."

"Well," Tom answered, "I haven't been happy for a long time. And I've never forgotten her."

"So, what are you saying? What happens next? Do you have plans?" These were interrogatory questions. Giovanni asked them almost the way detectives do. Except that they were warm, friendly, and genuine.

"Well, we're going to have dinner again. We didn't set a date, though. My call took her by surprise and I don't want to rush things."

"Tom, as you know, I haven't had much reason to celebrate since last fall. But I'm happy about this. I have a bottle of twenty-five year old Talisker single malt. I was saving it for a special occasion. Why don't we open it now?"

"Sounds good to me," Tom replied.

Few things are as warming as a peaty, smoky scotch. And this one ranks high on the list. It's just a superb after-dinner drink. They spent the next forty minutes in relaxed conversation, comfortably setting aside the cares and struggles that had consumed them for so many months.

CHAPTER 6

"Politics is the art of the possible." Otto Von Bismarck was so known for laconic statements, some might think that this shrewd admission of the power of diplomacy was an endorsement of democracy. Far from it. It appears that he was unintentionally voicing a confession of the limits of his own authoritarianism. For throughout his political career he was more interested in his own puissance than in sharing governance, willingly instigating wars in service of his vision of a united Germany. From a historical perspective his comment invites the witness of generations of people the world over who have suffered from a subversive use of power. From dictatorships to democracies, this pursuit of the possible continues to expose the lack of a moral compass among many politicians. And yet, Bismarck's observation speaks to something more than power, something at the heart of democracy.

The art of the possible is best achieved through the art of compromise. Unlike war, democracy is not about defeating the enemy. It is about the give and take necessary to attain a common good, about fending off the natural tendency toward tyranny. The best of laws do not beat down an adversary. They lift everyone higher. So it is understandable that politicians would pride themselves on their ability to forge alliances and pass difficult, even seemingly impossible legislation while maintaining political peace. When it works, politics in a democracy is a noble calling and a lofty endeavor. As in any walk of life, some leaders are more gifted than others. But there is one skill that only the rarest politicians possess: inscrutability. And it is valued above everything else. The true masters—and they are few—exude an aura beyond suspicion. They are able to mask ulterior motives and forge a false sense of security, facilitating a zone of comfort for both ally and adversary. Still, goodwill is not always enough and there are times when an accord is not forthcoming.

The historic fifty-fifty split in the United States Senate was not nearly as dramatic as the pundits predicted. Between January and June, the month that Jim Jeffords defected to the Democratic Party, Vice-President Dick Cheney cast only two tie-breaking votes. Though neither was earth shattering, the first, and more critical one salvaged the framework for President George W. Bush's tax cuts. Cheney knew the importance of that vote and its long-term ramifications. He had served as a member of the House of Representatives before being appointed as President George H. W. Bush's secretary of defense in 1989.

During the intervening years, between the two Bush presidencies, Cheney maintained good relations with Republicans in both houses of Congress and with some Democrats. After being elected vice-president, he was welcoming and receptive to the new senators and representatives. I briefly encountered him on several occasions, at meetings and in the halls of Congress. For some reason, I was ill at ease in his presence. I did not know the reason until we were formally and personally introduced on April 3, 2001, following his tie-breaking vote on the budget. The meeting occurred in the office of Majority Leader Trent Lott who had taken me under his wing, helping me learn the ropes and navigate the Senate. Only Cheney, Lott, and I were present, but it was a decidedly different encounter than my meeting with the president. In some ways it was even more formal. And it briefly caught me off guard causing a rare moment of self-reflection.

I don't spend much time in front of a mirror. It's not that I don't keep well-groomed or am unconcerned about my appearance. To the contrary, I dress quickly and can Windsor my tie on the run. I just don't like the reflection that stares back at me. Unlike the queen in *Snow White*, I am not tempted to deceit. I need not question a mirror in search of answers I already possess. Whatever image I may project in public, the one in the silver glass is true, perceptive and accusatory. What I see is an empty, hollow heart. And I avert my eyes to avoid confrontation. This reflection had been darkening for some time, but it began haunting me after my family was murdered. Not unlike the teenager entering puberty, and exploring the joys of a changing body, I thought I was alone. Then I met Dick Cheney.

He was friendly and easygoing. But I was too familiar with both the look and the demeanor. It was not his crooked smile or half-closed eyes. In fact, it wasn't physical at all. It was something emanating from within, something dark and deeply personal. When I looked in his eyes I perceived what few others could. He and I were kindred spirits. He seemed to notice it also for there was a momentary pause, a knowing glance, imperceptible to Lott, intended only for me. People like the two of us can hide our true selves from almost everyone, but not each other. He might have been vice-president of the United States, but that was only a job. I saw something else, someone else, when we met. What disturbed me most was what I saw behind his eyes—my image in his soul. Behind this mirror was another man just as dark, just as empty. He was at the pinnacle of his career. I was still ascending mine. But we were both skelms. Twinned in a world of evil and deception. This was an uncomfortable acknowledgement. As much for him as it was for me. And one I did not anticipate.

The problem for most people is that evil is a word we banter around with too much abandon and too little thought. Hence, its incarnation is rarely recognized. For some this pedestrian identification of evil shrouds their fear and insecurity making a complex world seem simple. In reality it merely makes the world simplistic. From the dinner table to the playground, from religious sanctuaries to political chambers, we use the word to identify anyone we perceive as a threat, anyone who does not share our monolithic view, who thinks, believes, acts, or looks differently. As a result, we are blinded, incapable of knowing or identifying real evil. And so it walks freely among us needing only to present itself as friend. In the world of politics, the masquerade is so successful, that it often corrupts the very principles of democracy.

When I met the vice-president I knew instantly that this relationship would need cautious coddling. I also knew better than to make an enemy of Dick Cheney. He was to be trusted as much as I, which meant not at all. If this sounds like exaggeration, there is no grievance or animus between us. I simply knew on the day we met how to handle him in the future. And he knew how to handle me.

Congress was a different matter. It was not populated with many Cheneys or Lozanos. I found most members, especially my fellow Republicans, quite congenial. Though I had limited political experience, they accepted me. Still, I have never been stupid and I knew their approval was primarily due to the fact that I could reliably deliver a vote, rather than to any innate abilities. In spite of developing camaraderie during the first few months, I was keenly aware of my status as newcomer if not outsider. I lived alone and had no genuine confidant. I could share ideas with my staff and other representatives, but I had no one to share my feelings with. More than anything else, meeting Dick Cheney startled me into the realization that I needed a true friend in Washington. And though I usually strategize every move with the precision of a chess master, I needed no time to address my sense of alienation. There was only one place I could turn.

•   •   •

Since the funeral I had remained in contact by telephone and letter with my friend, Jackson Carver, and I looked forward to seeing him again when I took my oath of office in Washington. As it turned out, he was unable to attend. I was understandably disappointed, for I also anticipated being introduced to his partner, Jean-Paul Lecuyer. They had been together for fifteen years and, although same-sex marriage was not legal in Massachusetts, they were husbands in every sense of the word. I wanted to meet the man who made my friend happy. Boston and Washington, D.C., are in the same time zone, so I knew nine o'clock would not be too late to place a call. The phone rang three times. My impatience generated a momentary anxiety. Maybe no one was home. Then I heard the receiver lifted from the cradle. Connection was made.

"Hello?" As I'd hoped, it was Jackson and not Jean-Paul.

"Hello, Jacks. This is Sep." I was certain that the tone of my voice conveyed my feelings of friendship.

"Oh Sep, how are you? How's Washington?" Neither of his questions was inane. They were imbued with genuine sentiment and transported me back to graduate school. Here was the only person I could ever truly be myself with—to a point.

As always, conversation with him flowed easily. I answered, "Well, I'm still getting used to the city and to my new job, but I've settled into a home and so far, I like it. And it's exciting being a senator."

"Listen, Sep. I want to apologize again for missing your oath of office."

He had explained his absence back in January and the circumstances were beyond his control. Jean-Paul's family still lived in Brussels and his mother had become ill. She lost a significant amount of weight and was experiencing heart irregularities. They had flown to Belgium only days before the ceremony. Several years earlier Madame Lecuyer had been diagnosed with Basedow's disease, what we call Graves' disease here in the U.S., but it was never treated properly. She had not been consistent about seeing her doctor and had developed complications. The week before my swearing-in ceremony she had a heart attack.

"You already told me, Jacks. You don't need to say it again. How is Jean-Paul's mother doing?"

"She seems better now, but we're still concerned. One side benefit is that she quit smoking."

"Well, that's good to hear," I replied.

Jackson continued, "Sep, she's my mother-in-law, even though Jean-Paul and I are not married, at least not yet. She has accepted everything about the two of us and has always treated me like her son. She is a good woman and certainly the reason he is so loving. I'm really sorry if I let you down."

"Would you please stop apologizing? You sound like a damn fool. I told you before, Jacks, that I understand. You made the right decision. You belonged with Jean-Paul and his mother. Besides, I had family here at the time. And now that we both live on the East Coast we'll have plenty of opportunities to get together. How often do the two of you get to see his mother?" I asked.

"He goes to Belgium more often than I, usually once or twice a month. It's just a few hours' flight. I stay here most of the time. After all, someone has to keep the house going. As she continues to improve, he will probably visit less frequently. But I know you did not call to ask about her. What's on your mind?"

"Well, I have a two-bedroom house in Georgetown, and I would like to invite the two of you to come down and spend a weekend with me. I want to talk to you about something, but I want both of you here."

"Sep, that sounds a little ominous," he replied.

"Not at all. I do have a proposition that I want you to think about, but it's important to present it to you together."

"We live a fairly simple life here when we're both in town. So I don't see a problem. I'm sure Jean-Paul will agree. Do you have a weekend in mind?"

"Let me check my calendar," I replied. Not that it was necessary. The Senate hardly ever works over the weekend. I came back on the line and said, "Any weekend in April, including this coming one and even the thirteenth, which is Easter weekend."

"Religious holidays don't hold any significance for me. But aren't you going home for Easter?" he asked.

"Well, not if you guys are going to be here. If you don't come for Easter I might fly to California. But believe me, meeting with you is more important."

"You sound very serious, Sep."

"I am, Jacks."

"OK. Let me talk to Jean-Paul. It probably won't be this weekend, but I'll call you back tomorrow regardless. Thanks for calling. Good night, Sep."

"Good night, Jacks."

I hung up the phone, elated at the possibility of them visiting Washington. But would they accept my offer?

.   .   .

True to his word, Jackson called back the next day with plans to come to Washington on Good Friday. Although Georgetown is accessible via the metro rail, I chose to meet them at the airport. With a flight time of approximately one-and-a-half hours, their midafternoon departure meant a four thirty or five o'clock landing. To be on the safe side I left my home early and was waiting at the gate as they disembarked.

I had anticipated meeting Jean-Paul ever since Jackson told me about him the previous September. But it was really Jackson I wanted to see and I was not disappointed. As they walked off the plane, his broad smile and sparkling eyes reminded me of our years at Harvard. The joy he emanated might leave one to suspect that his life had been easy, free of care, or perhaps the exact opposite. After all, joy comes from deep within and Jackson had never been a superficial person. Perhaps for him it was the result of struggling with and overcoming serious obstacles. Regardless, I was pleased to see him again.

"Hello, Jacks," I said.

"Sep. It's so good to see you. This is my partner, Jean-Paul." I don't know what I expected. I had never even seen a picture of him. He was not as tall as I anticipated. Maybe about five feet eleven inches. For some reason I thought he would have olive skin, but no. He was white, although not pale, slender and had light brown hair and blues eyes. In truth, they made a handsome couple.

"*Bonjour*, Jean-Paul," I said in my best French accent. "It's a pleasure to meet you. *Bienvenu* to Washington, D.C."

"*Merci beaucoup*, Giuseppe. Jackson did not tell me that you speak French."

"Oh, I don't," I replied with a slight laugh. "I know a couple of phrases but they would quickly exhaust the limits of my knowledge. We're better off speaking English." I addressed them both saying, "Let's get your luggage and head over to the house." As we walked toward the baggage carousels I continued, "Have you been in Washington before, Jean-Paul?"

"Once," he replied. "When I first came to the United States I traveled along the East Coast. But I did not spend nearly enough time in the capital. I remember it being a spectacular city. And even though I'm a European, I think Washington has the world's most magnificent monuments."

I am sure that comment came from his heart. He had no reason to impress me. As the conversation continued, I found that listening to Jean-Paul speak was a thorough delight. His English was impeccable and it was graced with a charming accent. In one respect, Washington D.C. is like Los Angeles. On every street, in every store or restaurant, one hears accents from around the world. And yet, his stood out. Lilting and lyrical, it had a calming effect. It was clear to me that he was a sensitive man.

When we arrived in Georgetown, I gave them a quick tour, driving around the university, along Canal Road and M Street and up Wisconsin Avenue to Thirty-Third Street where my home is. Once we arrived I showed them around the house and let them settle in their room. Afterwards we enjoyed cocktails and hors d'oeuvres on the patio. This relaxation gave them time to fill in the gaps of their story. I attempted to regale Jean-Paul with tales of my time in graduate school with Jackson. Not surprisingly, most of my recollections were positive. I never mentioned Helena, Jackson's former therapist and love interest. I figured that was not territory I should trespass. Anything he wanted Jean-Paul to know about that experience was Jackson's purview.

I was struck by their relationship. All of us were in our mid-forties and none of us innocent to worldly ways. But I noticed something each time they looked at each other. There was a purity of love between them. I always knew that Jackson, like Nathaniel in the Gospel, was without guile. I discovered that night that so also was Jean-Paul. They did not just make a handsome couple, they were a match. I admired the depth of their love and was perhaps a little envious. The two of them had an unnerving effect. I found myself plaintively thinking about Yolanda. I could feel emotion welling up inside me and was not prepared to handle it. Fortunately, it was time for dinner.

"Listen, guys," I said. "I'm not the cook that my brother is. If we were at his house, he would have prepared a spread worthy of our Italian heritage. I live alone, and I don't enjoying cooking. I took the liberty to make a reservation at 1789 Restaurant. It's a historic building right here in Georgetown, named for memorable events of 1789: the adoption of the Constitution and the incorporation of Georgetown, to name just two. It's also walking distance from here and we're fortunate to have pleasant weather this evening."

"Sounds good to me," Jackson replied. "But tomorrow night you have to let us fix dinner. We're both pretty good cooks. We almost never go out to eat in Boston these days."

"It's a deal," I said. "Although I might not be good in the kitchen, I do know my way around a wine cellar. I'm a little partial to California cabernet if that's OK. But I promise not to disappoint you. I have a 1985 Caymus Special Selection. I've been waiting for the right occasion to open one of those. I also have a St. Clement Oroppos from its inaugural year, 1991. Let me get them and we can be on our way."

I had not exaggerated the beauty of the night. We were only two weeks into daylight savings time. The sun was setting later each evening and we were bathed in twilight as we sauntered through residential Georgetown.

The maître d' greeted us on our arrival. I had reserved a table to the far side of the fireplace, where it would be reasonably quiet. I wanted this evening, indeed this entire weekend, to go well. As a small gesture, I had requested a 1789 Restaurant souvenir gift card and coin be placed at their settings. We each selected different options for our main course: Jackson chose lamb, Jean-Paul the pork loin, and I had red snapper. The food was superb and the wines magnificent. I favored the Caymus, but had no criticism of the St. Clement.

Jackson must have been restraining his curiosity for days. Finally, he spoke up. "Giuseppe, what is it you need to talk about?" I took a drink of wine, a breath, and began.

"I've been in Washington for four-and-a-half months. I realize that I am still adjusting, but something has been missing. At first, I thought I was just a little anxious. But that's not really my style. I know what I want and where I want my career to go. Self-confidence has never been a problem for me." I said this matter-of-factly. I did not want to come across as cocky. "But a couple of weeks ago, just before I called you, I realized that I don't have anyone to share my confidence. This goes beyond the business of governance. I have a good rapport with my staff, but that's professional. I don't have anyone I can talk things over with on a truly personal level. I want you to be my advisor, Jacks."

He looked at Jean-Paul and then said, "I don't know anything about politics, Sep. And I'm not a lawyer."

"I'm not looking for that," I interjected. "I have lawyers and lobbyists in my office every day. It's tiresome. I want someone who can tell me how the average American feels and thinks; someone who can challenge me on the issues; someone I can be myself with; someone I can trust. That's you, Jackson."

There was a brief pause. Again he looked at Jean-Paul, but their glance did not reveal much to me. He asked, "What would this entail?"

That was not yet a commitment, but at least it indicated some interest. Hopefully, it portended that he was not closed to the idea.

"It won't interfere with your job. And you won't need to move to Washington. I'd like you to visit occasionally, on a weekend. Especially when there are critical issues before the Senate." I looked at Jean-Paul and said, "You're both always welcome." Then I looked back at Jackson and continued. "I just want you to be the person who tells me what's right and what's wrong. You're the only one I know who will be honest with me."

"What about your brother?" he asked.

"No," I said, perhaps a little too quickly. "His religious bias would get in the way. I don't want a Catholic perspective. Besides, there are enough of them in Washington already. I want something more secular, more balanced. That's what I'd get from you."

He drew a deep breath and said, "I can't give you an answer right now. This is something Jean-Paul and I need to discuss alone. We live a quiet Bostonian life and you know about his mother. He needs to go to Brussels frequently. Give me—give us—some time to process this. I'll let you know soon."

"Thanks, Jacks. I appreciate it."

Night had completely descended over Georgetown during our meal. The temperature was mild and a gentle breeze accompanied us on the walk back to my home. The next day I committed to showing them around the city. Between the monuments and the museums it's really too much to absorb in one day. But I hoped there would be more to come. On Sunday morning I drove them back to the airport.

I shook hands with Jean-Paul and said, "It was good to finally meet you."

"*Merci*," he said with a smile.

"Take care of Jackson," I replied.

Then I turned to Jackson and said, "Thank you for coming down this weekend. It was great seeing you again."

"Same here, Sep. And thanks for your hospitality. You're a great host. I promise to be in touch and give my answer soon. Goodbye."

As I returned home I had reason to hope. I guess I could not have asked anything more of the weekend.

CHAPTER 7

As far back as high school, Tom had always been more sensitive than I when it came to relationships. For me, girls were merely conquests, each one another notch. Tom, by contrast, was always concerned about their feelings. To my knowledge he never lied to any of them or merely used them for his pleasure. For that same reason I am certain he never cheated on Emily during their marriage. In fact, with her alluring charm and depth of character she tamed whatever roaming instincts he may have possessed. His commitment to Emily came as easily as sex itself. Even after their divorce, Tom could not dislodge her from his heart. That is probably why he never married again, unlike many of his fellow police officers who seem unable to live alone, many of them approaching marriage with the ease and frequency of a bar.

Over the course of several months, they continued to meet for lunch, dinner, and an occasional movie. They were dating all over again and Tom, wanting to be gentlemanly, did not push the idea of sex. Nonetheless, it was unavoidable. Even if they had not previously been married, neither of them was burdened by Victorian values. Tom had hungered for Emily since their dinner in April, but it was she who first ventured into that memorable territory. And if it was planned, it was on a subconscious level.

In June Tom picked Emily up at her apartment. They went to dinner and then to see the newly released film *Pearl Harbor*. The love story in the movie was unconvincing, but even bad acting can spark desires. Tom walked Emily to her front door and was about to kiss her good night. She stepped back and asked, "Do you want to stay here tonight?" Her eyes revealed a sincere invitation and betrayed a surprisingly deep longing. Tom hesitated ever so briefly before replying, "More than you know."

Upon entering the apartment they were enveloped by a long forgotten passion. He had never met anyone like Emily and yearned to be with her again. To him she was as beautiful as she was in her twenties, and he just as nervous as the first time they made love. His brief disquiet did not last and gave way to a kiss of overwhelming intensity and duration. This was not a kiss that had to be practiced. It sprang naturally and from deep within the lovers. He leaned back against the door and drew her close, her suppleness melting in his arms. She stood between his legs and even as he felt himself grow hard he could focus on nothing but her kiss. Their tongues entwined in a rhythmic dance, slow then fast then slow, exploring every inch of each other's mouth. He was certain the neighbors could hear the pounding of their hearts because that was all he could hear. They snatched quick breaths when possible but refused to quit their embrace. Their minds were in such a state of disorientation. They had so much to say to each other, but were afraid to speak. Neither was willing to end the kiss for fear the whole experience would evaporate into a harsh and unwelcome reality. Tom refused to let go. He couldn't take the chance that there would be nothing more. He was willing to remain forever lost in this wonderful world they had created. That one kiss seemed to dissolve sixteen years of emptiness. There was no fantasy here. This was true love.

When at last Emily stepped back, the glow in her eyes kept reality at bay. "Let's go to bed, Tom." She didn't have to say it twice.

•　•　•

As Neil Diamond famously sang, "It was a hot August night." The midsummer month's scorching heat frequently drives Angelenos to one of the southland's many social or cultural distractions: amusement parks, museums, and a plethora of concert venues including the Hollywood Bowl, Universal Amphitheater, the Greek Theatre, and various city parks. Or they just go to the beach. One such evening Tom and Emily had dinner at the Chart House situated on prime real estate along Pacific Coast Highway in Malibu. The restaurant is built on the edge overlooking the sand and the Santa Monica Bay. Diners can watch seagulls perch on wooden posts, pelicans brim the waters in search of food, and the waves delicately enfold the beach. As picturesque and enchanting as the scene may be, romance descends from above as the evening sun sets the California night afire. With magical wonder, the waning star inches beyond the horizon leaving intense hues of the rainbow in its wake. Then with a finishing touch this drowning Midas of the sky imparts a shimmering layer of gold upon the sea. This is California romance at its finest.

After dinner Emily suggested a stroll on the shore. They ambled along, reminiscing about earlier times. The two had become quite comfortable in their intimacy, opening more and more doors of conversation.

"Tom," Emily began. "The last few months have been wonderful. The more I see you, the more I realize that you are still the good and decent man I fell in love with so long ago. Why didn't you ever marry again?"

He laughed and said, "I asked you the same question five months ago. But you didn't answer."

"True," Emily replied with a wry smile. "But that was our first meeting in sixteen years. We've been seeing quite a lot of each other since then and the question is more natural now." She darted in front of him, looked back, and said, "I'll answer you, but tonight I asked first."

That response conjured up the perpetual interplay of children, leading to a little laughter from both of them. Tom caught up to her. As they continued their walk he said, "For me, it was a combination of two things. First, I didn't want to be bothered."

"Because you were hurt?" she interjected.

"No," he replied. "I mean, I was hurt, but that wasn't the reason. I didn't want to be tied down again. By the time I adjusted to living alone, I saw no need for change. Hell, the last couple years of our marriage, we were both practically living alone, anyway. I let my job take precedence over everything else, including you. I regret that, Em. I've regretted it for a long time." He suddenly realized that he had never had this discussion with anyone. No one else had ever asked him. The question itself was simple, but the response was potentially deep—deeper than he thought the evening warranted. Instead, he moved on.

"The second reason is somewhat related. I was afraid of relationship. I figured that I was at fault for our marriage falling apart and I didn't want that to happen again."

"You were not at fault, Tom," she insisted. "Relationships are never one-sided. Besides, you've changed. You're not as ambitious or driven. You don't even seem to care whether or not you please your superiors. You're calmer and more balanced."

"A lot of it has to do with that damn murder. I was certainly driven by the investigation. For months I could think of nothing else. In spite of that our work went nowhere. Now that it's over I refuse to consider my job the most important thing in my life."

"But the case isn't closed," she replied.

"No. But it's not active, either. I told you before. I know who did it. There's just no proof. And there never will be. I'll have to live with that. But I won't let it or my job consume my life again."

"Tom, are you going to tell me what you know about the murders?" she asked.

They had been strolling hand in hand. He stopped to face her and looked intently into her eyes. "For the time being I can't, Em. It would put you in danger." She started to interrupt but he waved his hand and continued, "I know you've been in precarious situations before, many times. But you've got to believe me. This is far more serious than any of your assignments in the Middle East or Asia. At least you can be somewhat prepared in the center of a war zone. Most of the time you know who your enemy is. And often where he is."

"I'm a seasoned journalist, Tom. I've handled myself in perilous places before and I've survived."

"But Em, you don't understand this case. It was so high profile there were things we kept from the media and the public."

"For example," she egged him on.

He decided to give in a little. "There were subsequent killings connected to the Lozano murder investigation. Yolanda and the kids were the center of a three-dimensional net, the human version of the redback spider's tangled web. Treachery continues to lie in every direction and a simple trip of the thread means death. No one, not even the police, knows where the next strike will take place."

"Then you think there will be more killings?" she asked.

"I don't know. I'm only certain that if people outside the LAPD begin sniffing around, if they get too close, those threads will be tripped."

"Why is the LAPD immune?" she asked.

"Because we have no usable information. I've never seen nor read of a murder planned so efficiently." He placed his hands on her shoulders and said, "I'm serious. Stay away from this. I won't take the chance of losing you again."

She had never before seen fear in his eyes. Indeed, this was more. It was equal parts fear and anxiety. She knew he was concerned for her, but this angst was broader than the two of them. It embraced anyone who might decide to do some private investigation.

"OK, Tom. I'll stay away from this case for now. But if my editor should want anything, we'll have to revisit this whole discussion. Fair enough?"

"Fair enough," he reluctantly replied. He thought that returning to the previous part of the discussion would ease some tension. He asked, "So, Em, it's your turn. Why didn't you marry again?"

"I can answer that very easily," she said. "At least I can now. You know I'm a romantic, Tom. I've always believed that there is one person for each of us. For me it was always you. I've never loved anyone else. I didn't even try. No one could be for me what you were. I was content to live that way. Then you came back into my life."

She smiled and he drew her to himself. He wanted to take her right then, but at their age the beach was an undignified place to yield to sex. Besides, there are laws against public nudity, even at night.

As Tom kissed her neck, she whispered his name. He didn't want to talk and responded only with a groan, "Hmm?"

"Will you marry me?" she asked.

He had to admit that he had similar thoughts but he was not ready for her to ask the question. Tom was not a sexist but he thought it was his place to propose. And yet, he knew how to respond. He looked into her eyes and said, "Nothing would make me happier. But are you sure you want this?"

"I'm certain, Tom."

"Do you know what you're getting into, Emily?"

She had lost none of her insight or wisdom over the years. She replied, "No one ever does. But we've been there before. We're different people now. And this time we're prepared."

"Then my answer is yes," he replied. Then he took her in his arms and kissed her.

CHAPTER 8

It was seven o'clock in the morning. Giovanni had finished celebrating Mass and was having breakfast when the telephone rang. He hated being disturbed while eating, but welcomed the sound of the voice on the other end.

"Hello, Gio. This is Tom."

"Hi, Tom. You're up early today. How are you?"

"Better than you can imagine. Are you free for lunch today?"

"I can be," Giovanni replied. "What's up? You sound different. Almost excited."

"I'll tell you later. Can we meet at Taix? My treat."

Taix is a landmark Los Angeles restaurant specializing in French country cuisine. It originated in the early nineteen hundreds in L.A.'s French quarter. In the early 1960s it relocated to its current location on Sunset Boulevard overlooking downtown. It is not too expensive and the food is always reliable. Of particular note are Taix's lamb shank and coq au vin.

"Let's make it after the lunch rush," Giovanni suggested. "Say one o'clock?"

"OK," Tom said. "See you then."

Giovanni hung up the phone and wondered. He had not seen Tom for a while. Yet he was not as surprised by the phone call as he was by his friend's enthusiasm. It had been almost a year since either of them had experienced anything approaching happiness. They had been friends all their lives and could read each other impeccably. Giovanni had his suspicions but would have to wait to have them verified.

When he arrived at the restaurant, Tom was waiting. They greeted each other and the maître d escorted them to a booth. Giovanni spoke first. "Tom, what's going on? Something is different about you."

Tom smiled as he replied, "Emily and I are getting married."

At another time Giovanni would have had an immediate reply. Such a response was not forthcoming that day. Still he could not disappoint his friend. He smiled, took a sip of water and replied, "That's great news, Tom. I can't say I'm surprised, and I'm very much delighted. But isn't this a little soon?"

The words were authentic, but they were not conveyed with a great deal of conviction. Tom's expression changed as he said, "Come on, Gio. We're not kids anymore. Emily and I were married before. To each other! I think I knew as soon as I saw her back in March. I really want this." He almost pleaded with him. "She makes me happy, Gio."

Giovanni saw a sparkle in his eyes that he had not seen in years. It reminded him of when Tom and Emily first met.

"Well, Tom. I always thought you two were made for each other."

Tom quickly interjected, "She said the same thing. You know, Gio, Emily and I have seen a lot of each other the last several months, and this is not impetuous. Talk of marriage did not come up until the other day."

"I had no idea things were getting so serious," Giovanni said, still avoiding the enthusiasm Tom anticipated.

"Yeah," Tom responded, almost sarcastically. "But you haven't exactly been available lately, have you? Sometimes I think if I didn't call I'd never hear from you."

Giovanni hastened to answer. "That's not true."

"Isn't it?" Tom asked. "When was the last time you picked up the phone and called me?"

There was some truth in what he said. Giovanni had to admit that much. But it was not just Tom. He did not really want to talk to anyone. He had begun an almost irreversible journey into isolation. The only friends he saw regularly were other priests, and then only on his day off. He welcomed the distraction these Tuesdays brought, even the fact that they had become almost as routine as Sundays. He did not have to open up to anyone.

"I'm sorry, Tom. I really am. I don't know what's happening to me."

"I do," Tom replied. "You've cut yourself off from everyone. I know things have been difficult. And even if I hadn't been raised Catholic, on some level I suppose I'd still understand this confession dilemma. I get that. But what's happening to you isn't healthy. I know you can't talk about what your brother told you, but you have to share your feelings with somebody. Unfortunately, we're too close and both of us too affected by the murder. Still, you need to find someone."

Giovanni thought for a minute and then replied, "Ironically, you didn't speak like this before Emily came back into your life."

"No, I didn't," Tom said. "That's the point. Just sharing with her has helped me tremendously."

"It's more than that, Tom. You're in love. That's a luxury the priesthood does not afford me. And it's a risk I don't want to take."

"You don't have to fall in love, Gio. You just need to share your feelings. You need to be human." He realized that did not come out right. "I'm sorry. I'm not expressing myself well."

"Never mind, Tom. Forget about me. Tell me more about you and Emily."

Tom related the events of the last several months and their most recent dinner. He and Giovanni were not in high school and he did not need to exaggerate his prowess, so he left out the sexual details. Then he said, "Emily and I would like you to perform the ceremony. And she wants another religious one, but I'd rather not do it in church. What do we have to do?"

"Actually, you don't have to do anything except get a marriage license from the state. As far as the church is concerned, your marriage is still binding. You don't even have to exchange vows in a church building. We can use the official rite, but do it anywhere you want. As far as I'm concerned you can have as big or small a wedding as you want. We just need to set the date and place."

"Let me talk to Emily," Tom said, "and we can all coordinate our calendars." He looked directly in Giovanni's eyes. "Thanks, Gio. This means a lot to me."

"You're still my best friend, Tom, but I'd do this no matter what. And I really am happy, even if I sometimes act like a shit."

Through the rest of lunch Tom continued to talk about Emily. Giovanni could tell that this was not an adolescent infatuation. He was witnessing the rebirth of love. He didn't say anything, but it left him wondering if the priesthood was worth it.

•   •   •

Tom and Emily had no desire to duplicate their first wedding. This would be a simpler, more intimate, family-only affair. Labor Day fell on September 3, and with many people traveling out of town for the holiday weekend, they scheduled the wedding for Friday, August 31. My sister, Bianca, and her husband offered their home in South Pasadena, a comfortable dwelling with a large backyard. Tom's parents were present, as was his sister, Karen, and her family. Andrew and Margaret Cartwright, Emily's parents, flew in from London. With Bianca hosting the celebration, Giovanni officiating the ceremony, and my parents in attendance, everyone was there but me.

Over the previous eight months I had developed an enviable talent for making excuses. No one in the family knew the inner workings of Congress. True or not, I could always claim some Senate business as a reason to remain in Washington. Only Tom and Giovanni suspected the truth—I was avoiding them as much as they wanted to avoid me.

For the ceremony an arch was placed in the back corner of the yard. It was decorated with white and yellow roses, complementing the tables that were draped in white cloth, each with a centerpiece displaying yellow jasmine. In spite of all he had been feeling, Giovanni knew that he had to come through for this service. He owed it to Tom and Emily to be in top form. He orchestrated a special beginning to the ceremony.

The previous November, following the murders and election, I entrusted Giovanni with some boxes containing family memorabilia, mostly pictures, but also many of Yolanda's papers. He had been perusing them during the spring as part of his personal grieving process. I did not know it, but mixed among the papers were some of Yolanda's poems, including lyrics she had written to movie themes. One of them was from the film *Bad Girls*. Jerry Goldsmith had written the music. Having been born in Pasadena, California, where we grew up, he was more than a celebrity. He was a local hero. Goldsmith was such a prolific composer that it is difficult to measure one score against another. Nonetheless, an argument can be made that the *Bad Girls* theme was his most romantic. It is certainly no surprise that Yolanda would want to write equally amorous lyrics for it. I suspect she had planned on using it for one of our daughter's weddings. Whatever her intent, Giovanni was certain she would have approved its use for Tom and Emily.

From childhood Bianca always had a beautiful voice. As an adult, however, it had become resonantly seasoned. Giovanni asked her to sing Yolanda's song at the ceremony, but he had not told Tom and Emily. After everyone had taken their places, Tom and Emily stood at the back, she in a yellow cocktail dress with white lace, he in a white tuxedo with pale yellow tie. Giovanni stepped forward and addressed the small gathering.

"Less than a year ago we were all struck with tragedy when my sister-in-law, two nieces, and nephew were inexplicably murdered. At the funeral we all learned that Yolanda had a hobby. She wrote lyrics to movie themes. A few months ago I discovered some of them. At the time I did not know we would be here today. But once Tom told me that he and Emily were getting married, and unbeknownst to the two of them, I decided this was an appropriate time to use one of Yolanda's songs. I imagine that if she were alive today she would willingly sing it herself. Since she is not here, I asked Bianca to sing. Let's now stand to welcome our bride and groom."

Giovanni had cued the music system so that as Tom and Emily began walking down the aisle, the song would begin.

Bad Girls

Track 1:

The John

I have lived but once before
Only in a passing dream.
Life and love itself mean so much more
Here with you, oh my love!

When you fold into my arms
Strange the stirrings that I feel.
So bewildered by your mystic charms,
Not a dream this is real, my love.

Now I know that my search is at end,
Nevermore a glance.
You are all I could ever need or tend.
Here we hold one glorious chance.

Lay beside me day is done.
Feel your body warm with mine.
Here our breath and hearts become as one.
Evermore I am yours, my love.

The song had the emotional effect Giovanni hoped for. If possible, it made Emily look even more radiant and Tom more heartened. No one present harbored any doubts. This time their union would thrive.

CHAPTER 9

September 11, 2001

September weather in New York City can be oppressive. Although not as hot as July and August, eighty degree temperatures frequent the days, often accompanied by ninety percent humidity. But there are exceptions. On 9/11, as we would come to call it, the waking hours were perfect. The morning air was brisk and above the city gleamed an azure sky usually reserved for picture postcards. Hurricane Erin had been threatening the Northeast but was pushed out to sea by the combined forces of a cold front and high pressure. Had the storm moved onshore, the day and the world might have been different. As it was, Tuesday morning was simply beautiful. Until 8:36 a.m.

When constructed in the early 1970s, the Twin Towers of the World Trade Center were the tallest buildings in the world and loomed above the Manhattan skyline like two steel and concrete sentries. Symbols of power, prestige, and permanence they assured that life in New York City was shielded and stable. But like many a man–made fortress they offered a false sense of security. Tuesday, September 11, New Yorkers would learn the lesson of ancient Troy: the enemy can always find a way in.

American Airlines flight 11 left Boston Logan Airport en route to Los Angeles. The time was 7:59 a.m. Unknown to the airline, and with no apparent reason to raise suspicion, five terrorists had boarded the plane. About a quarter after eight the plane was hijacked, the transponder turned off, Boston air traffic control lost contact, and the plane began to deviate from its scheduled flight plan. At the time, this information was unknown to the authorities. Given the number of flights over the U.S. on any given day, it is not uncommon to lose contact. But at 8:28 a.m., a message was broadcast from the cockpit to the passengers stating that the plane was returning to the airport. This announcement was necessitated due to the course change, for everyone onboard would notice the plane turning around. Although the message was intended for the passengers, it was overheard by a traffic controller in Boston. He understood. Something was wrong and a report was communicated to the Federal Aviation Administration.

Ben Sliney was serving his first day as national operations manager for the FAA. It was his responsibility to manage all flights over the United States. This included more than five thousand commercial flights just between the hours of seven o'clock and eight o'clock in the morning. Most hijacked flights, while tense and inconvenient, have a favorable ending, so he was not overly concerned.

At about the same time as the cockpit announcement, Betty Ong, the number three flight attendant, managed to get a call through to American Airlines reservation center in Raleigh, North Carolina. She informed them that the plane was being hijacked, and that two of the flight attendants had been stabbed.

Dave Bottiglia, at the air traffic control center on Long Island, was overseeing sector 42 of U.S. airspace. He received a message from Boston stating that American flight 11 might have been hijacked. With the transponder off he had no idea of the plane's altitude or speed. He was only able to follow the radar that indicated it was heading toward JFK International Airport. After repeated attempts to reach the cockpit met with silence, another controller contacted the Northeast Air Defense Sector requesting F–15 support. His request was escalated to Colonel Bob Marr who put the fighters at Otis International Guard Base on alert.

At 8:46 a.m. American Airlines flight 11 crashed into the North tower of the World Trade Center. The speed of the aircraft, the force of the impact and the fully fueled tanks created an instantaneous conflagration. From the South tower, Rick Rescorla could see the building engulfed in flames and smoke. When he heard the Port Authority announce over the public address system that people should remain where they were he sprang into action. He was director of security for Morgan Stanley financial services, and had previously drafted emergency evacuation procedures. Ignoring the Port Authority announcement, he grabbed his bullhorn and walkie-talkie and directed the employees to evacuate, sending them down a stairwell from the forty-fourth floor. He saved more than two thousand people that day. In his attempt to rescue yet more people he perished when the tower collapsed.

A few minutes after the plane struck the building, the FAA command center received a CNN report that a small aircraft had crashed into the World Trade Center. No one conceived of the possibility that CNN got it wrong; that it was actually the hijacked airliner that was involved. The military, still unaware of the reality in New York City, sent two F–15 fighter jets to search for American Airlines flight 11.

Dave Bottiglia became increasingly concerned about another plane, United Airlines flight 175. It also had changed its transponder code and its flight path was erratic. At 9:03 a.m. flight 175 flew into the South tower. As soon as he realized that the World Trade Center had been attacked, Colonel Marr ordered the F–15s to New York to control the airspace over the city. From the FAA command center, Ben Sliney ordered an immediate national ground stop order—no airplane would be allowed to take off anywhere in the nation. This, however, would not end the day's horrors.

At 9:05 a.m. American Airlines flight 77 from Washington, D.C., to Los Angeles was observed to be off course. Again the transponder was turned off and air traffic controllers could not make contact. Radar indicated it had turned around and was headed back to Washington. At 9:25 with still no confirmation that the first plane to hit the towers was American flight 11, two F–16 fighter jets were deployed from Langley Air Force Base in Virginia to search for the missing flight.

There were multiple reports of hijacked aircraft that Tuesday, and the military was left to decipher reality from fantasy. Assuming that Washington was a target, the F–16 jets were ordered to turn around and head for the Capital. The time was 9:36 a.m. They were too late. At 9:37 American flight 77 dived into the Pentagon building.

That was too much for Ben Sliney. He immediately made the unprecedented and extreme decision to force every airplane in the sky to land at the nearest airport regardless of their destination. All planes began to clear the skies, save one. Unknown to any authority, United Airlines flight 93 had already been hijacked—the fourth that morning. At 9:44 what had become an all too familiar and frightening pattern emerged. The transponder had been changed, and the flight had deviated from its scheduled plan. Radar indicated that it was headed to Washington, D.C. Like the F–15s in New York, the F–16s out of Langley were preparing to secure the airspace over the Capital. As it turned out, heroic efforts by passengers and crew onboard United 93 foiled the hijackers' plan. They overpowered the terrorists and crashed the plane into the ground twenty minutes shy of Washington.

America was in shock. Within one hour three hijacked airliners had hit their targets. The South tower of the World Trade Center collapsed at 9:59 a.m. followed at 10:28 by the North tower. The world was in shock, too, for nearly three thousand people from ninety countries lost their lives that morning. The attacks were so terrifying that it seemed as if the entire world were in a single time zone. Everyone received information, both accurate and false, at exactly the same moment. Around the globe people were mesmerized by what they saw: smoke, dust, and debris engulfing Manhattan Island; thousands scurrying for safety, fleeing death and destruction; New York City fire and police personnel heroically rushing to the scene within minutes of the first plane crash. This was a science fiction movie turned ominously real.

•   •   •

If knowledge is power and power is the currency of the realm, the nation was bankrupt. In the early hours of the morning, as chaos gripped the city of New York, official Washington was slow to go on alert. Once United Airlines flight 175 slammed into the South tower, everyone realized these were no accidents. Still, believing the attacks were restricted to New York City, Congress continued its business as usual for the next thirty-five minutes.

I had already eaten breakfast at home, but was in the Senate dining room having coffee with Senator Don Nickles of Oklahoma. An aide rushed into the room and shouted, "Washington's under attack." I looked out the window and could see a huge plume of smoke rising above the Pentagon. Nickles had already stood up. He turned to me and said, "We've got to get out of here."

Cell phones and electronic communications were quickly rendered useless—too many people trying to contact offices and loved ones. The president, vice-president, secretary of state, and CIA director could not rely on their secured phones, cell phones, or even landlines. It seemed as if the entire Capital were cut off from meaningful communication. Hundreds of congressional members crammed into the Capitol Police Department seeking some kind of news. This was the beginning of the twenty-first century, and our nation's leaders were getting all their information from television networks over a small black and white TV!

President Bush was particularly slow to react. Less than twenty minutes after the first plane was missiled into the WTC he entered a second grade classroom at Emma E. Booker elementary school in Sarasota, Florida. He had been informed about that first crash, but had no reason to suspect either that it was deliberate or that it was an act of terrorism. A few minutes after nine o'clock, Andrew Card whispered into the president's ear that another plane struck the second tower and that the United States was under attack. Now there was reason for concern. But President Bush's Secret Service detail made no attempt to move the president to safety. His staff did not whisk him into an emergency briefing. Bush did not even flinch. He really did not know what to do. In hindsight he could have stood up and said something innocuous so as not to frighten the class. After all, they knew he was the president. "Excuse me, children I have to take care of something very important. I will come back as soon as possible," would have sufficed. He did not stand. He did not say anything. He just reached for a book and read with them for nearly eight minutes—not reacting, seeming instead, as if everything was normal.

To be fair, the United States, indeed no country, had ever prepared for such an event. Being unready also meant we had no response plan. After all, we were not at war. And even if we had been, certainly no enlightened mind could have devised using passenger jets as rockets to strike civilian centers. Even the attack on Pearl Harbor targeted warships and military installations. The terrorism of 9/11 was unprecedented. But it did not excuse the lack of leadership. As much as I needed to support Bush, I made a mental note of how I would handle a similar incident when I became president.

In times of panic and angst great men and women, especially true leaders, prove their worth. Not unlike a loving parent, they rise to tame the terror of the night, their mere presence producing comfort and calm. They promise peace and guarantee that the people are being watched over and cared for. For over one hundred eighty years, through wars and civil strife, American presidents have provided that assurance. On September 11, 2001, for alleged security reasons, President Bush did not return to the White House until ten hours later, long after the airspace above the Capital had been secured. It was the first time that a president had abandoned Washington since 1814, when the British set the White House and Capitol buildings ablaze. Bush did address the nation at 8:30 p.m. but the people expected and deserved more. For the second time that day I made a mental note regarding my future occupancy of America's highest office. To be fair to Bush, however, the president was not alone.

Most of Washington seemed asleep at the wheel that morning. The FAA warned that a hijacked plane, United flight 93, was headed to the Capital. And yet, it was not until twenty-four minutes later that the Capitol Building was evacuated. Had the takeoff not been delayed by forty minutes, there may have been few, if any, surviving members of Congress.

In the midst of this chaos one person was astutely alert—Vice-President Dick Cheney. He lived by a personal mantra chosen from *Odes,* a poem by the great Roman writer, Horace: *Carpe Diem* (Seize the Day). Cheney always believed that his time for greatness would come. His first real opportunity occurred while he was in Congress as a representative from Wyoming. It eluded him, however, even though he briefly served as the House Minority Whip, the second highest-ranking member of his party.

Then Cheney gained national prominence when President George H. W. Bush selected him to be secretary of defense. In this role he oversaw Operation Desert Storm, the first Iraq war. But he was frustrated by his inability to call the shots, to make the ultimate decisions. That prerogative belonged to the president. As part of a band of ideologues known as Neocons (neoconservatives) Cheney wanted to continue the war into the streets of Baghdad and remove Saddam Hussein from power. The president, however, was far more skilled in international affairs and knew that such an action would not be supported by our allies in the Middle East. He was also aware that it would have had disastrous effects, including further loss of life. Additionally, it was beyond the scope of the justification for war. When the Iraqi army was expelled from Kuwait and coalition forces controlled the requisite part of Iraq, the conflict reached its desired end. President Bush called a ceasefire and an agreement was signed bringing the war to conclusion. No one is more adept at revisionist history than Neocons, and Cheney would later state that he agreed with the president. However, in secret he vowed that he would never again allow someone to deny him his destiny—and 9/11 provided his long awaited moment.

Shortly after 9:00 a.m., it was evident to Cheney that America was under attack. He descended into the White House basement and through a tunnel to the Presidential Emergency Operations Center, an underground bunker. He was joined by his wife, Lynne. Also present were National Security Advisor Condoleeza Rice and Transportation

Secretary Norman Mineta, among others. Cheney understood the importance of maintaining a functioning government and a chain of command. Speaker of the House Dennis Hastert and President Pro Tempore of the Senate Robert Byrd—respectively the second and third in line for the presidency—Senator Tom Daschle, Representative Dick Gephart, and other congressional leaders were taken to secure locations. Cheney told the president not to return to Washington. His *Carpe Diem* had arrived.

•   •   •

Tuesday was Giovanni's day off and he had driven up to Lake Arrowhead in the San Gabriel Mountains with two of his close priest friends, Perry Leiker and Bill Messenger. On the way they were all struck by the same sensation. Something eerie was in the air. They had watched news coverage of the attacks before they left Los Angeles and knew that all planes had been grounded throughout the country. Perhaps their observation was partly induced by that knowledge, but it was nonetheless unsettling. On the freeways of Southern California no one actually hears jets flying 35,000 feet above them. Most of the time people do not even see them. They just know the planes are there. But on September 11, they were not. There was nothing above but empty sky. Perry was the first one to comment.

"Something's wrong today," he said. "Can you feel it?"

Bill, being a bit of a smartass, replied, "No shit. The World Trade Center just collapsed! And the East Coast is under attack."

"That's not what I mean," Perry continued. "There's something ghostly about the atmosphere today. Even though we already know it, you can actually sense that there's not a single plane in the sky. Not even a helicopter. I can even feel it here in the car."

Giovanni agreed. "It's like that trip we took to Puerto Vallarta ten years ago for the solar eclipse."

"Oh, don't remind me," Bill said. "We had to fly out of Tijuana because the flights were booked from L.A. and that meant spending the night at the roach motel they call Hotel Leon. It still gives me the creeps. I didn't sleep at all."

"Don't be such a wuss," Perry replied. "Besides, the point is not the hotel in Tijuana. It's the moon shadow: the instantaneous cooling of the earth as the moon passes in front of the sun; everything, including the birds, abruptly going quiet, the sudden lunar breeze that sweeps across the land. It's preternatural."

Bill responded, "How poetic, Perry! But you're right. It's an amazing experience. And today does feel somewhat the same. Except that it's hot, the sun is shining bright, the birds are singing, and there's no lunar breeze." Only Bill can compliment without ever complimenting.

"You're such an asshole, Bill," Giovanni replied.

"No. I'm serious," Bill continued. "I really do agree with Perry. Today does remind me of that feeling during the eclipse. But you're also right, Gio. I am an asshole. That's part of my charm!"

"Not always," Giovanni said.

"What are you going to do, though?" Perry said, exasperated. "You've got to love him."

"Thanks, guys," Bill replied.

When they arrived at the cabin Giovanni said, "I'm going to the bedroom for a few minutes. I need to make a private phone call."

•   •   •

As a very junior member of the Senate I contributed to a functioning government, but was not at all important in any chain of command. When it appeared that the immediate wave of terror was over and Washington airspace was safely patrolled by the military, I returned to my office. About half-past twelve, nine thirty on the West Coast, I received a phone call. In a Shakespearean play, the ringing would have startled me into reality. But in this case that would not be true. It was not the ring that astonished me. It was the voice. And far from reconnecting me with the activities of the world, it suspended me in disbelief. I was momentarily frozen by a familiar sound. It was my brother, Giovanni. He had not spoken to me since late December. He had not even tried. In truth, neither had I, for I was driven by an instinctive certainty that he would not have responded.

"Hello," I said as I picked up the receiver.

"Giuseppe, this is your brother. Are you all right?"

"Well this is a surprise," I replied. "I didn't expect to hear from you."

"Listen," he said. "I'm not calling to have a conversation. Mom and Dad have not been able to get through to your office, and they're worried. I promised that I would try to reach you and find out if you're OK." I could not help but notice the curtness in his tone. So I decided to be a bit playful.

"Are you saying that you would not have called on your own? That you're not concerned?" I asked.

"That's exactly what I'm saying," he replied. "I really don't care. Mom and Dad do." The anger in his voice was palpable. But I heard something else. Whatever his words conveyed, we were raised to love family above all else. The tremor in his voice betrayed a powerful effort to reject any remnants of brotherly love. But he was not fully equal to the task. He never was. I once told our friend Tom that neither of them could cross the line when needed. Giovanni was hampered on two counts. He was my brother. And he was a priest. But I did not want to embarrass him. I could not let him fail at this most minor of encounters. As directly and emotionlessly as possible I answered.

"Then you can tell them I'm fine. I was in the dining room when the plane hit the Pentagon. It now appears that the worst is over." Then almost as an afterthought, I threw in, "And Gio, thanks for calling."

"You can thank our parents," he said icily. Then he hung up.

• • •

Given that the United States is a country with six time zones, including Alaska and Hawaii, no one could have anticipated the speed with which all aircraft across the nation would be grounded. Since no additional flights were allowed to take off, tens of thousands of people were stranded wherever their planes happened to land. To the FAA this was a minor inconvenience in service of possibly saving untold numbers of lives. That decision had a great impact on the country's police, and the zeal of their response cannot be exaggerated. As the magnitude of the terror attack became clearer, agencies around the country sprang into action.

In Los Angeles, for example, officers were dispatched with alacrity. Even with the skies cleared of planes, the LAPD had to consider other means that might be used in attacking the greater Los Angeles area. All of its resources were shifted to address terrorism. Teams were sent to secure the ports, the airports, Hansen Dam, the DWP and the federal buildings in downtown Los Angeles and Westwood. The LAPD had learned some significant lessons from the Rodney King riots, one result being that when there is a UO—an unusual occurrence—everyone switches into high gear. They all want a piece of the action. And they get it. It is the only way for the LAPD to present a coordinated and united force for the common good.

Once flights resumed across the nation, the LAPD sent teams to New York to find out how their forces consolidated in the face of the attacks. They offered assistance to officials in both New York and Washington.

CHAPTER 10

All Tuesday Giovanni, Perry, and Bill watched the news: the looping visuals of the second plane hitting the South tower; the repetitious video of the collapsing WTC buildings; the smoldering Pentagon; a hole in a Pennsylvania field; the frequently shallow and redundant comments of news anchors competing with each other to maintain viewership. Watching the carnage, the three friends began to discuss how they and their congregations should respond. What would be an appropriate religious reaction?

The Los Angeles Archdiocese has long had an unsurpassed Office for Ecumenical and Interreligious Affairs, developed over many years by Monsignor Royale Vadakin. Ongoing religious dialogue groups that exist nowhere else, meet regularly throughout the diocese. But openness can never be forced on people. Despite successful committees spearheaded by the Catholic Church, getting many evangelical Christian leaders to accept people of other faiths remains impossible. To begin with, many of them are highly skeptical of Catholics, but in their narrow-mindedness they have no use at all for anyone who does not believe in Jesus.

Perry was a member of an ecumenical ministers' association in Hawthorne, and Giovanni belonged to one in the West Adams district of Los Angeles. Neither of them included rabbis or imams. Even for Thanksgiving Day celebrations, the nation's only true religious holiday—at least the only one that crosses all faith divides—the Hawthorne Evangelical ministers would not participate with non-Christians.

Bill, on the other hand, was regularly involved in inter-religious activities at the University of Southern California. The rules of the university require all religious leaders to attend a monthly meeting regardless of their attitudes toward people of different faiths. The group even includes the leader of the Atheist/Free Thinkers association. But a special relationship developed among the Catholic, Lutheran, and Episcopal communities.

In the late 1990s Bill joined with the Episcopal and Lutheran directors, Glenn Libby and Sean Ewbank, to implement a groundbreaking document signed by the Catholic, Episcopal, and Lutheran bishops of Los Angeles, respectively Cardinal Roger Mahony, Bishop Frederick Borsch, and Bishop Paul Egertson. Entitled *"One Lord, One Faith, One Baptism: A Covenant among The Episcopal Diocese of Los Angeles, The Evangelical Lutheran Church in America – Southwest California Synod and The Roman Catholic Archdiocese of Los Angeles,"* it was an attempt to bring these three closely related churches together for prayer, Bible study, and some liturgical activities, including joint baptismal ceremonies. The three bishops even participated in an Ash Wednesday service at USC—the first time ever that bishops from these three denominations had come together for an Ash Wednesday liturgy.

When national crises occur, many people immediately begin to question their faith. Some express doubts about God's existence, or at least ambiguity regarding his whereabouts. In such cases the burden always falls on priests, rabbis, ministers, imams, and other spiritual leaders to make sense of tragedy. On 9/11 the media instantly began reporting some of the religious reactions, in the process singling out the more inflammatory remarks. But not in an effort to spark a national discussion. They were engaged in a ratings race. Nonetheless discussion did occur.

As the news continued to unfold on Tuesday Perry asked, "How are you guys going to respond to this when we get home? What are you going to say to your parishioners?"

"Well," Giovanni answered. "Obviously we need to address it this weekend during mass. We can't pretend it's just another Sunday, or ignore what has happened."

"But how?" Perry repeated.

Bill interjected, "My situation's a little different from yours. Most of your parishioners will only be around on Sunday. The students at USC, however, are around all the time. I think I'll talk to Glenn and Sean about having a joint prayer. We've been celebrating Ash Wednesday, Holy Thursday, and Good Friday together for a few years now. It will be an easy progression for us to do something around this. I'm more interested in what you plan to say when you preach on Sunday. It will help me put my reflections together."

Giovanni thought for a moment and then said, "I suppose we need to call for calm, openness, and peace. To caution against rushing to judgment."

"Are you kidding?" Bill asked. "You know damn well that we're going to war. Against somebody. It doesn't matter who. This is just the kind of thing Bush needed."

"That's a little harsh and uncalled for," Perry sternly replied. "No president would wish this kind of thing to happen. You can't make this political."

"Well, maybe he didn't want it," Bill said dismissively. "But everything's political. How much are you willing to bet that Bush uses the word "war" before the evening's out?"

"You're still being unfair," Giovanni commented. "He has a duty to lead the nation's response to this attack. And most of the people probably feel the same way he does. You just don't like him."

Bill felt as though he was in the minority. He said, "You're right. I don't like him. But I guarantee you. We are going to war." He said it with deliberation, emphasizing his point. "Are you two OK with that?"

"I'm not in favor of war," Perry replied. "But I think there's something else we need to address. Something right here in America. Imagine what it will be like for Muslim women to go to the market or the mall—especially those who wear the hijab. They'll be pariahs.

They'll be rashly and unfairly judged by people who don't even know them. The reaction of many Americans will not be kind. War is beyond our scope of influence. Maybe we should focus our attention on innocent American Muslims."

Giovanni replied, "I think we need to focus on all of it, the war and the bigotry. That means it's not going to be easy to preach this Sunday. I have no idea how to bring all the different realities together without losing the congregation in the process. This presents a difficult challenge for each of us."

"But not insurmountable," Bill said thoughtfully. He was beginning to formulate his own response. "We will just have to do more preparation than usual. And pray that we do it well."

It had been a tense day and the three of them decided to return home that night rather than the next morning.

Across the land reactions to the terrorism varied. Many were afraid, but anger seemed to stoke people's passions more than fear. There was good reason for outrage. The terrorism was unprovoked; there was an immense loss of life; daily routines were disrupted the world over. But it was the breathtaking scope of the attack that drove emotions. At first it was a mere question: How could this have happened here? The U.S. is protected by oceans to the east and west and friendly countries to the north and south. But it was a query without an answer, leaving people in a state of anxiety.

In the wake of fury, reason is frequently unrestrained and September 11, 2001, was no exception. The events of that day fueled ignorance and bigotry with otherwise good citizens surrendering to Islamophobia. Whatever my own faults, I was dismayed by the rapidity with which Americans embraced violence. Hundreds of attacks took place against Muslims and people of Arab descent in just the first week following 9/11. This included vandalism at Mosques and even murder. Sikhs were also attacked simply because people thought they were Muslim. This embrace of violence was not patriotism. It spoke to something deeper in the American psyche; namely, most Americans believe the hype that the United States is the greatest nation on earth. The truth is more becoming and certainly far humbler. The United States is, indeed, great. But no nation is the greatest. Only people overwhelmed with self-doubt feel a constant need to proclaim their superiority. And nobody knows that better than politicians. We play to that sentiment every election cycle. In retrospect, much of the anger in America was rooted in the fact that a nation's pride had been wounded.

Adding to civil insecurity were the foolish and self-serving comments of so-called religious leaders like Jerry Falwell. In the irrational web that constrained his mind he blamed the terrorist attacks on abortionists, gays and lesbians, the ACLU (American Civil Liberties Union) and even People for the American Way. Fortunately, his and other such discordant voices were drowned out by the example of President Bush and representatives of the country's legitimate religious authorities.

On September 14, 2001, three days after the attacks, an interfaith service was held at Washington's National Cathedral as part of the president's National Day of Prayer and Remembrance. In attendance were Presidents Bush and Clinton, along with their wives. Formally participating were the Very Rev. Nathan D. Baxter, dean of the National Cathedral; Dr. Muzammil H. Siddiqi, imam from the Islamic Society of North America; Cardinal Theodore McCarrick, Catholic Archbishop of Washington; Rabbi Joshua Haberman, from Washington Hebrew Congregation; Rev. Kirbyjon Caldwell, pastor of Windsor Village United Methodist Church; and Rev. Billy Graham.

President Bush delivered an address at the service. Although he acknowledged that a war had begun and promised that we would respond in defense of our country and our freedoms, he also spoke to the deeper and better parts of our nature, praising the tireless work of rescuers, the generosity of blood donors, and the selflessness of those who died saving others. He echoed President Franklin Roosevelt who, speaking sixty years earlier, invoked "the warm courage of national unity." In sharp contrast to those who would divide us, Bush spoke of the unity of every faith, of togetherness among political parties, and cooperation between the houses of Congress. He had become the leader that we sorely needed and that he had failed to be only three days earlier. Here was a president people would be willing to follow.

·   ·   ·

Upon returning to Hawthorne, Perry made an overture to the imam of the local mosque in an attempt to seek interfaith understanding. He sent the imam a letter assuring him of his personal support and committing his parish to work with the Muslim community to bridge whatever divide existed between them. He received a most grateful and positive reply and published both letters in the parish Sunday bulletin. Sadly, Perry was unable to convince the narrow-minded evangelicals to let the imam join the ministers' association. Even after so great a national tragedy they could not accept anyone who did not believe in Jesus. It was left to the Catholics and Muslims to draw from their shared heritage as descendants of Abraham and children of the same God.

Back at the university Bill called Glenn and Sean and invited them to lunch on Wednesday, September 12. Over Chinese takeout they discussed what kind of joint response they could make. The Dean of Religious Life, Rabbi Susan Laemmle, was already arranging a multi-faith memorial service for the following week. But something more specific, more uniquely Christian, was also needed. Sean had often referred to their three denominations as the liturgical churches, and that was the direction Bill suggested they take. Once the food was served he started the discussion.

"I think we need to do something as Catholics, Episcopalians, and Lutherans. Something that reflects our liturgical traditions and builds on other things we've been doing here for the last few years."

"Bill, I've known you for eight years," Glenn said. "And I think you already have something in mind."

"I do. But I don't know if you guys will go for it." He paused for a moment and then continued, "I think we should share a full eucharistic celebration—Concelebrate Mass."

There was a brief hesitation as each imagined the potential power of such prayer. Sean responded, "That's not a problem for me or even for Glenn. The Catholic Church is the one that stands in the way of us sharing communion."

He was correct. The Catholic Church has a firm position, but it represents a clash of theology. By definition, communion is an act of unity that says, "We are one." History, however, has left the various Christian churches divided. They are not one. Among Catholics, Lutherans, and Episcopalians, many of those differences are modest, but they are not insignificant. On the other hand, by virtue of baptism a Christian has a fundamental right to approach the Eucharist table. This is an unresolved conflict decided by church edict. The terrorist attacks gave the three churches the perfect opportunity to make a counterstatement.

"But we've already done that," Bill reminded them. It's been a little surreptitious. We've only shared Communion on Good Friday, when there is no Mass, using the Eucharist left over from the Catholic celebration of Holy Thursday. So far there hasn't been any objection. Of course, I doubt that Cardinal Mahony knows anything about it. But if there's ever a time for us to share the Eucharist, this is it. I don't see how anyone can object."

"Sometimes I think you're naïve," Glenn replied. "Either that, or you just like being a rebel."

"That much we already know," Sean said laughingly.

"Come on, guys," Bill said. "We've been wanting to push this envelope for some time. What better opportunity could there be for us to take this step then having our nation under attack?"

Glenn was thoughtful for a moment. Then he suggested, "We can't be the only ones who are contemplating this idea. But we might be the only ones willing to act on it. My vote is yes."

"Well," Sean replied. "I already said I have no problem. When and where do you suggest?"

"I think we should do it here at the Catholic Center," Bill said. "It's the largest space at our disposal. However, there are some conservative students here and they could create a problem. As a minor caution, and a way of covering my ass, I don't think we should use the chapel. Let's celebrate the Mass in the community room."

"Which prayers should we use?" Glenn asked.

"I've thought about that, too," Bill said.

"You'd have disappointed me if you hadn't," Glenn joked.

Bill continued. "When we began our joint Ash Wednesday services, we combined prayers from each of our three churches. I think we should do the same with this celebration. I'll be the principal celebrant since it will be here. We should wear albs and stoles but no chasubles. It will be a little less obvious that way. I don't think we all have to preach and since I'm leading the service, you two can toss a coin for that task. We should combine prayers for peace and reconciliation from each of our traditions. If we plan it for next Wednesday or Thursday we'll have enough time to prepare and announce it to the students."

They agreed on the date, and Glenn volunteered to merge the Catholic, Episcopal, and Lutheran prayers for peace.

Throughout the week interfaith prayer services multiplied around the nation. For believers it was a natural response to terror. But there are limits to cooperation, even when national unity and a common faith in God are on display. The Lutheran Church Missouri Synod (fortunately not the Lutheran Church Sean belonged to) specifically forbids its ministers to participate in any interfaith or interdenominational prayer at any time. The Catholic Church, on the other hand, welcomes such prayer but refuses inter-communion. Except at USC. A full Mass of peace and reconciliation was held on September 19, 2001, at Our Savior Catholic Center. For the moment, the Catholic, Lutheran, and Episcopal communities were truly one in a shared faith in Jesus Christ. It was a profound witness, and no one raised an objection.

.   .   .

The groundwork for a religious response had to be laid the weekend immediately following 9/11. As with many a crisis there would be a momentary surge in pious expression. More people would flock to mosques, synagogues, and churches than at any other time, including high holy days. But if faith was to exercise any influence over the national response, there could be no delay.

Giovanni and Bill lived within a mile of each other so they met Friday evening to share final thoughts on their sermons for Sunday. Despite their close friendship, their ideas were not in sync. Bill was committed to nonviolence and speaking against any concept of war. He was not about to give into or be guided by feelings. Nor would he allow his agenda to be set by the president or Congress. Giovanni, on the other hand, saw the attacks as an opportunity to seek the justice he was denied when my wife and children were murdered. It was only vicarious, but it was a way to play out his own quest for vengeance.

"Gio, I can't believe how apropos Sunday's readings are," Bill said.

"Apropos of what?" Giovanni asked.

Bill smiled and said, "Don't try to be so cute. I get the musical reference. But this is serious. The readings are tailor-made for this week's tragedy. They set up a near perfect call to forgiveness."

"We're not on the same page this time, Bill," Giovanni replied. "I've been thinking a lot over the last few days, as I'm sure you have also. But the more I contemplate what happened, the more personal it becomes for me. And I'm not in a mood to forgive. I happen to agree with the president. We need to hunt down the terrorists and exterminate them if we are to be free, if we want to prevent this from happening again. I'm not opposed to war, at least not in this case."

"You're kidding!" Bill exclaimed. "The Gospel is bigger than terrorism. And the call to forgive is clear. Jesus's call is more compelling than Bush's."

"Not to me. I'm not going to endorse violence specifically. But I intend to speak about national unity. And if the president calls for war, I won't object."

"There's something else going on, Gio. What you say is too superficial. It's what I'd expect to hear from a Pat Robertson or a Jerry Falwell, or any of those other people who think the United States is synonymous with the kingdom of God. This is not like you. Then again you haven't been yourself for months."

"Maybe I've changed," Giovanni suggested.

"That much is obvious," Bill replied. "I understand that you're still grieving over what happened last September."

"You don't understand. You don't know the half of it," Giovanni said.

"Then tell me," Bill continued. "You can't let what happened last year alter your basic beliefs and fundamental principles. You're still a priest. You're called to preach the truth, to help people view the world through the lens of the Good News. You and I both know that no matter what tragedy occurs, the Gospel is bigger than the United States. We can't surrender that belief."

"I don't intend to," Giovanni replied. "But maybe God is using the United States for purposes we don't see."

"Now you're being equivocal. I'm still going to pose a challenge this Sunday and call for a different kind of response."

"Well," Giovanni said. "We have different things to say to our parishes. Maybe I'll come by and listen to you."

One of the Masses at the university was at ten o'clock at night. Since Giovanni's own Sunday commitments had concluded by that time, he went to the Catholic Center to hear his friend preach.

The 10:00 p.m. Mass was always standing room only. This particular Sunday was an overflow crowd. Once the seats were filled, Bill invited the students to come in and sit on the floor. It had been a difficult week and a challenging Sunday. This was his fourth Mass of the day, but he drew energy from the crowd. Part of the homily included an African-American spiritual. As he had at the earlier liturgies, when he came to the lyrics he sang them. He was in no hurry to rush this particular sermon.

CHAPTER 11

September 16, 2001
24th Sunday in Ordinary Time

Reflections on Terrorist Attacks of
September 11, 2001

First Reading: Exodus 32:7–11 13–14
Responsorial Psalm: Psalm 51:3–4, 17, 19
Second Reading: 1 Timothy 1:12–17
Gospel: Luke 15:1–32

"Periodically, there are events that change the world. A look through human history sadly demonstrates that most of these events were violent acts sprung from the seeds of prejudice, hatred, poverty, and oppression. Even the death of Jesus, the single most earth-changing event in all of history, was a violent one. Tuesday's attack on the World Trade Center and the Pentagon is the latest such earth-changing event, and our lives will never be the same. Even our thinking and language have changed for we now believe the unbelievable and so speak the unspeakable.

"These horrific acts of violence spark terror in the hearts of millions, as all of us are touched by the attacks either personally or collectively. I have two friends in New York City and I was anxious to hear about them. Fortunately, on Tuesday I was able to ascertain that Marianna Pisano, Jane and Mark's daughter was all right. She works a block away from the WTC. The day of the attacks she was an observer for a scheduled election at a polling place many miles away. Still she lost friends that morning. My other friend is a lieutenant on the NYPD. Not only because it is her job, but also because of her personality and commitment to service, I knew that she would be in the thick of the rescue efforts. For days I tried to find out what happened to Theresa Tobin. Finally, on Thursday, I was able to get through to another friend who informed me that Teri was injured. She had been at the WTC when the first building collapsed, and was thrown with such force that she suffered a broken ankle, multiple bruises and lacerations, and head and back injuries. She is alive and recovering.

"Three thousand miles across the nation I am alive and well. But I am angry. Why should my friends, or any people for that matter, be put through such terror? Why should there be thousands of innocent people dead? Yet my anger pales in comparison to others—those whose relatives and friends died last Tuesday. I am also afraid. I am not so much afraid that there will be an attack on the West Coast. And given the mobilization of the nation's intelligence and military personnel, it will be a long time before I fear another such attack on the East Coast. I am not suggesting that we are safe, either. If we have learned anything, it is that no one and no place is safe from terrorism. I only say that I do not fear an attack. Still I am afraid. I am afraid of what we will do in response to this terror, and I am afraid of what will result from our response. We are being drawn into a whirlpool of violence from which there may be no escape.

"Throughout the week, I have spoken with many people about how we should respond to such evil. I have been concerned and critical of the language used by all of our political leaders. From the outset they have spoken only about punishment and retaliation. Although that language does not necessarily mean violence, I believe that is what our leaders have in mind. I hope I am wrong. But even if I interpret our leaders incorrectly, our citizens have violent retaliation on *their* minds. You would think that by this time in our history we would have learned that violence only breeds more violence. No war has ever resulted in peace. Rather, every war has sown the seeds of future conflict. I have been confronted with one question over and over this week: If punishment and retaliation are not the answers, then what kind of response do we make?

"My starting point is to look back at the crucifixion of Jesus—a violent act that I have already suggested is the most earth-changing event in history. And what response did Jesus make? Hanging from the Cross, as his enemies unjustly orchestrated his death, Jesus simply said: "Father forgive them." To be honest, however, that forgiveness does not come easily. Nor can it come too quickly if it is to be real. Jesus had three years during which he healed, forgave, and taught how to love. When he died he was ready to extend that love, that forgiveness, and that healing to those who unjustly put him to death. What about us? We have had two thousand years of Christianity, of reflecting on the teachings and example of Jesus. Are we finally prepared to ask and give forgiveness, to extend healing and love?

"During this past week there has been an understandable rise in patriotism accompanied by an almost uncontrollable emotion. As a result, most every store that sells American flags has had their stock depleted. We have all seen the cars on streets and freeways with the Stars and Stripes waving proudly in the breeze. I resisted that temptation. I resisted both individually and as leader of this community. Instead, I stood outside a flag store yesterday for two hours waiting my turn to enter the building. And when I did, rather than purchase an American flag, I purchased the flag of every member of the United Nations. Tuesday was not just an American tragedy. It was a tragedy for all peoples. It was not just an attack against the United States. It was an attack against all of humanity. Over eighty countries lost citizens in the destruction of the WTC. So how do we respond?

"My reflections this week took me back to another time in American history—when people were forcibly brought to these shores in chains. During the awful period of slavery, the imprisoned Africans and their descendants frequently turned to the stories of the Old and New Testaments to draw strength and courage and hope. In the midst of their suffering, which often took the form of violence and death, they found faith in a God who was not distant from them, but intimately a part of their pain and their struggle for freedom. They expressed that faith in the only international language we have—music and song.

"Although many spirituals emerged in those days one stands out this morning. Through a quirk in the English language, it is easily misunderstood, in part because singers are not too careful with the pronunciation.

There is a balm in Gilead, to make the wounded whole.
There is a balm in Gilead to heal the sin-sick soul.

"I was a child the first time I heard that hymn, and I thought the singer sang about a bomb in Gilead. I knew it was a religious song, so I was a bit confused. How could a religious song be about a bomb, and how could that bomb bring healing? But then I grew up and realized that the song spoke of a balm—a soothing, healing ointment. What I hear from people today takes me back to my first encounter with that spiritual. For it is not a balm many seek to bring healing. They look for a bomb.

Sometimes I feel discouraged
and think my work's in vain.
But then the Holy Spirit
revives my soul again.

There is a balm in Gilead to make the wounded whole.
There is a balm in Gilead to heal the sin-sick soul.

"I have been searching this past week for a symbol of what unites people around the world. Most of us would like to think that we are united by a common humanity: a concern for justice and a quest for peace. The truth is less hopeful and far less convincing. It is also cynically paradoxical. I had planned to bring a gun into church today—

just a theatre prop. I wanted to bring a gun, because while it obviously divides us by violence, it is also the most real symbol of what unites us as a people around world. We are not linked by common desires for good. We are linked by a common surrender to violence in all its forms. The single most defining element in international relations is power—power exercised through violence. There are two worlds on this planet: some countries have power and the ones without power want it. I did not bring the gun because I contacted the School of Theatre too late. I did, however, bring something else. This is a symbol of what should unite us. It is a copy of a painting I have previously used as a visual aid in my preaching.

"This is a picture of the head of Christ. From a distance, like many other things, it seems perfectly obvious. This is an artist's rendition of how Jesus looked. But its depth is only seen with clarity when one examines it closely. For this head of Christ is made up of the heads of many other people. Some of them are famous and easily recognizable. They include people of every race and culture, people of various faiths and even people who do not believe at all. Other images are unknown, just a representation of all human beings. Two thousand years ago in ancient Palestine, Jesus walked among us as we walk today. But now the only way Jesus is present is through us. Each of us. Each person.

"I continued to grow up from the day I first heard the song of Gilead. Eventually I came to realize that it is not an ointment that is the balm, but it is Christ himself—his compassion, his healing, his forgiveness, and his love for all people. Jesus, by rejecting violence and embracing mercy, became the way to peace.

If you cannot preach like Peter
If you cannot pray like Paul
You can tell the love of Jesus
And say he died for all.

There is a balm in Gilead to make the wounded whole.
There is a balm in Gilead to heal the sin-sick soul.

"Crafting a national response to last week's terrorism is treacherous. Before we take refuge in our indignation and our democratic history, we must remember one thing: We are not defined by lofty rhetoric, or even by the values we treasure. We are defined by how we respond when that rhetoric and those values are challenged. We have a right to be angry, for there is no moral judgment placed on feelings. We also have a right to feel outrage, hatred, and even a desire for revenge. These feelings are all neutral. But it is precisely in the midst of these feelings that Jesus reaches out and into us. Jesus calls us to something different. Jesus calls forth from us the power to transcend our feelings. Yet it takes time. I, for one, do not feel like forgiving today. There is still anger that must subside within me. But I cannot overcome the anger until I admit that it is there, and surrender the disease of my own heart to the love and the power of God. I know I will not be healed until I recognize the presence of Jesus even in my enemies.

"Although the healing process will take time, it begins today. I draw inspiration and hope from the nineteenth century slaves. Indeed there is a balm in Gilead, and that balm is Jesus."

Giovanni found the service—the lateness of the hour, the number of students, and even the homily—moving. He was transported backward. He kept thinking about the previous September. But he could find no pathway to peace. Even his friend's preaching could not tempt him to forgive.

CHAPTER 12

With the LAPD on high alert and the media in a whirl, Tom and Emily did not see much of each other that week. Once flights resumed over the country, the *Los Angeles Times* dispatched Emily first to New York, then London, and on to Washington. Sixty-seven citizens from the United Kingdom died in the 9/11 attacks. The *Times* wanted its best correspondents covering every aspect. Emily was not only the chief correspondent for the paper, she was born and raised in England. As such, she was the natural choice to report on the British response to terrorism.

Her first stop was in New York where she met with the family members of British victims. She had always despised the gauche, tabloid-style reporters who thrust microphones into the faces of grieving families while uttering inane questions—"How do you feel?" "Do you have anything to say?" That was not her style. She chose to meet people in private, unaccompanied by cameras, in order to develop trust. This allowed mourners to grieve and express their anxiety and bewilderment with the dignity they deserved.

Emily spent the entire first week in New York City, the center of the attacks. She established contacts and coordinated stories with her colleagues in London, ensuring that Great Britain and its citizens would not be lost among the WTC rubble. In spite of the now ancient American Revolution, Great Britain continues to hold a fascination for Americans. There are still many British descendants in the United States, and England remains America's closest international ally. The *Los Angeles Times* also had to ensure that its foreign coverage would not be overshadowed by the *New York Times* or the *Washington Post*. She spent the following week in England, meeting with British families. The BBC willingly offered her a desk in its headquarters from which she was able to report on the British government's response to 9/11.

The third leg of Emily's trip was Washington, D.C. Unbeknownst to Tom she made an appointment to meet with me on Monday, October 15. As a widower, I thought it would be good for my image to be seen about town with a beautiful woman, and dinner seemed appropriate. I would have liked some French cuisine and nothing surpasses L'Auberge Chez François. But Emily and I had not spoken in years, and I did not want to stress the evening with a ride out to Great Falls, Virginia. Normandie Farm, another French restaurant closer to the heart of D.C., would possess too loud an ambience. I decided to save these restaurants for the next time Jackson and Jean-Paul came to visit. Instead, I chose The Monocle. It is walking distance from my office and would provide an opportunity to show Emily around the Hill.

Emily checked into her hotel in the early afternoon and agreed to meet me at my office. Although much time had passed since we last saw each other, there was a comfortable familiarity about her. She was still a beautiful woman—a little more seasoned, and aging with remarkable grace. But her beauty was not superficial. It never was. Her inner charm had always been her draw—captivating and alluring, rooted in a confidant depth of character. It was easy to understand why Tom had fallen in love with her.

As she walked into my office, I greeted her with a kiss on the cheeks and said, "Hello, Emily. You look stunning."

"Thank you, Giuseppe," she replied. "I can see politics already has a grip on you. I assure you I can handle the truth, and I realize that, like all people, I am a victim of age. But as long as we're complimenting each other, time has been good to you, too. You look much more distinguished these days."

"That's just the touch of gray," I acknowledged. "And who knows? Maybe a little dignity comes with my office. Then again, we are only in our forties. Who knows what will happen in the next ten years?"

As she sat down I remained standing and leaned back against my desk. Her smile faded and was replaced with an intentional sincerity. "Tom, I'm very sorry about Yolanda and the kids."

"Thank you, Em."

She smiled again as the shortened moniker slipped from my lips. It was not planned but even after all this time it was the most natural way of addressing her.

"The funeral was beautiful, Giuseppe."

I was as surprised as Tom had been when she spoke the same words to him.

"I didn't know you were there," I replied.

"I didn't speak to anyone or allow myself to be seen. I was looking for personal healing. I felt guilty that I had distanced myself from the family following my divorce from Tom. But you always did everything together, and I didn't think I would be at ease. I was the outsider, the foreigner. I may have been wrong, but I did not see a place for me."

"You would have always been welcome, Em," I assured her.

"That's kind of you, Sep, and I'm sure you mean it. But there was another problem. I still loved Tom and I don't think I could have handled seeing him at all those gatherings. By the way, Tom and I are remarried—to each other." She beamed as she showed me the ring.

"I know," I replied. "Bianca told me. I'm sorry I couldn't be there." There was some truth in that. Just seeing Emily that afternoon, I could imagine how radiant she must have been at the ceremony. And I would have liked to see the rest of my family. On the other hand, I had no desire to encounter either Tom or Giovanni, a mutually shared feeling among the three of us. But she did not need to hear about that. I continued, "I understand it was a very small and simple wedding. Bianca said you looked beautiful."

"Thank you. But tell me, Sep. How are you doing? It's been just over a year now, and you're all alone here in Washington."

"I'm not really alone, Em. I mean, I don't have family here, but I have a great staff that carried over from my campaign, and several of them have moved to D.C."

I looked away to conceal my emotions. I did not really want to have this conversation. At least I did not want to share my feelings about Yolanda and the kids. I adroitly changed the subject. Glancing about I said, "I know you've been to Washington before, but have you ever seen the inner sanctum of the Senate offices?" As she shook her head I continued, "Follow me." Then I proceeded to lead her on a brief tour of the Hart Senate Office Building and introduced her to a few of the senators we found roaming the halls. As it was late fall, just a couple of weeks prior to returning our clocks to standard time, the sun was setting early and nightfall was quickly approaching.

"Emily, I made reservations for us at The Monocle. Have you ever been there?" I asked.

"No. Usually when I'm in Washington I'm on a deadline—and a budget," she joked.

"Well, it's an exceptional restaurant. They have a good selection of meat, seafood, and even vegetarian courses."

She quickly quipped, "You can forget about the vegetarian. My British family would disown me."

"Do you still have an affinity for oysters on the half-shell?" I inquired.

"What a memory," she replied. "They're among my favorites."

"Then I think you'll like the rest of the menu, also."

We sauntered over to The Monocle, commenting on the monuments and landmarks that were beginning to sculpt the darkening sky. As we entered the restaurant Nick Selimos, the maître d, immediately greeted us.

"Good evening, Senator Lozano," he said. "Your table is ready."

"Thank you, Nick," I replied. "Let me introduce Emily Moran. She's married to an old friend of mine, a lieutenant on the LAPD. And she is the *Los Angeles Times*'s best, and certainly most beautiful, correspondent."

He took her hand and kissed it. "*Enchanté, Madame,*" he said. It was a formal but graceful greeting, filled with old-world charm.

"Thank you," Emily replied. "I haven't been greeted like that in a very long time. I didn't know such charismatic maître d's still existed. I'm accustomed to the perfunctory greeting of the average host or hostess."

With a touch of exuberance Nick responded, "Ah! But not at The Monocle, *Madame*, I assure you. Every guest is special. Please follow me."

As we were shown to our table, I quietly remarked to Emily that Nick was completely truthful. "He's been greeting customers in the same manner for many years. He remembered my name on my second visit. He'd make a good politician."

"I thought you said he was truthful!" Emily said laughingly.

After we sat down a waiter came up and asked if we would like anything to drink. Emily requested her signature Smith and Kearns, and I ordered a Beefeater martini, not too dry, extra olives on the side. I have never understood the pretense of bartenders who merely spritz vermouth over the glass. Why don't they just serve straight gin and be done with it? Give me that additional flavor of vermouth. Not only does it make a perfect martini, it gives the bartender a reason to shake or stir.

The Monocle is elegant without being stuffy. As we waited for our drinks, we noted the photographs that lined the restaurant, especially those of presidents going as far back as John F. Kennedy. There is a story that someone once removed a photo of Richard Nixon, tore it up and left it in the restroom. The pictures are now more securely attached to the walls. We were in no hurry to begin our meal, but I asked that the oysters be served with our cocktails. When the drinks and appetizer arrived, Emily began a new conversation.

"Sep." Her tone was gentle and cautious. "I noticed that you deflected my question earlier about how you are doing."

"Well, Em. It's an ongoing process and there are times when I just don't want to think about it. I'm content to let my job absorb my attention and avoid the subject altogether. I know it's only a temporary solution, but it works. At least for now." That was an honest enough statement. Over the previous year I had been confronted with a range of responses and emotions, receiving sentiments of sympathy from the president on down to my fellow legislators. I had developed an automatic defense system and a superficial facade. There were aspects about the murders I was not willing to face—not personally and certainly not publicly. "Besides," I continued, "there is a lot to learn about being a senator."

"Do you mind if I ask a slightly different question?" she queried.

I shrugged my shoulders with a casual disregard.

"Now that Tom and I are back together we have sixteen years to catch up on. But during that time nothing has been as momentous as the murders. He's an excellent detective and I'm surprised that no arrests have been made. As far as the press knows there aren't even any persons of interest. I've asked him about the investigation, but he's very tight–lipped. Do you have any thoughts about it?"

Even before she arrived in Washington, I suppose I knew this discussion would take place. It was unavoidable. In part because she was a journalist, but more so because she was like family. Her rhythm had picked up as she moved into journalist mode. Maybe she could read my expression because she hastened to add, "I'm not trying to make you uncomfortable, Sep. I guess it's just the reporter in me."

Either Emily was a better actor than I credited or Tom really had told her nothing. I certainly had no intention of revealing anything. I felt competent enough to steer the conversation.

"You're right about Tom. He is a good detective. As a result, he doesn't give out any information he can't prove. Only a careless cop would be so cavalier. He shared bits of information with me, but he never told me who his suspects were." I chose my words with factual precision, skirting the edge of truth.

"I just can't believe there are no clues," she said.

As if ponderously recollecting I said, "I do remember him telling me that he had never come across a crime so carefully planned. Something about not leaving any useful evidence at the scene. The only thing he had to go on was the tape from a video camera, but it did not show any faces. I guess that didn't go anywhere, either."

"I've been a journalist for a long time, Sep. And although murder was never my beat, I've certainly never heard of anything like this. I don't believe in a perfect murder. There's always a mistake. But if Tom can't find the killer, then I don't know what to make of it."

Her voice trailed off and she looked away. Just then the waiter came by and asked if we needed more time.

"I think we're ready," I said. "Order anything you want, Em. This will be my celebration for your wedding."

Emily ordered a baby arugula salad and filet mignon. I had the same salad, but chose the lamb chops.

"We can share the sides, Em," I suggested. "Everything here is good. I'm partial to onion rings and I'm going to order them. You can choose whatever other side dishes you want. Does anything grab your attention?"

"There are only two of us and I don't need to eat a lot. How about some creamed spinach?"

"Excellent choice," I said.

After the waiter left, I asked, "Em, do you mind if we change the subject?"

"I apologize, Sep. I think I was insensitive. That, and I've been away for so many years."

"There's no need to apologize," I said. "I understand."

The truth is that while I was sure I would not slip in the conversation, I also knew that Emily was a hound of a reporter. She had an uncanny ability to surface what most of her colleagues missed. She wasn't scrappy. She was sophisticated and insightful. And those are the most dangerous.

We spent the rest of the time talking about her and Tom and her recent travels. She was so clearly in love that I found it easy to hide my indifference about their relationship. Her recent visit to the Middle East was far more interesting to me, as it contained political dimensions that I would have to deal with in the Senate. At the end of the evening, she took a cab back to her hotel and I walked for a while around the capitol. I had not anticipated Emily coming back into my life, but at first I figured it would have no impact. She had always been a genuine and remarkable woman, and on some level I was pleased for her and Tom. And yet, she was a penetrating correspondent and I had a discomforting foreboding. Emily could be potentially dangerous. And my life was so neatly packaged. I had held off Tom and Giovanni. I was not about to let a reporter unravel my plans.

•   •   •

Tom was waiting for Emily when her plane landed at LAX. Even in post–9/11 security he was allowed to meet her at the gate. The Transportation Security Administration (TSA) had not yet been created, but LAX security stepped up and carried the load for much more intensive screening and restricted access to the gates. Although the LAX police and the Los Angeles Police Department are separate entities, there is a small LAPD contingent assigned to the airport. The two departments participate in a number of joint ventures, including detective duties, specifically when investigating airport crime. Being an RHD (Robbery and Homicide Division) lieutenant, Tom was given special entry to the gates. As Emily stepped into the terminal, he greeted her with a huge hug and a long kiss.

"I missed you so much," he said. "How was your trip?"

"I'll tell you all about it later. Right now I want to get home. Having the military roaming the airports with AK–47s is supposed to be a sign of security, but it leaves me very uncomfortable. This is what I've come to expect in the Middle East or from authoritarian dictatorships, but not here in the U.S."

As they walked toward the baggage claim, Tom replied, "It's necessary, Em. The events of last month have taught us that no one is immune from terrorism. The increased security is a sign—and a warning—to anyone who would attempt another attack."

"So what?" she asked. "We end up with a gun battle in broad daylight in an open airport? That's not my idea of security. This is all an overreaction and an oversell—an attempt on the part of the government to create the illusion that people are safe."

He had seen this side of Emily many times in the past. Her passions were not easily quelled. That was part of the reason she was so skilled at her job. He hesitatingly asked her, "Aren't you overreacting yourself?"

"Oh, Tom," she replied. "You can be so naïve. As a detective you're always looking backward, piecing together evidence and trying to identify a culprit. Your hindsight is remarkable, but you don't have very good forward vision."

It did not help that on the way to the baggage carousel, they had to pass several soldiers in full combat gear, square-jawed with menacingly "I dare you" stares. She was beginning to make even him paranoid. He wondered if their voices were too loud, or if their conversation was being overheard by well-hidden Orwellian microphones. It didn't matter, though. Emily was not to be deterred. She continued, "The administration and Congress are going to use 9/11 as a pretense, as a reason to govern from fear. The freedoms we have long treasured are going to vanish."

"I think you're reading too much into this heightened security," he replied.

"No," she insisted. "I'm not. I've seen it everywhere in the last three weeks. One of the great harbingers and proofs of our freedom has been that in America we only saw armed military personnel on the streets during parades. Now they're everywhere. We are frightfully in danger of becoming what we despise—a totalitarian country."

He smiled at her phrasing and use of the word "frightfully." Like a bilingual person who reverts to his native language during moments of excitement or agitation, one of Emily's charms was that she became so fully British, forsaking the more refined English of America.

It was a short drive from the airport. As they approached their apartment he told Emily, "I planned a simple meal for us tonight, at home. I hope you don't mind. I'll even cook."

"Dear Tom," she said with much affection. "You are so sweet. I was afraid you might want to go out for dinner and right now I am tired of restaurant, hotel, and airplane food. Then again, your culinary skills are somewhat limited." Her sparkling eyes and mirthful voice indicated no umbrage whatsoever.

"Don't be so sure," he replied slyly. "How do you think I survived the last three weeks without you?"

"Perhaps a few trips to Tom Bergin's?" she suggested. Bergin's is a landmark Irish pub on Fairfax Ave. It opened in 1936, holds the second oldest liquor license in Los Angeles County and was the first establishment to introduce Irish coffee to the United States. The ceiling of the bar is covered in personalized shamrocks—each clover named for a regular customer, collectively conjuring up a colony of leprechauns showering lucky charms, if not pots of gold, upon the clientele. Each month the bar staff nominates patrons for possible inclusion in the club with the lucky winner granted a party to celebrate the induction. It is a rite of passage particularly coveted by USC and UCLA athletes but also by many a drinking Angeleno.

"Would you believe," he asked, "that I did not once go to Bergin's? I spent three lonely weeks alone, bemoaning your absence." He spoke whimsically knowing she was not that gullible.

"I believe the first part," she said foxily. "And I'd like to believe the second. But then I wouldn't really want to see you miserable simply because I was absent." Their exchanges had become increasingly playful since their reunion several months prior.

"Truthfully, Em, I did miss you."

"I missed you too, Tom. It was a tiring trip."

As they brought in her luggage and began to settle down, Emily told Tom about the devastation in New York, the fear that had gripped London and the near chaos in Washington's halls of Congress. No one expected this to be the end of terror, and security had been beefed up around the Western world. The British, at least in London, seemed less consumed by Islamophobia than their American cousins. This may have been due in part to Great Britain's colonial past. Its domination of India and Pakistan prior to Mahatma Gandhi's drive for independence resulted in many Hindu and Muslim immigrants. Being a much smaller country than the U.S., Englanders tend to interact more openly with their Islamic neighbors.

Tom had told the truth about their simple meal. He broiled steaks, and for sides he sautéed mushrooms, asparagus, and onions. The entire supper took no more than thirty minutes to prepare. But to Emily, sitting in her own home and being attended to by her husband, made the food ambrosial. After dinner they snuggled together on the couch relaxing with a glass of Dow's vintage port.

"Tom," she said, "when I was in Washington I had dinner with Giuseppe." Was it her imagination or did she feel his body tense up at that revelation? There was certainly no need for jealousy on his part. Maybe it was something else.

"Did you?" he asked, feigning inattentiveness. "I would have expected him to be very busy."

"It was only one dinner, Tom. And he does have to eat. But yes, he was busy. The entire Capital was buzzing with reaction to the attacks."

"What did he have to say?" Tom warily asked.

"Are you angry with me?" she inquired.

"No."

"Then perturbed?" she pressed.

"No, Emily. Neither one."

"Then why did your muscles tighten at his name? And don't try to deny it."

"I told you before, Emily, that the murders, the failed investigation, everything about the case leaves me unsettled. Hearing you speak his name just reminds me. That's all."

She was too perceptive and her memory too constant to believe that. "There's something more," she said. "Ever since we got back together I've noticed that neither you nor Giovanni talks about Giuseppe. And he didn't have much to say about either of you."

"Then what did you talk about?" he asked, attempting to veer the conversation in a less awkward direction. Emily picked up the hint.

"First, I asked how he was doing," she replied. "I couldn't imagine how he was able to assume his new position, leaving everything and everyone behind. He didn't divulge much, choosing instead to change subjects. Much like you," she observed. Tom did not react.

She continued, "Later I asked him if he had any ideas about the investigation." This time Emily noticed a clear discomfort. "Tom, what's wrong?"

"Nothing," he replied. "Tell me what he said."

Tom was less than convincing, but she continued nonetheless. "He agreed with me that you are an excellent detective and that you had said something about the murder being perfectly planned. He did not want to pursue the discussion. But his not mentioning you or Giovanni caused me to wonder all the more. I was not trying to pry or play the reporter. But you know that I have been wondering about the three of you for months now."

Tom sat up, took her hands and looked directly into her eyes. "Emily," he said. "I promise you that when the time is right I will tell you what I suspect, what I know, and what I cannot prove."

Tom was feeling uncertain. He did not know if he could control this conversation. But his words were deliberate and firm and Emily was willing to let it go—for now. He escaped by voicing a desire he had contained for three weeks.

"Let's go to bed."

In the bedroom he drew her close and held her in a tight embrace. Feelings raged and clashed inside him. His hatred for Giuseppe surged as he worried that Emily had waded into a danger she did not and could not perceive. But, for the moment, he surrendered to love and an instinct to protect. He slowly undressed her, kissing each inch of her sensual flesh. As he laid her down he said, "Tell your bosses—no more three week trips." Then he slipped between her legs, and with aching penetration satisfied a lost and longing passion.

CHAPTER 13

Independent of the confusion created by the shifting Senate leadership, it was clear from the beginning that Bush would not sail smoothly through his presidency. He had to deal with churlish and recalcitrant Democrats who had been unable to thwart and were unwilling to embrace the U.S. Supreme Court decision that appointed Bush the forty-third president of the United States. Yet it was a fait d'accompli they had to accept. Unfortunately, the Court had further poisoned an already toxic atmosphere in Washington and no one expected much bipartisan legislation to reach the president's desk. One exception was the Public Safety Officer Medal of Valor Act, signed by Bush on May 30, 2001. The authorization itself was simple:

"After September 1, 2001, the President may award, and present in the name of Congress, a Medal of Valor of appropriate design, with ribbons and appurtenances, to a public safety officer who is cited by the Attorney General, upon the recommendation of the Medal of Valor Review Board, for extraordinary valor above and beyond the call of duty. The Public Safety Medal of Valor shall be the highest national award for valor by a public safety officer."

The Act was not in the least controversial. President Clinton established the award by executive action on June 29, 2000. The Congressional medal supersedes Clinton's citation and the president now presents it in the name of Congress. Awards such as these do not just recognize the dedication and bravery of the recipients. They also acknowledge the justifiable pride of the people being served. At the time of its passage, no one could anticipate the irony of the law. Only ten days after it took effect, we would see public safety officers demonstrate immeasurable valor hundreds of times over. However, the criteria established under the law made the 9/11 first responders ineligible for the honor. It would take years before the Congressional Gold Medal would be awarded to anyone connected with September 11, 2001.

In contrast to legislative inactivity throughout most of the year, following 9/11 Congress rushed to pass the USA Patriot Act (Uniting and Strengthening America by Providing Appropriate Tools Required to Intercept and Obstruct Terrorism Act of 2001). This is precisely what I had in mind when I asked Jackson to be my personal advisor. The Senate vote was scheduled for October 25 and I was fairly certain how I would cast mine. After all, America was in the grip of fear and we in Congress needed to create at least an illusion of addressing the crisis. Still, I wanted to talk to my friend. It wasn't just professional, either. I had a personal reason to meet with him.

It had been just over a year since my family's murder. I don't know if it was the anniversary, the terrorist attacks or Emily's visit, but I was feeling vulnerable, and with that came an unwanted anxiety, a new experience for me. I realized that if not controlled it threatened to derail my political ambitions. A jumble of nonsensical dreams began disrupting my sleep. In one I was about ten years old riding my bicycle. As I rode down the street faster and faster, I reached under the crossbar and pushed a button. As if scripted by Ian Fleming, a set of wings sprung out in Bond-like fashion, locked themselves in place, and I began to soar into the sky.

Another night I was caught in the midst of a bizarre invasion. Beings not unlike dinosaurs were threatening the city. Inexplicably they all walked on two legs and spoke English. I had managed to befriend one of the creatures, for he was sympathetic to the plight of the human population and worked with me to subvert his own kind. By the end of the dream, the dinosaurs had been defeated although I woke too early to discover what had happened to my friend.

Mixed with silly and bizarre dreams were several commonly threaded nightmares—what a less enlightened mind might call visitations from beyond the grave. But I am not a simpleton and don't believe in ghosts. The visions were hallucinatory, but seemed real enough in the dark of night. Yolanda and the kids were simultaneously there and not there, phantom apparitions drifting about the bed. I found myself in dialogue with them, or more accurately, monologue.

"I don't know what to say to all of you. Carmen, Gina, Leonardo, you will never know the depth of my love or the emptiness I feel without you." I was not trying to convince myself. The words I spoke were true, and in my mind they did not contradict reality. I was resurfacing a remorse I had tried to bury with their bodies. "It was such a joy watching each of you grow and embrace life with excitement and curiosity. In waking hours I frequently think of you, and when I do the sun is less bright, the world less beautiful." This was almost a soliloquy and I felt as if I were teetering on the very edge of dreamland— somewhere between consciousness and slumber, unable to ground myself in either. I was aware enough to know I was not heard, but sufficiently disoriented that I felt compelled to speak.

In these dreams Yolanda had become my conscience. Even though I could not clearly distinguish her features, I could see her frowning judgment and disapproval upon me. "Yolanda, I don't know if you can forgive me. Perhaps to you that no longer matters. But I want you to understand. I always loved you and the kids and I was a faithful husband. For a time you seemed to bring out the best in me. Maybe you were just too good and I not worthy." Even in my sleep I was aware of my emotions. Only on this subconscious level could I confront my past. I was pleading with her, trying to assuage my guilt. "I always said we had to sacrifice, Yolanda, but please believe me: this is not what I had in mind. I was talking about material things. But as I set my goals higher, I realized that I did not have what it takes to succeed and losing you became inevitable." I began to sound downright defensive, much like an accused man protesting innocence, trying fiercely to escape an incriminating truth. My thoughts and words were almost robotic, as if attempting to control a disturbed subconscious desperately seeking to materialize in the animate world.

I invariably would wake awash in perspiration. Yet feeling no need to justify my past, I tried not to give the dreams cognizance. I had taken great pains to protect myself and was not about to let family history protrude into my present or compromise my future. At the same time these dreams further underscored my personal isolation. I had no one to share them with. On October 10 I placed a call to Boston.

•   •   •

When Jackson answered I said, "Hello, Jacks."

"Hi, Sep. How are you? Are things still chaotic in Washington?"

"I wouldn't use that word, but we've been quite busy trying to find an adequate response to the attacks. In fact, that's why I'm calling. There's a bill making its way through the Senate with a similar version in the House. I haven't read all of it, but it will stir a great deal of controversy and I'd like your opinion. Can you fly down for the weekend?"

"Well," he said hesitatingly. "This is short notice. Jean-Paul and I were planning on a quiet weekend together. He's been out of town more than usual lately and we haven't had a lot of time to ourselves."

"Forgive me, Jacks," I replied. "I don't mean to be insensitive. It's not just the bill. There's something personal I need to talk to you about. But I guess that can wait." I spoke with a slightly dejected tone knowing that I was subtly putting pressure on him. I had called him on the spur of the moment hoping that if he came to Washington, he would be alone, since I would not be able to have the conversation I wanted if they both visited. Nonetheless, with genuine interest I continued, "How is Jean-Paul's mother?"

"Thank you for asking, Sep. She's not critical but she's been having a difficult time lately. That's why we haven't had much time together."

"I'll tell you what, Jacks. Suppose I send you a confidential copy of the proposed legislation and see how much you can read within the next seven or ten days? You and Jean-Paul will be able to have your time together, and I'll still get your advice."

"What about the other issue?" he asked.

"Ah, don't worry," I said almost dismissively. "The next time Jean-Paul is away for the weekend and you're in Boston, just come down here and we can talk then. I promise you it will keep. It's not a crisis. It's just something I would like to talk over with you."

"Thanks, Sep," he replied. "I'll give the bill as much attention as possible. And I promise to fly to Washington soon."

"It's a deal," I said. "I'll send the papers to you tomorrow."

I was disappointed as I hung up the phone, but my troubled sleep was not urgent, and could certainly await another time. I did not expect it would be long before his next visit, anyway.

As he promised, Jackson read the bill and called back the following week with some serious concerns.

"Sep," he began, "what exactly do you want me to comment on regarding this legislation?"

"I want to hear everything you have to say, Jacks. Are you suggesting it's not straightforward?"

"Oh, it's hardly that," he replied. "It doesn't even make a pretense of being candid. There are some good elements in it, but I have objections with a number of items."

"Tell me," I prodded.

"On the surface," he continued, "there is much to be commended in the proposed law: The anti-money-laundering provision; the paying of awards for information regarding terrorist acts; increasing the speed with which victims of crimes are compensated; improving communication about terrorism among various governmental agencies.

"On the other hand, there are some totally unnecessary and potentially divisive issues. Title II tramples on any concept of freedom as Americans have come to understand it. As you know, I have often expressed the belief that our freedoms are more imaginary than real, the result of slick and successful government propaganda. But this goes too far—as if the authors of the act have conjured the spirit, if not actually resurrected the body, of Senator Joseph McCarthy."

"You're such a drama queen, Jacks! But tell me. Do you think people will object?"

"Probably not," he replied. "Congress isn't really going to give the general public enough time to think and to respond. I suspect you're also taking advantage of the insight of Cicero."

"Cicero?" I asked.

"I forgot," Jacks responded. "You didn't have a classical education at Stanford." That was intended as a putdown. In actual fact, I did not study the classics in college. I was focused on business from day one. Jackson continued, "While defending his friend, Milo, against a charge of murder, Cicero gave an address entitled, '*Pro Tito Annio Milone ad iudicem oratio.*' In it he employed the expression, '*Silent enim leges inter arma*' (the law falls silent in time of war). Cicero suggested that murder, which is usually contrary to the law, was justified in self-defense, thus the law becoming silent. But I don't use the phrase that way. I think what you're doing in Washington is far more sinister. The Patriot Act plays upon the people's fear and uses war as a justification for eviscerating the rule of law. In a not surprising display of ignorance, many Americans are more than willing to have the government suspend freedoms."

"You're being way too cynical, Jacks."

"Am I?" he asked. "Do you really think this law would have any hope of being passed if 9/11 had not occurred? After reading the draft of the bill I'm left wondering if it had already been written, and held in abeyance for just such an occasion. I'm also puzzled as to why the rush. The only reasonable explanation I can devise is that the Patriot Act is perverse, a scenario worse than the world of George Orwell's *1984.* If you do not rush passage of this law, it will generate powerful opposition and possibly a death knell for the legislation. I have other concerns, too.

"While I acknowledge that protecting citizens is one of the prime responsibilities of any government, the language of Title IV reflects a siege mentality. It appears motivated more by a political agenda, indicating that it was conceived long before September 11. There is something obscene about detaining anyone indefinitely, even an immigrant suspected of criminal activity.

"There are also problems with the redefinition of many terms, particularly terrorism. But I guess I am most concerned about the expansive authorization of secret surveillance."

"But," I protested, "according to the proposed act, that surveillance must be approved by a Foreign Intelligence Surveillance Act court."

"And the FISA courts are secret," he responded. "Look, Sep. I realize you are now part of the government. For my part, I am not willing to entrust anyone with that much power. If there is a saving grace to all this, it is that we are still a democracy."

"Well, Jacks, I really do appreciate that you took the time to read the bill and shared your thoughts with me. I had not anticipated so much opposition to the sections of the bill. What if I don't agree with you? "

"I don't suppose you will, Sep. But what does that matter? You asked me to serve as an advisor, not a puppeteer. I will tell you what I think, but you have to calculate more things than I do. You need to satisfy your constituents as much as you do your own conscience. And you need votes to remain in office. I don't envy you."

"Jacks, you are far too understanding. You would never make a good politician."

He chuckled and said, "Thank God." And quickly added, "It's just an expression."

"Well, thanks again," I said and hung up the phone.

There was much depth in Jackson's observations. But he was also right about my career. The Senate voted on the Patriot Act on October 25. The final tally was ninety-eight to one, Senator Russ Feingold of Wisconsin casting the only dissenting vote.

CHAPTER 14

Before running for the Senate, I set a personal goal. I intended to become president. To accomplish that, I would need to create and complete a number of objectives: developing name recognition beyond the state of California; creating a comprehensive voting record in Congress; and demonstrating an ability to work with others. Being from California, that last item included working across the aisle with democratic members of Congress.

Throughout the election cycle that landed me in Washington, I had already begun creating an impeccable public persona. I was seen as a family man, a faithful husband and loving father. My wife attended many campaign appearances with me, even though she was a democrat. I frequently altered my calendar to attend functions at my children's schools. Following the murders of my wife and children, I was seen as the devastated husband and father. But I did nothing publicly to capitalize on their deaths. Once I was in Washington I needed to set about developing a legislative career, and I anticipated that being the most difficult task.

I was not delusional. My objectives were achievable and my goals attainable. But I was engaged in a fierce internal battle, which no one, not even Jackson, could be allowed to observe. Within my soul I discovered that God is not the sole dispatcher of avenging angels, not the only guarantor of justice. I sought to entomb this conflict of conscience, falling ever deeper into a cavern of personal deceit. As I did so I found it more difficult to trust others. With decreasing options for friendship, I would need to survive on wit and caution.

When I arrived in Washington, I had no circle of trust. I was content with that. Besides, initially I did not know most of my fellow legislators. But my long-term plans required me to develop some cordial working relationships on the Hill. I was cool and collected in my deliberations with others, giving them no reason to question or even doubt my sincerity. I didn't particularly want friends and I had no time for scruples. I wanted someone to control. Selecting my target was easy, but moving in for the kill took careful preparation. It was an exercise of planning and power befitting Cardinal Richelieu and the court of King Louis XIII of France.

I found a representative with a questionable past. That was rather an easy task given the nature of politics and the membership of Congress. But the politician I chose was from my own backyard. Unlike other people, I do not rush to judgment. I like to be sure of my facts. Although my company, The Pegasus Group, had been placed in a trust for my time in office, I maintained access to unparalleled resources including skilled investigators. Once I was certain of my information and possessed the necessary evidence, I was ready.

•   •   •

Following the 2000 election, I was not the only new face from California in the nation's capital. The forty-eighth district, based primarily in San Diego County, elected Darrell Issa to replace retiring U.S. Congressman Ron Packard. Two years earlier Issa attempted to challenge Barbara Boxer for her seat in the U.S. Senate, but lost in the primary election to state treasurer Matt Fong. Boxer easily won in November and would have just as easily beaten Issa. Although his primary race was not successful, it gave him name recognition and left him free to run for Congress in 2000 in a heavily Republican and fairly safe district.

Issa and I did not campaign together. We had different agendas and I needed to appeal to a much broader electorate. We did, however, make one joint appearance in Oceanside, California. That campaign stop probably helped me more than it did him, although neither of us had reason to worry about the forty-eighth district. It was solidly in the Republican camp. Issa handily won the election, defeating his Democratic rival, Peter Kouvelis. After moving to Washington we both attended a welcome party for newly elected Republicans in March of 2001, co-hosted by Senate Majority Leader Trent Lott and Speaker of the House Dennis Hastert. But we did not have frequent contact after that.

The Senate and the House of Representatives operate under different rules of procedure. At times a similar version of a bill will be introduced in both houses. On those occasions it is a good idea to have a reliable colleague in the other chamber. Issa was a natural ally given that both of us were moderate Republicans and hailed from the same state. There were also correlations in our business histories. We had a similar approach to ethics, though we were both accused of lacking integrity. Some people may have read Lt. Tom Moran's previous exposé of my business background. I needed to develop one for Issa, also, but keep the information private. He had no idea what I knew about him, but he was about to find out. And I would use that knowledge to my own purpose.

In order to establish camaraderie I invited Issa to lunch. That was in June of 2001. My secretary, Catherine Stripling, greeted him, showed him into my office, and then left closing the door behind her. I stood up, walked around my desk and greeted the congressman with a smile and a firm handshake. The warmth of my greeting belied my ulterior motive.

"Hello, Darrell, and welcome. I'm glad you had the time to come over." We were not yet on familiar terms, but by choosing to use his first name, I hoped he would relax. Later in the conversation that same technique would become a means of control. He surrendered to the familiarity.

"Thank you, Giuseppe. It's a pleasure," Issa replied.

To the right of my desk and near a window was a small round table draped with a white cloth. There were two place settings, modest but tasteful, and a healthy amount of food.

I pointed to the table and commented, "I hope you don't mind having lunch here in the office. It's quieter than the local restaurants and more private. I had some food brought in from Lebanese Taverna." Issa smiled and I quickly continued, "I'm not catering to your ethnic background. I miss the great Lebanese food I had back in L.A. One of my favorite dishes is ground beef kibbeh from Sahag's Basturma on Sunset Blvd. It so happens that here in D.C. one of Taverna's specialties is a delicious lamb kibbeh. Not knowing your tastes I decided to play it safe and also ordered chicken and lamb kabobs, shrimp arak, and ouzi with grape leaves."

"It looks like a small feast and more than I usually eat for lunch. But it is too enticing to decline. I look forward to it. I've heard about Taverna but haven't managed to get there yet. I appreciate your thoughtfulness."

Over lunch we spoke of our elections and our moves to Washington. Unlike me, Issa rented a small room. As a senator I would be in the Capital for at least six years, whereas he was only guaranteed two. His family maintained their home in Vista, California, and he would fly back when possible.

I possessed good skills when it came to disguising my thoughts, feelings, and intentions. I expected the same from Issa and was surprised by his complete lack of acumen. Given his history I had naturally presumed that he would be more sagacious. To the contrary, he gave the distinct impression that he was not very bright. He would probably muscle his way through Congress the same as he did in life—without finesse, relying on pure thuggery. This would make my job much easier, for if there is one thing a bully recognizes and even fears, it is someone with genuine power. In this case, that power was knowledge.

After we had finished eating and sharing insignificant pleasantries, I opened a new course for discussion.

"Darrell, both of our careers are just beginning, and they have different trajectories but remain linked by the fact that we are Californians. However, given that the Golden State is frequently at the forefront of progressive social issues, our state's priorities do not always match the national Republican trend."

"I understand that, Giuseppe, but what are you driving at?" Issa asked. "What does this have to do with our careers?"

"To begin with, Darrell, your district is strongly Republican. Most of your choices should be simple. You have only to please a few people. But I represent the entire state and it is predominantly moderate to liberal. Secondly, my political path is different from yours. I need to begin building a support base not just with voters, but also among elected officials, and I need to create a track record on public policy. That means that I'm looking for someone to support my political agenda."

"Meaning what?" Issa asked cautiously.

"Meaning, that if I introduce or sign on to a piece of legislation in the Senate, I expect you to do the same in the House, regardless of what the party leadership says."

"You want me to be your lackey in the House of Representatives?" Issa protested.

I considered telling him about "the Silencer," the security device I brought from my office in California. But I really did not want anyone to know. It was part of my plan to build a power base in Washington. Compromising conversations can be so convincing when turned into blackmail. If people knew why my office was secure, they would refuse to meet there. Alluding to the privacy would suffice.

"Darrell," I replied coyly. "Let me be upfront about the real reason we had lunch here. My office is more secure than the president's. It is impossible to bug, wire, or record anything said in this room. You and I are the only two people able to repeat what is discussed during this conversation. Should our recollections disagree it would be purely a matter of credibility. And to be honest, Darrell, I think you would come up short."

Issa looked irritated. The hooligan of his past was surfacing. He started to stand but I continued sternly, "Sit down, Darrell, and hear what I have to say."

"I don't think I'm interested in what you have to say," he responded.

"You will be," I said manipulatively. "You see, Darrell, the past can be such an ugly world, especially if it refuses to die." My cadence and tone barely concealed my contempt for him or the extent of my threat.

Issa paused and sat back down, overcome by an unnamed fear and a drive for self-preservation. His personal history was corrupt—more so than most lawmakers. He was exactly the kind of person who gives politicians a bad name. He had much to hide and had no idea what information I possessed. I did not need to muster much of my own guile to get the better of him. Issa's smarts extended only as far as the streets. He had never been confronted by anyone as plotting or cunning as I, and it was necessary for me to clearly convey that he was outmatched.

After he sat down again he said warily, "Go on."

"Here's the problem, Darrell." I addressed him with a well-deserved disdain. "You're rich. But I'm richer. More to the point, I have an unequaled and extremely thorough intelligence network." I was not being boastful. The truth is that my people can uncover information that escapes even the NSA and the CIA. "Your past is very much present to me. And I don't mean the youthful mistakes we all make."

At this point, by way of emphasizing that I had the upper hand, I became almost playful. "Shall I tick off those indiscretions? For most of us our adolescence does not include grand theft auto." Twice Issa was involved in automobile theft. Though there was no question of his involvement in either case, the second one actually included an indictment. "Tell me, Darrell. How much does it cost to get an indictment quashed? And let's not forget that you were arrested for carrying a concealed weapon. Of course that makes you a darling, if not a poster child, for the National Rifle Association. No harm done there. The fact that it was illegal and a felony is a minor consideration to the NRA."

I enjoyed watching him squirm and was not about to let up. I continued enumerating. "Then there is the exaggeration of your military service, falsely asserting that you provided security for President Nixon and claiming that you had a stellar career when, in fact, you were a substandard soldier and were demoted. But, hell. Who cares about that? I don't."

Issa was fuming inside and I could tell from his demeanor that he feared I had more compromising information. I saw no reason to drag out the suspense.

"I'll tell you," I continued. "I don't really care about anyone stealing automobiles, carrying guns or padding their military resumes. And I don't think most other people do, either. Sure, the cars and gun are felonies, but they would not disqualify you from running for, or being elected to, office. The average citizen doesn't give a rat's ass about those things. And as for military service, even President Bush deserted his post in the National Guard. But when a pattern of offenses leads to ever greater transgressions, that's when I take note, unleash my team, and secure the upper hand. You see, Darrell, like you I'm a businessman. I know you've heard the rumors about Quantum and Steal Stopper."

Issa's eyes narrowed at these words. Wondering if my knowledge surpassed innuendo, he peered across the table as if trying to read me. It was a task way beyond his skill set. What he did not know was that my knowledge was more than gossip. It was solid gold.

Quantum and Steal Stopper were a combined company in Ohio that, among other things, made car alarms. Issa wrested control of the firm from Joey Adkins. The method of gaining sole ownership did not bother me. It was an adept business move and the kind of thing I might have done. What happened after he gained ownership is what perked my interest and led me to believe that I could control him.

The company was struggling when Issa took over. He managed to secure lucrative contracts from Ford and Toyota. But that was not enough. On September 7, 1982, at 2:35 a.m. the plant caught fire. According to Adkins, three weeks prior Issa had increased the fire insurance by over four hundred percent. He had also removed the computer equipment, accounts, and customer information, and had taken circuit board silk screens from a file cabinet placing them, instead, into a fireproof box. That was actually a clever move that I admired. A less cunning criminal would have taken the silk screens home with the other equipment and files. Both the fire department and insurance company determined that it was arson. None of this information was new. The blaze had happened nineteen years prior and Issa had occasionally had to answer questions, which he mostly managed to deflect. What I brought to the table was the danger of evidence.

"What puzzles me, Darrell, is why you were so careless." In truth, I was not at all perplexed. I knew Darrell Issa. We were cut from the same cloth, with the exception that he lacked shrewdness. He was cocky without reason, a recipe for recklessness. "I've never hired an arson," I continued. "Still I can't help but wonder why you would leave a loose end. Why not just set the fire yourself? It would be so much easier to cover your tracks. My people are the best, Darrell, and they have traced the arson back to the source. It's information I am prepared to use if necessary."

Issa was not prepared for this confrontation. His fitful response indicated a combination of fear and dejection. "What do you want from me?" he asked.

"I already told you." He looked so pathetic that I could not resist condescending. "Aw, don't look so down, Darrell. It won't be every vote. I'm quite selective about my plans."

"I could just deny your accusations," he feebly suggested.

I was reminded of the conversation I had with Lt. Moran in my Pegasus office the previous December. I started to laugh and said, "More than half the members of Congress are criminals. The questions are, 'What crimes did they commit?' and 'What are their constituents willing to accept?' You've been denying accusations, particularly about the arson for years, but you don't want to test me," I assured him. "I could become your worst nightmare. You're just beginning in politics. Your district is reasonably wealthy, and if you can manage to get elected to a fourth or fifth term, none of this will much matter to them. Your constituents are not likely to hold it against you, particularly if they determine your time in office has helped their bottom line. But if my information is disseminated now, that knowledge will suffocate your career just as it's beginning to breathe."

Issa's expression had continually changed through the course of our conversation. He looked helpless, almost pathetic, clearly unsure of what response to make. I sat back and gazed at him, neither smug nor self-congratulatory. But I would not allow myself to pity him. It occurred to me that goons are like adolescents. They think they are invincible. The goon expects people to cower before him at the mere threat of doing harm. It is rare for one to end up where Issa was that day—completely emasculated. He was so used to manipulating others that he did not know how to respond. Viscosity clogged whatever wheels of intellect might have once inhabited his brain.

"You're despicable, Lozano," Issa said.

"That's your best shot, Darrell?" I laughingly asked. "How disappointing! You miss the sheer simplicity of it all. You don't seem to realize that you're looking at a reflection. You and I inhabit the same world. I just do it better. Still, your value to me is limited. In a few years, I will no longer have need of you. For now . . ." I let the sentence drift unfinished and simply stared at him.

Realizing that our conversation was over he stood up again. This time I did not object. As he walked out I said candidly, "Remember. What transpired here is just between us."

In my twisted and sadistic reality, I usually enjoy these kinds of conversations. And I must say that I really wanted to like Issa. As it turned out my desire was inconsequential. He was gifted with neither a keen nor agile mind. Like many a politician he was merely mediocre. He elicited no sympathy from me at all, for he put his future in jeopardy the day he decided to become a punk.

CHAPTER 15

Many senators and representatives who live on the East Coast return to their own homes on weekends. Senator Joe Biden of Delaware actually commutes every day by Amtrak in order to be with his family. It was a practice he began when first elected in 1972. For his first five years, he was a single father. Biden's first wife and their one-year-old daughter had been killed in an accident a few weeks after his election, leaving him with two boys who survived the crash. He needed to be with his sons every night, and the train ride was more than worth the time. For those of us further west, frequent trips home are inconvenient, impractical, or both. Instead, we mostly rely on Senate recesses to be with family and reconnect with voters.

I decided to go home for Christmas in 2001. My absence would have been conspicuous. Besides, I really wanted to spend some time with my parents and my sister and her family. I also needed to strengthen my outreach to my constituents. California is large both in population and size, so I scheduled meetings in my six district offices located throughout the state. It allowed me to be both home and not home at the same time. However, Christmas Day was set aside for family. I could find no adequate excuse for being absent, but spending time with them meant seeing my brother Giovanni, and possibly Tom and Emily as well.

When I was growing up, I knew of families for whom the holidays were anything but pleasant. There was either someone who wasn't on speaking terms with someone else or family gatherings ended in a fight with one person storming out of the house. But we are Italians and regardless of our disagreements, family is everything. For us arguments are part of communication and rarely lead to lingering hurt or someone exiting in a fit of anger.

Then again, the problem between my brother and me, one that also included Tom, had nothing to do with an argument. We were not on speaking terms for a very different reason that no one in the family was privy to. And none of us was in a position to explain it. More accurately, only I could explain it but I knew better. By necessity, the cause of division would continue to puzzle everyone else.

Christmas dinner was at the home of my parents, Luciano and Carmela. My sister, Bianca, had recently had another baby—a boy whom she graciously named Leonardo, after my late son. She, her husband, their firstborn, Henry, and the baby were all there. Tom's parents, Thomas and Susan, were present, as well as his sister and her husband, Karen and Sean. They were expecting their first child in early March. And, of course, Tom, Emily, and Giovanni were there. This was a year, almost to the day, after Giovanni and Tom learned the truth about my wife and children and I wondered just how the reunion would unfold.

I have to give both of them credit. Acting is a part of my political career. I constantly assuage people's concerns by making them believe I care. Most Americans are not interested in truth—only in hearing what they want to hear. Since politicians are only interested in maintaining their office, it is a perfect match. The key is knowing how to convince. If constituents' minds are already made up, pretense becomes the key ingredient to success.

As a priest, Giovanni also inhabits a public world in which people's minds frequently are already made up. I've often thought that many priests and ministers would make good politicians. They read people the same way I do, in their case recognizing that congregants do not attend church to be challenged by the teachings of Jesus. They go to Sunday services wanting to be comforted and assured that their way of seeing the world is correct. Although Giovanni has always been aware of that, he takes the risk of making people uncomfortable by embracing and preaching a gospel of inclusion and forgiveness. Yet, when challenged he also must engage a certain charade and maintain his composure. My very presence on Christmas challenged both his gospel and his poise.

Tom is entirely different. He has never been a public speaker. Contrary to making people comfortable, he does his best investigative work when he can throw a suspect off balance. He usually has no need to pretend, except when possible offenders do not realize they are persons of interest. Then he also is called upon to distract them, to make them ill at ease and hopefully careless.

I was the only one of the three of us who actually was calm on Christmas. Neither Giovanni nor Tom was visibly uncomfortable. In that regard they proved themselves well practiced. On the other hand, there was unaddressed tension among the three of us, not quite palpable but nonetheless real. Beyond exchanging cursory hellos, neither they nor I asked any questions—not even how are you.

With Bianca's new baby and Karen's pregnancy, we were able to keep most of the conversation focused on their families. Having Emily back in the fold engendered many questions about her job and her travels, and age was creeping up on our parents, enabling us to discuss their plans for the future such as retirement and where they would live. As was to be expected, everyone had questions about Washington and the Senate—everyone, that is, except for Giovanni and Tom. The rest were concerned about the terrorist attacks, the government's response, and whether they were safe in Southern California, as well as what kinds of things I did in the Senate, and whether I had met any famous politicians such as the president. While trying to assure them Washington is relatively boring, I managed to hold their attention with stories about political intrigue and the machinations of Washington's elite.

As frequently happens at family gatherings, we divided into different discussion groups. Someone filming Christmas Day at the Lozano's would have noticed that Giovanni, Tom, and I never interacted. We wandered different parts of the rooms and even sat at separate tables. Most of the family was oblivious. Even Bianca, who had previously expressed concern about the apparent deteriorating relations among the three of us, had her attention consumed with baby Leonardo. Only Emily seemed to notice.

As she and Tom drove home, he said to her, "Emily, it was wonderful having you with all of us at Christmas again."

"Thank you, Tom. It's been a long time. I always loved those gatherings and I almost forgot how wonderful they are. I missed Yolanda and the kids, though. Very much."

Was she testing him? He had no reason to doubt the sincerity of her words, but there was something ambiguous in her tone. Tom should have let it be, but he knew the subject would continue to surface. He was going to have to confront it eventually, but not tonight.

"It was worse last year," he replied, attempting to control the conversation. "There was no joy at all. I think Bianca's new baby and Karen's pregnancy helped a lot. You made a big difference, too." They both smiled. Tom knew where this might go, so he tried to head it off by saying, "Em, I know what you want to ask. I already promised you that I would share the investigation and tell you what I discovered. Tonight, however, is not the right time. I just want to go home and be with you for our first Christmas together. The second time around."

She leaned over and kissed his cheeks. "Tonight," she promised, "I'm all yours."

·   ·   ·

February 2002

There had been so much activity in Washington during the fall that I decided to invite Jackson and Jean-Paul to visit in February. They arrived on Friday, the eighth, and stayed through Sunday. This trip was primarily for relaxation and we spent the weekend touring D.C., something I had done little of since my arrival. As a result, much of what we saw was new even to me.

As many visitors have found, Washington is not a quick-tour town. It is possible to exhaust several days strolling along the national mall taking in all the monuments and wandering the many museums. Since I anticipated more visits from Jackson and Jean-Paul in the future, there was no need to absorb everything that weekend. On Saturday I showed them around some of the administration buildings that are not on the typical sightseeing list. One of them was the Robert F. Kennedy Department of Justice Building. Only one year before it had been renamed to honor the late attorney general, senator from New York, and presidential candidate.

In the Great Hall of the Justice Building stand two cast aluminum statues commissioned in the 1930s, one depicting *Lady Justice*, the other *Majesty of Law*. However, they were both covered in blue drapes. The reason is rather embarrassing. George W. Bush had appointed John Ashcroft attorney general, and he objected to the fact that Lady Justice is only partially clothed and has an exposed breast. Fortunately, her male counterpart is only unclothed above the waist. Still, Ashcroft found them offensive.

Jean-Paul started to laugh. "After all these years in the United States, I still don't understand some of your prudish ways, particularly your obsession with avoiding anything public that refers to sex. So many great paintings and sculptures in Europe are completely nude and society voices no moral disapproval. In fact, the only objection would arise if someone painted over or covered them."

"Well, Jean-Paul," I explained, "there is a history of such nonsense in the U.S.—all of it the remnant of a puritanical past. When the liberty quarter was first released in nineteen seventeen, Miss Liberty was holding an olive branch and shield, and her right breast was bare. It was a beautiful design, and given the turmoil of WWI, it made a statement about American values—the country's willingness to stand firm in the face of freedom while pursuing its desire for peace. But there were some people in America who remained anchored to the Victorian age. As a result, the artist, Hermon MacNeil, redesigned the quarter and not only was Miss Liberty's breast covered, but she was depicted wearing a chain metal shirt. Whether intentional or not, the new design invoked and mocked the memory of chastity belts."

"Maybe," Jackson suggested, "the mint's anatomical knowledge was deficient and they did not know the real purpose of a chastity belt!"

"I don't know about that," I replied. "But there will always be those in American society whose minds and morals are firmly rooted in the sixteenth century."

"I still don't understand why the statues had to be covered," Jean-Paul said.

I responded, "Ashcroft's Assemblies of God Church is more than a little religiously and morally conservative, and the attorney general makes a number of speeches in front of those statues. Apparently, Ashcroft objects to being photographed in front of them. He sees it as government-sponsored pornography."

"So there was nothing wrong with the statues until Ashcroft became attorney general?" Jean-Paul mused.

"Apparently not," I said. "Ashcroft is just living in the wrong century."

During the visit I wanted to speak about my disturbing dreams. Jean-Paul knew that I had something private to discuss with Jackson. After Saturday lunch he offered to tour the National Museum of Natural History by himself, thus providing Jackson and me with some time alone.

We meandered along the mall, slowly covering the distance between the Washington and Lincoln memorials. Despite being outdoors, the walk would provide privacy for our conversation. It was early February and although the temperature was warmer than normal, it was still quite cold, and we were bundled appropriately with overcoats, scarves, and hats. Jackson even wore a pair of rabbit-lined leather gloves. As we began our walk, I told him about the different kinds of dreams I had been having, but focused more on the nightmares involving Yolanda and the kids.

"The strange thing is, Jacks, that in spite of what seems like restlessness, if I wake up during the night I quickly fall back to sleep. And in the morning, I am not tired. For the most part I feel refreshed.

It's only during the day, when I have time to remember the previous night that I am bothered."

"Sep," he replied, "I am not a psychologist and I certainly do not know how to interpret dreams. In fact, I'm a little suspicious of those therapists who claim to be experts at it. I know people say that dreams are signs of the subconscious trying to break into reality. But even if that's true there must be more than one way to decipher them. I don't know what to tell you. How long has this been going on? The first time you mentioned it was last October."

"That's about when the nightmares began," I replied. "I figured they were somehow connected to the events of 9/11 and the fact that it had been a year since my wife and children died. And they don't occur every night. Plus, I don't think I told you that Emily, Tom's wife, had come to visit. Seeing her again also brought up a lot of memories."

"You didn't mention that part, Sep. But I have to tell you, I really don't know how you've managed any of this. I admire the fact that you did not give up the election after their deaths. I don't think I could have continued. But when I think back to our days at Harvard you always had a certain determination. I guess it's not really surprising that you kept going."

"Yeah, but this is unlike any challenges we faced in graduate school."

"You're right," he said. "But it's not your fault. If you could have prevented their deaths you would have."

I counted on his innocence and compassion. We had spent a year-and-a-half rebuilding our friendship. And each time we talked, there was more to reveal. Jackson was an easygoing person, but he had deep feelings and felt he had to make up for the past. It was as if he did not deserve the relationship we had rediscovered and that he should not be the one whom I confided in.

"Sep, for many years I have regretted what happened back at Harvard. I was such an asshole. I didn't realize what a good friend you were trying to be. No one had ever cared for me the way you did or been concerned about what happened to me. Certainly not Helena. I was such a fool, but I was in denial. And then after the funeral, I . . ." His eyes wandered and his words trailed off.

"You don't have to explain, Jacks."

"Yes, I do. For the last year I have been wondering what would have happened if I had listened to you all those years ago. At the very least we would not have lost twenty-five years. We would have remained a part of each other's lives. You know, I really regret never meeting your children. If they were anything like you and Yolanda, they were very special. And now that you are having so much trouble, I want to help. I want to be there for you. I just don't know what to do."

I needed something more than his assurances. I was looking for a way to survive the nightmares. But I began to realize he couldn't help with that. There were still things he did not know and truths I would not reveal. Maybe his gift to me was simpler and more valuable than analysis. "Just the fact that I can talk to you is a comfort, Jacks. It's not as though I have a lot of places to turn."

"What about your brother or Tom?" he asked.

Everyone not directly connected to the murder or the investigation always came back to that damn question. Sometimes I wish I could relive my past and never have the relationship I did with either Giovanni or Tom. It was like a millstone. I was either drowning or choking. I felt as though one or both of them would eventually be the death of me. I got to the point where I hated hearing their names. But I could never express that to anyone, not even to Jackson. In some ways, Giovanni and Tom were worse than the nightmares. The various iterations of that question had become so oppressive that I developed many different ways of answering it.

"Jacks, they have been through as much as I have. I can't share my problems with them. Who knows? They may be going through something very similar and trying to help me would verify the old adage of the blind leading the blind. There's another dimension, too. Sometimes when I'm alone reality kicks in and I suddenly realize that I've been talking to myself. Not full-on conversations, of course. Mind you, I'm not crazy or anything."

"Of course you're not," Jackson replied. "You're suffering and in pain. You'd be crazy if you weren't—if you didn't feel the loss of your family. It just proves what a loving husband and father you were. Talking to yourself and having nightmares are completely understandable after such a tragedy. I want you to know that whenever you need to talk or just have someone listen, you can call me anytime, even in the middle of the night."

Jackson was one of the truly good people I had met in life. He might have been a little naïve, but he was kind and accepting and always looked for the best in people. As a result, he could see things others could not. He could even see good in me.

"Thank you, Jacks. But I doubt I will call you at three o'clock in the morning. It wouldn't be fair to either you or Jean-Paul. Anything that happens to me, anything I need to discuss, can probably wait until daylight."

We met up with Jean-Paul outside the Natural History Museum and went across the street to the Smithsonian Castle. Although Jackson had shared much with me, I did not yet really know Jean-Paul. I had only met him one time, on their visit the previous year. Still, I did not want him to feel superfluous, and when it was time for dinner I suggested a restaurant I knew they would enjoy and one that would give him a taste of home.

Whether entertaining friends or manipulating enemies, it has always been my habit to provide exceptional food. My choice that night was quite fortuitous, because Robert Wiedmaier had only opened his restaurant two years earlier. He had named it after his son, Marcel, and it specializes in exquisite Belgian cuisine. It also offers top-flight French wine. It was the perfect way to end a Saturday in D.C.

Surprisingly, or maybe not, I did not have any disturbing visions the two nights they were in town. On Sunday afternoon Jackson and Jean-Paul flew home to Boston, and I wondered how long before Yolanda and the kids would return to haunt my dreams.

• • •

I was committed to the Republican Party, but I was elected from a liberal state because I was viewed as a moderate. That was essential for drawing support from independent voters and even some Democrats. Not only was California liberal, but it was perhaps the most environmentally conscious state in the union. It was not about to become conservative, nor would it abandon the environment. On those issues, my allegiance was to the state, not the party. In April Congress handed me my first opportunity to demonstrate independence in my carefully calculated political universe.

Although the Environmental Protection Agency was created as the result of bi-partisan legislation in the 1970s, in more recent years my own party had been attacking anything that smacked of preserving nature. Instead, the Republican leadership attempted to chip away at virtually all protections with the hope of ultimately dismantling the EPA, thus subjecting the entire land to the whims and desires of industry. The strongest onslaught was in the area of oil exploration and development. A full-fledged battle had emerged over drilling in the Arctic National Wildlife Reserve, the largest protected wilderness in the United States.

The Organization of the Petroleum Exporting Countries (OPEC), initially created to stabilize oil prices around the world, had, at various times, taken advantage of market demand to over-inflate crude oil prices, thus driving up costs for the importing countries and for the consumer. The Republican Party seized on the concept of energy independence and used it as a counterattack. The approach would mean more drilling both on land and offshore.

However, oil spills and environmental damage have long plagued the industry. One does not need an elephantine memory to recall the damage caused when the *Exxon Valdez* ran aground in Prince William Sound in Alaska and the thought of destroying the pristine ANWR, coupled with an irreversible threat to wildlife, galvanized opposition from conservation groups and many in the Democratic Party. This provided the perfect opportunity for me to test the waters of autonomy and demonstrate my commitment to my home state. For years California had been a leader in establishing environmental requirements, including fuel efficiency standards for automobiles that required the manufacturers to build cars with special emissions systems. As a whole, the state was extremely pro-environment. It would be easy for me to buck the party leadership with few repercussions and in the process establish a good working rapport with Democrats.

The two Republican senators from Alaska, Frank Murkowski and Ted Stevens, had harangued the chamber for months in their demands that ANWR be opened for oil production. They invoked every imaginable negative image of the wilderness and spoke in near-apocalyptic language of America's future without drilling in this part of Alaska. No matter anyone's position on drilling, it was clear who owned these two senators.

In the final tally, nine Republican senators voted against drilling including Gordon Smith of Oregon and me. The West Coast was solidly on the side of the environment.

CHAPTER 16

On Wednesday, October 2, a resolution was brought before Congress—*Authorization for Use of Military Force Against Iraq Resolution of 2002 (AUMF)*. It proffered amazingly weak evidence to suggest that Saddam Hussein had weapons of mass destruction. If true, those weapons could never reach the United States, but he would be able to attack America's interests elsewhere.

Support for the resolution was far from unanimous and although there was a deteriorating atmosphere in American politics with partisanship superseding any genuine concern for the country, the congressional leadership of both houses wanted to speed passage of the resolution in order to demonstrate that the two parties could work together. Apparently, it was too much to hope that after a year of war in Afghanistan and constant fear-mongering at home the two parties could have come together on a peaceful endeavor. Even with the feigned bi-partisanship, most of the support and opposition fell along party lines.

Senators Robert Byrd of West Virginia, Carl Levin of Michigan, and Dick Durban of Illinois all introduced amendments designed to limit the scope and duration of the authorization, specifically in terms of Iraq's alleged weapons of mass destruction, and to require a new resolution from the United Nations Security Council. All these amendments failed, and it quickly became evident that there was a rush to bring this legislation to the floor. I called Jackson and asked if he could possibly come to Washington that weekend. This vote was going to cause me some consternation and I wanted to test the waters outside Washington.

Jackson arrived at Reagan National Airport on Friday afternoon, this time coming alone. It was not a social visit, so we settled right into reading and discussing the resolution, a process that continued most of Saturday. He was neither a lawyer nor a legislator. But he was a thoughtful and penetrating reader with an acute intellect. Whatever reservations he may have had about the Bush administration, he was careful to exclude them from his analysis.

"Sep, I'm reminded of something from philosophy class. Always question the assumptions. All of them. It's a piece of advice I should have given you regarding the Patriot Act. It may not have changed your vote, but it's good guidance for everything you do in the Senate."

"Give me an example in reference to this authorization," I said.

"OK. Let's start with the whereases. In any resolution they are intended to support, or in this case justify, the 'be it resolved.' However, several of the whereases in this resolution are conspicuously lacking in evidence. They are stated as matters of fact when, in truth, they are presumptions.

"Several of them assume that Saddam Hussein possesses weapons of mass destruction and is pursuing a nuclear weapons program. That kind of accusation cannot carelessly be made, especially in a war resolution, without including evidence. It is vague and demonstrates a casual disregard toward the import of the resolution. It is as though the authors presume passage is a foregone conclusion.

"There is also an assumption in another whereas that Iraqi civilian life should be the same as in America. Take a look at the seventh whereas regarding the oppression of Iraqi citizens. First of all, the oppression is not spelled out. It's too generic and ignores the fact that Iraq is not a democracy."

"But," I objected, "Saddam Hussein is a brutal dictator."

"That may be," Jackson replied. "But we support despotic leaders all over the world. That's hardly a justifiable basis for war."

"But if you put them all together, don't they add up?" I asked.

"Not necessarily. Let me use the example of the Catholic Just War Doctrine."

"Have you suddenly discovered God and turned religious?" I asked.

"That's for another discussion," he replied. "It has no bearing on this conversation."

I may have been imagining it, but he seemed slightly irritated by my comment. And a bit evasive. He continued.

"The title 'The Just War Doctrine' may actually be a misnomer. It was conceived by St. Augustine and further refined by other theologians as a way to make war *un*justifiable. There are seven principles that comprise the doctrine. However, for a war to be called just it must meet all seven criteria. A preponderance is not sufficient. Even if a war fails in only one category, it is not just. I think the idea is difficult for many people, including our political leaders to grasp. The doctrine was created from a bias in favor of peace. The same concept should be at work in this resolution. Simply saying that most of the whereases are accurate neither validates not justifies the 'be it resolved.'"

By Saturday night we had exhausted our conversation about the resolution. Jackson had given me much to ponder and even left me undecided as to how I would vote. I would make that determination after further debate in the Senate, where I would hear very different perspectives.

·   ·   ·

When Jackson and Jean-Paul first visited me in Washington, I treated them to dinner at the classic Georgetown restaurant, 1789. He was so impressed with the ambience, the service, and the meal that he requested to return. It was the least I could do. However, before heading out to dinner, and with our discussion completed, Jackson and I had time to relax.

It was a cold October night and we had cocktails indoors. Jackson brought me up-to-date with the health of Jean-Paul's mother. Then he talked about his own family. He had not spoken of them since we reconnected two years before. I thought that he was assiduously avoiding the subject, so I never broached it. As he began to speak, I recalled his fear back in graduate school that his family would never accept his being gay. Of course, in those days he was in the closet and was spared confronting his fears. But after he and Jean-Paul entered into a relationship he could no longer hide.

"Sep, when we talked after the funeral, I explained, or at least I tried to, about our days at Harvard. I could not accept your intervention, because I could not accept myself. I was running away from the truth of who I was. When we were in school, I told you that my family would never accept me. I was so wrong about them.

"When I was thirty I came out of the closet. The first person I told was my youngest brother, Kaden. We always had a special relationship and communicated on a different level than our other siblings."

"What did he say?" I asked.

"There was not the slightest hesitation. He said he didn't care if I was gay. He saw nothing wrong with my orientation. He even joked that it was not as if I had committed some horrific crime. The only thing that mattered to him was that I was his brother."

If Jackson only knew. But I didn't want to interrupt and certainly had no intention of comparing brothers.

"Kaden made me feel very comfortable," he continued. "He was still in college and his university was very tolerant of gay rights. As in other schools, this created a general ease with homosexuality. Through one of his friends and at various university functions, Kaden had met many gay and lesbian students and he was quite relaxed around them."

"How did the rest of the family respond?"

"Everybody was OK with it, although it took more time for some of them. They were not all as comfortable as Kaden. But I don't think any of them were truly surprised. In fact, my oldest sister and another brother had a secret bet. He was convinced I was gay; she was convinced I was straight. She lost. When I found out about it, I offered to pay her debt. She refused. It was all of five dollars."

We both laughed and then headed off to dinner. When we arrived home, I fixed a nightcap. He had his choice of anything in the house but selected a vintage port while I had an eighteen-year-old Laphroaig single malt. As we started to sip I looked across the room. This was the Jackson I remembered from graduate school. I still believed that he could read my every thought, every emotion. He sensed there were things he did not know about me, things I was not ready to reveal. His look intensified.

"Sep, a few times tonight I noticed you staring off into the distance. Just briefly. As if something was bothering you."

"To tell the truth, Jacks, I was a little jealous as you spoke about your family. I'm happy that you are on such good terms with your brothers and sisters. I only have part of that. I get along fine with Bianca, but not Giovanni. And yet, now I don't really care. Tonight proves something."

"Tell me," he said encouragingly.

"Jacks, you know that I'm not a poet. I don't even like reading the stuff. But ever since the murders I've been thinking, first about being alone. I was OK with that. I had no desire to be with anyone else and certainly had no intention to marry again. Then when I saw you at the funeral, I began to think about when we were younger, what had happened to us over the years, and where we are now. No one else, not even Yolanda, had ever really known me. When I stepped back to look at myself from the outside, I saw a tapestry of people woven together, moving in and out of the picture. And then I realized something unexpected. You stand out as the dominant thread. Even after all those years of separation between us, you stitch all the fibers together into a single tableau, imbuing even the darkest scenes with vibrancy and life."

"And you say you don't like poetry!" He smiled and then asked, "You got all that from the funeral?"

"Well, the funeral was a good start. Your presence was totally unexpected, especially since we had not spoken in some twenty years. But seeing you there lifted my spirits. Somehow I knew I could get through the tragedy."

"I hardly knew what to say, Sep. I wasn't even sure you'd see me. I just knew that I needed to be there."

"Well, it meant more than you can imagine," I told him. "And the next day, the time we spent together talking and catching up on our lives, brought me comfort. For the first time since the murders, I felt peace. Thank you for that. I hope someday I can be just as good a friend to you."

He smiled and said, "You already are. You have accepted me for who I am, without judgment or condemnation."

It was getting late and although we had nothing particular planned for the morning, it was time for sleep. We had spent a long day going over the war resolution, and I could tell he was tired.

I gave him a totally unnecessary, but desirable, hug good night, lasting slightly longer than normal. Neither of us displayed any discomfort, except that my muscles tightened defensively. I was careful to maintain a few inches between us, keeping only my body erect. Where did these feelings come from? As far back as graduate school we had a strong, secure emotional connection. But there was never anything physical. I was crossing a threshold I did not anticipate and stepping into a world I feared I could not control. I was surprised to feel my hand tremble as I touched his back. It could have been only my imagination because he didn't seem to respond. I was fighting with myself. I desired more but was afraid. Cautiously, I moved my fingers slowly, slightly stroking the nape of his neck and hair. He paused for a brief moment, then stepped back and looked at me. It was more than a glance, his eyes once again penetrating my being as they had so many years before.

"Sep," he said, "we cannot walk down this path. Maybe it would have been possible in our youth. But we are no longer young, and rash behavior does not suit either of us. We have moved in different directions and given our lives to other goals."

I felt torn. I wanted to reach out and draw him back to me, but I couldn't move. I was frozen by my foolish impetuosity. I suspect that even in the dim light of evening I was red with embarrassment. He continued, speaking with a gentle grace, neither accusatory nor defensive.

"Perhaps more than most people I know your feelings—what you have lost and the emptiness you must be suffering. I offer comfort and solace but if you're looking for more, I cannot be the one. I am in a committed relationship that is neither casual nor open. I love Jean-Paul with my whole being. And when the day arrives, when it is legal, we expect to be married. But even if I were free, it wouldn't work, Sep. I don't think you're gay. You're just alone and lonely. I doubt this is how you would find satisfaction."

I really did feel like a fool at that moment, deserted by both wit and wisdom.

"I'm, sorry, Jacks." It was a lame reply that benefitted only from its honesty. What a stupid thing to do!

"Don't be sorry, Sep. I'm not embarrassed. Actually, I'm flattered. And I treasure the fact that you could be so open and comfortable with me. But it's time for sleep. Good night."

"Good night, Jacks."

With that we withdrew to our separated bedrooms and separate beds.

·　·　·

I don't know if it was Jackson's presence in my home or my lapse of judgment, but my sleep was more fitful than usual. Yolanda and the kids appeared again, but this time they were not hovering over my bed. They passed by as if they could not even see me, as if I were the ghost. Their eyes were empty as they started to leave. I could see in their expressions that I did not matter to them.

I began to cry out, "Yolanda! Can you hear me? Don't you see me? Carmen, Gina, Leonardo. My kids. Wait for me."

This was not my usual hallucination. I had seen them before. But I was always home alone. Not this time. Jackson could hear me from the other room. Nothing distinct, just loud and painful noise. Awakened, he tried to distinguish my words but could not. I was asleep and though

I did not know it, I had begun to perspire. I must have been almost shouting, "Yolanda, I could have saved you!"

Jackson entered my room and shaking my shoulders tried to stir me to consciousness. "Sep, wake up. Wake up."

I opened my eyes and asked, "Jacks, what are you doing here?"

"You were talking in your sleep, loud enough that I could hear you in the other room. When I walked in you were practically shouting. So I woke you." He noticed the perspiration and said, "My God, Sep, you're drenched. You can't go back to sleep like that. You'll get sick."

"But—" I began.

"We can talk about it in the kitchen. Right now you need to get into some dry clothes. Go take a shower and I'll make us some tea. It'll be waiting for you when you get out."

Even in my semi-conscious state, I looked at him and thought, "Fuck. This is not how I pictured him in my room." Of course, it was not something I was about to say. I got up and took a shower. Then went downstairs where Jackson was waiting.

As I sat across the table and began to drink the tea I said, "Jacks, I wasn't actually asleep. I was at the cemetery speaking to Yolanda and the kids. They were standing before me. It was so real."

"Maybe it seems real to you, but you were asleep. And maybe I was wrong, Sep."

I looked at him hopefully, but he said, "Not about that. Maybe I don't understand what you're going through. You have never been a person to lose control. But in that nightmare you were not yourself."

We did not say much after that. When we finished the tea we went back to bed, again separate ones. Life can be really fucked up. I think I always wanted Jackson, even back in graduate school. I guess that is the real reason I confronted him over his relationship with Helena. But when we were in our twenties at Harvard, neither of us was ready. Now he was beyond reach, and I was out of luck. I was not interested in another woman, and I did not want another man. I discovered it that night—I would simply ride the role of widower right into the White House.

In the morning nothing more was said about the previous night's encounter. I still had vestiges of embarrassment, but Jackson did not seem in the least bothered. In fact, he was quite relaxed and comfortable in my presence. He initiated the discussion I had wanted to pursue the previous day. At the time it would have distracted us from analyzing the war resolution.

"Sep," he began. "Yesterday you asked me about religion. You know I've been an atheist all my life. I could never buy into any of the traditional belief systems. Even the philosophical "proofs" for the existence of God don't actually prove anything. They presuppose a belief or at least an inclination to belief. If that does not already exist, they are less than convincing."

"I know what your position's always been. That's what caught me off guard yesterday. I certainly did not expect you to reference religion in our discussion. I just didn't know where that came from."

"It doesn't spring from any one source," he replied. "I guess the first, and most important thing, was Jean-Paul. He was raised Catholic. But when we first met, he was not sure of his religious footing. During his internship in Boston, he never went to church. But when I would visit him in Brussels he always attended Mass, just to please his family. And I went along."

"Really?" I asked, somewhat skeptically.

"I didn't see any harm in it." His tone did not convey a defensive attitude. Rather, he was almost apologetic. "To me it was a matter of being polite. The first few times I really felt out of place. I didn't know what was going on with the rituals. And at the time I didn't speak much French. The thing is, as the two of us traveled around Europe, Jean-Paul continued to go to church, and I went with him. Hell, I would have gone anyplace with him. I began to ask questions and discovered that he couldn't explain a lot. And whenever we talked about church or faith I could sense a turmoil within him."

"You've always had that ability," I said. "But what was the problem?"

"Mostly, I think it was because the Catholic Church is not terribly accepting of homosexuals. Jean-Paul had known since childhood that he was gay, except that when he was little, he didn't have a word for it. He just knew he was different. By the time he could understand, he had no need or desire to test his orientation and he found himself the object of condemnation in the one place he expected solace."

"Then why didn't he just leave?" I asked.

"He tried. As I said, he didn't go to church when he was first in Boston. But as we fell in love and I watched him struggle, I felt I wanted to help. I wasn't interested in changing his beliefs and I didn't want to convert. On the other hand, I didn't want to see the person I loved in pain. So I decided to learn a little bit about Catholicism.

"I discovered that sexuality is not as black and white as some traditionalists claim, that there is room for gay and lesbian people in the Catholic Church. We found a couple of priests who did not condemn us. As Jean-Paul became more comfortable with his faith, I became a little less anti-God. I'm still not convinced, but I'm open."

"You sound more than just open, Jacks."

"Well, Sep. Maybe I am. Maybe I'm searching. I've learned a lot from my investigation of the Catholic faith. And I found support for some of my own beliefs—for example, war. I have always been committed to nonviolence and I am steadfastly opposed to war. I happened to be examining Catholic teaching when the first President Bush took us to battle in Iraq.

"Several times he made the claim that it was a just war. That's how I discovered the Just War Doctrine. What I found out is that the first Iraq conflict did not meet all seven criteria. And that's why I brought it up yesterday in response to your question. It's a pretty powerful doctrine and it should give everyone pause."

We had come full circle in our discussion, and it was time for Jackson to return to Boston.

"I promise you, Jacks, that I will consider everything you said about the war resolution, and I really do appreciate your insights."

With that, I gave him a normal embrace and we said goodbye.

. . .

On Monday I called Darrell Issa. I was about to test his appreciation of my power and to demonstrate my resolve. Although Issa represented a very strong Republican district, California as a whole was not enthusiastic about war. If nothing else, that strengthened my hand.

"Hello, Darrell," I said. We had not spoken much over the previous year. Even so, he would not have forgotten our conversation and was certainly smart enough not to question my steadfastness. His tone of voice was less than enthusiastic.

"Hello," he replied coldly. No query as to why I was calling. He just waited for me to continue.

I spoke as if he had no choice, which, in fact, he did not. He remained quiet as if thinking of a response. I continued, "I know that the Republican leadership wants this war resolution to pass. For that matter, so do the Democratic leaders. I want you to vote against it."

"Are you out of your fucking mind?" he asked.

"I don't think so," I said coyly. "But look, Darrell. You need to grasp the bigger picture. The resolution will pass. It's a foregone conclusion in the House, and I can guarantee it will clear the Senate. Since Californians are not pro-war you can't lose. And that's your cover. You can assure any concerned members in your district that you knew it would pass, but you wanted to cast your vote to stem the tide of war. Your vote was a statement, but in reality, it was futile. Besides, nobody's career hangs on one vote."

"I won't do it. I've already spoken in favor of the resolution."

"Darrell, why not let people think you are sufficiently flexible and intelligent enough to change your mind after careful consideration?"

"Hastert will be pissed if I vote against the resolution," he protested.

"I'm sure he will. But he'll be even more pissed if you lose the election next month. Right now you're a lock, especially considering the demographics of your district. Nobody can imagine you losing.

That is, nobody but me. There is still a month to go. I have the goods and the money. Can I count on your vote?"

"I got the message," he replied. Then hung up.

I admit to being a bit smug as I returned the receiver to its cradle. I leaned forward with a smirk on my face. Issa was not much of a challenge, though. He was more of a lab experiment—a beaker of ignorance, ambition, and weakness, mixed with a measure of criminality. I did not really care about his voting record or what his constituents thought. I knew the measure would pass and wanted to test my power over him. When the votes were cast, the *Authorization for Use of Military Force Against Iraq Resolution of 2002* easily sailed through the House of Representatives on Thursday, October 10, and comfortably passed the Senate in the wee hours of Friday morning, October 11. I imagine that I disappointed my friend, Jackson, for the second time. But I was building a career and I needed an unassailable record.

CHAPTER 17

The unsolved murders of my wife and children rippled through the LAPD's Robbery and Homicide Division. Detectives Gary Wharton and Philip Rose were unceremoniously transferred from RHD to less glamorous divisions, Wharton to the Foothill Division and Rose to the Southeast. Lt. Tom Moran who headed the investigation found his career arrested. He retained his rank of lieutenant and remained at RHD, but his reputation in the department had been diminished. By contrast, Captain Erick Haskell was promoted to the rank of commander, not because of, but rather in spite of, the failed investigation. It was another example of the upper echelon taking care of its own.

Tom bore no ill-will toward Haskell. In fact, they remained friends. Throughout the investigation, even in its darkest and most frustrating hours, Haskell was supportive of Tom's work. For his own part, the captain boasted an excellent resume. He was a model police officer from his first days on the force. His rise through the ranks was steady and sure, every promotion justified. In 1996 he was an original participant in the Los Angeles Police Department's West Point Leadership Program. Subsequently, he proved himself a skillful leader with an uncanny ability to read the potential in his officers. His appointment as commander was due as much to his proficiency as anything else, and it presaged the crowning achievement of his career.

Los Angeles Mayor James Hahn appointed William Bratton as the LAPD's fifty-fourth chief of police in October 2002. Bratton had already distinguished himself both in Boston and New York. After assuming the helm in Los Angeles, one of his first observations was that, like most major cities, it was ill-prepared for an attack similar to the one that shocked New York and the world on 9/11. The House and Senate were currently debating the Homeland Security Act. Bratton, like everyone else, knew that Congress was still in the throes of terrorist fear and grasping for legislation that would stem a growing sense of danger. The Act passed on November 22, 2002, and was signed into law by President Bush on November 25. In the meantime, Bratton wanted to be ahead of the curve.

He convened a number of meetings, initiating what was to become the LAPD Counter-Terrorism and Criminal Intelligence Bureau, and was actively pursuing John Miller to serve as bureau chief. They had worked together when Bratton was commissioner of the New York City Police Department. Miller had been a journalist before working as NYPD deputy commissioner. After his police service he returned to journalism, but with a decidedly pro-law enforcement bent.

In preparation for Miller's arrival, Haskell was brought onboard and charged with bringing together the best of the LAPD to work in the new bureau. He knew that Moran was a superb detective and that the Lozano murders were unique in the annals of Los Angeles crime. He also knew that the lieutenant had an unequaled grasp of the city. On November 19, 2002, Haskell called Moran and asked him to come to his office.

"Welcome, Tom," Haskell said.

Tom looked around. Someone in the department had exercised frugality. Although this was significantly better than Haskell's previous office at RHD, it was far from luxurious.

"Hello, Erick. How's the new job?" Tom asked.

"It's beginning to evolve and that's why I called you. The chief wants to establish a new bureau."

"What is it?" Tom asked.

"We're calling it The Counter Terrorism and Criminal Intelligence Bureau (CTCIB). The chief thinks we're vulnerable for an attack similar to the one in New York. In fact, according to him, Los Angeles is even more susceptible."

"Did he specify?" Tom asked.

"Just generalities," Haskell replied. "There's been no threat, but he wants to be prepared and I think he nailed his observations. As he noted, the greater Los Angeles Metropolitan area is the largest region in the United States, spread out over hundreds of square miles. On top of that, the chief listed the most obvious potential targets: the twin ports of Long Beach and Los Angeles, the skyscrapers, the airport, the power grid, aqueducts, the list goes on. This new bureau is being created not only to respond to terrorism, but to prevent it."

"What do you want with me? My reputation is shit right now."

"I'm not interested in what others think of you, Tom. I don't blame you for what happened, or didn't happen, in the Lozano case. I've known you for years and you are one of the best, if not the best, detective I have ever worked with. You were an excellent credit to RHD. More importantly, I trust you and want you to come over to CTCIB. My job is to gather the best people. Now it's your decision if you want to join us. What do you say?"

"Well," Tom answered. "At this point I'd love to get the hell out of RHD. And I'm more than interested. Most likely I'll say yes, but if you don't mind I'll tell you tomorrow. As you know, Emily and I are back together. Eighteen years ago she left me in part because of my job with the department. I don't want that to be a problem again. I don't want her to think that she's not consulted."

"I understand that, Tom." Haskell had been married to his wife, Sharon, for more than thirty years. It was one of those enviable relationships that just worked. Then again, Sharon did not have her own personal career. "I always thought you needed someone in your life, and I'm glad Emily's back. Until tomorrow, then." They stood up and shook hands.

That night Tom discussed the promotion with Emily. It was radically different from the conversation they had following his meeting with Chief Gates so many years before. This time she had few reservations.

"Emily, I've been offered a new job."

They had grown to be very trusting of each other, but she did not extend that same trust to the department. She had seen and experienced too much police malfeasance in her journalistic career. She knew her husband was not corrupt, still she was a little wary and wanted more information.

"Tell me about it," she said.

"As you know, a year-and-a-half ago, Haskel made commander. He deserved it. He's a good cop. Now he's been appointed to head a new special bureau that will focus on terrorism and intelligence. He wants to recruit me. There's no promotion in rank, but it will get me away from the assholes in RHD."

"What will it entail?" she asked.

"At this point no one knows for certain. Given the available targets in Los Angeles, the bureau wants to head off a possible threat using community policing and private sector resources. For me it will mean better hours and few, if any, calls at three o'clock in the morning. The two of us could develop a more normal home life."

"Is Haskell going to run the bureau?"

"Apparently not. Bratton wants John Miller for the post."

"The journalist?" she asked. That caught her off guard, and she protested, "But he's not really a cop." She had reason to be concerned, given his casual disregard for civil liberties. He was on the opposite end of the spectrum from Emily. Like many of her colleagues, she thought Miller had sold his soul to the devil when he took the police commissioner's job in New York. Nonetheless, this was not about Miller. It was about Tom.

"Did you give Haskell an answer?" she asked.

"I told him I wanted to talk to you first, but that I was pretty sure you'd like the idea."

"So you think you know me that well," she teased.

"Tell me I'm wrong," he bantered back.

"You're not wrong, Tom. I think it's a wonderful idea. I've always liked Erick, and I'm glad to know that he's looking out for you. He must know that things have not been easy for you in RHD since he left."

"I'm sure he does," Tom said. "He likes his replacement enough, but he understands the division better than most and he knows that I sometimes rubbed people the wrong way. Guys in the department have long memories. Erick knows it's been a bitch since he was transferred."

"Well," Emily mused. "On the surface it sounds fine. But I can already anticipate being at odds with this new bureau. I'm not particularly happy with the federal government's overreach since 9/11. Still, if you want to take the job, I'm all for it. I think it's time for you to leave RHD. I just wish I knew more about what it will involve."

"Thanks, Emily. I won't let it come between us."

That, of course, remained to be seen. Emily was not just a reporter for a major newspaper. She had a very vocal commitment to civil rights and had written extensively during her career about the abuses of police departments, including the LAPD. Nevertheless, Tom believed that he could fulfill his promise.

Haskell managed to fill the CTCIB with some of the brightest minds on the force. Tom worked closely with Haskell to identify critical sites around the city. When Miller assumed leadership, the bureau was ready.

Miller likes to think of himself as the personal savior of L.A. He claims that upon his arrival there was no threat assessment system for the city's critical assets. That was only partially true. Haskell, Moran, and others had identified more than six hundred critical sites and they were in the process of determining which were of highest risk. The problem was that, like the federal and state governments, the system for determining risk was a relic of the WWII. Something new was needed.

What Miller brought to the city was an outsider's vision and a broader concept of what constitutes Los Angeles. He selected Lt. Tom McDonald to head an operation code-named "Archangel." A key element of the program was to bring together diverse agencies and resources. The city had learned a lesson from the federal government regarding 9/11, namely, a refusal or inability to share intelligence information is a recipe for disaster.

Realizing that each agency knows its own critical needs best, Operation Archangel brought together the LAPD, Los Angeles Sheriff's Department, Los Angeles Fire Department, Department of Airports, Ports of Los Angeles and Long Beach, Department of Parks and Recreation, Department of Water and Power, Department of Transportation, and the Los Angeles Unified School District. Archangel immediately began to coordinate with both the U.S. Department of Homeland Security and the California State Office of Homeland Security. Within months, it developed a new modern threat assessment tool that could be exported to cities and areas around the country.

Lieutenants McDonald and Moran worked closely to map out a program for inter-agency coordination including training for first responders. Action plans were developed for both businesses and government that included an upgrade in electronic communications and the ability to disseminate information instantly and accurately.

Since attacks like those of September 11, 2001, do not occur without sophisticated surveillance and coordination, counterterrorism efforts would need to be equally good. Operation Archangel was designed to provide peace and security for the City of the Angels.

As a result of the 9/11 attacks and Al Qaeda's continued terrorist activities worldwide, Lt. Tom Moran, as a cop, and I, as a senator, were confronted with new challenges practically on a daily basis. By contrast, my brother, Giovanni, was stuck in the unchanging and relentless routine of a parish priest.

CHAPTER 18

Giovanni needed some distraction and some time alone. One evening in November, he went to see the newly released film *The Truth About Charlie,* a slightly above average remake of *Charade,* minus the sophisticated charm and chemistry of the original. On his way home he stopped at McDonald's on Hollywood Blvd. After picking up his order at the counter, he found a quiet corner table, sat down and began to eat. A few minutes later, a young black woman walked in. She was obviously a prostitute, but her pretty appearance was not deceit, her work not yet hardening her youthful charms.

She walked up to Giovanni and said, "Hey, baby. You want to go have some fun?"

"Not really," Giovanni replied.

"Then how about a blow job for ten dollars?" she asked.

"No, thank you. I'm a Catholic priest," he said.

"Five dollars, then?" she quickly replied. He smiled at the suggestion acknowledging the wit that accompanied her persistence.

"No, I'm just having a quick bite to eat before heading home."

She started to walk away, then stopped and looked at him. "I don't know much about priests. Is it true you can't get married?"

"Yes, it is."

"Well, I can see that you got some real mis'ry goin' on. You need someone. If you want, I got a brother at home."

Giovanni wondered, *Does she think everything boils down to sex?* As if that would solve all his problems.

"I'm not looking to be with anybody," Giovanni replied.

"Well, it don't really matter to me," she said. "If you wants to stay mis'rable, go ahead." Then she asked, "Do you mind if I sit down a minute or two? I can be good company—even in a public place like McDonald's." She smiled.

Giovanni was not seeking company of any kind. But there was something intriguing about her. He sensed in her a similar unhappiness. But he was not in a mood to commiserate, either. Nonetheless, he motioned for her to sit.

"Please. Can I get you something to eat or drink?" he asked.

"Baby, why you think I come in here? I always be lookin' for someone nice to buy me some food. Can I get a Quarter Pounder and some fries?"

"Nothing to drink?"

"I'll take some coffee. I ain't turned no tricks yet and I gonna be workin' all night."

As he went to place her order, she could not take her eyes off him. She was more than a little curious. She had never met a priest before. Plus, he was a handsome man, graying a little from the stress of the last couple of years. She guessed his age in his early fifties, just a few years older than he really was. He returned to the table with her food.

"Here you are." He hesitated for a moment and said, "You know, I don't know your name."

"Oh, baby, that's 'cause you're new around here. I'm LaQueesha."

"That's a pretty name, though a little unusual."

"Ah," she said brushing the comment aside. "We just make up names. We try to make 'em sound mysterious or exotic."

"Do you have a street name?" Giovanni asked.

She started to laugh and said, "You mean like Sugar or Chocolate?" All of a sudden he felt foolish, and chuckled nervously. She continued, "My, you really are new. Girls like me only have street names in the movies. In the real world, everybody just calls me LaQueesha. But hey, what's your name?"

"I'm Giovanni," he replied.

"I like that. Is it Italian or somethin'?"

"It is," he said. "My parents are from Italy. I was born here."

She looked at him quizzically and asked, "You said you're a priest. Should I be callin' you father or pastor or somethin'?"

"No, you can just call me Giovanni or Gio."

LaQueesha looked at him and said, "When I first saw you, you looked depressed. But you're different when you smile and relax, kinda cute, even."

She was no longer looking to turn a trick. She wanted to know more about this stranger. He was not the typical late night McDonald's patron she was used to. She sensed some strange turmoil inside him and was puzzled.

As Giovanni did with everyone, he tried to deflect her comment. "I guess I was just absorbed, my mind drifting," he said.

"I've been around, baby. I mean Gio. And you weren't driftin' or nothin'. Somethin's botherin' you."

Damn, Giovanni thought. Having avoided talking to his closest friends, he certainly would not bare his soul to a total stranger. Maybe he could satisfy her with some general priestly stuff.

"Being a priest is not always easy. I have to deal with a lot of people and their problems. Sometimes it just becomes too much. Then I go to a movie and stop by a place like this. It's an escape for me."

"Nah," she replied knowingly. "There's somethin' else."

"You wouldn't understand," Giovanni assured her.

She shifted slightly in her chair. Her facial expression changed as did her style of speech. She was suddenly an entirely new person. "You misjudge me. You think that because I work the streets I'm ignorant or uneducated."

Giovanni was embarrassed. He started to defend himself, but she stopped him.

"Look, I don't blame you. Most people I meet think the way you do. The truth is that this is just a job for me, and I'm expected to act and speak a certain way. Believe it or not I went to college."

He tried his best not to look surprised or condescending. She continued.

"I didn't finish. I left after my sophomore year."

"May I ask why?" he asked.

"It's the oldest story in the book," LaQueesha replied. "I got pregnant. That's another part of me you don't know. I was raised by a single mom. We didn't have much money and I was working my way through school. I met this guy. At first, he seemed really nice. In fact, that's exactly what my friends said about him. They encouraged me to go on a date with him, which I did.

"I didn't plan on having sex with him, so I wasn't taking any birth control. My mom raised me well and had warned me too often about that. She didn't want me to end up like she was—a single mom. Sometime during the evening, he slipped me a roofie. When I discovered I was pregnant, I finished the semester and left."

"May I ask— "

She cut him off before he could continue. "You want to know why I didn't have an abortion?"

"Yes."

"That's an interesting question coming from a priest," she mused. "My reason had nothing to do with law or morality. I am neither opposed to nor in favor of abortion, and I don't impose my views on anyone else. My decision stemmed from a personal conviction. In one sense it wasn't even about the baby, at least not in terms of him being a human being. It was simply about life.

"In many parts of Africa there is no distinction between the secular and the sacred. Everything is holy because it comes from God and because God is found in everything. I simply don't believe in any kind of killing. This might sound silly, but I even set spiders and flies free."

"It's not silly at all," Giovanni replied. "If everyone had your personal conviction we might not be constantly fighting culture wars in this country. When you were talking about the baby, you referred to 'him.' I presume you had a boy?"

"Yes. A beautiful baby boy," she beamed. "He's six years old now and the love of my life."

"His name?" Giovanni asked.

"Tyriq."

"I like that name, too," he said.

"Now I've told you part of my story. What about you? Why were you so down when I first met you?"

Giovanni took an instant liking to LaQueesha. She was genuine, and he was enjoying this spontaneous visit in spite of himself. But she was pursuing an area he would not transgress. How could he answer her and remain true to his priesthood and to himself? Perhaps he could just mention the funeral.

"Two years ago several members of my family were killed. It's something I can't forget."

"I'm sorry," she said. "I had no idea. Otherwise I wouldn't have asked."

"That's OK. You had no way of knowing. To make matters worse, the police were never able to arrest the killers. They aren't even actively pursuing the investigation anymore.

"In some ways I guess I'm a little like you—living two lives. What people see on the surface is not the real me—not anymore. Over the years I have preached about reconciliation and healing countless times. And I really thought I believed it and I forgave people from my own past. But when I think about the persons who killed my family, it's different. I don't know how to forgive them, and I'm not even sure I want to."

"And there's something wrong with that?" she asked. "I don't think you're any different from anyone else."

"That's the point," Giovanni said. "I'm supposed to be different. At least I'm supposed to lead by example. And in spite of everything Jesus said in the Gospels, all I feel is hate. I've preached about what hate does to a person. Now I'm personally experiencing it. I'm giving into it, and it's eating away at me. I used to be a happy man." As he said that she could see in his eyes that he was transported to another time. That observation was verified by his words. "That seems a lifetime ago."

A connection was made between Giovanni and LaQueesha. She looked at him and said, "It sounds to me as if you're too hard on yourself. Whatever else you may be—a priest for example—you're still human. You have feelings like the rest of us." She continued unflinchingly, "I don't go to any church, but if I did, I wouldn't want my pastor to be less than human. How could he understand my problems if he didn't have some of his own?"

"I don't think my parishioners are as understanding as you," he replied. "If they knew how I feel now, the depth of my hatred, they'd consider me a hypocrite. My preaching would lose any sense of conviction."

"I think you're wrong," she said. "I suspect you're a very good preacher, precisely because you do have feelings. And with them come understanding and compassion. I could see it in your eyes when I was talking. You made no judgments on me as a person."

He shrugged. "I'm not in a position to judge. That's not why I became a priest."

"That's another difference," she said. "Do you know how many people, including ministers, would condemn me? Some already do because I'm an unwed mother, others because I did not give the baby up for adoption. They don't think I can provide a good home for him and object to the way I do provide for him. And if I had obtained an abortion? Well, I'm sure you've met that kind. People like me just can't win."

"Now you're the one who's wrong," Giovanni said. "Tyriq may be too young to know it, but he's a lucky kid."

This entire encounter was unexpected and initially unwanted. But here Giovanni was, talking to someone he had never met, sharing his internal struggles and managing to maintain his commitment to the sacrament. What's more, this woman had completely disarmed him. He was relaxed and comfortable with her. He couldn't fully comprehend what was happening. For two years he had locked up his emotions, sharing nothing with his closest friends—unable, or at least afraid, to tell them what he was going through. They were all intelligent and knew him too well. He was sure that if he expressed any personal feelings they would figure out what he could not say, and that would be tantamount to a violation of confession. He was ashamed at the crudeness of his thought: *All this time the only thing I needed was a whore.* That's such a base word and it did not come near to defining her. His remorse caused him to look away. Whatever else this woman was, she was classy, compassionate, and a loving mother.

When he looked back, her expression was soft and gentle, putting the lie to the general perception of prostitutes. This woman was not callous and what she shared was no pathetic or superficial sympathy. The woman before him was deeply empathetic—more so than he deserved.

He looked at her and said, "Can I ask you something else?"

"Certainly."

"Whatever happened to the baby's father?" he inquired.

"At first I didn't want to tell him that I was pregnant. But then I figured he had a right to know. He wanted me to get rid of it. I think he was afraid that I would want him to support the child. But I didn't. I just wanted to give him a chance to be part of Tyriq's life."

"And is he?"

"No. I don't even know where he is. When I think about it, Tyriq is probably better off without him."

"You sound resolved and even at peace," Giovanni observed.

"I am. There's no comparison to what you're going through, but at first I hated him. Having a baby was not part of my plans at that time. I really wanted to finish school, get a good job, marry, and then have children.

"Before Tyriq was born, sometime after I decided to continue the pregnancy, I knew I had to forgive him. I couldn't bring a baby into the world if I was filled with resentment and hate. I didn't just want to love my child. I wanted to teach him how to love."

LaQueesha was more remarkable and impressive with every word she spoke. Giovanni was in a reversal of roles that only emphasized the inadequacy in his own life.

"Where is your church?" she asked.

"A few miles from here, near USC," he replied. "It's called St. Catherine."

"Do you mind if I go to church there sometime? I'll dress properly and I promise not to embarrass you."

How could she embarrass him after this conversation, he thought? Sure, if she looked like a hooker she would be shunned by some, maybe many of his parishioners. But that would be the grossest form of narrow-mindedness.

"You're welcome anytime, LaQueesha. I don't turn anybody away from church." He suddenly realized how that sounded and corrected himself. "What I mean is, there is room in church for everyone and I think you would be a welcome addition to our parish, even if you only visit a couple of times. But it's getting late. I need to go home and you need to go to work."

She started to laugh and said, "Yeah, I have to switch to my other personality! I really enjoyed meeting you."

"LaQueesha, it was an honor for me."

As they parted, Giovanni felt a calm he had not experienced for a long time. It was not really peace, and he was no closer to forgiveness. But he may have inched his way toward acceptance. Whether any permanent change would come of this evening remained to be seen.

CHAPTER 19

January 2003

I was not particularly concerned about what was going on in either Giovanni's life or Tom's. My focus was elsewhere. The 108th Congress commenced on January 3, 2003. By that time, I had been a United States Senator for two years and was comfortable with the way Congress, especially the Senate, operated. I was appointed to the same committees as in the previous Congress and was in no hurry to try out others. There would be time for that since I was fairly confident of my reelection in four years. Besides, my longer-term goal did not include a lifetime in the U.S. Senate and I did not see how serving on different committees would be of significant value or advance my plans.

I received a call from Vice-President Dick Cheney asking me to meet him on Tuesday, January 7, at his vice-presidential residence, one of three places he inhabited when officially at an "undisclosed location"—a phrase that became synonymous with his name in the post 9/11 world. His other two dwellings were Camp David and his family home in Wyoming.

Seeing Cheney at certain public events was unavoidable, as were the occasional meetings over Senate business. Then again, I was not trying to dodge him. We simply did not have much in common—that is, other than our competing roles for Washington's most devious politician. At the time that he asked to meet with me, he was leading in the rivalry if only for the reason that he was vice-president and was, through his activities, better positioned to claim the title. We had not developed any serious relationship, either professional or personal, yet I was only mildly surprised to receive the invitation.

The official residence of the vice-president is located at Number One Observatory Circle on the grounds of the United States Naval Observatory in Washington, D.C. The white nineteenth-century structure became the official residence of the vice-president in 1974, although the first one to actually reside there was Walter Mondale in 1977.

I arrived at the vice-president's home at twenty minutes after one for a one thirty meeting and was escorted into a sitting room. A few minutes later Cheney walked in and greeted me.

"Hello, Senator. Welcome."

"Hello, Mr. Vice-President. It's an honor."

"Please follow me." We walked into an office. He motioned and said, "Have a seat."

There was a desk in the room, but he wanted to create an informal atmosphere and we sat at chairs a couple of feet apart, similar to the photo-ops when the president meets with other heads of state at the White House. At five feet eight inches, Cheney was not a tall man. His head was inescapably balding and were he a little more rotund, he could have been a dead ringer for Humpty Dumpty. But what he lacked in physical stature and appearance he compensated with cleverness. Whether or not one agreed with him, he knew how to get things done. This was a man whom all the king's men would have reassembled.

We had never had a private meeting before and, as indicated by the time of day, this was clearly not a social call. Cheney spoke first and was faithful to his reputation for being direct and blunt.

"Senator, you've been in Washington for two years, and I know you have your bearings. Although few words have passed between the two of us, I've been following your career and especially your statements from the Senate floor and your roll call votes. It appears to me that no one can take you for granted. You're a natural politician."

"If that's a compliment, sir, I thank you."

"It's not so much a compliment as an observation. But I cannot quite figure you out. At times, you cast votes clearly as a Republican. On other occasions you side with the enemy."

Cheney and I were so much alike I had difficulty believing that he would attempt to play the same kind of game I played with Darryl Issa. First, he had no dirt on me. Second, I know it sounds arrogant, but as similar as we were, he was not in my league. At least that is what I told myself at the time.

"Well, Mr. Vice-President, our viewpoints diverge on the definition of enemy. Admittedly, I don't have to deal with the antagonism you get from the other side of the aisle, but I don't consider the Democrats the enemy. And I'm not being naïve. I have to answer to my constituents and to my own conscience, and they preempt loyalty to the party."

"That's part of what puzzles me, though," he replied. "I'm a pretty calculating politician. Since you hail from California, I can understand your votes regarding the environment. But why did you vote in favor of the war resolution? The people of your state are not looking to reignite the conflict in Iraq."

There was a mild tension rising in the room that did not escape either of us. I was not about to play the role of an elementary school child called into the principal's office. I did not answer to Dick Cheney and certainly owed him no explanation for my voting record. But he knew that. I wondered if he was testing my ability to remain calm. I did not know where the conversation was going, but I was beginning to feel manipulated. That, also, was not a problem. I was sufficiently skilled in that area and certain that I could defend myself.

"I'm sure most Californians are opposed to the war," I replied. "But I know how to gauge my votes and my constituency. Also, I see the bigger picture."

I did not want to convey any hints about my political future and ultimate goal. Nor did he seem interested in my personal plans. I got the distinct impression that he was appraising me for some other reason. He did not take much time between sentences but appeared to process everything I said instantly, knowing how to direct and pace the conversation for his own purposes.

"Senator, I understand that your company, The Pegasus Group, has a special device that renders a room secure from any kind of electronic surveillance or recording. I even have reason to believe that you installed one in your Senate office. I would like to obtain three of them."

That explained the what, but not the why. He knew of the device but did not know that it had been named the Silencer. I did not know how he found out about the device or that I had it installed in my Senate office. My best guess was that Issa had said something to him about our meeting and Cheney figured out the rest. So the maneuvering began.

"As you know, Mr. Vice-President, my company is held in trust while I'm in office. I no longer run it nor am I engaged in any day-to-day operations. You'll have to contact the current CEO, Michael Walton."

"Please don't be crafty with me," he suggested. "You wouldn't be here if it was that simple. I've contacted Walton. He tells me that you took personal control of that device, including its specifications, and that it is not available for production."

"That's correct," I admitted. "The device is not part of the assets of the company. The prototype was the only one ever manufactured and was installed at my Pegasus office. I brought it with me to Washington. It is a technology I do not share. Why would you need one anyway? Surely your offices are secure."

"I don't want it for my official office. I want it for this room and my other two residences. I meet with people in these three locations. They come from all walks of life, and much of what we discuss is above and beyond the vice-presidency and the normal enterprise of the government. Some subjects are even more confidential than official U.S. business. Decisions are made that have ramifications far beyond the White House or the halls of Congress, and these gatherings require the highest level of security."

I found it difficult to comprehend his meaning. Why would conversations at his undisclosed locations be any more classified than meetings in the White House offices? Cheney could see the consternation in my expression. He was also weighing how much to confide in me. He took a gamble.

"Senator, do you know why George W. Bush was selected to run for the presidency? It was not due to a stellar intellect. He was chosen because he possesses something I do not—a charming personality that appeals to average Americans. Bush is the result of an old-fashioned political machine. The powers in the Republican Party were not going to allow McCain to get the nomination. That would have guaranteed a loss to Gore. However, there was no way I could ever be elected to national office except as vice-president, so Bush was tapped for the top of the ticket."

"Then you owe him," I suggested. "He selected you to be his running mate."

He scoffed, his lips turning downward into a look of dismissive disdain.

"No, Senator. I chose myself. I helped him vet various candidates and in the process exaggerated their weaknesses and potential liabilities, making sure they all proved wanting. That was the hard part because there were excellent politicians in the mix. As we kept coming up empty, I had to plant the seed. George does not like to be pushed. If he feels manipulated, the game is over. I had to make him think that it was his idea to select me and then I had to simulate surprise and unworthiness. I played the game exceedingly well, and he insisted. But that's not the whole story."

Cheney settled into a fully relaxed, comfortable, and one might even say domineering posture. Then he continued, "Bush does what I tell him and I clear his speeches. Of course, I don't take any responsibility for his inarticulate babbling when he speaks off the cuff." Cheney actually managed a light laugh almost as if he were embarrassed by the president. "What I'm saying to you I would never repeat in public, but I run this government."

Forget the public. I was astonished at his brazenness and was baffled as to why he would share such statements with me. We were not friends and as far as I knew, he had no reason to believe that I would hold his trust. I wondered if his overconfidence would be his undoing. But he continued, undeterred.

"Senator, in spite of opposition around the world and even here in the United States, we are going to war with Iraq."

"That much seems obvious," I cautiously replied. "But I don't see the connection."

"You may already be aware," he explained, "that all countries, friend and foe alike, spy on each other. Two of our greatest allies, Germany and France, will not join our coalition for war. They would pay dearly to know what is discussed in secret, our motivations for action, and especially the evidence we intend to use to force the conflict. And our enemies?" He let the question linger ever so briefly. "They are even more desperate for that knowledge."

"I still don't understand," I said. I was not being obtuse. I sensed there was something he was not telling me. As a result, I could not comprehend the priority he was establishing for these locations. For the first time that afternoon he paused, and thought before replying. It was as if everything else he had said was prepared, and now he was left to wing his responses without a script. He stood up.

"May I offer you something to drink?" Cheney did not suffer from multiple personalities, but his demeanor changed quickly and remarkably. He suddenly became more casual, not quite friendly, but easygoing. Of course, I understood that it was a ploy to disarm my suspicions and allow him time to think.

I had no idea what new direction this conversation would take. But I was too practiced to be beguiled. Far from putting me at ease, Cheney's actions merely fixed my attention. I was not in a mood to spar with him, but that would not be necessary. He had successfully piqued my curiosity; I was intrigued and willing to listen.

"I would like a glass of red wine, if you have it," I said.

Cheney's attitude and actions did not admit his desperation. He wanted the Silencer, and he was searching for a way to win me over. Like any other practiced politician, he knew that even words spoken in private are irretrievable. As if he had not already divulged too much, he was willing to risk revealing even more. He felt forced to take a chance, although with it came a great deal of liability and possible peril to his own credibility. At the same time, Cheney did not have the appearance of a man struggling with his decisions. He maintained a natural poise.

As he handed me my drink he said, "My job does not come without some dangers and occasionally it requires a leap of faith. To demonstrate your importance to me, I'd like to draw you into my confidence. Are you willing to attend a meeting here next Monday, the thirteenth, at nine o'clock in the evening?"

"Who else will be present?" I asked.

"A small cadre of patriots," he replied. "All of them trusted advisors. People you should know."

I wondered if he had intended on inviting me or if the overture was a spontaneous change of plans. Cheney did not strike me as the type to play loose with his strategy, and I doubted he was interested in advancing my career. Then again, I had something he desperately wanted.

"I'll be here," I assured him.

With that we finished our drinks, making small talk, each keenly aware that the other was not sympathetic to such useless pleasantry. As I left, he offered one caveat.

"The meeting next week and the people in attendance are confidential. That's my only criterion. It would be best if you did not put it on your office calendar."

On my way home I began to mull over observations from our meeting. For the most part, Cheney had been straightforward. He wanted the security device. But I noticed that throughout the conversation he did not once mention national security as a reason. That was notable because it is the first refuge for politicians who choose not to answer questions about compromising or illicit decisions. My imagination began to run wild. I wanted to maintain control over my fantasies, but felt as though I were being drawn into a world of international espionage. The truth would be revealed in a few days.

.   .   .

I did not know what to expect when I arrived at Number One Observatory Circle the following Monday. On my previous visit I found that I did not personally dislike the vice-president as much as I had anticipated. But neither did I trust him, and I suspected that was a mutual feeling. He was using me, but that, too, was reciprocal. I was willing to meet Cheney's people because I believed that anything learned from them could only advance my own career.

I did not walk blindly into the gathering that night. One of the beauties of the Silencer is its portability. I was taking a risk because the device would frustrate any attempts to record what was said, and therefore might alert people to its presence. On the other hand, any failed efforts would only serve as a first-hand and real-time demonstration of its effectiveness. But I suspected that Cheney's interest in my security system was precisely to avoid any trail of evidence. No one would be recording that evening.

As was my custom, I arrived a few minutes early. I was immediately ushered into a room significantly larger than the one where I had met with the vice-president a few days before. Having mastered control of my facial expressions, I did not indicate how stunned I was by the list of attendees. If the United States were a parliamentary system, these men would have been an extremely right wing and minority party—and very exclusive, for the vice-president had assembled the country's leading Neocons. As I would later learn, these non-elected advisors to Dick Cheney would chart the course of the Bush presidency and alter world history.

It was an impressive gathering. Dick Cheney was the leader and not coincidentally exercised the most influence over George W. Bush. Paul

Wolfowitz was the major architect of Bush's Iraq policy. Elliott Abrams was the legal expert and also instrumental in devising Bush's "global strategy." In the Bush administration John Bolton was undersecretary of state, his expertise being arms control and weapons of mass destruction. He was positioned to shape and alter facts—which he did masterfully. Ably assisting him was Michael Ledeen who was tasked with manufacturing a completely dishonest case accusing Saddam Hussein of purchasing yellow cake from Niger. Scooter Libby was Dick Cheney's chief of staff. He coordinated the times and locations of these meetings, organizing convoluted flight plans to guarantee media blindness. Donald Rumsfeld was another key figure. As Bush's secretary of defense, he was able to coordinate a military posture for the U.S. Government. Richard Perle had no significant influence in the Bush White House, but he was this group's ideological leader. His personal lieutenant was Paul Bremer. No longer in public service to the U.S. government, he was willing, even anxious, to participate.

When I walked into the room, Cheney was quick to greet me and then he introduced me to the rest of the members one by one. Everyone in the room was pleasant, although a couple of them eyed me with some suspicion. I was, after all, not one of them. I was a businessman, new to politics, and had demonstrated no interest in international intrigue. But they all trusted Cheney and were willing to accept my presence.

If I was intimidated by the gathering, no one knew it. Actually, I was fascinated. As the meeting progressed I could see other hands at work, people who probably would not be so brazen as to secretly chart the course of a nation, but who would support the doctrines espoused in that room. I could almost hear the speeches of Henry Kissinger and Jeanne Kirkpatrick, and see the writings of Eliot Cohen, Charles Krauthammer, and of a recently devolving Alan Dershowitz.

In America, in 2003, an organization like this with its ideological conceit would hardly be believed in a work of fiction. But this was no novel. There I stood before what can best be described as a gang of elitists intoxicated with their own sense of superiority and intellectual arrogance. Through it all shown the genius of Dick Cheney. He knew better than most how to tap into the anger and fear that followed 9/11, and was remarkably candid with this group. They would not be deterred by the rule of law or the consent of the governed. Their mission was too critical to be subjected to plebeian interests or congressional oversight. If they were to change the world and remake it according to their vision, they would need to operate from obscurity.

Following the introductions and after everyone had settled in, Cheney began.

"Good evening. You all knew that I was inviting Senator Lozano to join us tonight. For those of you who had reservations, let me assure that he is a man to be trusted."

Now that was truly amazing. When I met with the vice-president the previous week, I believed that I was more than capable of holding my own with him. Now I began to doubt—both my own abilities and my estimation of him. I already knew that Cheney rarely spoke the truth to the American people or to their elected representatives. But this was a highly secret and sophisticated gathering, and there he stood blatantly lying to his most trusted allies. For he did not trust me. However, hearing him utter those words did not set off any alarms. It merely put me in an ever more cautious and protective mode.

"I had a special purpose for inviting the senator this evening," Cheney continued. "He has access to a truly unique security system, one that even the United States government does not possess. I believe we would do well to procure three of them from him, one for each of our rendezvous locations. It is a device that blocks all forms of electronic surveillance or recording within a designated area. It is my belief that once the senator understands what we are about and how we seek to protect the country, he'll acquiesce." He looked at me and nodded knowingly, as if we had already reached agreement.

As he spoke, I noticed that no one was taking notes. These men had impeccable memories, and they were not going to leave anything to chance. They certainly would not trust anything as potentially damaging as pen and paper. I was also fairly certain that no one was attempting to record the meeting. They did not know I brought the device with me, but everyone remembered Richard Nixon.

At that point I could only surmise the purpose of the gathering. For the time being I kept my questions private. I wanted to try to figure things out for myself and was content to take stock of the participants. One thing was clear, there was a certain fear and desperation in the room. They needed me, or at least my security system. Even in modern America treason carried the potential threat of death. And yet, the Cheney genius was unstoppable. Nothing they discussed, none of their plans, were technically treasonous. But if word of their operation surfaced, it would be abhorrent to the nation and they would lose everything in the arena of public opinion.

I do not know how he did it, but I began to suspect that Cheney might have learned of my security system before I ever took office. That would explain why he was following my career for two years. But if he had studied me as carefully as he claimed, how could he have so misjudged? The people in this room represented neither the America I knew nor the world I wanted.

Cheney continued speaking. "We are getting ever closer to war with Iraq. Regime change is now within our grasp." Had this been a speech they all would have applauded. As it was they just nodded their heads in agreement. I began to understand and decided to ask a question hoping it would feign innocence. If the people in the room perceived me as malleable, it might put some fears to rest.

"Excuse me, Mr. Vice-President, but when Bush was running for office he disavowed nation-building."

There were a few smiles in the room indicating that I successfully conveyed the image I wanted.

Cheney curled the side of his mouth in his signature half smile and said to everyone, "He's new here. Give him time." Then he turned to me. "I influence the president's thoughts and I assure you that he has come around to our way of thinking. Ten days ago when Congress began its new session, the president said, 'The Iraq regime is a threat to any American.' That was an attempt to prepare the nation for an imminent invasion and the removal of Saddam Hussein."

The vice-president then addressed Bolton. "John, where do we stand now with accusing Hussein of possessing weapons of mass destruction?"

"We've outlined a strong enough case even though the evidence is only anecdotal and circumstantial. But Scooter's having problems with the CIA."

Libby spoke up. "I still don't have McLaughlin (Deputy Director of Central Intelligence) onboard. He claims our WMD (weapons of mass destruction) intel is too weak. They didn't find any support for our position and he does not want to revisit their work."

"Then you'd better fucking get him in line," Cheney said. "I can't do it from my position. I have my hands full with George. I have to spoon feed him information every day. We can't have the CIA back off the weapons of mass destruction charge—at least not until we are already at war. We sold the idea to Blair, now we need our own people behind us." Even in bursts of anger or frustration, Cheney was a man who delighted in playing Richelieu to Bush's Louis XIII. Like the seventeenth century cardinal, he did not want to be the power behind the throne; he secretly wanted to be the throne.

As the discussion continued, the light of understanding began to glow brighter in my mind. I was not on the Senate Foreign Relations Committee, or the Select Committee on Intelligence, and as a senator I accepted the information they reported to the rest of us. But what if the information fed to them was wrong or worse, deliberately distorted? This meeting caused me to doubt the accuracy of any of the committee reports presented on the Senate floor. I was becoming a little uncomfortable. Yet, leaving would clearly send the wrong signal. My mistrust of Cheney was multiplied many times over in that room. People dying under mysterious circumstances were not unheard of in Washington, and these men were willing to sell the entire world down the river. Certainly I was expendable.

For the rest of the evening I asked no more questions. I was content to listen, to observe, to scrutinize. The men around me presented themselves as patriots, eagles hovering above their would-be realm in a protective and soaring surveillance. What I saw were vipers huddled in a darkened den, vision finely attuned to shadows.

I could not help but recall the movie *Seven Days in May*. In one scene, President Lyman has a confrontation with the treasonous General Mattoon Scott during which he says, "You want to defend the United States of America, then defend it with the tools it supplies you with—its Constitution. You ask for a mandate, General, from a ballot box. You don't steal it after midnight, when the country has its back turned."

Whether from backs turned or eyes closed, the ambitions of both the imaginary Scott and the real Cheney required a blind and acquiescent America.

I have always considered language our best means of communication, but it is as sharp as any sword with the power to ignite the imagination or impair the intellect. Words are capable of inspiring the mind or depressing the spirit, extending the reach of the soul or shattering the dreams of the heart, embracing falsehood or eradicating truth. Speech can unite and build. It can also divide and destroy. Throughout that night the language I heard was not unknown, nor were the speakers unfamiliar. The world had seen such masters of the universe before. This was, after all, the kind of group from which a Reich is born. And in a display of nefarious irony, most of those present as well as their absent allies were American Jews. In the midst of it all, Cheney showed himself a force to be reckoned with, and he commanded a surreal devotion from the men in the room.

By the end of the evening, I understood—war in Iraq was just the beginning. Removing Saddam Hussein was the first step in their plans to redraw the map of the Middle East and assert American power and control.

Reality was not lost on me that night. From Cheney on down, the room was full of men who had assiduously avoided military combat in their own lives but who were now itching to send American troops to certain death in service to their heinous ideology.

As the meeting was disbanding, Cheney asked me to stay behind. Libby was the last of the group to leave. He needed to check some calendar events with the vice-president—a title that took on new meaning for me that January night. After Libby left, Cheney came up to me and said, "This must have been a strange evening for you."

"Well," I replied, "it was not what I anticipated."

"Senator, I was watching you during the meeting. You may have some reservations, but after tonight I hope you realize that what we're doing is for the good of the country and the world."

I did not know what he expected me to say. I could not voice what I was thinking or share my real concerns. I had unwittingly walked into a trap. It appeared that Cheney was indeed cleverer than I.

"I have no problem with the idea of Hussein being out of power, but isn't it possible to achieve that same goal through legal means?"

"That's why Abrams is here," he said. "It's his job to create the legality. Even if the rest of the world does not follow suit, we'll at least have our asses covered with Congress and the American public. Besides, there are a lot of people in this country who don't trust the United Nations. We're going to operate from our own interpretation of law."

I do not know why I was engaging in discussion with him. He would never change his mind. He could not. He had already crossed his Rubicon, and burnt his only route of retreat. The Republican Party, at least the mainline leadership, would never support what Cheney was up to, and I did not want to be a part it. But how to extricate myself? As my mind began to race, one thing quickly became clear: Cheney would get his Silencers. That was my only hope of safety. If I did not produce them, I was as good as dead, for I was a liability no one from that meeting would tolerate. The security devices were also the only way I could disassociate from this group.

"I can understand why you need to protect these meetings, Mr. Vice-President. I'm not sure how much of your ideas I agree with, still I recognize that the stakes are high. I'll get you the Silencers, but it will take a couple of weeks. I have the only one. I'll need special engineers—my own people."

"Can you speed it up?" he asked.

"If I push hard enough, I can probably have them within ten days, maybe even a week. It'll be expensive to expedite the process."

"As you can tell from the attendance tonight, money is no object."

"Then I'll get started tomorrow," I assured him.

"Good, Senator. I'm glad we could do business." He shook my hand and flashed his wry grin. "Good night."

"Good night, sir."

As I drove home, I wondered just how safe I really was. Had I given in too quickly? I knew Cheney did not trust me. The beauty of his scheme was that if I did not deliver the devices, he could dispose of me without suspicion. If I did deliver them, he could ask me to be part of the group. And if I refused, he had little reason for concern. I was not about to reveal what I'd learned, and even if I did there would be no compromising record of any meetings. I was in the same situation I'd put Lt. Tom Moran in when we met in my office at Pegasus.

American democracy was forged in the flames of revolution, and I suppose revolution has always remained a possible path for its demise. I just never contemplated that in the modern era it could so easily be overthrown by such a small and narrow-minded ilk. This was beyond even the cartoonist Walt Kelly's prescience. Pogo's declaration decades earlier sprung to mind: "We have met the enemy and he is us."

But that was the Cheney genius. As his countenance concealed the witches' cave, he toiled from the shadows, brewing plans in such a way that no congressional committee or White House office knew they had been co-opted. The fire burned and the cauldron bubbled. And no one saw the enemy.

Cheney's every move was unconstitutional and I wanted no part of it. My allegiance was to the people of California and to the United States of America. His secret was secure with me. Although I did not want to multiply the number of Silencers in existence, I had to secure my own safety. I delivered three devices to him on January 30 and informed him that I would not participate in any future meetings. He seemed thoroughly unconcerned, almost imperious, his eyes surrendering to derision.

I had underestimated the vice-president. Whatever unsavory personal traits we shared, we differed on something very important. Power. It can be pursued from two directions. The first is to win it openly and let friend and foe alike know that you possess it. My intention was to achieve power in a national election—something Cheney could never do. Once elected, my skills would almost guarantee my agenda. After all, I was a man who usually got what I wanted, though on occasion needing to carefully exercise my manipulative art.

The other approach to power is to hold it in secret, to exercise it without anyone realizing. It is much more Zen, providing personal satisfaction without the need for adulation.

Maybe I had taken too much for granted during my first two years in office. I recalled my first introduction to Dick Cheney. At first sight and without words we were able to recognize the darkness in each other's souls. The night he received the Silencers, it was clear that of the two of us only I had been insufficiently cautious. It was a mistake I would not repeat.

CHAPTER 20

In the weeks that followed, the world was treated to an incessant clamor, for war and conflict had become almost inevitable. The United States was beating a path to battle—with Britain at heel.

Three of the five permanent members of the United Nations Security Council opposed the war. Two of our strongest allies, Germany and France, were steadfast against the invasion, with the French offering support only if the United Nations Security Council passed a follow-up directive to Security Council Resolution 1441, which gave Saddam Hussein a final opportunity to disarm. Japan refused to participate in or contribute to the fighting, its only participation being a self-serving willingness to accept reconstruction contracts. In the final analysis, the "Coalition of the Willing" comprised a mere ten percent of the world's population. This was America and Britain's war and it was clear that these two countries were marching to the beat of a different drum.

Although they continued to push the buildup for war, they were unable to extinguish all hope for preserving peace. Voices arose in the international community to counter the constant cry to battle. One of the more fervent addresses was delivered at the United Nations by French Minister of Foreign Affairs Dominique de Villepin on February 14, 2003. It would be some time before the world would recognize the prescience of his remarks and the near clairvoyant prophecy of what a post-war Iraq would entail. But when he stood before the United Nations the eloquence of his speech stirred the souls of all those willing to listen.

Villepin profoundly defended Security Council Resolution 1441, which the members passed unanimously. After detailing the progress of disarmament in Iraq and the successes, however inadequate or incomplete of the U.N. inspectors, he correctly challenged the alleged links between al-Qaeda and Iraq. And in what may be the loftiest part of his address he spoke to the core of what it means to be a world community: "In this temple of the United Nations, we are the guardians of an ideal, the guardians of a conscience. The onerous responsibility and immense honor we have must lead us to give priority to disarmament in peace."

Domestically, the Bush administration continued its own preparations buttressed by a docile media. Of course, there were prophets of peace even in the U.S., but their voices were barely audible over the fevered rumblings of war. Most prominent among them stood Senator Robert Byrd of West Virginia who, in several speeches beginning in February, sought to move the Senate toward a meaningful debate about the merits and outcomes of war. Through his rhetoric, he evoked the spirit of our Senate predecessors and ably filled the shoes of the great orators of the nineteenth century—those men who attempted to avert civil war rather than throw themselves and their country into chaos.

Two days before the French minister spoke at the United Nations, Senator Byrd addressed the U.S. Senate.

To contemplate war is to think about the most horrible of human experiences. On this February day, as this nation stands at the brink of battle, every American on some level must be contemplating the horrors of war. Yet this chamber is, for the most part, silent—ominously, dreadfully silent. There is no debate, no discussion, no attempt to lay out for the nation the pros and cons of this particular war. There is nothing. We stand passively mute in the United States Senate, paralyzed by our own uncertainty, seemingly stunned by the sheer turmoil of events.

As a fellow senator, I found myself moved by the depth of his conviction and his passionate desire for peace. And for a moment I felt as though he were speaking directly to me, challenging me to take a stand, to make a commitment. For me his words were an indictment because I, like many of my colleagues, was indeed paralyzed. I looked around the Senate chamber, taking special note of the empty chairs, an indication that many senators had made up their minds and refused to listen to a variant voice. And I suspected that most of them had done so without objective advice. I, at least, had planned for just such a contingency. On the evening of February 12, following Senator Byrd's speech, I called Jackson.

"Jacks," I said as he answered the phone. "I really need to talk to you. By telephone, if necessary. But I would prefer the advantages that accompany the give–and–take of a personal meeting."

"I suppose you want to talk about the impending war with Iraq," he suggested.

"Yes. It's the only subject of discussion these days. Can you fly down for the weekend? Or at least for one day?"

'Tell me, Sep," he said playfully. "Is it the nature of the Senate that you always call me on such short notice?"

"I hadn't really thought about it," I replied. "It would be a lot easier if you and Jean-Paul lived in Washington. But, of course, that's not going to happen. Still, when I make these calls, I want you to know that I understand if you cannot be here."

"Well," he said. "As it turns out, Jean-Paul is going to Brussels this weekend and I had planned on staying in Boston."

"Does that mean you'll come here?" I asked.

"Yes, Sep. But not until Saturday morning. I'll try to get there before lunch."

"Thanks, Jacks. Let me know what flight you're on and I'll pick you up at the airport."

I did not really expect Jackson to have the answers I sought. In fact, I suspected that we would differ on Iraq. But maybe a serious conversation between us would help surface my own convictions.

In truth, I wanted more than just conversation. Unlike many a politician I had no desire to dominate a neophyte. I had learned a valuable lesson from President Bill Clinton, but unlike him I would not be able to phoenix from the ashes of scandal. After all, my career was only in its infancy and I could not allow it to be sidelined by indiscretion. And in an echo of my days at Harvard, I could not confront the depth of my own truth—not completely. Introspection was not my problem. I knew myself well enough, but could allow my desires to rise to the surface only on my own terms.

It had been over two years since Yolanda had died, and I was not interested in pursuing a new relationship. To begin with, my primary interest was in laying the foundation for my own career. It was somewhat ironic that although I had never confided in my wife, I was in need of a confidant now. Jackson had already agreed to serve in that capacity. But even the most calculating of men have other needs.

For most of my life I projected an image of confidence and control. My weaknesses were on display to no one. But there are multiple hidden sides to every individual, and no one can be defined solely on what is revealed in public. I was not the man everyone thought I was and over the years had honed my persona carefully, as if Carl Jung were my personal tutor.

The last time Jackson was in Washington, I had not properly set the scene. A little too sure of myself I played my cards wrong and I misjudged him in the process. A good gambler knows how to play a bluff. I backed down because I was not bluffing and he held the high cards. The play I wanted would have to come from him. I was going to have to find a way to stack the deck or at least change the rules of the game. But it would not be this trip.

·   ·   ·

Jackson arrived at Reagan National Airport at eleven thirty in the morning and I was there to meet him.

"Hello, Jacks," I said as I cautiously and discreetly embraced him. "How was the flight?"

"Not a bit of turbulence," he replied. He had only a carry-on bag with him, so we went straight to the car. He brought me up-to-date on life in Boston and the health of Jean-Paul's mother. There was very little traffic as we left the airport and headed back to my place.

"Are you hungry?" I asked. "We can stop and grab some lunch."

"No, I'm not at all hungry right now. I had a snack on the plane." I was driving and focused my eyes on the road ahead. He turned to pensively look at me, then out at the road and said, "I started putting my thoughts together after you called. I think we should jump right into this conversation. But before we do, I want to ask you a question."

In spite of his desire to begin the conversation immediately, there was a slight hesitation. He looked at me reassuringly and said, "I want you to know that I'm willing to speak with you about Iraq, or anything else for that matter, but here's my question. Do you think that anything we discuss can possibly avert a war? I know you're only one of a hundred senators. You're not on staff at the White House, nor are you one of the president's advisors."

"You're right," I replied. "What I didn't say on the phone was that I called you right after Robert Byrd gave an address on the Senate floor. It was an impassioned speech about the need for us, as a Senate, to at least discuss the impending conflict with Iraq. He's also only one senator, and yet it was that speech that caused me to call you."

"So you want to start a revolt in the Senate?" he asked impishly.

"No," I said with the slightest hint of exasperation. "I don't know what I want. I'm conflicted about the war, and I think there's merit to Byrd's request for discussion. Right now, I want to process the facts with you. You're thoughtful and honest, two qualities sorely lacking in Washington today."

"All right," Jackson said. "Why don't you begin with the question that's really on your mind?"

"OK. Is this war justified?"

"Whoa! If that's your first question, you've missed a step. Do you remember what I advised you a few months ago when the war resolution came up in the Senate?"

"Of course," I replied. "I remember everything you say." That was a gratuitous comment, but it reminded him that I have an impeccable memory. "You told me to always question the assumptions." I looked at him as if searching for some further insight.

He replied, "I also said, 'All of them.' You need to question all the assumptions and you should wear it like a mantle. You can't take anything for granted in your job. Even when people do speak the truth, you need to know what's behind it, what their motives are."

I did not respond right away. I was thinking. Just then we pulled up to my house and went inside. He put his bag in the guest room and I went to the living room, picked out and loaded one of my favorite pipes, the Killarney by Peterson, similar in style to the ones that Bing Crosby used to smoke. As he walked into the room he said, "When did you take up smoking again? I haven't seen you do that since we were in Boston."

"I took all my pipes out of storage last Christmas. It was cold here in Washington and I always find that smoking both calms and warms me. I also have some cigars if you'd like one."

"It's tempting," he said. "And I know they're probably first class."

"As a matter of fact," I replied, "I have an authentic Cuban Cohiba, an Espléndido."

It took but a moment's thought.

"OK. Consider my arm twisted," he said.

The weather was cool in Georgetown that Saturday, but not cold. I suggested a walk down by the Potomac River. This was not exercise. It was a pensive stroll.

"Jacks," I said, "there are only two people I have ever been able to open up to and reveal myself. To my shame, I sometimes deceived Yolanda, or at least misled her. She's gone now. That's one reason I asked you two years ago to serve as my advisor."

"And have you deceived me?" he asked.

I was not prepared for that question, but I guess I deserved it. After all, I had just confessed dishonesty with my only other confidant.

"No, Jacks. I actually never even tried. You're different from Yolanda. I don't think I could ever delude you even if I wanted. I always had this idea that you are the one person who can really see me, that you would know if I was being dishonest or holding back."

"What does this have to do with war in Iraq?" he asked.

"Jacks, I want to be president. I won't challenge Bush next year, of course. That wouldn't sit well with the Republican establishment. Besides, I need more time to build my reputation. But that's my endgame. The problem with Iraq is that I don't trust what the administration is saying. And yet, I think it would be political suicide for me to oppose the war. Besides, I think it's now inevitable, no matter what the Senate does. I would like to find a way to support Byrd's call for discussion without appearing weak on national defense or disloyal to the president."

"That sounds suspiciously self-serving, Sep. If you really want to be president someday, shouldn't you build a legacy of standing on principle rather than expediency? I don't want to think that I'm wasting my time today. I could have stayed in Boston if you already have your mind made up."

Maybe I referenced my long-term goal too quickly. His comment was a little harsh. On the other hand, in spite of what I told him, I really was disguising my true intentions and he could not read it. Still, I did want to hear what he had to say. But I also had to be careful.

"I already told you, Jacks, that I'm conflicted about the war. I hope that talking this out with you will clarify things for me."

"Fine. Then let's come at this from another angle," he replied. "Ever since 9/11 there's been a growing anti-Muslim sentiment in the United States, especially from people like Pat Robertson and organizations like FOX News. The constant talk of a conflict of cultures between the Islamic world and Western civilization is both ignorant and destructive. Unfortunately, it's also become pervasive."

"But the president spoke positively of the Islamic faith following 9/11," I protested.

"Yes," Jackson replied, "that's part of the problem. Americans, for the most part, are not discriminating. No matter what the president says, they only hear what they want to hear. How many people do you think realize that most Muslims do not even live in the Middle East?"

"I suppose not many."

"Exactly. They hear talk of al-Qaeda, the Taliban, Saddam Hussein, or the Ayatollah, and they don't comprehend an isolated handful of enemies. All they hear is Islamic extremists. All of Islam ends up conflated with the Middle East and that gets exploited as a conflict with the West."

"And just how do I counter that? How do I suggest that there is another way to respond to violence besides war?"

We had been strolling along Wisconsin Avenue and upon reaching the river paused, sat down, and looked out across the water. It was too early in the year to see rowers or kayakers and Thompson's Boat Center would not open for at least another month. Too bad, because the water was clean and smooth as glass, creating photo-still reflections of the banks and trees. A dozen or so people were walking along the river and above us was a variety of birds, some quite lively in flight and song. It was a setting conducive to reflection and memory.

"You know, Sep. I've always loved cities that have rivers flowing through them. Sitting here reminds me of our days in Boston, of our walks along the Charles River discussing everything from the girls we were dating to the great problems of our day, both foreign and domestic."

"Yeah, I wish I had known you two years before that. When Nixon resigned. We could have celebrated together."

"You take too much delight in that, Sep. The presidency is bigger than one man. I blame Nixon for what happened, but that was a dark day for the United States, and it began the decline that has brought us to where we are today."

"What do you mean?" I asked.

"There's very little respect for the presidency today and practically none for Congress. No one believes what elected officials say—even other politicians. You said yourself that honesty is sorely lacking in Washington. So, tell me. What is it that you do not trust about the administration's case for war?"

I briefly contemplated sharing with him my experiences with Dick Cheney and the manufactured evidence regarding Saddam Hussein. But that knowledge was something I chose to keep to myself, at least until it would serve my own purposes. When I made my run for the highest office, I would be more than willing to expose and destroy the vice-president, thus building credibility with both the moderate and liberal elements of the American electorate. I would probably even be able to gain support among a fair number of conservatives. They would only need to know the truth about Cheney. He was worse than Nixon could have ever been. But even then I would have to manipulate the information so as not to raise questions about why I remained silent when I might have been able to derail his pursuit of war.

Jackson was a man of principle, which meant that I would have to be cautious of what I shared with him. If he possessed my knowledge about Cheney, he would pressure me to come forward. He would not betray me but neither would he let up.

"The first problem, Jacks, is that this war is not a response to any violence. In spite of what you have heard, there is no link between al-Qaeda and Iraq. Saddam Hussein is just as vile in the eyes of Osama bin Laden as he is in ours."

"How do you know the claim is false?" he asked.

"I've met certain people. At this point I don't want to say who they are or how we met. But I know they've been manufacturing false evidence. I don't think the president knows it, though. He's being manipulated. And although I'm sure he believes what he says, he's wrong."

"You're not giving me much to go on, Sep."

"I realize that. But that's not my only concern. Going to war against Iraq would be a violation of international law. Also, there's no reason to rush. The people pushing invasion are afraid that if they wait, if they allow the United Nations' inspectors to complete their work, they will lose any justification for war."

"So you're beginning to question assumptions," he observed. "Name one of them for me."

"Some people think the upcoming war is about oil. But as long as there is no current conflict, there is also no danger to the world's oil supply. Another assumption I would question is that peace and freedom would result from war. Yesterday's speech by the French foreign minister called that into question."

"That's an excellent start, Sep."

"There is one that has been stated outright; namely, that U.S. troops will be greeted as heroes because Saddam Hussein is a tyrant. But his people are much more at peace than those under other dictators. There is no ongoing civil war in Iraq. Of course, there is a suppression of Western ideals, e.g., freedom of speech, but that can be found in many countries.

"Finally, Jacks, I know this will sound cynical at best, but there's a fortune to be made from a war with Iraq. On that point, at least the Japanese are being honest. But they have no stomach for conflict."

"Sep, you need to speak to more than just me. You already have the information you need. Surely you can deliver a passionate address to the Senate," he suggested.

"Eloquence has never been my weakness," I replied. "I'll be honest with you. What I lack is integrity."

"I don't believe that, Sep. If you did not have integrity, you would not have asked me to serve as an advisor."

If he only knew!

"Jacks, although many Americans are opposed to the war, there is a growing sentiment in favor. Many, although misguided, see this as patriotism, as defending our country. If I oppose the war it will haunt me when I run for president. I would be portrayed as weak by my opponents."

"Is that what people think of Senator Byrd?"

"No. Many just see him as a relic and they mock his oratory, referring to him as a man out of time. I admire him, though. I'm in awe of his style, his poise, particularly the content of his speeches, and I would like to see a discussion on the Senate floor. But in the end, I will probably still support the war. As I told you, I'm conflicted about it."

"Why can't you be as honest with other people as you are with me?"

"My ambitions are too strong to withstand honesty. In this town, principles and integrity are not a recipe for success."

"That may be the truest thing you've said to me all day," he responded. I could hear the disappointment in his voice and I knew there was an accusation beneath the surface. But we were friends, and he believed he could reach some deeper part of my being.

•   •   •

We went to dinner, after which we returned home quite satiated. I poured an after-dinner drink and loaded a hookah with triple apple tobacco. We sat in the living room relaxing with the smoke and drink. The time had arrived for a little truth between us.

"Jacks," I began. "I was not satisfied with the way things ended the last time you were here."

"You don't need to say anything," he said.

"Yes, I do. I apologize for what happened, or almost happened, but not for the feelings. You see, you were wrong about me.

"Earlier when I said that you and Yolanda were the only ones I could ever open up to, I also told you that I had occasionally deceived Yolanda. It was never about anything critical. I never cheated on her or anything like that. Sometimes I just did not want to admit certain things to her. Mostly about my business practices. Her moral compass was too true to understand or endorse my actions."

He sat there, just listening. At times he was cloaked by the tobacco smoke, but I could see through the haze and knew that he was taking in every word. I paused for a few moments.

"You told me before that I was alone and lonely. And you were correct. I had no idea what life would be like without Yolanda and the kids. But that is only part of the problem. It runs much deeper.

"I look back at our time in Boston. I treasured your friendship, but I think I was attracted to you on another level. At the time, I didn't realize it. I couldn't even imagine it. When you ended our friendship that made it easy. For twenty years, I was able to forget. But seeing you again at the funeral three years ago stirred feelings I wasn't prepared to confront."

"Sep—" He started to interrupt, but I continued.

"Let me finish, Jacks. We may not have this chance again. When we talked after the funeral, I could sense a certain joy about you. You were happy and seemed to have your life together. You weren't chasing unfulfilled dreams. You were very different from me. I envied that and saw in you something I sorely lacked. I saw in you someone I would have liked to be. I also recognized that our lives were set on different courses, and I could never be like you.

"But when you came to Washington last October, feelings surfaced in me. And it was not just loneliness. I pride myself on control. But for a moment I thought—just maybe—I could have what Jean-Paul has with you. I realize now that I was wrong. I just needed to tell you tonight that those feelings were real."

It was difficult to read his expression. Was he confused, uncertain? He did not look at all concerned or uncomfortable. He sat across the table, and I could see he was still a handsome man. Over the years, I imagine that many people, both men and women, had found him attractive. He did not say anything. He just let me continue.

"You know, Jacks, I'm actually glad that you didn't give in. I respect the love that you have for Jean-Paul and your unwavering commitment to him. And I appreciate the friendship we have."

When I finished, he did not reply immediately. He took a sip of scotch, then a long draw on the hookah. When he did speak, he could not have been more compassionate or understanding.

"I told you," he said. "You didn't have to say anything." He paused and looked away, wondering if he should add more. I knew he did not share my feelings, but he had not been offended on that last trip. Neither was he the type to be cruel. When he looked back, it was with the gentleness that had come to define him as an adult, his loving acceptance of others—of me—no questions asked. He decided to change the subject. "Are you still suffering nightmares?" he asked.

"They come and go," I replied. "I think I've been too caught up in world events lately to allow my past to intrude into my sleep. But I haven't resolved anything, either."

"Then I'll say good night, and I'll see you in the morning."

The next day we had breakfast and Jackson took an early afternoon flight back to Boston so he would be home when Jean-Paul returned from Belgium. As I drove home from the airport, I put Jackson out of my mind and focused on other challenges. I found myself swirling through history, a world confronted by political and military blunders. As a young man, I had opposed the war in Vietnam. Not just because I did not want to go, but because I thought it was wrong. Yet here I was, simultaneously opposing and supporting another war that was, morally, even more insidious.

CHAPTER 21

The night before Jackson visited me, Giovanni's support group met at the Henderson home in San Marino, California. Foremost on their minds, as indeed most of the world, was the impending invasion of Iraq. None of these members was a warmonger, but Brian Henderson was probably the only true pacifist among them. The rest, although they opposed the coming conflict, were open to arguments defending war in certain circumstances. But none supported the Bush administration's plans against Iraq. Giovanni almost elected to skip the gathering. With the impending war, he was afraid the discussion would include Congress and lead to questions about me. Nobody seemed to know that he and I were not on speaking terms. Nonetheless, he joined the rest of the group that night.

Most of their gatherings opened with prayer, and of the four priests, Tim McGowan was the least likely to lead it. He tended toward the jocular and avoided conversations that were too serious. In fact, at one meeting he interrupted the conversation to say, "Can't we talk about something happy?" After that, he became a target of harmless humor. When he would show up for a meeting, Judy Henderson would say, "Oh, Tim's here. Let's all be happy." On this particular night, however, Tim actually volunteered to lead the prayer.

Father of peace, hope, and love,

We are reminded to lay
our care and concerns at your feet.
You have always taken care of us—

you, who are all-consuming love.

We come to you today in a time
of trial and tribulation.
We beseech you to heal our world,
to heal our nation and so to heal our souls.

We beg your curative grace for those
who suffer injury or confusion.
We humbly ask strength for those
who have lost loved ones in violence,
for those whose security has been threatened.

Today, especially, we ask that you cast
your loving watch over all peoples.
Do not let the master of deceit
weave a new web of lies.
Do not let him draw us into a conflict
counter to your love—
a combat without end or resolution.

You hold us in the palm of your hand,
let us now and always
feel your comforting touch.

We ask this in Jesus's name.

AMEN

Ever the smartass, Bill Messenger spoke immediately after Tim finished. "I didn't know you could pray like that, Tim. Spontaneous and everything. It was so poetic." His comment was not meant to be as sarcastic as it sounded. Intentions aside, no one laughed and Tim was not bothered.

But Sister Barbara Nixon responded. "Come on, Bill. We're trying to be serious here." Then turning to McGowan she said, "Tim, that was a beautiful prayer."

"Believe it or not," Tim said, "I'm not all fun and games. I've been following the political situation and the buildup to war. And I'm very concerned. I'm not sure what we can do about it, but prayer has to be in the mix. And since several of us are parish leaders, hopefully we can have some impact on others."

"Well," Brian said, "given the world situation, war is going to be the main focus of our meeting tonight. It takes precedence over problems in our parishes, even our personal lives."

"But what can we do?" Judy Henderson asked. "In the past we've marched against nuclear weapons and arms manufacturers; we opposed the first Gulf War; we've seen our friends arrested. And nothing has changed."

Giovanni ventured into the discussion carefully, hoping he could direct it in a more general direction despite Brian's comment. He suggested, "The fact that violence persists does not mean nothing has changed. We're in a long–term battle here to move the minds and hearts of a nation."

"Gio's right," Barbara said. "We can only change our leaders when we change the people. Remember the 1960s' slogan opposing the Vietnam War: 'Suppose they gave a war and nobody came?' When the people refuse to support violence, the politicians will not be able to make war."

"We have no impact over the president or Congress," Perry Leiker said. "We can only influence the people we serve and turn their minds to peace."

"Like that's going to happen," Bill interjected. "We're up against forces far more powerful than we are, including government propaganda."

"You sound defeatist, Bill," Brian commented.

He replied, "Perhaps I am. At the USC Catholic Center, we have a couple of graduate students from Iraq. Both are born and raised

Catholic, yet one of them felt compelled to change his given name from Abdul to Andrew because of the anti-Muslim and anti-Arab sentiments in the U.S."

"But that's not the fault of the U.S. government," Perry suggested.

"Isn't it?" Bill asked. "I've had many discussions with Andrew about Iraq. One of the things he told me is that although the people do not like Saddam Hussein, they are relatively free. Not by our standards, of course. They do not have freedom of speech. But Hussein does not restrict their religious practice. They can go to mosque or church anytime. As long as the imam or priest does not speak against him, there's no problem. At the same time, they have good infrastructure. Everyone gets paid and life goes on. That's not the way the Bush administration portrays it. We are being indoctrinated. And like all propaganda, its purpose is to distort the facts, manipulate the truth, and stifle dissent—very effective on a non-discriminating public. And nobody does it better than the current administration."

"You don't think you're exaggerating?" Tim asked.

"I think I trust someone who was born and raised there, someone who doesn't like Saddam Hussein, more than I trust our government. They have ulterior motives. Andrew does not. Let me tell you something else.

"Andrew returned home from the university one day when the FBI showed up at his door. They were interrogating everyone from Iraq. They walked into his house and saw a crucifix on the wall. When they asked what it was doing there, he told them he was a Catholic. They told him that was not possible because he was from Iraq. He proceeded to point out that Christianity was born in the Middle East and flourished in Iraq for five hundred years before Islam was even conceived."

"But that's just two ignorant FBI agents," Judy said.

"No. It's the result of a duplicitous government and an ignorant public."

"Then we have to make the public more discriminating," Barbara said.

Judy turned to Gilbert Cruz and said, "You are very quiet, as usual."

"Well," he answered. "I don't see how this conversation is going to help the people of our parishes. We're just sitting around talking to ourselves."

"Perhaps if you were a little more involved," Bill suggested, "you'd understand. We need to challenge each other and define our principles if we're going to preach about them."

"I know that," Gilbert said with exasperation. "I just don't see this conversation going anyplace."

"Then let's move on," Perry said. "Maybe we can't stop war. If we're going to influence and change peoples' minds, it will be around peace. Let's talk about that. I remember a letter that Dietrich Bonhoeffer sent to his brother, who was an agnostic, during WWII. He wrote about the Sermon on the Mount and said, 'There are things for which an uncompromising stand is worthwhile and it seems to me that peace and social justice are such things.' Maybe this is our time—the opportunity to be modern-day Bonhoeffers."

Perhaps it was merely invoking the great Lutheran pastor's name or maybe it was the idea of embodying his commitment to peace and justice, but for a moment silence reigned over the group.

Barbara noticed Brian looking into the distance and asked, "Brian, are you still with us? You seem lost in thought."

He replied. "I was just thinking about the talk that Bill and I gave a few years ago at the Religious Education Congress. We titled it, 'Peace: the Call to Personal Nonviolence.' We did not reference Bonhoeffer, but I think we shared a common idea with him. If we want peace in our world, if we want wars to cease, we have to begin by rejecting violence in our own lives. That becomes a statement, a witness and a challenge to others. It also becomes a movement. But it is not a quick fix."

Bill responded, "I don't think we're going to avert the coming war, so maybe on some level we should, instead, take responsibility for it and preach about that."

"Meaning what?" Barbara asked.

"Well, I for one have spoken about peace and nonviolence many times over the years. And I have tried more or less successfully to live it in my own life. But I think my preaching has been too academic. People have told me that it's been powerful and moving. Yet I think something's been lacking. I have not been vulnerable. Not publicly, at least. That limits the effectiveness of my preaching. It would be more compelling if I shared my personal struggles, like we do in this group."

"Sharing vulnerability requires trust," Tim replied. "There's a limit to wearing one's heart outwardly."

"But as a people of faith," Barbara said, "we are on a common journey. Those of us who are leaders in the community are not exempt from the call of the gospel and the challenges that entails. Sharing our own struggles shows our humanity and can encourage others."

"But how many will listen?" Tim asked.

"That's not the point," Brian answered.

Perry interjected, "It's not a numbers game, Tim. Ultimately it's a question of progress, and that takes time."

The talk of vulnerability struck Giovanni particularly hard. "Perhaps I have been the most lacking of all," he said. "I have limited my personal exposure even in this group, in spite of the fact that you have all reached out to support me. I don't mean to change the subject, and I don't want to talk about the things I've been going through. But if I can't open up to all of you I don't know how I can share my struggles with the parish."

"It might actually be easier in public, Gio," Barbara suggested. "At least in one sense. There is no immediate conversation or dialogue and you don't have to share any details. I think your manner and demeanor will carry you."

"To me," Perry said, "the question seems to be whether this is a risk any of us are willing to take."

Gilbert always tended to be both quiet and pensive. As a result, his comments, while few, were often thoughtful. "It almost sounds like we are relying too much on ourselves," he said. "We cannot discount the power of prayer. Rabbi Abraham Heschle once wrote that prayer is 'like the strap we grab hold of when tottering on a rushing streetcar or subway that seems on the verge of turning over.' That's where our world is again."

"Amen to that," Barbara said.

At that point, Tim suggested opening the bar. He had, indeed, been serious long enough.

•   •   •

The following Sunday Giovanni was celebrating the eleven o'clock Mass at St. Catherine. As he looked out over the congregation, he caught sight of LaQueesha, the prostitute he had met three months previously at McDonald's. He was not entirely surprised to see her. After all, she had asked if he minded her attending his church, but in the intervening weeks he thought maybe she had changed her mind. She wore a black dress that slimmed her figure, something it clearly did not need. In fact, it was a touch seductive, though her manner was prudent and forthright. After the service was over, he stood outside and greeted the parishioners. When they had all left LaQueesha came up to say hello.

Giovanni said, "Hello, LaQueesha. You dress up very nicely."

She looked at him in his church robes, smiled, and said, "So do you. I'm pleased you remember my name."

"You're not easy to forget. How did you like mass? I suppose this Catholic stuff is a little foreign to you."

"Well, I didn't understand some things, like all the standing, sitting, and kneeling. But then I really came to hear you preach."

"And?" he asked.

"I was right—about what I said when we first met. You are a good preacher. You made me think. Especially about violence and war. Mostly I thought about my son, Tyriq, and what kind of world we are leaving for him. Usually when I think of violence it's the street kind that we see around us, and I worry about keeping my son safe from gangs. Your focus on war, on the international community, made me realize that we are perpetuating a world of hate and revenge that will almost certainly circle back to us. No matter what I do to keep Tyriq safe in Los Angeles, there is still the danger of terrorism and international conflict."

"Thank you, LaQueesha." This was a new experience for Giovanni. "Sometimes people say that they appreciated the preaching when they didn't pay attention. It's just the polite thing to say. Most of them probably couldn't even repeat anything I said. You really did listen."

"It was my first time. Maybe I had more riding on it. If I didn't like it, it could easily be my last," she laughed.

"But you did more than listen. You've already begun to process. I'm impressed by that. Do you have time for lunch?" he asked. His work was finished for the afternoon and he wanted to talk more.

"I think so. I have no plans right now."

"Do you like Mexican food?" he asked.

"I'm from Los Angeles. It's one of my favorites."

"There's a restaurant a half-block from here, just up Vermont. It's called La Barca. In fact, you can almost see it. It's very popular, both with the college crowd and with the Latino community. The margaritas are OK, but the food is very good. Besides, they make special salsa for me."

"Sounds good," she replied. "Let's go."

"Just let me change out of these vestments. I'll be right back."

Since the restaurant was so close, they chose to walk. Less than five minutes had elapsed when they entered. Although there were only two of them, they had to wait a few minutes since Giovanni had requested a booth. At a regular table, their conversation would have been less private. As they were being seated, Guillermo, one of the owners, acknowledged Giovanni.

Sergio, one of the waiters, came to the table with chips and the normal salsa. "*Buenas tardes, padre*," he said. "Would you like something to drink?"

Giovanni looked at LaQueesha and asked, "What would you like?"

"I'll have a margarita," she replied.

"And I'll have a Bohemia," Giovanni said.

As the waiter left LaQueesha asked, "What's a Bohemia?"

"It's my favorite Mexican beer. In fact, I rank it among the world's best—at least outside of a microbrewery."

They looked over the menu and LaQueesha asked, "What do you recommend?"

"Most everything here is good," he replied. "I'm going to have huevos rancheros. If you're hungry I'd recommend the carne asada super burrito. It's excellent. And it's big. If you don't finish, you can take it home to your son. He'll definitely thank you."

Sergio returned with the drinks and a freshly made salsa that Guillermo had prepared just for Giovanni.

"*Muchas gracias,*" Giovanni said. Then to LaQueesha he added, "Every time I come in here, they make a special salsa for me. It's always different but always good. Fair warning, though, it's always hot."

"I think I'll pass on that," she said.

They placed their food order and Giovanni said, "It really is good to see you again, LaQueesha. I've thought about you and Tyriq and wondered how you are." There was no subtext or hidden meaning to his comments. He simply felt relaxed in her presence. On some level even more than with his other friends. They hardly knew each other but he didn't have to play a role with her and he felt no need to be on edge. "Tell me more about your reaction to Mass."

"As I said, I don't know much about Catholic worship, but I really like the way you preach. And I like what you had to say today." She thought for a moment and then asked, "Gio, the pope is really important, isn't he?"

"For Catholics he is. He's the head of the universal Church. And he is a recognized world leader. Why?"

"Well, I was thinking about those two quotes you used today from one of the popes."

"Actually," Giovanni interrupted carefully, "the first was from Pope John XXIII and the other from the Second Vatican Council, which was a meeting of all the world's bishops backs in the 1960s."

"You pulled a paper out of your pocket to read them. But I got the impression that was just for show, a little bit of drama to focus people's attention. You have them memorized, right?" she asked.

"Yes. John XXIII wrote 'Therefore, in this age of ours, which prides itself on its atomic power, it is irrational to think that war is a proper way to obtain justice for violated rights.' The other passage is from one of the Council's documents. 'The horror and perversion of war are immensely magnified by the multiplication of scientific weapons . . . Such considerations compel us to undertake an evaluation of war with an entirely new attitude.'"

"How important are these statements?" she asked. "Do Catholics take them seriously?"

"I do. And I think everyone else should also. They are part of official Catholic teaching. Why do you ask that?"

"Because, Gio, when I listen to politicians, even the Catholic ones, they never talk about war this way. They try to justify it from some political perspective. I don't hear anyone speak from philosophical or religious principles. I get the idea many of them have their minds made up, and the kind of things you were talking about today would be a great inconvenience."

"You're right," he said. "But it's not just the politicians who pursue peace through the crosshairs of violence. A lot of average Americans are content to be herded into a world of war. Unfortunately, I don't hear people speak like you very often. You amaze me, LaQueesha."

"Well, it's not like I've never thought about these things before. What you had to say in church fits in with what I already believe. But I'm interested in something else."

"What's that?" Giovanni asked.

"Something I noticed when we first met. I told you then. I can see that something is bothering you. When you were preaching today there was a passion in you that had nothing to do with war. You told me that night at McDonald's that your family had been killed. But there's more to it, isn't there?"

Giovanni did not really know how to answer. He could not tell anyone what he knew. He was bound by a sacramental seal. And while ordinarily that would pose no problem, this was not ordinary and it had been eating away at him for more than two years. Everyone could see the stress, no one knew the reason. He believed in his church and its sacraments and knew that the rules were neither capricious nor casual. In the aftermath of death and confession, he was resolved to never divulge the secret.

Then came this woman from a seemingly random encounter. No one had introduced them. They appeared to have nothing in common. Giovanni had wanted to be left alone and what could be a more innocuous location than McDonald's? Somehow, on first meeting, LaQueesha had sensed his turmoil and elicited personal information he would never have revealed to a mere stranger. Giovanni did not possess an extraordinary imagination and was not given to flights of fancy, but legitimate questions began to crowd his mind. Why LaQueesha? Where did she come from? Was this some kind of sign? She was no temptress. She was not even truly mysterious. But he felt calm in her presence, even more than with his friends. He almost wanted to tell her everything. But he could not do that.

LaQueesha could tell that he was struggling and said, "Gio, I apologize. I'm not trying to intrude. If you don't want to say anything, you don't have to. I just want you to know that I'm here and I'm a pretty good listener."

"It's a little more complicated than that, LaQueesha."

"Is it because we're still strangers?" she asked.

"No. In fact, I don't think of you as a stranger. I feel a real connection with you. That's part of the problem. We have both been hurt, even betrayed, but you have found a way to forgive. I have not."

"What do you mean? You're an expert on forgiveness."

"Maybe for other people," he said dismissively. "I've given plenty of advice over the years, but applying it to myself is not so easy. There are things I can't say, but there's one thing I can. I told you my family had been murdered and that I could not forgive the murderers." He paused, then continued. "I think I know who they are." This was treacherous territory and Giovanni was not merely trying to be clever. He reasoned that using the qualifiers "think" and "they" would technically preserve his commitment to the sacrament and the anonymity of the murderer, thus not allowing her to deduce anything confidential.

"Why don't you tell the police?" she asked.

"I don't have any information they can use. I can't prove anything. I've resigned myself to the fact that the killers will never be caught or prosecuted. I look at the road and see a bridge that leads to forgiveness and healing, but I can't cross it. How did you do it? How did you manage to forgive the man who raped you? He completely upended your life."

"It's hardly the same thing, Gio. My situation did not involve murder. It's true that nothing has turned out the way I had planned, but does it for anyone? Besides, in my case there was a blessing. I have a wonderful son who means everything to me. At first I had no idea what it would be like to bring a child into the world under those circumstances. But I wouldn't trade him for anything.

"I believe in a contingency of events. At any point in our life, everything that we are is dependent on everything that has come before. Even the good things are, in part, the result of bad."

"That sounds a little fatalistic," he said.

"Not at all," she replied. "I'm not saying that we have no control in our lives. And I certainly don't want to suggest that we shouldn't choose good over evil. But we are the sum of all that has happened to us. We cannot deny our past and still be the people we are today."

"I wonder if I do the same thing to other people that you are doing to me," he said.

"What's that?"

"You make it sound so easy. I wonder if I do that when I'm trying to help others through a crisis."

"Every situation is different, but I doubt it's ever easy. I hated Tyriq's father at first, even before I found out I was pregnant. I wanted him to be punished. I wanted him to suffer. At first I thought it would make me feel good."

"But something changed," Giovanni suggested.

"Yes. The healing process took a while. It was a combination of time and distance. At first I tried to forget. Of course, that was impossible especially after I discovered I was going to have a child. When I decided to keep the baby, I had to find a way to forgive. Otherwise, I would have probably ended up blaming him for my life. That wouldn't be love, and it wouldn't do either of us any good."

"So how did you forgive?"

"I talked to a lot of people, to my mom and to counselors. Especially my mom. I came to realize that in some way I needed to own the rape."

As startling as that statement was, Giovanni did not react. He said nothing and continued to focus on what LaQueesha was saying.

"I suppose that sounds strange since you've probably never been raped."

She paused as if she were waiting for him to say something. This was supposed to be a dialogue, after all, and she wondered what he was thinking.

"No, I haven't," he replied. "However, I've had to counsel and support people who were. I never thought of suggesting ownership."

"I said 'in some way.' Let me try to explain. By ownership, I don't mean that I let the rape happen. But I can't run from it, either. I could have chosen to be only a victim to be pitied. Instead, I chose to make it a part of me. It has contributed to who I am today. And without that I wouldn't know what it means to love my son. As I said, Gio, my crisis does not compare to yours. But that's how I handled it. For me it has made joy possible."

This was only the second time Giovanni and LaQueesha had met, and it was the second time she had reversed their roles. He was supposed to be the priest, the spiritual director, the counselor. She did not intend this *volte-face*, but as she told her story he knew he was being counseled. She never mentioned God, and yet there was something transcendent and divine in her words and the peaceful manner in which she spoke. Her narrative also exposed a chasm between them. Before him was a woman who had no hate. He envied her.

For a few moments Giovanni did not speak. He was deeply moved but that was not the reason for his silence. In her wonderful simplicity, LaQueesha had shamed him. Without realizing it, she had imitated the teaching style of Jesus, invoking the power of storytelling to speak truth.

In a quarter century of preaching, Giovanni may never have presented forgiveness as powerfully as she did. And for good reason. He never had to forgive anything significant before. For him it had always been theoretical, theological. He was being challenged now for the first time and was found wanting. For even though he was stirred by what she said, he still could not see his way to forgiveness. Nor was he prepared to pursue that conversation now. Instead, he changed the subject.

"LaQueesha, may I ask you a question?"

"Of course."

"I understand what you do for a living and maybe even why. But I think you're a remarkable woman, and you have a lot more to offer."

She smiled and said, "Gio, I've tried before. I have at least two things against me. First, I did not finish college. Although now that Tyriq is a little older, I've been thinking of going back."

"What's the second thing?"

"I know that some of my job applications have been overlooked because people see my name and make judgments. Who wants to hire a LaQueesha? I get passed over because of prejudice."

"I can't believe that," he said.

She chuckled and replied, "You live in a different world, Gio. Maybe in the church that prejudice doesn't exist, but I live in the real world. And that's the way it is."

"Maybe we can change that," he said.

They had long finished their lunch. Giovanni picked up the tab and they walked back to the church.

"Thanks for lunch, Gio," she said as she got in her car.

"You're welcome. I'd like to do it again. And thank you for sharing. I think I got more out of today's visit than you did. Goodbye, LaQueesha."

"Goodbye, Gio."

Giovanni watched as she drove off and then decided to go for a walk. Their conversation had given him a lot to think about. How could he own the murders the way that she owned the rape? He did not want to answer that question just yet. In fact, he was not sure he ever wanted to. An answer might lead to forgiveness and for the time being that was not a consideration. He was unhappy, but was adjusting to his world of hate.

CHAPTER 22

Buildup to War

In early February I had breakfast with Robert Byrd at his home. It would not necessarily have been conspicuous for us to dine together in the Senate dining room, but due to his vociferous denunciations of the Bush administration and its preparations for war, Byrd was becoming more and more of an irritant to other senators, and I did not want to stir up or answer any questions that might arise from our association. Saturday, the eighth, proved a perfect opportunity for the two of us to discuss the president's international policies. I wanted to share with him what I had learned about the vice-president, but that would have been wholly unproductive. Knowing Byrd, he probably would have believed me. But I was without proof and, given his opposition to the war, would have been unable to contain his response or swear him to silence. Instead, I chose to explore the idea of a Senate debate on Iraq, the very thing he had been calling for.

"Bob, unlike many other senators, I have listened to your speeches about the impending war. You have not convinced me, but you make several salient points. I, for one, would welcome renewed debate. Perhaps we rushed the war resolution last October."

He laughingly replied, "Perhaps? There's a reason I filibustered the bill, Giuseppe. You're still new to the Senate, but you have already seen the worst of us. I have been around a long time and consider politics a noble calling. During my years, I have discovered that to serve effectively requires a broad and long-term vision. Heralding from the

South I arrived in Washington with some pretty clear-cut ideas. They were mostly provincial and many were wrong. It wasn't always easy, but I learned from my colleagues that the United States is bigger than Virginia and the world is bigger than the United States. I'm afraid that's a lesson many young senators have yet to learn and that many elder statesmen have forgotten."

"I respect that, Bob, but your criticisms of the Bush administration often sound strident and harsh. It's not easy for others to hear, especially those of us who are Republicans."

"It's not a partisan issue, Giuseppe. I may be a Democrat, but George W. Bush is my president, too. Still, as a member of Congress I have a responsibility, in fact a duty, to point out when he's wrong. This is an arrogant administration that has already squandered the sympathy we gained after 9/11. I'm very concerned for our country today—and for our world. I have lived through enough wars. Now I ardently strive for peace."

"It sounds a little more convincing this morning than it does on the floor of the Senate."

"Because we're actually speaking and listening to each other," he continued. "That's all I really want from the Senate."

I was still uncertain how to respond to the war, and wanted to probe his thoughts a little more.

"Bob, I grew up with the idea that we need to be strong in order to guarantee peace. If we back down to Saddam Hussein now, we will look weak and diminish our role in the world."

"How very Reagan of you!" he said somewhat sarcastically, then quickly continued, "I apologize, Giuseppe. But I've heard that argument endlessly for twenty years now. And I'm left wondering whose peace we're guaranteeing and what you mean by 'strong'? Shouldn't everyone have a voice in the pursuit of peace? Especially when it involves the whole world? What you suggest sounds like the man whose voice gets louder as his arguments crumble. Shouting never sways minds or wins debates, and military conquests never truly vanquish foes."

"At this point I don't think anyone or anything can stop war," I replied with resignation.

"Giuseppe, you're too young to be so defeatist. If you oppose the invasion, then stand with me."

"That's just it," I said. "I'm not sure about the war and don't know where to stand."

"It's a little late to be on the fence," he continued. "Time is not our ally here. I'm not a simpleton and don't expect to change everybody's minds. But neither can I just sit by and watch us rush headlong into wanton destruction without objecting. If the Senate overwhelmingly opposed war—at least for the moment—even this president would have to listen."

If he only knew! Bush wasn't calling the shots, and Cheney was not about to be corralled by Congress. But Byrd had a point. There was already a growing international protest against invading Iraq. If there was a significant uprising in the Senate, the United States would be unable to go to war.

"Giuseppe, I cannot decide for you. If it helps, let me assure you that I have not become weak in my old age. I've matured. An America-centric vision of the world is no better than the old Eurocentric one. As political leaders we must find a way to work for the good of all peoples—of all nations."

Byrd watched patiently as I lifted my head and stared at the ceiling. He had no desire to interrupt my thoughts. Neither did he know what they were. As in my youth, I could appear focused in a conversation, yet be absorbed by other concerns. For the moment, I was in a quandary. I really did want to avert war. But, at this point, the American public had swallowed Cheney's lies. If they supported the invasion of Iraq and I objected, my career might never recover and I could forget about being elected president. No. I would not stand against the war unless a significant majority of the Senate did. That was the only way to win over the people.

After what seemed like several long minutes, I said, "Bob, I'll support your call for debate if I can get a couple of influential Republicans to join the cause."

Byrd said nothing, but his stare was accusatory. Or so it seemed to me. I continued, "Let's be honest, Bob. I've only been in the Senate for two years and previously never held any other elected office. I'm a novice and people view me with some suspicion. No one will listen to me. My voice will only carry weight if I get others to speak up first. I can see you're disappointed, but that's the best I can offer."

"Then it will have to do," he said.

On the way home, I thought. I did not see myself as cowardly or lacking in conviction. I saw two problems. First, despite Byrd's years of faithful service in both the House of Representatives and the Senate, despite his leadership in the Democratic Party, despite his position as senior member of the Senate, no one was really listening to him. Other senators condescendingly considered him a relic. He was consistent, raising the same concerns in his dining room as he did on the Senate floor. But in the chamber his words were falling on deaf ears. Even though he was a Democrat, I admired him, or at least his tenacity on this issue, because his position forced me to confront a part of myself. That led to my second problem, namely that I remained conflicted about the war.

If anything, I tended toward opposition. But I would not hang my career on this one issue, nor would I go down with Robert Byrd. My first inclination was to seek the counsel of John McCain. Age aside, we had much in common: both representing Western states, both members of the moderate wing of the Republican Party. But McCain was a unique paradox.

One might have expected his experiences in Vietnam, especially his heroic years as a prisoner of war, to direct his passions toward peace. Sadly, that was not the case. He returned a hardened man, his approach to international diplomacy irrepressibly savage. There is no duplicity in McCain. He projects outwardly the same image he sees in the mirror: a hawk, wings spread, talons open, eyes fierce, dedicated to the belief that violence is the first, best response to any international crisis. My studies in psychology suggested that forays into new wars are McCain's unconscious revenge for torture at the hands of the Viet Cong. Or worse, that he had become the enemy he so despised. There was no hope of winning him over on the issue of Iraq.

·　　·　　·

I decided to discuss the matter with Senator Kay Bailey Hutchison of Texas. If there was any prospect for success, it lay with her. We had developed a good relationship since my election. She and the president were both from Texas and she was one of his ardent supporters. Hutchison was also Chairwoman of the Senate Republican Conference. Her name and reputation lent credibility. I reasoned that if I could garner her support it would be possible to get the full Senate to formally reconsider the issue of war. It was a stretch, but it was my best shot.

We agreed to meet in her office on Sunday, at three in the afternoon. Unlike with Byrd, there were no concerns about dining in public, but she already had lunch and dinner plans.

When I arrived, there was no staff around. We were very much alone. I always felt comfortable in her presence and was indebted to her for escorting me down the aisle for my oath of office. Although we were both professionals and technically equals, she had been a senator since 1993 and saw herself as an older sister tutoring me in the ways of Congress.

She had already set some coffee on a table between two wingback chairs. As we sat down, I got right to the point. "Kay, have you been listening to Robert Byrd's speeches from the Senate floor?"

"Not really. He's made his stance clear and seems intent on imposing his will and ideas on the rest of us. It's easier not to listen." Her voice lacked its characteristic charm and grace. She almost sounded dismissive of him.

"It's not really that simple," I replied. "Bob is a good man and deeply principled. Would it be such a bad idea for us to discuss his concerns?" I tried not to sound too innocent or overly solicitous. She was aware that I was one of the youngest senators by age, and the most junior by time in office, and I used that to my advantage. Still, she remained unbending and took on a lecturing demeanor.

"By my recollection we did that last October. The war resolution was given full Senate debate and passed with ease. We knew then that the president was targeting Iraq. The only thing that's changed is the imminent start of war. I thought you support the president."

"I do," I quickly replied. "This is not about support. If one of our colleagues has serious reservations regarding something as momentous as war, he deserves a hearing."

"He's getting that," she insisted. "He harangues the Senate every time he stands up to speak. He has clearly detailed his resistance to war and his opposition to the president. That does not mean we need to debate it. I don't see what's to be gained by humoring him."

Her comments did not bode a favorable outcome to our discussion. I knew that a number of senators did not respect Byrd. Still I was a little surprised by her scorn and was further amazed because I always thought women would be less inclined to war if only because they bore the sons who would die in battle.

"Kay, what if there's more going on than we know?" I proposed.

"If you're talking about evidence against Hussein, the Senate cannot run the State Department or the CIA, nor can we second guess every White House decision on foreign affairs. The administration must be free to act on intelligence that we are not privy to."

Once again, I felt the unwelcome burden of knowing Dick Cheney. I already knew that the supposed intelligence on Iraq was faked. Even if there were weapons of mass destruction, the idea of a preemptive strike was illegal and immoral on multiple grounds. It was also duplicitous. Hell, several nations possessed WMDs, and not all were our allies.

It seemed there were people in the Bush administration who understood that possible possession of WMDs was not a justification for war and that a majority of Americans would oppose such a move. That was the reason for concocting a false link between Iraq and 9/11. But even if that had been true, allowing an incident—even one as significant as the terror attacks—to drive major policy decisions is fraught with dangerous complications. I decided to try another approach.

"Kay, what do you think of Donald Rumsfeld?"

"Why do you ask?"

I was winging it and wanted to be careful in my response. I took a moment and said, "President Bush has surrounded himself with a good team of advisors, but Rumsfeld is a weak link and perhaps even a liability."

Her response was relatively quick, suggesting that she had already formed her own opinions about Rumsfeld. "I agree that even in a darkened room he would provide no light. But why do you call him a 'weak link'?"

"Let me answer with this question. Do you really think war with Iraq will end quickly?" I asked. She was personally friendly with Bush and not just because they both came from Texas. I decided to play on her loyalty. "Our only significant ally is Britain, and Iraq is a large country. If the war drags on, as most reasonable people suspect, we will lose hundreds, if not thousands of troops. Yet Rumsfeld continually forecasts an early end to the fighting. I think his predictions are one reason senators are reluctant to question the administration. But if the war begins to look endless, Bush will lose credibility, even here at home."

"I don't think so," she thoughtfully replied. "Every war runs the risk of being a lengthy conflict. Right now the president is riding a wave of popularity and the country supports his decision."

"But look what happened to President Johnson during the Vietnam War," I pressed.

"That was different on too many levels. The time, the politics, the lack of world consensus regarding the cause—they were all different. There is no disagreement about the reign of terror in Iraq, even among those nations that do not support the president's plan. Saddam Hussein is simply a tyrant."

Throughout the conversation, I kept inching toward the edge. I wanted to tell Hutchison the truth about Cheney, but realized that without evidence I would sound like a lunatic—shadow governments are the work of literature and film. Worse, I might sound like a traitor. How ironic! Treachery had become the province of the vice-president. So skilled a Machiavelli was he that no one could separate fact from fiction, truth from lies. American politics had become a tornado whose path was directed by the vagaries of an illegitimate despot, a whirlwind touching land in attempts to satisfy the inexhaustible cravings of the neocon elite. And I had to remain mute.

"Kay, I only want to make sure we're doing the right thing. I'm not opposed to all war, but there is one specific way in which this war compares with Vietnam."

"What do you mean?" she asked.

"The American military is the best trained in the world and when we send them into the right battle they conduct themselves with dignity and reflect the excellence of that training. WWII is a classic example. We entered the war reluctantly, but when we did, our cause was just, our course and objectives were clear, and our soldiers performed admirably, instilling pride in our nation and grateful esteem around the world.

"When we engage in the wrong war, those same warriors are reduced to barbarians. The atrocities of Vietnam are now legendary. I have reason to doubt the justifications for this war. But even if they are correct, I don't think it has been thought through. A protracted conflict will produce the same results as Vietnam. That's why I question the predictions of Rumsfeld."

I could tell from her expression that I was making headway, but was still not convincing.

"Talking with you helps, Kay, but it seems as though the whole Senate should take one last opportunity to discuss war. Are you at least willing to consider that?" I wanted to convey sincerity but could not ask her to do it as a favor to me. That would have been pleadingly childish.

Instead I noted, "No one is dying right now and Hussein is no closer to a nuclear weapon than Iran."

"You don't know that," she insisted.

Ah! But I did. I said, "He will also never reach the United States."

"But he could target Israel."

There it was—the myopic hysteria of the neocons! I was not about to wade into those tricky waters. As much as I enjoyed and respected Hutchison, she was like so many other politicians—unable to distinguish between the right of Israel to exist and particular policies of the Israeli government. Strange that we have no such dilemma with ourselves or any other nation. By this time, it was clear to me that she would not lend support to opening a discussion in the Senate. I needed to find a graceful and noncommittal way out.

"Well, Kay, I'm still learning how things work here in Washington. I guess at some point we really do have to make decisions and stand by them. I just hope we've made the right one in this case. For both the president's sake and the country's."

"I'm glad you came to talk to me, Giuseppe. You're already a credit to California. You have a lot of enthusiasm and dedication. And I'm pretty sure that someday you will be a major player in our party. Just don't let people like Robert Byrd cause you to second-guess your decisions."

"Thanks, Kay, for your time and for putting my concerns to rest."

After leaving her office, I decided to stroll aimlessly around the National Mall, too engrossed by my thoughts to pay much attention to my surroundings. I was accustomed to being in charge. Having planned my personal choices and actions in detail, I rarely encountered difficulty making decisions. This war was different. I was being controlled in a very real way by decisions in the both the Senate and the White House, and I did not like it.

On a fundamental level, I was opposed to the invasion of Iraq. In part, that may have been my brother's influence. He had always preached against violence. In the years before our estrangement, I had heard him deliver many a homily on forgiveness and reconciliation, and listened as he expounded on the inescapable cycle of the violence wrought by war. But my problem did not lie with Giovanni.

I realized that war actually grates against my own style. My interaction with others, while clearly manipulative, was rarely violent. By contrast, I have always delighted in the challenge of shrewdly outmaneuvering my opponents. War represents weakness rather than strength, a clear acknowledgment of failure.

After a while, I found myself at the Lincoln Memorial among a typical throng of tourists, their cameras capturing hundreds of moments. There is an odd reverence when people gaze on the nineteen-foot behemoth statue of America's sixteenth president. One can almost see them being swept away by the legend and myth surrounding Lincoln, calling to mind images of the Civil War—American heroism and valiancy from both the North and the South. As I stood there that afternoon, my mind also wandered to the past, and I wondered.

The mystique surrounding President Lincoln obscures much of his humanity and flaws. As a result, few people are aware of either. In its own way, nineteenth-century American politics were as deceptive and manipulative as the twentieth, and certainly Lincoln was a product of his time. His speeches are as inspiring today as they were in the 1860s. Perhaps even more so. Still, there was treachery and manipulation in the successful efforts to preserve the union and expand the Constitution. If he had not been slain, would history have so lionized him? Without question, he deserves the respect of generations. But I shuddered at the thought that the politicians I served with could ascend to such lofty heights and gain similar stature simply by falling victim to an assassin's bullet. If I were a praying man, I would have entreated the Lord to endow a keen and quick response upon the secret service agents attending the vice-president.

. . . .

War preparations and the stated rationale ramped up precipitously in the next few weeks. On March 18, 2003, President Bush certified to Congress that he had determined that:

"(1) reliance by the United States on further diplomatic and other peaceful means alone will neither (A) adequately protect the national security of the United States against the continuing threat posed by Iraq nor (B) likely lead to enforcement of all relevant United Nations Security Council resolutions regarding Iraq; and (2) acting pursuant to the Constitution and Public Law 107–243 is consistent with the United States and other countries continuing to take the necessary actions against international terrorists and terrorist organizations, including those nations, organizations, or persons who planned, authorized, committed, or aided the terrorist attacks that occurred on September 11, 2001."

The difficulty here was that most Americans and even members of Congress were being lied to. The president had no such information except by way of Dick Cheney, who had already determined that war was in his personal best interests. Bush, as he had been since 9/11, was simply being used by Cheney. There was no evidence linking Saddam Hussein or Iraq with any facet of the September 11, 2001, attacks. Bush was proposing a preemptive strike, an action roundly condemned in religious, moral, and theological circles. An action opposed by the United Nations and most of the international community, and supported only by the questionable patriotism of the neocon elite who had assumed secret and unconstitutional roles of power.

Senator Robert Byrd did not know the whole truth either. But he was from the South, had been serving in Congress for sixty years, and, as Southerners are wont to say, could smell a skunk. He knew something was deeply wrong and feared the long-term outcome of a precipitous war. Several months prior, he had challenged the Senate with uncompromising truth and astounding prescience:

"This administration has turned the patient art of diplomacy into threats, labeling, and name calling of the sort that reflects quite poorly

on the intelligence and sensitivity of our leaders, and which will have consequences for years to come.

"Calling heads of state pygmies, labeling whole countries as evil, denigrating powerful European allies as irrelevant—these types of crude insensitivities can do our great nation no good. We may have massive military might, but we cannot fight a global war on terrorism alone. We need the cooperation and friendship of our time-honored allies as well as the newer found friends whom we can attract with our wealth.

"Will our war inflame the Muslim world resulting in devastating attacks on Israel? Will Israel retaliate with its own nuclear arsenal? Will the Jordanian and Saudi Arabian governments be toppled by radicals, bolstered by Iran, which has much closer ties to terrorism than Iraq?"

While the Bush administration spoke to the country's lowest common denominator, demanding medieval fealty to its call for war, and castigating anyone not in agreement, including America's allies, Senator Byrd chose to address and challenge the nation's concept of loyalty. Although few had paid him heed, he was relentless in his pursuit of peace.

On March 19, 2003, the day after the president spoke, Byrd rose once again to address the U.S. Senate, and delivered the last great demonstration of oratorical truth in opposition to a preemptive war in Iraq. This speech was a capstone to his sixty years in the United States Congress, and arguably, was his finest moment in forty-four years as a United States senator. This magician of a statesman stood before his colleagues conjuring up the ghosts from Senates past. Closing their eyes each member could see Byrd ringed by the likes of Daniel Webster, John Calhoun, and Henry Clay—men who placed the good of the country above party loyalty, and now stood in apparition beside the senator from West Virginia. Although Quakers did not coin the phrase "speak truth to power" until the 1950s, the concept has long been core to grand Senate speeches, and the truth of Senator Byrd's words were further amplified by the history of every great man to address that august body since 1789. Sadly, not even the ghosts of senators past could move the minds and hearts of a body whose intellects were manacled by endemic partisanship and a thirst for power. In one last effort to preserve and secure peace, Senator Byrd fearlessly took to the floor:

I believe in this great and beautiful country. I have studied its roots and gloried in the wisdom of its magnificent Constitution. I have marveled at the wisdom of its founders and framers. Generation after generation of Americans have understood the lofty ideals that underlie our great Republic. I have been inspired by the story of their sacrifice and their strength.

But, today I weep for my country. I have watched the events of recent months with a heavy, heavy heart. No more is the image of America one of strong, yet benevolent peacekeeper. The image of America has changed. Around the globe, our friends mistrust us, our word is disputed, our intentions are questioned.

Instead of reasoning with those with whom we disagree, we demand obedience or threaten recrimination. Instead of isolating Saddam Hussein, we seem to have isolated ourselves. We proclaim a new doctrine of preemption, which is understood by few and feared by many. We say that the United States has the right to turn its firepower on any corner of the globe that might be suspect in the war on terrorism. We assert that right without the sanction of any international body. As a result, the world has become a much more dangerous place.

We flaunt our superpower status with arrogance. We treat U.N. Security Council members like ingrates who offend our princely dignity by lifting their heads from the carpet. Valuable alliances are split. After war has ended, the United States will have to rebuild much more than the country of Iraq. We will have to rebuild America's image around the globe.

The case this Administration tries to make to justify its fixation with war is tainted by charges of falsified documents and circumstantial evidence. We cannot convince the world of the necessity of this war for one simple reason. This is a war of choice.

There is no credible information to connect Saddam Hussein to 9/11. The Twin Towers fell because a world-wide terrorist group, al-Qaida, with cells in over sixty nations, struck at our wealth and our influence by turning our own planes into missiles, one of which would likely have slammed into the dome of this beautiful capitol except for the brave sacrifice of the passengers on board.

The brutality seen on September 11th and in other terrorist attacks we have witnessed around the globe are the violent and desperate efforts by extremists to stop the daily encroachment of Western values upon their cultures. That is what we fight. It is a force not confined to borders. It is a shadowy entity with many faces, many names, and many addresses.

But, this Administration has directed all of the anger, fear, and grief which emerged from the ashes of the Twin Towers and the twisted metal of the Pentagon towards a tangible villain, one we can see and hate and attack. And villain he is. But, he is the wrong villain. And this is the wrong war. If we attack Saddam Hussein, we will probably drive him from power. But, the zeal of our friends to assist our global war on terrorism may have already taken flight.

The general unease surrounding this war is not just due to "orange alert." There is a pervasive sense of rush and risk and too many questions unanswered. How long will we be in Iraq? What will be the cost? What is the ultimate mission? How great is the danger at home? A pall has fallen over the Senate Chamber. We avoid our solemn duty to debate the one topic on the minds of all Americans, even while scores of thousands of our sons and daughters faithfully do their duty in Iraq.

What is happening to this country? When did we become a nation which ignores and berates our friends? When did we decide to risk undermining international order by adopting a radical and doctrinaire approach to using our awesome military might? How can we abandon diplomatic efforts when the turmoil in the world cries out for diplomacy?

Why can this President not seem to see that America's true power lies not in its will to intimidate, but in its ability to inspire?

War appears inevitable. But, I continue to hope that the cloud will lift. Perhaps Saddam will yet turn tail and run. Perhaps reason will somehow still prevail. I along with millions of Americans will pray for the safety of our troops, for the innocent civilians in Iraq, and for the security of our homeland. May God continue to bless the United States of America in the troubled days ahead, and may we somehow recapture the vision which for the present eludes us.

It was a forceful oration. More than that Byrd laid bare the soul and aspirations that had defined America, and attempted to stir the very conscience of a nation. His speech should have been compelling, but as I listened to him and watched the reactions of my colleagues, I realized that politics is rarely as principled as elected representative's claim, or the voters expect. I also developed a perverse appreciation for Vice-President Dick Cheney. His genius lay in empowering a host of lies to overshadow and defeat the truth and in enlisting the unsuspecting as co-conspirators. These were both on display as John McCain rose to respond to Senator Byrd:

Madam President, I observed the comments of the distinguished Senator from West Virginia concerning the events which are about to transpire within the next hour or so, or days. I did not really look forward to coming to the floor and debating the issue. It has been debated. It has been discussed in the media. It has been discussed at every kitchen table in America. But I felt it would be important for me to respond to allegations concerning the United States of America, its status in the world, and, in particular, what happens after this conflict is over, which I do not think we have paid enough attention to, perhaps understandably, because our first and foremost consideration is the welfare of the young men and women we are sending in harm's way. But to allege that somehow the United States of America has demeaned itself or tarnished its reputation by being involved in liberating the people of Iraq, to me, simply is neither factual nor fair.

The United States of America has involved itself in the effort to disarm Saddam Hussein, and now freedom for the Iraqi people, with the same principles that motivated the United States of America in most of the conflicts we have been involved in, most recently Kosovo and Bosnia, and in which, in both of those cases, the United States national security was not at risk, but what was at risk was our advocacy and willingness to serve and sacrifice on behalf of people who are the victims of oppression and genocide.

We did not go into Bosnia because Mr. Milosevic had weapons of mass destruction. We did not go into Kosovo because ethnic Albanians or others were somehow a threat to the security of the United States. We entered into those conflicts because we could not stand by and watch innocent men, women, and children being slaughtered, raped, and "ethnically cleansed." We found a new phrase for our lexicon: "ethnic cleansing." Ethnic cleansing is a phrase which has incredible implications.

The mission our military is about to embark on is fraught with danger, and it means the loss of brave young American lives. But I also believe it offers the opportunity for a new day for the Iraqi people.

Madam President, there is one thing I am sure of, that we will find the Iraqi people have been the victims of an incredible level of brutalization, terror, murder, and every other kind of disgraceful and distasteful oppression on the part of Saddam Hussein's regime. And contrary to the assertion of the Senator from West Virginia, when the people of Iraq are liberated, we will again have written another chapter in the glorious history of the United States of America, that we will fight for the freedom of other citizens of the world, and we again assert the most glorious phrase, in my view, ever written in the English language; and that is: We hold these truths to be self-evident, that all men are created equal and endowed by their Creator with certain inalienable rights, and among these are life, liberty, and the pursuit of happiness.

The people of Iraq , for the first time, will be able to realize those inalienable rights. I am proud of the United States of America. I am proud of the leadership of the President of the United States.

It is not an easy decision to send America's young men and women into harm's way. As I said before, some of them will not be returning. But to somehow assert, as some do, that the people of Iraq and the Middle East are not entitled to those same God-given rights that Americans and people all over the country are, that they do not have those same hopes and dreams and aspirations our own citizens do, to me, is a degree of condescension. I might even use stronger language than that to describe it.

So I respectfully disagree with the remarks of the Senator from West Virginia. I believe the President of the United States has done everything necessary and has exercised every option short of war, which has led us to the point we are today.

I believe that, obviously, we will remove a threat to America's national security because we will find there are still massive amounts of weapons of mass destruction in Iraq.

Although Theodore Roosevelt is my hero and role model, I also, in many ways, am Wilsonian in the respect that America, this great nation of ours, will again contribute to the freedom and liberty of an oppressed people who otherwise never might enjoy those freedoms.

So perhaps the Senator from West Virginia is right. I do not think so. Events will prove one of us correct in the next few days. But I rely on history as my guide to the future, and history shows us, unequivocally, that this nation has stood for freedom and democracy, even at the risk and loss of American lives, so that all might enjoy the same privileges or have the opportunity to someday enjoy the same privileges as we do in this noble experiment called the United States of America.

It was obvious that I had made the correct decision in not seeking McCain's support for debate. It was not just that his personality was bent on war. By swallowing the lies and deceptions of Cheney, McCain, like many senators, had been reduced to sophomoric rhetoric. And their assertions would all be proved wrong.

I did not know how to counter the events unfolding before me. During Senator Byrd's speech, I grew ever more uncomfortable by the split between my sense of right and my personal desires. I could have addressed the Senate, supported Byrd, and challenged the assertions of McCain. But I calculated this crisis as I did everything in my life and decided that political suicide was not in my plans. Politics was a game that I was playing to win and I remained silent. Hours later bombs fell on Baghdad and the war began.

CHAPTER 23

McCain had been right about one thing—the war had been discussed at every kitchen table in America. No conflict in U.S. history had been the subject of so much debate and so thoroughly scrutinized before it even began. Nor was any corner of the country immune. The personnel who would fight this conflict had been culled from every state in the union; from modest rural towns to small suburbs to major cities. Every facet of life was affected, from the farmer to the banker, from the preacher to the cop and, of course, the reporter.

On Thursday, March 20, the day after the bombing began, Tom and Emily had planned a simple meal at home. Tom had spent the day as part of a regional task force consisting of both law enforcement and civilian agencies. Retaliation against the United States, particularly from a cell of terrorists already in the country, was a real possibility. Response teams and contingency plans were created and surveillance escalated. Southern California was prepared for any eventuality.

As the largest and most prominent newspaper in Southern California, the *Los Angeles Times* alone had the resources to dispatch reporters to foreign countries to cover international affairs. Years before, Emily had become the *Times'* chief foreign correspondent. This position had necessitated many trips abroad, most commonly to England, the land of her birth. Once again, she received orders to fly to London in order to cover the British involvement in the Iraq war. The *Times* was not looking for information on the government's war effort. As if twinned from the same womb, Prime Minister Blair was in lockstep with President Bush and there were sufficient sources to identify England's military activities. Emily would provide something that was indiscernible from other authorities including international wire services.

One measure of Emily's brilliance was the way she captured the mood of the populace. Where many reporters raise suspicion, she engendered trust.. Her gentle, caring and poignant manner enabled people to open up and share their darkest fears and deepest thoughts. With an incisive intellect and incredible insight, she tracked the pulse of Britain's citizens.

Emily had anticipated dinner with Tom since early Thursday morning. Then came the call from her editor and her assignment to London. She faintheartedly argued to stay in Los Angeles knowing her efforts would end in vain. No one knew how long this war would last nor how it would end. She was booked on a flight Friday morning and dreaded informing her husband.

Emily arrived home a couple of hours before Tom. She packed her suitcases and began preparing the meal. Her new assignment hampered her choices. Did this night call for a favorite meal, for simplicity or elegance? There was no telling how long she would be in England. She settled on the simple—baked chicken breast with lemon and capers, garlic butter rice, and asparagus.

Tom walked in the door without suspicion, but he could immediately tell that Emily was nervous. She had a glass of scotch waiting for him, in itself not an abnormal gesture. But she greeted him a little too quickly and with unusual longing, especially considering that they had seen each other only hours before.

As she threw her arms around him Tom said, "Thanks for the drink, Em. What's wrong? Or should I guess?"

"Oh, Tom. Can't a wife throw herself at her husband anymore?"

He smiled and said, "I welcome that. But something else is going on."

She lingered a few moments and whispered in his ear, "Let's talk about it at dinner. Doesn't the food smell good?"

He replied, "Your food always smells good." Then he stepped back, looked at her, and said, "You're going on assignment, aren't you?"

She sighed. "Yes. And I don't know how long it will last. It's the war."

"Everything is these days," he said. "People are on edge. All they can talk about is Iraq. Where are they sending you?"

"To England. Don't worry, Tom. I won't be embedded with the troops, or be in harm's way. I'll cover the war from London. There won't even be reason for me to go to the continent."

With resignation in his voice he said, "This is not really a surprise. I expected you'd have to go sometime. I just hoped it would be later."

"You know I'd stay if I could." She did not really have to convince him.

"I know, Em. I also know this is important. Not just to the paper, but to you. You're an outstanding reporter. I knew that when we remarried. I can't ask you to give up your career. But I won't pretend that I'm happy about it. When do you leave?"

"Tomorrow."

"Then let's not waste time," he said as he drew her close. "Let's go to bed."

"What about dinner?" she asked.

"It can wait."

"Well, let me turn the stove off and set the food aside."

"OK. I need to clean up anyway. Meet me in the shower."

When they awakened the next morning the food had still been untouched.

· · ·

Across town, Giovanni had originally planned on spending a quiet evening at home, but he had been asked by his friend Fr. Bill Messenger to lead a discussion for students, faculty, and staff at the University of Southern California. Every Thursday the USC Catholic Center held a weekly social night. These ranged from pure entertainment to serious discussions of faith. One recurring event was called "Theology on Tap."

The concept originated in the Archdiocese of Chicago and involved priests meeting with young Catholics in a local pub to discuss concerns the young adults had about their faith and its relevance in their lives. Over the years, Theology on Tap has been appropriated by many parishes and dioceses around the nation as a way of engaging people on their own turf. The Catholic Center version of this program took place on site instead of a bar, since many students were under twenty-one and not allowed to publicly consume alcohol. The center kept a supply of sodas on hand, thus enabling everyone to share in the format of these theological reflections.

Messenger frequently invited guest speakers to address the community and on occasion he was joined by the Episcopal and Lutheran chaplains, Rev. Glenn Libby and Rev. Sean Ewbank, respectively, to discuss areas of faith common to all three churches.

With the bombing of Iraq just underway, the topic for the evening was the Just War Doctrine of the Catholic Church, a subject Jackson and Giuseppe had briefly discussed the previous October. The university discussion, however, would be more than a casual conversation. Giovanni would need to detail the principles of the docrtine. Having been in seminary together, and having remained friends over the years, Bill knew that Giovanni was a perfect choice to make the presentation and lead the discussion.

The university students were not unlike most U.S. citizens—many did not even know such a teaching even existed. The common American practice has always been to say, "This is a just war" simply because the enemy is portrayed as evil or because one approves of the objective of the conflict. Even in the early days of Vietnam, most Americans supported the war. In the case of Iraq, they either supported the war from a misguided sense of patriotism or opposed it for personal reasons. The Catholic Church's teaching, however, challenges this kind of expediency with deeply rooted principles for determining the validity of any war.

Augustine of Hippo originated the doctrine, and it was further defined and developed by philosophers Thomas Aquinas and Francisco

Suarez. The Just War Doctrine is based on a presumption *against* war and *for* a peaceful settlement of disputes. As a result, seven conditions are set to determine if a war is just. On the surface, they seem rather reasonable and obvious:

1. The war must be declared by a legitimate public authority possessing the power to do so.
2. A real injury must have been suffered.
3. There must be a reasonable hope of success.
4. Every possible means of settlement must have been exhausted.
5. The nation waging the war must do so for a humanitarian reason, not for selfish ones.
6. Only legitimate and moral means may be used in prosecuting the war.
7. The good to be achieved must outweigh the harm done (proportionality).

.   .   .

A casual reading might lead to the conclusion that justifying war is relatively easy. Certainly that is the prevailing attitude in the Pentagon and military institutions the world over. Modern politicians quickly follow suit driven by their quest for military endorsements.

The task for this Theology on Tap meeting was to engage centuries of philosophical and theological reflection, to develop an understanding of the principles and generalities of war, and to refine the means of applying that knowledge to modern warfare.

However, as Jackson had reminded me in our conversation, there is an inescapable caveat: each of the seven principles must be met in order to determine that a particular war is justified. Failing this there is no justification. A more careful reading might suggest that no war can meet the criteria, at least not in the modern era, but the seven principles continue to serve and indispensible role when considering the issue of war.

I know the Just War Doctrine well. When Giovanni was in seminary we were on good terms and spoke frequently, and he would often share what he learned in his studies. This particular teaching had a deep impact on me. My faith was already waning, and in a twisted paradox, the Just War Doctrine contributed to my growing agnosticism.

I was deeply captivated by both the brilliance and the high moral standards set forth in the doctrine, but at the same time I found the church's history hypocritical and repugnant. St. Augustine lived between 354 and 430, yet in 1095 the Catholic Church launched a series of crusades in the Middle East. After almost nine centuries of theological reflection, the church failed both Jesus's call to nonviolence and its own teachings. Christianity had surrendered to the primal forces of violence. But it was not just past failings that concerned me.

In more recent memory, a majority of U.S. bishops ceded allegiance to truth and supported every international conflict in which the United States was engaged. Even the first Gulf War did not meet all seven criteria of the doctrine. But this one did not come close.

I acknowledge that I am an uncertain voice of criticism, having previously succumbed to the use of violence myself. But the scope of war is broader than an individual act of brutality. Besides, I did not espouse lofty principles of nonviolence as did the church.

One hallmark of leadership is knowing how far the people are willing to follow—not taking them too far too fast. That's one reason politicians rarely speak the truth. At least not the whole truth. Leadership is a delicate balance. It requires a clear vision that cannot always be fully articulated.

My own lack of faith notwithstanding, I could shake neither the truth nor the power of the Just War Doctrine. That was one reason I was uncomfortable with this Iraq war. That and the fact that I knew the reasons had been manufactured. At the same time, I refused to stand against the war. I guess I learned one thing from the U.S. bishops: all principles can be set aside if they are inconvenient. Hell, I didn't need the bishops to teach me that.

CHAPTER 24

The war in Iraq occupied the front page of all the world's newspapers and was the daily lead item on most television and radio broadcasts, even those of France and Germany and other countries that refused to participate in the so-called "coalition of the willing." Even if it had not been so widely covered, it is doubtful that any media would have reported an obscure event in Belgium, with the exception of *De Morgen*, *Le Soir*, and *La Libre Belgique*. Yet those three papers buried the news deep inside their pages. On Sunday morning, April 13, 2003, three days after the fall of Baghdad, a trio of men in their late forties were found dead on a quiet street in Brussels.

Saturday night I stayed up late watching news analysis of the fall of Mosul, which gave U.S. and British forces control of all of Iraq's major cities. At about one o'clock in the morning I went to bed, then was awakened forty minutes later by a ringing telephone. It was Jackson.

"Hello," I said somewhat groggily.

"Sep, this is Jackson." I needed no more words to realize that something was terribly wrong. His voice, choking as he fought back tears, startled me into consciousness.

"What is it, Jacks?" I asked.

"Jean-Paul is dead." He was barely able to speak the words, clearly overcome with emotion.

"I'll catch the next flight to Boston," I said.

"No," he replied. "I'm flying to Belgium later this morning. It happened there, while he was visiting his family."

I wanted to be sensitive and supportive, but could not avoid the question. "What happened?" I asked. "Has he been sick?"

"No," Jackson replied. "He went out with some friends last night, and they never came back."

"Was it an accident, a robbery?"

"I don't have any answers yet," he said. "But his brother said something about murder. I'll tell you what I find out after I get to Brussels. Right now I just want to be with his mom."

"Of course, Jacks. I didn't mean to press you."

He began to cry. "Sep, they found him and his friends on the street."

"Oh, Jackson. Are you sure you don't want me to come to Boston?" I asked.

"Not now," he assured me. "I'll call you in a day or two." With that he hung up.

Once before, when we were studying at Harvard, I had seen Jackson really upset, but never in tears. This was far beyond that experience. In Boston he was struggling to find false love by holding on to a lie. Now he was coping with true love slipping from his grasp. I could tell from his voice that he was genuinely distraught. I wanted to console and support him, but I also understood his need to be with Jean-Paul's family. The night my wife and children were murdered was interminable, and I can't imagine what it would have been like to be alone. My brother's presence was critical and Jean-Paul's mother would need Jackson now, especially since her health was precarious.

After the call I could not go back to sleep. Suddenly the war in Iraq was of no interest to me. Nonetheless, I turned on the TV, tuned it to CNN and realized just how little actual news the cable stations broadcast. They simply set their information on a seamless loop. But the background noise did fill the house with sight and sound, pretending to keep me company.

I sat alone for hours, thinking. No one to talk to, no one to call. All of Jean-Paul's family lived in Belgium; I did not really know any of Jackson's siblings; and my brother and I were not on speaking terms. Jackson was my closest confidant and ordinarily he was the one I would talk to. I sat with no information to digest, my mind imagining various scenarios, occasionally recalling times from our youth and his recent visits to Washington.

For breakfast, I had no desire to cook and settled for drinking a pot of coffee. But when lunchtime came I decided to go to Cantler's restaurant. It is located in Mill Creek, Maryland, just outside of Annapolis. Soft shell crabs were just coming into season, and Cantler's is *the* place to go. Even if they were not available, the restaurant has some of the freshest seafood and one of the largest selections in the Washington area. Besides, the drive would be worth it, and hopefully take my mind off Jackson's crisis. He would not yet have arrived in Brussels, and it would be a while before I would hear from him. I was concerned for my friend, and, for the moment, felt helpless.

Throughout the day, I wondered. What had happened? Simply hearing that someone was dead did not constitute knowledge. I did not know Jean-Paul well, having only met him on two occasions. But what I was able to discern through Jackson and my own brief encounters, was that he was a man of simplicity and integrity. Had he been the target? Or was it one of his friends? And if it was Jean-Paul, why?

Violent crime is rare in Belgium, so a robbery was the most probable cause, except that neither Jean-Paul nor his family were wealthy, and it was not likely that he carried much cash. A hate crime was doubtful because he was a native Belgian, not part of an ethnic or religious minority. Jealousy could not have been the cause. Jean-Paul had been living in the United States for over twenty years and was no longer a known person in the community over there. I supposed that it could have been drugs. Brussels was not immune to the scourge of substance abuse and addicts always have to pay for a fix even if only in small amounts. A crime of passion seemed ludicrous for the same reason that it could not have been jealousy. A mob contract was out of the question given that Jean-Paul's life, even though he was a banker, had no connection to organized crime. Of course, mental illness, however unlikely, was a variable not to be discounted. And yet, timing strained the theory of mere coincidence.

Jean-Paul visited his mother regularly and his trip would raise no suspicions. I couldn't buy the idea of a drug deal gone wrong; as far as I knew, Jean-Paul was not connected to any narcotics traffic either in the United States or Belgium. Some kind of irrational randomness seemed the most likely culprit suggesting that solving the murder of him and his friends would be next to impossible. But a solution was not my concern. Jackson was. How would he handle this? How would he survive? I made a decision to go to Brussels for the funeral. He did the same for me when my family was killed, and I owed him that.

•　　•　　•

Jackson called from Brussels on Monday.

"Sep, this is Jackson."

"Hello, Jacks. I know you're having a difficult time, but I want to know how you are. And how Jean-Paul's family is doing."

"Everybody's struggling here, but they're a strong family and very supportive. I'm glad I came. It helps me, and I think it helps all of us."

"Have you learned anything yet?"

"A little. He and two of his friends were shot. That's almost unheard of over here. I'm not even sure the police know how to handle it. The doctor says they did not suffer. Apparently they died instantly."

"Do the police have any suspects?" I asked.

"Not yet. Until they can determine a motive, it's unlikely they will apprehend anyone. It's all very shocking, Sep. It's still hard to believe it really happened."

I could tell this was not a conversation he was ready to have.

"Jacks, we don't have to talk now. Will you let me know when the funeral is?"

"Of course, Sep."

"And," I quickly added, "call if you need anything."

"I will. Goodbye, Sep."

"Goodbye, Jacks."

• • •

A funeral Mass was held on Saturday, April 19, at ten o'clock in the morning at Notre Dame de la Chapelle (Our Lady of the Chapel), a Gothic style church located in the Marolles District. I had taken an evening flight on Friday and arrived at the Brussels Airport at seven in the morning where Jackson was waiting. He had already purchased train tickets for us, so once I cleared immigration and customs we took the train from the airport to Gare de Bruxelles-Chapelle station, only a few blocks from the church.

Most of Jean-Paul's family spoke English as well as French. But I presumed it was in deference to Jackson that the Mass was bilingual. The priest, Fr. Vincent Lejeune, was fluent in both languages. Laurent, Jean-Paul's older brother, gave the eulogy. As at any funeral, he spoke of Jean-Paul's life, enumerating his good qualities, such as his generosity, and focusing on his tenderness and compassion toward others. Although his family had known for years and fully accepted him, I was somewhat surprised by the openness with which Laurent addressed his brother's sexual orientation. He suggested that Jean-Paul's loving and caring nature may have been precisely because he was gay. He spoke affectionately of his life in Boston, referring to Jackson as another brother and full member of the Lecuyer family. These remarks were clearly comforting to Jackson. There was no burial since Jean-Paul had requested to be cremated.

Jackson had planned on spending the next week in Brussels while I was returning to Washington Saturday night. The family held a reception following the funeral, and Mr. and Mrs. Lecuyer seemed particularly proud to have a United States senator in attendance. Although Jackson was my reason for being there, I was also glad that my presence pleased Jean-Paul's parents.

This was my first trip to Brussels, but there was no time for sightseeing. I could not postpone commitments in Washington. After a couple of hours Jackson suggested that we head back to the airport early, allowing us some private time to talk. I checked in for my flight, and we found a place to drink coffee and sit for a while.

"Sep, I want to thank you for coming to the funeral. Having you here meant a lot to me, and Jean-Paul's family was very honored."

"Well, I hope you'll explain to them that I'm not a very important politician. I'm just one of one hundred senators and don't even have a position of leadership in my party."

"You don't have to downplay your role to me," he suggested. "After all, you do represent the largest state in the union."

"Well, the important thing was for me to be here for you, Jacks. I wish there was something more I could do."

His eyes wandered off, and though he was able to visibly control his emotions, I could still hear distress in his voice. He heaved a big sigh and said, "Jacks, I have no idea what I'll do without Jean-Paul. We never even had a chance to get married."

"Jacks, you've told me many times of your love for each other. I think everything about your life together was a marriage. And from my perspective, better than most."

"Thanks."

"I'm serious," I continued. "I'm sure you had difficult moments, like any other couple. But when I saw you together the two of you radiated joy and a very deep love. I envy you that."

He didn't respond; just closed his eyes wistfully. After a few moments, he opened them again and asked, "How long did it take you to get over Yolanda's death?"

I guess I expected that question at some point, but did not know how to reply. There were too many complications surrounding Yolanda's murder and that of our children. And there were lingering effects I had not anticipated. It had been two-and-a-half years and what stood out most was the fact that I found being alone much more difficult than I would admit to anyone. I was good at putting on fronts, did not display emotion, and would not allow any personal weakness to derail my plans. No one knew how I actually felt. I fumbled for an answer.

"I'm not sure I'm over it now," I said. "On one level I suppose no one ever is. You just find a way to live. Some people fall in love again. Others simply survive on memories."

"I'll never love anyone like Jean-Paul."

That was not the time to contradict him. Besides, he might have been right.

"Perhaps not, Jacks. For now, I can tell you from my experience that you won't truly rest until the police have some answers. In my case, they never arrested anyone. The murders have never been solved, and I think everyone in my family remains unsettled."

"Sep, you know I'm not a vengeful person. But I hate whoever did this. I hope they find him."

"So do I, Jacks."

My plane began boarding, we said our goodbyes, and I started to make my way toward security. Suddenly I turned, walked back, and reached out to embrace him. This time it was he who held on a little longer—no hidden agenda or disguised desire. He just needed support, as if his legs could no longer hold upright the weight he was bearing, and only my embrace prevented a week's worth of burden from collapsing. His shoulders did not heave nor did he sob. But he did cry. As I moved through security check and boarded the plane I wished I could have stayed longer. But it was time for me to leave. I quickly turned back and said, "Keep me informed, Jacks, and call when you're back in Boston, or anytime for that matter. And remember. You're always welcome in Washington."

"Thank you, Sep. And thanks again for coming."

It was a short trip. I had spent only hours in Brussels. But it was worth it. A couple of people from Boston had attended the funeral, but I knew that I was the one Jackson wanted most to see. Our situations were different, but maybe I would be able to help him when he returned.

CHAPTER 25

Crime is not unheard of in Belgium, but the murder rate is reasonably low and the police in Brussels were not accustomed to investigating a scene of multiple killings. Fortunately, the world was distracted by war and the detectives were not being pressed for information by the media. This provided them a comfort zone for examining the evidence and attempting to determine a motive. The scene was puzzling. There had been no robbery and no struggle. Luckily, the three men all carried identification. The authorities were able to determine who they were and how to notify the families. This also enabled them to retrace the victims' activities the previous evening.

Jean-Paul and his friends had gone for dinner and drinks, enjoying a leisurely meal at L'Estrille du Vieux Bruxelles, an old literary café at 7 Rue de Rollebeek. Following their meal, they stopped for drinks and dancing at Le Belgica, across the street from Le Boys Boudoir in the gay district. It was while walking along Rue des Pierres that they were ambushed by fate.

Brussels had been installing CCTVs (closed-circuit television cameras) on many of its streets, beginning with major thoroughfares. But there were none on Rue des Pierres. Nonetheless, the assailant exercised extreme caution. As he approached them, he kept his head slightly down, appearing to be just an anonymous pedestrian. Had they seen his face they still would not have known that he was Vincent Gillmore. They paid him no attention nor did they see his weapon. He shot Jean-Paul once through the heart. "Thuup." At first, his friends did not know what had happened. The stranger passed them quietly. As Jean-Paul began to sink, they both grabbed an arm. And as they did so, the killer turned back, shooting twice, one shot to each head. Only a professional of Gillmore's skill could so easily dispatch all of them with a total of three shots. He dropped the gun, a silenced Glock 9 mm, and continued on his way as if he were an uninterested passerby. The street was deserted, there were no witnesses, and the friends were not found for several hours. The police initially estimated that the murders occurred around two o'clock in the morning. The families were notified at seven.

. . .

In preparation for the 1984 Olympics, a joint task force was created in Southern California involving federal and local law enforcement agencies. As a representative from the LAPD, Tom was sent to the FBI National Academy in Washington, D.C., for training. While there, he met Lt. Miguel Moreno, a Puerto Rican detective from the New York Police Department. After a stellar career as a topnotch NYPD detective, Moreno (having risen to the rank of deputy inspector), retired in 1988 and was appointed U.S. Marshal for the Northern District of New York by the director of the U.S. Marshals Service (USMS). Eleven years later, he retired from USMS and was hired by INTERPOL Washington, United States National Central Bureau (USNCB), eventually becoming assistant director in the State and Local Law Enforcement Liaison Division. In 2001 Moreno was stationed in Lyon, France, the international headquarters for INTERPOL, as the chief U.S. liaison.

At the time, INTERPOL consisted of 176 countries, divided by regions, each operating independently. The European agency is known as EUROPOL and contrary to suggestions in movies and television, the International Police Organization is not a police force. It is a communications center for agencies around the world. There is no international database of crimes, although member agencies do have access to each other's list of wanted persons and cooperate in apprehending fugitives and preparing for extraditions.

None of the officers investigating the triple murder in Brussels were aware of the similarity with the six murders three years earlier in Los Angeles. But information about the killings in Brussels reached Moreno.

Because I was running for the U.S. Senate from the state of California and the election was only weeks away, the murders of my wife and children made the news in many countries, including Belgium. But the inability to bring the case to conclusion caused it to fade from the public mind. It remained of interest only to law enforcement personnel. One person who took notice was a skilled detective from Brussels, Chief Inspector Briek Dusmet, who was overseeing the investigation of the murders of Jean-Paul and his friends.

Dusmet worked in the Directorate of Crime against Persons (DJP) a division of the General Directorate of Judicial Police in Brussels. This arm of the Federal Police is charged with investigating all crimes against individuals, including murder, terrorism, and human trafficking. In May 2000, Dusmet had attended a symposium in Washington, D.C. While there he met Moreno. They struck up a friendship that continued after his return to Brussels. And when Moreno was sent to Lyon, Dusmet was there to welcome him.

The investigation in Brussels surfaced two key elements of the crime that caught his attention: the single shot to each victim and the weapon left at the scene. Prior to Jean-Paul's death, the most recent case to be covered by journalists and draw the scrutiny of law enforcement was my family's murder. Dusmet remembered. But it was not just the Los Angeles murders. Similar crimes had occurred in other countries over the years. None had been solved and there was no known suspect. This led to the conclusion that they were all the work of the same master criminal, a man capable of eluding police the world over.

It quickly became clear that the investigation by the Belgian police was going nowhere. No evidence, no suspect, no solution. In comparing the Los Angeles and Brussels murders, Dusmet recalled that Moreno and Moran were friends. It was he who contacted Moreno in Lyon and shared his suspicion that the same assailant was responsible for all the killings.

Miguel Moreno called Tom Moran and informed him of the murders and the stalled investigation. There was nothing for Tom to do. He had no authority in Belgium and agencies do not reach out to their counterparts in other countries to supply detectives. However, Moreno was not concerned about solving the case in Brussels. But from his own experience he knew that just being on the scene can occasionally provide that last piece of information to link to or solve another case. A spark of recognition that pieces everything together. If Tom was willing to fly to Belgium, Moreno would furnish an introduction to Dusmet.

Tom thought the matter over briefly. He had questions. What could he possibly discover in Brussels? He already knew of the similarity between the crimes: each victim killed by a single shot, weapon left at the scene, no fingerprints, no other evidence. What could his presence offer the Judicial Police? Nothing. He certainly suspected, as did Dusmet that they were dealing with the same assassin. Tom was not as infuriated by the news as he was forlorn. It was unlikely this would lead to a solution of the Lozano murders, but Tom had a personal reason for going. Emily had been in London for more than a month and he missed her. He decided to take some personal time. He had amassed weeks of vacation, and there were no threats to the security of Los Angeles. Commander Haskell was more than willing to let him leave.

•　　•　　•

On Tuesday, April 22, two nights before his trip to Europe, Tom went to St. Catherine Parish to speak with Giovanni, but he asked that they not meet over dinner and drinks. This needed to be a more formal encounter. He had pre-arranged the meeting so that Giovanni would come home early from his day off. Tom arrived at 7:00 p.m. and was shown into Giovanni's office. About five minutes later Giovanni walked in.

"Hello, Tom. I apologize for being late."

"Not to worry," Tom said. "It was only five minutes."

253

"You asked to meet in the office, no food, no drinks. It sounds pretty ominous."

Giovanni's office was simply but tastefully appointed. The floor was made of Brazilian rosewood. One wall was lined with books; another, dubbed his "justice wall" featured a hand-drawn sketch juxtaposing images of Mahatma Ghandi, Martin Luther King Jr., and Dorothy Day. Beside that were works of *Los Angeles Times'* political cartoonist Paul Conrad, each satire evoking reflections on world peace. In front of one window stood his modest oak desk, across from which were two chairs covered in a checkered black and burgundy pattern. Tom motioned to them. "Gio, let's sit down."

His demeanor was quite sober. After they were both seated, he continued. "Have you heard about the murders in Belgium?"

That seemed like an odd question and Gio was tempted to make a smartass comment about there being sufficient murders in the U.S. without needing to go to Europe. But he noticed that there was no humor in Tom's expression. He simply answered no.

"Well, a couple of weeks ago three men were killed in Brussels." That statement brought no recognition to Giovanni's countenance. Tom continued, "Do you remember Jackson, Giuseppe's friend from Harvard?" he asked.

"Of course," Giovanni replied.

"One of the three dead men was Jackson's partner, Jean-Paul Lecuyer."

Giovanni began to feel uneasy and suspected where the conversation was going. Still, he did not want to jump to conclusions. Instead he queried, "Why does this matter to you? You're a policeman here in Los Angeles."

"There is an eerie familiarity. Let me recap for you. When we were investigating the murders of Yolanda and the kids, we were pursuing some persons of interest. One was actually a suspect, Gary Bass. We were pretty sure he was one of the two assassins. He wound up dead at MacArthur Park. The other man we were looking into was Christopher Coker, Giuseppe's attorney. We suspected he knew something about the murders. After all, he only had two clients, The Pegasus Group and Giuseppe, himself. Coker was found dead on Aberdeen Avenue in Los Feliz. Both men died of a single shot through the heart. Glock 9 mm pistols with silencers were found at all three murder scenes.

"By the placement of the bullets and ballistics analysis of all six murders, we're sure that Bass killed Yolanda and Gina. We don't know the other assassin's name, but believe he shot Carmen and Leonardo as well as Bass and Coker."

Giovanni could not even look at Tom. He cast his eyes downward as his friend continued, a cloak of despondency descending over him.

"Here's where it all connects, Gio. The deaths in Brussels were too similar to be mere coincidence. The assailant was facing Lecuyer and shot him once through the heart. The other two men were both shot from behind in the head. I think the assassin was trying to be a little too clever, combining his modus operandi with that of Bass. You know me. I'm not easily thrown off track. The killing of Jean-Paul replicates the deaths of Carmen, Leonardo, Bass, and Coker. In my mind, the killing of his friends mirrors the deaths of Yolanda and Gina. Finally, there was a Glock 9 mm, with silencer, left at the scene in Brussels."

Giovanni thought for a moment, then said, "Tom, you told me once that the men who killed Yolanda and the kids were professional assassins. They must have killed people in many countries. Why do you think my brother was involved in these murders?" Tom had not actually made that accusation, but he had implied it. And, of course, Giovanni already knew the answer.

"If the murders in Brussels were merely random, or if the M.O. were different, I wouldn't. But Jean-Paul was connected to Giuseppe through Jackson, and the murders were too similar to the ones here in L.A."

"And the motive?" Giovanni asked. "You've always claimed that Giuseppe was responsible for having his family killed. If so, it was twisted, evil, and reprehensible. But at least there was a motive. I can't see it here." He opened his hands with those last words, to emphasize his incomprehension.

"Neither can I. Not yet," Tom replied. "I just don't accept that that these murders were coincidence. And I don't think you do, either. I can see it in your eyes. I'll find the motive, Gio. Tomorrow morning I'm flying to Europe to meet with the chief inspector in Brussels." He paused for a moment and then asked, "Gio, don't you think it's time for you to say something?"

This was not really a rhetorical question. And even though he wanted an answer, he didn't expect one. Nor did Giovanni offer one. Although Tom no longer went to church, he understood the sacraments and the hold that confession had over Giovanni. Despite their differences about God, it was not easy for Tom to sit in judgment on his friend.

Stress had taken an evident toll over the last three years and Giovanni could feel himself decaying from within. The mere memory of his brother was like a parasitoid slowly killing him cell by cell. Tom had not intended to cast such a pall over the evening. He only wanted to disclose the news. But he looked closely at his friend. Giovanni just sat there, overwhelmed by a battle he knew he could not win.

Usually when the two of them met, they shared a drink or two. But tonight there would be no camaraderie. It would be impossible to make small talk after this conversation. During the silence, Tom had risen and walked to the side window. He stared out, looking at nothing in particular. After a few moments, he turned back to Giovanni.

"Emily's in London right now, covering the war. I'm going there first. And I intend to tell her everything."

Giovanni wanted to object, but knew it would be a fruitless venture. They had grown up together and he knew Tom's resolve. There would be no dissuading him. Instead, he shrugged off that last bit of information.

"Say hello for me," was the most he could muster.

"I will. I'll call you when I get back, Gio." With that he left, seeing himself out.

Giovanni sat alone in the office for a while. He did not know how to react. He had spent the past three years agonizing over his commitment to the church, three years with few moments of joy or peace, three years grasping at faith trying to avoid descending into retribution and violence, three years measuring the cry for earthly justice against a higher truth. And three years of constant remembering. Yolanda and the kids were never far from his thoughts and always in his heart.

Once again, he was sickened by the reality of death and the possibility that his twin brother was the culprit again. As much as he hated and tried to disavow Giuseppe, he was still a priest. There was a place deep in his soul where once he felt the warmth of God's love. It was cold now. And empty. At best, God was a mere shadow, not quite invisible. From deep in that darkness, Giovanni clung to a belief that there is good in the most evil of people. No one had tested that faith more than his brother. To survive he would have to confront Giuseppe.

CHAPTER 26

Tom called Emily on Wednesday to inform her of his trip.

"Em, I have to go to Europe for a few days, but I want to stop in London and spend the weekend with you. I understand if you'll be working part of the time. My flight is scheduled to arrive Friday afternoon."

"I'll meet you at the airport," she said.

"No. I get in at 3:00 p.m. and Heathrow is chaotic at that time. I'll just take the Tube from the airport to Putney Bridge Station and meet you at your folks' home."

"Tom, where are you going in Europe?"

"To Belgium; specifically, Brussels."

"Can you tell me why?"

"I'll explain it when we meet in London. Em, I have a lot more to tell you, too. I think it's time to share what I know about the murders of Yolanda and the kids. But it's a conversation we can't have over the phone." He knew that would only further peak her interest. "Don't worry. I'll explain everything. See you Friday, sweetheart. I love you."

"I love you, too."

As they hung up Emily could not help but wonder. Did she detect a hint of resignation in Tom's voice? Or perhaps agitation? For the most part, he sounded normal. Maybe it was just her imagination. Then again, he had warned her that knowing about the Lozano murders was dangerous. Also, it was unusual for him to go to Europe on police business. As far as she knew he had never done that before—certainly not while they were married the first time. Well, whatever it was she would find out on Friday. She needed to get back to work and finish her latest column for the *Los Angeles Times*.

. . .

On April 24, Tom arrived at Los Angeles International Airport at 5:00 p.m. He checked in for British Airways flight 268 departing LAX at 9:45, then took a seat at the bar. He never enjoyed flying. He did not like the idea of placing his life in someone else's hands, at least not thirty-five thousand feet in the air. A scotch or two usually helped to settle his nerves. According to his watch he had more than three hours before boarding, enough time for a hamburger, fries, and a couple of drinks.

One good thing about long flights is that Tom never had trouble sleeping on a plane. He tried to time his rest so he would get a decent night's sleep and be fresh on arrival. Sleep came easily on this trip and he woke around 12:00 noon British Summer Time (BST). He had the opportunity to eat a little food and clean up in the lavatory before deplaning at London Heathrow Airport. After clearing immigration, he retrieved his luggage from the baggage carousel and was passed through customs without question.

Immediately he heard his name called and saw Emily waving her hand. She rushed into his arms. "Surprise! I left work early."

He embraced her tightly and said, "I'm glad you did. I have missed you so much."

"And I, you," she replied. She stepped back and gazed into his eyes. "I hate this war, Tom. And this assignment. I'm ready to come home."

He drew her back to him and said, "Shh," then took a deep breath, filling his lungs with her intoxicating fragrance. "Um. You smell so good," he said as he slowly exhaled.

"That's the perfume you bought me last Christmas," she replied.

He smiled and said, "I know."

"I put a little on before I left the office. Is it too much?"

"It's perfect. But right now you'd smell good to me no matter what."

Since she had already purchased tickets for the Tube, they passed through the doors and waited for the train.

"Tom, you don't mind staying with my parents, do you? We could always get a hotel for the weekend, if you'd prefer."

"Why spend the extra money? Besides, I like your folks. But I do need some quality time with you. And not just in the bedroom," he laughed. "I have a lot to tell you and it won't be easy . . . for either of us. I just can't keep it to myself any longer."

Emily assumed he was referring to the Lozano murders. She had never pressed Tom on the issue and since it was no longer newsworthy, it was not a subject of conversation at the *Times*. If he was going to talk about it now, then something momentous must have occurred. She was willing to take everything in stride and give Tom a wide berth.

"We can go out after supper. Mom's making bangers 'n' mash in your honor."

"She's almost as thoughtful as you are," he replied. Unlike most Americans, Tom enjoyed traditional English fare, notwithstanding its general lack of flavor and seasoning. The simpler, the better for him. When it came to comfort food Emily's mother was a good cook, and on this occasion she did not disappoint. Out of fondness for Tom, she added garlic to the potatoes and prepared braised red cabbage to go along with the sausages. It was a perfect welcome to England, and just what he needed after a night–long flight.

After dinner, Tom suggested going to the River Cafe for dessert and after–dinner drinks.

"Across from the Putney Station?" Emily asked, somewhat incredulously.

The restaurant was a local hangout. What Americans would call a greasy spoon, and certainly not the choice for an evening out or a fine dessert.

"No," Tom replied. "I mean the real River Cafe. The Italian restaurant at Thames Wharf."

"I'm not sure we can get in there just for dessert," she said. "It's very popular. Besides, on a Friday night we would almost certainly need reservations."

"Well, what I really want is to walk along the water. Dessert and drinks don't matter."

"Then let's just take a ride down to the river and go for a stroll. I certainly don't need anything more to eat tonight."

Rising in Gloucestershire, the Thames flows through London and past many famous suburbs, including Oxford and Windsor. Driven by a strong current, and with an average width of more than eight hundred feet, it remains a mostly peaceful river with a calm sheen. The changing of clocks for spring and summer extended the daytime hours, providing light for a generously lazy walk along the riverbank. As dusk began to settle, the surface of the water became a stage for the colorful lights of bridges and buildings to shimmer in un-choreographed ballets.

Tom had been anticipating this conversation for months and supposed that his thoughts were sufficiently organized. After all, he had been living with a burdensome knowledge for almost three years. But it would be new to Emily—difficult for him to say, and even more painful for her to hear. With or without an organized process, this was the moment of truth.

"Let's stop for a while and watch the dancing lights," Emily suggested, not realizing that her cheerfulness countered the mood Tom sought to create. But it did snatch his attention and set him to his task. They sat together on a bench overlooking the water. Tom appreciated the view. He would be able to glance into the distance and away from Emily whenever necessary.

"Emily, ever since we began seeing each other a year ago, I have deflected your questions about the murders of Yolanda and the kids; about Giuseppe, Giovanni, and me; about the inability to apprehend a suspect. I wasn't just dodging the discussion. I was and still am concerned about your safety. I continually pleaded that the time wasn't right. It is now. In fact, it's the reason I'm going to Belgium. This is not work, Em. I'm using a week of vacation."

Emily reached out and took his hand. "Tom, whatever you have to say, I'm ready. In fact, I suspect I know what it is. Not all of it, of course. Certainly not the details. But I've observed too much over the last year. Remember I'm a reporter."

"And a damn good one," he assured her. "Em, do you remember Miguel Moreno, a lieutenant from New York City?"

"Vaguely," she replied. "You met him . . ." she paused. "It must have been nineteen eighty-three or eighty-four, when you were training in Washington for the task force."

"What a good memory!" he replied. "Well, we've kept in contact over the years, even though our career paths were decidedly different, his advancing much further than mine. After retiring from the NYPD he joined the U.S. Marshals Service and was assigned to upstate New York. After that he was hired by Washington INTERPOL just before the millennium. Last year he was sent to INTERPOL headquarters in Lyon, France." Tom paused for a moment before continuing. "He called last week."

Emily did not question why. She just listened.

"Miguel told me that three men were killed in Brussels on April 13. He had been notified by a friend of his, an inspector for the Belgian Judicial Police. The authorities were experiencing difficulties in their investigation because they had no witnesses and the only evidence at the scene was the murder weapon, a Glock 9 mm with silencer. Needless to say, there were no fingerprints on it. Nor on the shell casings.

"What caught Moreno's attention were the circumstances, or more specifically the M.O. Each man was shot once with fatal precision, one of them through the heart, the other two in the head. After speaking with the inspector in Brussels, Moreno began thinking and noticed a parallel to the Lozano family murders. But even he did not know the half of it."

Tom fidgeted a little, adjusting his posture. He had been looking at Emily most of the time. But now, he was growing uneasy. She sensed that and squeezed his hand for support. He glanced out over the water for a moment and then continued.

"I'm sure you remember that Yolanda and the kids were each shot once, two of them in the heart and two in the head." Even after all this time Tom could not help but shudder as he retold the event. "There's more," he said.

"Em, John Puerner has been publisher of the *Times* for three years now and he knows your skill and reputation as a journalist. I'm sure he trusts your judgment." At that point Tom turned, looked straight into her eyes, and said, "I want you to speak with him about the *Times* doing its own investigation into the Lozano murders."

"What do you think we can accomplish that the LAPD couldn't?"

"I have an idea about that. There are still some things I can't share with you since this is technically an open case and people at both the newspaper and the department know that we're married. If the *Times* had access to confidential information, everyone would know the source and it would mean the end of my career. But I can point you in certain directions and help you connect some dots. If Puerner goes for it," he stressed the next few words, "then whoever is assigned will be in danger. I'd rather it not be you."

"Local murders are not my beat, Tom."

"No, but considering that we're married, and that there is a likely link between those murders and the ones in Brussels, you'll be a natural choice."

"If so, I'll be careful, Tom."

"I wish it were that simple. I think the murderer is an international assassin. At least I think the Brussels and Los Angeles murders were the work of the same man. He only approaches his subjects at night and has a preference for deserted streets or locations that will not draw suspicion."

"Only the murders in Belgium were on the street," Emily replied. "Yolanda and the kids were killed at home."

Tom paused again before proceeding. He was dangerously close to compromising classified information. This was a delicate balancing act and there were risks involved—to both of their careers and possibly even Emily's life. But it was too late to turn back. He had already committed himself before he even left Los Angeles.

For the average person, cloak and dagger scenarios are the intrigue of spy stories and crime novels—fictional worlds in which the perils and thrills of adventure never pose any threat to one's life. But this was neither a book nor a movie. Tom was an experienced detective on the trail of a cold, careful, and deliberate assassin. Real lives had been lost and real lives hung in the balance. He could not allow himself to get lost in musings. He had to go on.

"There's something else you need to know, Em. But you're not hearing it from me. Make sure whoever gets the assignment looks into two other murders that occurred in late 2000. One happened in October in MacArthur Park, the other in December in Los Feliz. Both at night, both on the street, and a silenced Glock 9 mm left at each scene." This was Tom at his clandestine best. A side of himself that even he did not know existed. In over thirty years of police work, he had never considered divulging confidential evidence. He rationalized that the fact of the murders was public knowledge and therefore he betrayed no police secrets. "That's all I can tell you. But it's a good place to start."

"That's all you can say as an LAPD detective," Emily corrected. "You're holding something back that you don't want to say."

Tom stood up, walked to the water's edge and turned around. As he looked at Emily, he saw a seasoned journalist who had traveled the world over and reported on the worst of humanity. She had witnessed the malevolence that enslaves and degrades entire cultures, the conceit born of insecurity, the hate rooted in revenge, and the arrogance bred by power. Three decades later all that collective evil had not hardened her. This was a woman who believed in the innate goodness of all people and her writing reflected sensitivity and compassion. Yet she was neither fragile nor naïve. Emily was capable of standing up to power, of chiding generals, even calling presidents and prime ministers to account. In spite of her complex character, he almost feared speaking anything more.

Tom knew better than most the danger of knowing. His investigation of the Lozano murders had upended his life, drawing him down an unexpected path to face incomprehensibly personal evil, daring him to respond in kind, to sip from his own cup of anger and hate, a poisonous brew he came perilously close to consuming. Instead, he walked away, weak and struggling for balance of mind and spirit. Emily had no idea how much she now anchored his life, or that her return enabled him once again to hope. He hated himself for what he was about to say, for what his words might do, how deeply they might hurt. Yet even if Emily's resolve had its limits, she deserved to know the truth. He walked back to the bench and sat beside her.

"I can give you one more piece of the puzzle, but officially you're going to have to discover it on your own. There is a common link to every murder—those in Los Angeles and the ones in Brussels." He looked in her eyes, heaved a sigh, and said, "Giuseppe is the link. I am certain that he planned the murders of his family and at least one of the other ones in L.A. And I think he was behind the deaths in Brussels. This is not just theory or circumstantial.

"All the leads I uncovered eventually led back to Giuseppe. What I lacked was proof. I made an appointment to meet him at his office. That was in December of 2000. By that time, six people were dead. I can still vividly recall that day. As I walked in, he was clearing his office so that the Pegasus Group could be put into trust during his time in the Senate. He treated my visit as if it were a game, playing coy and innocent. Finally, I got him to admit that he had his family killed."

Emily did not react. Not visibly. Her mind began to race, however, as if inside it contained an atom smasher where opposite thoughts— what she knew and did not know—collided. For the past year she had noticed Giuseppe's absence at family affairs and commented on the fact that neither Tom nor Giovanni spoke of him. Unlike others, she could not dismiss these observations as collateral damage to the murders of Yolanda and the children. Her instincts were too keen.

At first, Emily said nothing. She was considered a wordsmith among her colleagues but there was nothing in her vocabulary for this occasion.

She rested her head on Tom's shoulder and began to cry. Not sobbing. Little more than a whimper, tears rolling down her cheeks. He put his arms around her and held her tight.

"I don't know why I'm crying, Tom. I half-anticipated this. I mean, it's worse than I thought. But I knew something was wrong. When we were young, you, Giovanni, and Giuseppe were all close friends. And I cannot imagine you and Gio deserting Sep. But since I've been back you haven't once talked about him. It may have passed unnoticed by others, but that first Christmas after we remarried, all three of you were at their parents' house and I noticed that neither you nor Giovanni were alone with Giuseppe and that you did not engage him in conversation. I just didn't want to believe that it went this far."

However much she might have expected this news, or whatever she thought Tom would say, just hearing it was physically exhausting. They sat a while longer in silence. Emily had questions but they could wait. Finally, she said, "Tom, can we go back to the house? I don't really want to talk anymore Not tonight."

.   .   .

Tom slept through to the morning, but the weight of knowledge had merely shifted—from his shoulders to hers. Emily tossed restlessly the entire night. She woke him at daybreak saying, "Tom, we need to hurry. My mom's cooking and I can already smell the coffee. Come on, get up. There's no breakfast in bed in this house."

They hurriedly dressed and headed downstairs to the kitchen. Emily's mother, Margaret, was determined to make this weekend special. English breakfasts are frequently extensive and leisurely, at least on Saturdays and Sundays. Margaret held nothing back that morning. She served up a hearty plate full of food for everyone: eggs, juicy sausages, thick back bacon, a combination of cremini and oyster mushrooms, potatoes, and lastly, tomatoes and bread, both fried in the bacon fat. This was not a meal to be rushed. And not to be repeated too frequently.

After breakfast, Tom and Emily sat in the backyard and continued their previous night's conversation. During the meal, Tom noticed that Emily looked tired. "I guess you did not sleep well last night," he said.

"No, I didn't. You had that covered for both of us," she said smiling. "At times when I was awake I thought about everything you said. Along with digesting the horrible story of Giuseppe, I realized that you never told me why the *Times* should start an investigation."

"I guess I got caught up in all the other stuff. My thinking is that if the paper begins to look into the murders all the information will be made public in a series of articles. Publicity tends to throw criminals off their game. If you follow the directions I suggested last night, you'll be able to reach the same conclusions I did. Minus the confession, of course."

"Why didn't you arrest him after his admission?"

"I had no evidence. It would only have been my word against his, and he had just been elected to the U.S. Senate."

"How much does Giovanni know?"

"He knows most of it, but it's actually worse for him. Giuseppe is pure vile. He knew that I was closing in, so he went to Giovanni to confess in the Sacrament of Reconciliation!"

"That's unbelievable," she said. "How do you know that?"

"We were tapping Giuseppe's phone. Immediately after one of my confrontations with him, he called his brother and said he wanted to confess his sins. Of course, he didn't say what they were over the phone. But I knew."

"No wonder Gio is so different these days," Emily replied.

"Yeah. That's been a major source of tension between us. I think he should break the seal of confession and say something. With his testimony we could put Giuseppe behind bars."

"Come on, Tom. You know better than that. Gio will never betray his faith or his church. You've always said what a great priest he is."

"That was before all this. You see, there's more, Em. I went to see Gio on Tuesday to tell him about my trip and let him know that his silence has allowed Giuseppe to commit three more murders. He said nothing."

"He's not responsible for what Giuseppe does."

"Maybe not, but if he spoke up there would be one less murderer running free."

"That's unfair to him, Tom. Do you really want him to change? He can't alter his principles according to the circumstances."

"There's one final thing for whoever starts investigating for the *Times*. Giuseppe has a device that he calls the Silencer. It renders all electronic activity null. That's why there was no recording of him admitting to the killings. I had taken a recorder with me. When I drew it out of my pocket he just laughed and assured me it was blank."

Emily sat for a few moments in silence. She was getting used to it. She was not given to making impulsive decisions, but she had been thinking most of the night. When she finally spoke, she was steadfast. "Tom, I'll speak to Puerner about investigating and maybe doing a series on the crimes. But I'm going to ask for the assignment."

Damn, Tom thought to himself. He did not tell her everything so that she would take on the story herself. But he knew it was always a risk, and he knew Emily. She was strong and strong-willed. She would not turn back. For the moment, he had time on his side. He would have to figure out a way to keep her safe.

CHAPTER 27

Tom's meeting with Giovanni further complicated my brother's already unsettled life. He knew in his heart that I could not have been involved in Jean-Paul's death and was aware that the unsolved investigation of my family's murders left Tom an obsessed man. Even after being transferred out of RHD he could not let the case go. He was always hoping for some new piece of evidence, some clue that would vindicate him and his accusation against me. Connecting the Los Angeles crimes to those in Brussels was tenuous, the evidence circumstantial at best; and it failed to raise Giovanni's suspicions. Far more likely was that the murders in Belgium were the work of some unknown European assassin. Possibly it was the same person who killed my family, then again, maybe not. After all, the world of felons is known for many inhabitants including copycat criminals and killers with similar M.O.'s.

Over the last three years, one defining distinction surfaced between Tom and Giovanni, though only the three of us knew the reason. Weekly, if not daily, Tom grew in his contempt for me whereas Giovanni, straining the limits of his faith, kept a firm grip on compassion. Two disparate feelings threatening, like swords, to split the bond of friendship. For contempt and compassion are not two sides of some biblical or philosophical weapon. Sharpening one does not hone the other. They are two separate and distinct blades: one razored in allegiance, prostrated before the altar of revenge, the other blunted in a quest for reconciliation and peace. And neither man wielded his with much wisdom. Both were blinded—one by hate, and one by faith.

It was easy for Tom to feel scorn. As a cop, a detective, he looked down on criminals. They were not his equal. As a result, contempt came naturally and with it, a lack of empathy. Contempt was the only emotion he could allow to surface. But it is not an innately powerful one. It gains strength in direct proportion as empathy diminishes. The two cannot inhabit the same mind or spirit. As a result, the more condescension rises, the less one can feel for another.

For his part, Giovanni tried to live by principles, to model his life after the teachings and mission of Jesus. This Son of God, as Christians call him, ruled out judgment and condemnation. He commanded his followers to love their enemies and pray for their persecutors. If practiced assiduously, this leads to the empathy denied the accuser. It leads to compassion rather than revenge. More often than not it falls—a victim of its own pretensions. For the human spirit is instinctively given to retribution.

·   ·   ·

From the first rumblings of the Iraq invasion, I had misgivings. The Bush administration had predicted an early end to the combat and a swift handing off of power. But no war had ever gone that smoothly. Still, I was surprised at how quickly the first cracks began to appear in the war's foundations. The major U.S. news on Friday, April 25, was the resignation of Thomas E. White as Secretary of the Army. When Donald Rumsfeld was appointed to lead the Department of Defense, he laid out a plan to streamline the military, creating a leaner, faster, and more precise attack force. But his goal was marred by his methods. He wanted to run the department like a business and sought out appointees who had solid corporate experience. He was of the opinion that good business leaders could run a war department better than experienced military personnel who had put themselves and their soldiers on the line in battle. White was a retired brigadier general, but more importantly had served in the private sector as vice-chairman of Enron Energy Services, a subsidiary of Enron Corporation. He was unfortunately burdened with some financially shady deals while at Enron. He worked hard to secure contracts for his company, even when Enron was the only bidder. Upon learning in a private meeting that Enron was chasing after the Dodo bird—an extinction that would render its portfolio worth less than the paper used to print it—he managed to dump some $12 million of Enron stock, a healthy return on his investment, to be sure. Nonetheless, he fit the profile desired by Rumsfeld.

White's military record and his Pentagon experience were valuable assets. He served as executive assistant to Joint Chiefs of Staff Chairman Colin Powell, and was described by Harlan Ullman, a friend and a retired U.S. naval commander, as Powell's "alter ego." That endorsement carried weight with Rumsfeld, for Ullman was also the architect of the Rapid Response strategy, popularly known as "Shock and Awe," during the bombing of Iraq. Euphemisms aside, this is a modern version of the allied bombing of Dresden and the B-29 firebombing of Tokyo during WWII. Like its historical counterparts, Rapid Response violates the Hague Convention of 1907, and is just as immoral. In Rumsfeld's view, White was a man more than capable of fulfilling the requirements necessary to serve as Secretary of the Army. But then they had a falling out.

General Eric Shinseki, 34th chief of staff of the United States Army, testified before the Senate Armed Services Committee that occupying post-war Iraq would require several hundred thousand soldiers. Rumsfeld expected White to publicly rebuke and challenge Shinseki's estimation. He refused. He recognized the same reality as Shinseki. Rumsfeld was beginning to appear more and more a buffoon and incapable of fulfilling his job. As I predicted, he was also becoming a liability for the president. But Bush always prided himself on his own loyalty, on standing by his appointments.

Eventually every advisor to the president and every major player in the Republican Party would force Bush to let Rumsfeld go. And calculating the damage he did as Secretary of Defense would be a task left to historians. In the meantime, Thomas E. White became a casualty of Rumsfeld's foolhardiness and lack of vision.

I was engrossed in this news when the telephone rang. It was 10:00 p.m. and the voice on the other end shocked me, quickly drawing my attention away from the Department of Defense and the war effort.

"Hello?" I said.

"Giuseppe, this is your brother."

The introduction was pure formality. I, of course, recognized his voice. Any communication from him was unexpected, but unlike previous occasions, I was in no mood to be snarky.

"Hello, Giovanni. I'm surprised to hear from you. Has something happened at home?"

"No. Everyone's fine. But I'll be in Washington next week and wanted to stop by and see you."

That was even more curious than the phone call. He had scrupulously avoided me for more than two years. Why a sudden desire to meet? Giovanni was my brother, my twin. But there was not much trust between us. I suspected some ulterior intent, but had not the slightest idea what it could be. At the same time, he could do me no harm. If he had business in Washington, then returned home without seeing me, it would raise concern and even suspicion. Whatever was going on between us, we each had reasons to keep the family in the dark.

"I would welcome that, Giovanni." That might have been an exaggeration, but I said it without exuberance. "How long will you be here?"

"Just two days," he replied. "I arrive Monday afternoon and leave on Wednesday morning. I was hoping you could be free sometime on Tuesday."

"I'll make a point of it. Would you like to have lunch or dinner?"

"No, thanks. I have a tight schedule. Are you available in the afternoon?"

At the time, I had no idea that he was lying to me. His only business in Washington was meeting with me. He would have been able to join me for lunch or dinner, or both. But he had no intentions of socializing.

"How about two o'clock?" I asked.

"That's fine. I'll take a taxi to your office."

"OK, I'll see you then."

As I hung up the phone, I wondered. In almost three years, we had barely spoken a dozen words—why did he want to see me now? Well, I would find out in a few days. In the meantime, it would not cause me any lack of sleep.

.   .   .

I made sure to clear my calendar for Tuesday. As the middle of the afternoon approached, there was no excitement or sense of anticipation. My brother would be on time and I would welcome him graciously, but not warmly. I decided to be merely an adequate host. As such, my secretary had prepared both coffee and tea.

Giovanni was early, nearly ten minutes. Having no appointments I was ready, and met him in the outer office. The two of us together in the same room must have been a startling sight. We were no longer a mirror image of each other. Our features were still identical, but he had grayed substantially more than I in the last few years, was a little more haggard, and now looked more an older brother than a twin.

"Hello, Giovanni," I said. "Welcome to Washington. You remember my secretary, Catherine Stripling?"

"Yes. Hello, Catherine."

"Hello, Father Lozano."

He smiled at her and responded, "I'm much more informal than that. You can call me Giovanni."

"Catherine," I said, "we'll be in my office, and I don't want to be disturbed."

"Yes, sir," she answered.

As we entered the other room I offered him a choice of coffee or tea.

"No, thanks."

He looked around. In every respect, this was simpler than my Pegasus office. It was smaller and less cluttered and the few keepsakes scattered around the bookshelves stood out more easily. Giovanni glanced over the decor, taking note of various items. He gave a slight start when he saw a picture of Yolanda and the kids, but said nothing. He just kept perusing. Finally, he spoke. "I notice that you're still wearing your wedding ring."

I tried to detect some emotion in his voice, but there was none, not even a hint of judgment. It suddenly dawned on me that no one had ever mentioned the ring before, not even Jackson or Emily. I don't know if that was due to a lack of observation or fear that the comment would be uncomfortable. It certainly would have raised unpleasant memories, on multiple levels.

"Yes," I said. "I've never even taken it off."

"Why not?" Again, his words were without a detectable feeling, not even casual concern. The question was somewhat idle, of throwaway interest, a breaking of the ice, a necessary prelude to some unrelated discussion. Although never previously queried about the ring, I had a ready response.

"I'm not looking for a relationship," was my simple answer. "I wear my wedding band so that anyone who meets me knows I'm not free. Even if they know that Yolanda is dead, the ring sends a signal, and they leave me alone."

"And the picture?" he asked, motioning toward my family.

"A lot of visitors and constituents come into this office. I may be a senator, but I want them to know that I'm just like they are."

"You don't find that hypocritical?"

At most there was only a hint of cynicism. Both the question and his manner were cold, and I was amazed by his control. He betrayed none of the feelings that I was sure were raging inside. I knew he was examining me, that he had a purpose for being here, but his facial expression was almost vacant.

"I don't expect you to understand, Giovanni," I said without defense. "I miss my family." That was a true statement and the only explanation I intended to offer. "But tell me, you did not come here to look around my office. What do you want?"

"I think I'll have that coffee now," he said, deflecting the question. He helped himself and then sat down. After a few moments he looked at me and said, "Jackson's friend, Jean-Paul, was killed in Brussels. Actually, he was murdered."

"I know. Jackson called me after it happened and I flew to Belgium for the funeral. I wanted to support him as he had supported me." Now I knew *what* brought him to Washington. I still did not know the *why*. It was my turn to probe. "You didn't have any meeting or any business in D.C., did you? Other than coming to see me, that is."

"No. This is exactly why I'm here."

"And what is it you hope to gain from this visit?" I asked.

"That's yet to be determined," he replied.

"I'm curious. How did you even know about Jean-Paul? You never met him and you're not friends with Jackson."

In spite of his outward demeanor, Giovanni felt as though his sanity was strung so tight that the strings would snap with the slightest touch. But he would not give me the satisfaction of seeing such stress. He continued as matter-of-factly as possible.

"Tom told me about it last week. He said there were three people killed at the scene. He's in Brussels now."

"What business is it of his?" I asked attempting a slight disinterest. "It's in a whole different country."

"He thinks you were involved."

That was blunt. I guess it did not surprise me, but I could not allow any expression to betray my thoughts. I cocked my head, turned up one side of my mouth, cast my eyes downward, shook my head slightly from side to side, and exhaled.

"Why would he think that?" Of course, I knew Tom. And I was fully aware of what he thought of me. I could even understand why he might think I was involved. But it was all in his imagination so I played innocent as to Tom's motives.

"He described the murders in Belgium as resembling the deaths of Yolanda and the kids."

"I still don't get it," I said, feigning incomprehension.

"Giuseppe, you at least have to acknowledge the similarity—single shots to either the heart or head of each victim."

"Come on, Gio." He winced at my use of the diminutive. "More than a quarter of a million people are killed by guns every year. How many ways can there possibly be to shoot someone?"

"It sounds as though you're evading the issue. The murders in Brussels were not random. They were the work of an assassin."

"Even so, that does not constitute a connection."

"There is one link," he said deliberately. "You. Tell me truthfully, Giuseppe. Did you have anything to do with Jean-Paul's death?"

In an interrogation or accusation, even by an amateur like my brother, reaction time is everything. Too quick or emotional a response would be unconvincing and defensive; too slow or cautious a reply would seem calculating and imply guilt; and a simple sigh of resignation would convey cunning and deception. This was my opportunity to go on the offense. And what better way than to answer one question with another? One tinged with disbelief and innocence.

"Why would you even ask such a question?"

"Don't play games with me, Giuseppe. I'm not in the mood. After what you did to your own wife and children, I believe you're capable of anything." Score one for me.

"Well, well," I said with an accusing smile, and light laughter, "so much for the sacred. You're not supposed to speak of what I told you in confession, not even to me. I guess you've finally found a way to bend the rules!"

"You're right," he replied. "I'm supposed to stay silent. And I have. But you are not in a position to lodge a complaint. And just between the two of us, I don't give a damn about the rules. I won't break the seal in public, but I have no problem pursuing the discussion with you."

I never thought I'd see the day that my brother would willingly violate so hallowed a duty, and with such feistiness. He was right, though. I was not about to object to any authorities.

He continued, "We never finished our discussion that night in confession. Actually, we didn't discuss much then, either. The fact that you were not repentant and I refused you absolution did not relieve me of my commitment to the sacrament. Just listening to you confess your sins was the most repugnant thing I have ever done. It wasn't just your admission of guilt. It was your cavalier manipulation of my life as a priest and of everything I believe. I realized that night that I don't matter to you. Neither did your family. In fact, I don't think anybody does. I really had no idea you were so evil."

There was no argument for me to make. What he said was true. Well, some of it. He was wrong about my family. They did mean something to me. I wanted to make him understand, but I could tell while watching him that it would not be that day. Perhaps if we talked more regularly, but the very idea of conversation was distasteful to him, evidenced by the fact that we had not really spoken in over two years. Instead of explaining myself, I chose to attack.

"You know, Giovanni, I had a couple similar conversations with Tom during the investigation. I did not try to justify anything with him, just as I did not with you. I knew that he has always seen the world in black and white, but you're a priest and I expected more from you."

"You wanted me to condone your actions?"

"No. But we both know that life is complex and our choices often nuanced."

He parted his lips in an incongruous sneer. "Nuance? You have four people killed, people you supposedly love, and you call it nuance?"

"Not 'supposedly,' Giovanni. I did love my wife and children. I still do. You'll never understand that." I was not about to share with him my loneliness or the recurring nightmares.

"You're right. I won't. Tell me something, Giuseppe. I realize that in comparison to Yolanda and the kids, I am nothing. But why did you deceive me that night by requesting confession?"

"Because Tom was getting too close. I didn't think he'd gather sufficient evidence, but I had to make sure you wouldn't help him. I told you then that I had to bind you to silence. You were just too innocent to suspect me."

"Well, there's no sacrament this time. Does that mean that you will not tell me about Jean-Paul?"

"There's nothing to tell."

"You know, Giuseppe, Tom told me about your little device. I think you call it the Silencer. It seems to me you don't have anything to fear. I'm sure you have it installed here."

"I do. And if I compromised myself in this conversation there would be no record. However, your testimony combined with Tom's suspicions could prove problematic. But then, that's not really the point. I simply had no motive. If I did, both you and Tom would probably already know it."

He didn't believe me, but neither could find grounds for distrusting. And I was getting bored. I decided to unmask his impotence much as I had Tom's three years earlier.

"Giovanni, you've been friends with Tom too long and I think the worst of him is wearing off on you. You came here thinking you could get some kind of admission from me. Something to give him so that I could be brought up on charges and my career brought down. He did the same that fateful December. I can still see it.

"He came to my office desperately wanting me to admit to the murders. God, he was so pathetic. I had already sworn you to silence, and, given the security of my office, I was more than willing to accommodate him and told him what he wanted to hear. In the end, however, he had nothing."

Giovanni had not told Tom about coming to Washington. That was something he wanted to do on his own. I don't know if he really expected to learn anything. Maybe he thought it would assuage his own feelings of incompetence and failure if I confessed to new murders. But I didn't. Nor did I give him reason to suspect me further. Reading his expression suddenly became easy. He knew his trip would prove futile. But I wasn't finished.

"Giovanni, I was not the only one who made a choice three years ago. You and Tom had choices, too. Did you know that Tom actually pulled his gun on me?" He did not look startled, but I could tell that this was obviously news to him. I smiled. "You didn't know. Well, no matter. That day I could see weakness in Tom's eyes. He was not going to pull the trigger. He lacked the courage." I looked at Giovanni with a certain amount of antipathy and continued. "I see the same thing in your eyes. If you were going to violate the seal of the sacrament and tell someone, you would have done it by now. And you wouldn't have bothered to come here and warn me.

"I know Tom despises me. But I don't know why he has decided to try to hang another set of murders on me. My advice to you, Giovanni, is to simply let it go. Otherwise, it will eat away at you, as it apparently does Tom."

Time had passed rather quickly that afternoon. I stood up and walked toward the door. He followed. In spite of having engaged in a lengthy conversation, neither of us could draw upon any pleasantries for parting. It was not particularly good seeing him again, a feeling I'm sure he shared.

All of a sudden a thought occurred to me. "Does the rest of the family know you're in Washington?"

"Yes. By the way, they asked me to say hello."

"Tell them I send my regards."

I closed the door, poured a drink, sat at my desk and lit a pipe, then pushed the intercom button to the outer office.

"Yes, Senator?"

"Catherine, close up for the day and send everyone home."

"Are you all right?" she asked.

"I'm fine. I just want to stay here for a while, alone. I'll see you in the morning. Good night, Catherine."

"Good night, sir."

For fifteen minutes, I practiced blowing smoke rings. I had never been good at it and did not get any better that afternoon. But the effort did focus my thoughts.

EPILOGUE

I had had a similar meeting with Tom in December of 2000—at least the environment was comparable. We met in different offices but both were mine and each was electronically secured. Meeting with Tom was inescapable and I was prepared. Even admitting to having had my family murdered was not improvised. I had been playing Tom throughout the investigation, leading him along a labyrinthine path, anticipating his every turn. I had one goal that December: to entomb any evidence against me and secure my move to Washington.

Meeting with Giovanni, however, was unanticipated and required some spontaneity. I had not known beforehand the reason for his visit and therefore had to improvise. Jean-Paul's murder was not international news, so I did not expect Giovanni to mention it. They had not even known each other. For a moment in our conversation, I thought I had slipped up, but did not allow any facial or ocular expression to give away that fear. For of one thing I was sure—there was no evidence against me. He had nothing more than supposition to work with.

Perhaps if Tom and Giovanni pooled their resources and intellectual skills in a single conversation they could outwit me. Doubtful. Certainly, when on their own, neither was equal to the task. Giovanni's visit had one positive effect, however. It put me on alert. I would be even more cautious of my brother and his friend as I pursued my goal of becoming president.

Purchase other Black Rose Writing titles at <u>www.blackrosewriting.com/books</u>

and use promo code PRINT to receive a 20% discount.